NIGHT
BOAT

Also by Alan Spence

Fiction
Its Colours They Are Fine
The Magic Flute
Stone Garden
Way to Go
The Pure Land

Poetry
Glasgow Zen
Seasons of the Heart
Clear Light
Still *with Alison Watt*
Morning Glory *with Dame Elizabeth Blackadder*

Plays
Sailmaker
Space Invaders
On the Line
Changed Days
The 3 Estaites

NIGHT BOAT

A ZEN NOVEL

ALAN
SPENCE

CANONGATE
Edinburgh · London

Published in Great Britain in 2013 by Canongate Books Ltd,
14 High Street, Edinburgh EH1 1TE

www.canongate.tv

1

British Library Cataloguing-in-Publication Data
A catalogue record for this book is available on
request from the British Library

ISBN 978 0 85786 852 7

Typeset in Baskerville MT by Palimpsest Book Production Ltd,
Falkirk, Stirlingshire

Printed and bound in Great Britain by
CPI Group (UK) Ltd, Croydon CR0 4YY

This book is printed on FSC certified paper

To the memory of
Sri Chinmoy
(1931 – 2007)
with eternal gratitude

Contents

ONE

The Gates of Hell	3
Tenjin	21
Wise Crane	29
One Time, One Place	41

TWO

Floating World, Flower-Path	57
Mu	84
Tsunami	92
Clear Severity	97
The Wild Horse of Mino	102

THREE

Wind and Rain	125
Fire and Brimstone	130
Return to Mino	140
Shoju Rojin	148

FOUR

The Zen Road 169
Zen Sickness 179
Mount Iwataki 202
Shoin-ji 222

FIVE

Hidden-in-Whiteness 239
Beating the Dharma Drum 251
Dharma-Thugs 265
Chikamatsu 272

SIX

Is that So? 285
Satsu 292
Teashop Zen 299
Two Good Monks 305

SEVEN

Ohashi 329
The Sound of One Hand 339
Precious Mirror Cave 357
Illusion and Play 369
Stone Garden 383

EIGHT

Dust under the Pines	393
Opening the Gates	403
Daimyo	407
Tall Tales	413
Ryutaku-ji	424
Bodhisattva of Hell	432

ONE

THE GATES OF HELL

My childhood name was Iwajiro, and I was eight years old when I first entered at the gates of hell. The old monk looked like one of the *gaki*, the hungry ghosts. He was gaunt and skeletal, cheeks caved in, skin shrunk tight over the great craggy dome of the skull, fierce eyes bulging in their sockets under thick black eyebrows that met in the middle just below the third eye. (When he glowered I could see it there, blazing.)

My father had brought me to hear the monk deliver a sermon, on the Eight Burning Hells. When the monk started to speak, voice dry and cracked, rasping, I felt he was talking directly to me, as if he had singled me out. He glared at me, pierced me with his gaze, cut me to the core.

I whimpered, grabbed my father's sleeve. My father shook me off, smacked the back of my legs.

Sit, he said. Listen.

The hells, the monk explained, descended in order of severity, down and down, ever deeper into the underworld. The first of them was the Hell of Reviving, and even here, he said, the heat was unbearable, far beyond endurance. The ground was a searing expanse of white-hot iron and it was impossible to rest your feet even for a second without being scorched.

I felt my feet twitch. It was a hot day and the shoji screens were open to the temple courtyard, shimmering in the glare. Inside at least it was shaded, cooler. The old wooden beams smelled of pine incense. I watched a little lizard, bright green, flick and dart across the wall.

In the Hell of Reviving, said the monk, you will be consumed by perpetual rage.

He looked at me, he definitely looked at me.

Think how angry you can get if you are thwarted in some small desire. You are ready to smash and destroy if you don't get your way. Well, increase this a thousandfold so you would kill anyone who obstructed you. This is what you will feel in the Reviving Hell.

I wondered, why Reviving? How could coming back to life be hell?

In this realm of the angry dead, said the monk, there will be countless millions of others like yourself, like your self, so many, so many, all consumed by their own incandescent fury. You will fight and tear and hack at each other with weapons you can only imagine, forged from your own karma. You will slash and cut and gouge, you will stab and rip till you fall down dead, a death within death, a death beyond death.

The monk paused.

And then, he said, looking at me again, answering my unspoken question, you will be revived immediately, you will wake up, you will once again be fully conscious, and the whole process will start again. You will fight, you will die in agony, you will be revived. And so it will continue for what seems like endless time. The scriptures are quite clear. You will fight and die in this realm for millions on millions of years. To be precise, for a hundred and sixty-two thousand times ten million years, you will fight and die in anger and pain. And this is the first, the least, of the Burning Hells.

A young monk bowed and placed a small tea-bowl of water

4

in front of the old man who nodded, took a sip, just enough to wet his thin old lips. I felt my own lips dry and parched. I looked up, saw the little green lizard scuttle across the ceiling, upside down.

The old monk coughed, loosed the phlegm in his throat. He sipped more water, continued.

The next level down, he said, the second level, is Black Line Hell. Again the ground is burning iron, hotter than the level above, and the demons of the underworld will lay you out on this white-hot surface and mark your naked body with black lines, dividing you up into ever smaller sections – four, eight, sixteen, thirty-two. And they will use these marks as guidelines for their burning saws and axes, and they will cut you into smaller and smaller pieces – sixty-four, a hundred and twenty-eight. And no sooner will you be reduced to tiny pieces of flesh and bone, than you will be reassembled, only for the whole process to start again, repeating, over and over, for twice as long as the first hell, for three hundred and twenty-four thousand times ten million years. And this is only the second of the Burning Hells.

Only the second, that meant six more to go, each one hotter and deeper and more terrible than the one above. The lizard had gone now, into the freedom of the world outside, and I wanted to follow, to run out, find my friends and play. My legs ached from kneeling on the hard wood floor, but when I shifted, tried to ease the discomfort, my father prodded me, cuffed the back of my head.

Be still, he said. Listen.

The third level, said the monk, is Crushing Hell. It is even deeper, even hotter. Here you will be rounded up with the millions of others suffering for their sins and you will be cast into a long valley between two ranges of fiery mountains. You will be packed in with these millions, piled on top of one another till there is no space to move and no air to breathe, and all that can be heard are the screaming and weeping of the damned in their agony and terror. Then the giant demons of this world will raise their mallets of red-hot metal, each one as big as Mount Fuji, and pound you to nothing. For a brief moment, an infinitesimal part of a second, there will be oblivion, then in a blink you will be awake, and immediately the whole cycle will begin again, the rounding up, the casting down, and this time the walls of the valley will close in on you, like great beasts butting each other, and once again you will be crushed. And this will continue for twice as long again as the previous level. Six hundred and forty-eight thousand times ten million years.

The numbers meant nothing. I could count, a little. But I couldn't imagine a million. Ten million. Grains of sand on a beach. Snowflakes falling through a whole winter day. My mother would laugh when I asked about these things. How could they be numbered? But I knew the way the old monk spoke, he meant they went on for ever and ever. And every time you thought the torture was over, it would start again.

The sermon hadn't even lasted a day, maybe not even an hour.

Howling Hell, said the monk. This is the next level down. Here you will be herded with all the rest into a gigantic red-hot building. And once you are inside, crammed together, suffocating, you will realise there is no exit, no door, no way out. You are trapped there, unable to move, as the intolerable heat increases even more and all you can do is howl and scream and cry and add to the cacophony of all those millions howling and screaming and crying all around you. And this you will endure for twice as long as the previous level. Ten million years, times twelve hundred and ninety-six thousand.

He looked at me again. I felt sick in my stomach.

You may think the exact numbers don't matter. But when you are there, and every single second is agony, it matters very much indeed.

Thinking of the numbers made my head feel like stone.

Now, said the monk, we descend ever further, from the Howling Hell to the Great Howling Hell. Here you will be crammed into an even bigger, even hotter building with thick burning walls, and outside those walls are thicker, hotter walls. You will be in a box within a box, a prison within a prison, a tomb within a tomb, where the space between the inner and outer walls is filled with molten metal, sealing it completely. And all the time you are there, you are tortured by the knowledge that even if by some miracle you could break through the first wall, you could never ever broach the second. So you howl and scream and cry, endlessly, or at least for twice as long as before. Some of you can add it up for yourselves, I'm sure.

Did his features twist a little as he said this, into a kind of grimace that might have been a smile? That was even more unsettling, and already he was racing ahead, ever deeper.

The sixth level, he said, is known simply as the Heating Hell – as if the other levels were not hot enough. Here you will be impaled on red-hot spikes, you will be flayed and wrapped in strips of white-hot iron. And for how long? Yes, twice as long as the hell before.

I noticed at the corners of his dry lizard-lips were little flecks of spit. He closed his eyes for a moment, continued.

And what is below the Heating Hell? What is the next level down? By now you should know it will be even worse, even hotter, for this is the *Intense* Heating Hell. Here you will be boiled in vats of molten bronze, then dragged out and impaled on larger spikes that tear your insides apart, the pain so intense

7

you lose consciousness for an instant, only to wake to the same torment, again, again, again, for twice as long as before.

He opened his eyes again, looked out from some deep dark place. His voice was low and gravelly, incantatory, the way he would chant the *Nembutsu*.

You have heard of the first seven hells, and the tortures and agonies that await you there. But these are as nothing compared to the last, the worst, the deepest hell. This is the Hell of Ultimate Torment.

I could read the words, blazing in the air, a sign written in flame.

In this realm, he said, the intense heat is seven times hotter than all the previous hells combined, and the pain is seven times greater. Here you will be trapped for seven times as long, in an immense edifice of blazing hot metal, at the centre of a mountain of white-hot iron. An army of demons will devise ever greater tortures, pouring molten bronze into your open mouth. Your body and the bodies of all the others suffering this damnation will be indistinguishable from the flames engulfing you. You will be separated only by the sound of your anguished screams which will echo back up through all the other hells. At times they can even be heard here in this world of ours, in the darkest night when you are racked with misery and despair. For surely these hells exist deep in your own being, and you can be pitched into them at any time.

Was that a bird shrieking out there in the courtyard? And was that an owl I'd heard screeching in the night? And was that really a cat that had woken me in the small hours, yowling like a baby stolen from its parents?

Don't whimper, said my father.

Existence is suffering, said the old monk. Its cause is desire. To conquer desire you must follow the Buddha-path. There is no other way.

8

His sermon was finished. He bowed and folded his hands, sipped a few more drops of water from his bowl. I was anxious to get out, to get home, to see my mother. The monk stood up, his old legs stiff as he creaked and unfolded himself. He walked slowly towards the door and I bowed my head as he passed. But he didn't pass. He stopped right in front of me. I kept my head down, stared at his gnarled old feet in their worn straw sandals, the thin toes bony and splayed, the blackened toenails thick and cracked.

So, he said. Have these words put the fear in you?

I looked up at him, that great domed head, that ferocious gaze, and my whole body shook. My mouth was dry, my throat closed. I couldn't say one word.

A man of silence, he said. This is a good place to begin.

He held up his right hand, fingers spread, and for a moment I flinched, expecting him to strike me. But instead he closed his hand again, made a fist, clenched it in front of my face.

Ha! he said, shaking the fist. Then he let out a terrifying roar of a laugh, sprayed spit, wiped his mouth with the back of his hand. He looked at my father who tensed beside me.

Look after this one, said the monk. Teach him well.

He glared down at me again, nodded, gave a kind of rough grunt and moved on. I watched his old feet in their straw sandals, shuffling across the polished floor, then he was out the door and gone.

My father smacked the back of my head. Why didn't you speak?

I had nothing to say, I said.

Useless, said my father.

All the way home I kept my head down, looked at my own bare feet leaving their mark in the dust with every step. The sun had baked the ground all day and it burned, made me

9

walk quick, not linger. I looked up at Mount Fuji in the haze. I imagined it throwing up fire and smoke. Beneath me were all these worlds, deeper and deeper underground. I was walking on the roof of hell.

Back home I still had nothing to say.

My mother laughed, but she was gentle, not mocking.

That old monk's a holy terror, isn't he? He'd put the fear of death into anybody.

I still said nothing.

Sometimes it's good to be just a little afraid, she said, so we'll do the right thing.

She had made noodles with my favourite broth, ginger and scallions and the thing I loved most, *tororojiru* with the rich earthy taste of mashed-up yams. I ate it in silence apart from the slurping. I drank the last of the broth, pushed the empty bowl away from me.

My older brother came into the kitchen, made a face at me behind my mother's back, tongue out, eyes popping, a demon.

She turned and saw him, laughed and waved him away. Then she stroked my head, ran her hands over the short cropped hair.

Go out and play a while, she said.

Outside, it was the same old place, the same old world I knew, but it was different. It was still Hara, way-station on the Tokaido, at the foot of Great Fuji. I was Iwajiro of the Nagasawa family, and my father ran the inn, Omodaka-ya. This was my life, here in this place. But it had changed. It was like somewhere I had dreamed. My friends looked the same, but they were strange to me. They moved around in their own dream, playing, not knowing.

At night, before I went to bed, my mother told me my favourite story, of the Dragon King's palace at the bottom of the sea. It calmed me and soothed me a little, imagining the coolness in the depths of the ocean. But when I lay down to sleep, I fell into dreams of fire and torment and I woke in a fever. I burned and howled till my mother came and held me and hushed me, said it was fine, it was fine, it was just a dream and everything would be all right, and she lit a stick of incense, chanted the Nembutsu to protect me from all harm.

But from that day on, everything had changed. The fear was always there.

*

One day my mother took me to the bathhouse. It was something I loved, to soak in the warmth, surrounded by it, to drift away.

To purify the mind, she said, chant the Nembutsu. To purify the body, sweat out all the poisons, soak in a hot tub.

The attendant at the bathhouse was a young girl. My mother nodded to her, told her to make the water good and hot.

Turn it up, she said. The hotter, the better.

The girl bowed, gave me a smile, set to stoking the fire under the iron tub. She prodded and raked with a poker so the embers glowed, she added more firewood and topped it with chopped logs when it caught and flared. It was hot work. The girl's face was flushed and a strand of her hair came loose, fell across her face. As she pushed it back, she left a smudge of soot on her cheek. She saw me looking and laughed. The flames flickered. I started to sweat.

Right, said my mother. Let's get you scrubbed.

I stepped out of my sandals, took off my robe and hung it up. I sat on the low three-legged stool and my mother washed me thoroughly, filled a little wooden bucket and poured it over my head, twice, three times, rinsed me down till I stood there dripping, clean and ready for the bath.

11

I turned and stepped forward, aware of my own nakedness, this little body of mine so tiny and fragile, so vulnerable, soft flesh. The heat in the room had grown intense. Steam rose, swirled in the air. The water gurgled and churned. Two merchants had come in and their voices boomed. I stood still and could not move. Through the steam I saw the girl's face as she smiled at me again, nodded encouragement. My mother pushed me forward. The fire was roaring under the tub. A huge flame suddenly leaped and the wood crackled, sent up sparks and cinders. There was a panic in my chest, a trapped bird desperate to escape. The waters would boil and scald me to death, my flesh would melt off the bone. I would plunge into the deepest hell and burn there forever.

No!

I heard my own voice, screaming, filling the place, till the girl covered her ears and the two men stopped their talking and stared, and my mother picked me up and wrapped me in my robe and carried me outside.

That night my father heard what had happened. He raged at me.

Why do you behave like this? Are you a baby?

I said nothing.

If you're going to scream and cry like a little girl, at least tell us why.

I'll tell my mother, I said, and no one else.

He looked for a moment as if he might slap me. Instead he let out a huge, long-suffering sigh and rubbed his face with his hands. Then he called my mother to come and talk to me.

So, little one, she said. That was quite a performance.

I stood with my head bowed, looked down at my feet in the straw sandals I wore indoors. This was me, standing here.

Well? she said.

It was the flames, I said. And the noise. And the heat.

Ah, she said.

I was afraid.

Of hell?

I nodded.

We have to put an end to this, she said. This fear is consuming you.

But how? If hell is waiting for us, how can we not be afraid? And if there is no escape, what is the point of anything we do?

There is a way, she said. But now it's late and you need to sleep. I'll tell you in the morning, I promise.

In the morning! That was no time, no time at all. She would tell me. I would know. I ran to her and she hugged me, stroked my back. The cotton of her robes smelled of incense from the shrine.

*

Some time in the night I heard a voice from behind the shoji screen, thin and wavery, a demon-voice wailing.

You're going to burn in hell . . .

I sat up, alarmed, but immediately the demon let out a chuckle and I recognised the voice of my older brother Yozaemon. I laughed and lay down again. Everything was going to be all right. I slept well, released from the fear. In fact my sleep was so deep I woke late, well after eight, and the morning sun was streaming in through the shoji screen. I jumped up and threw my clothes on, rushed into the kitchen to find my mother. But she was bustling about the stove, cooking miso soup in a heavy iron pot.

Not now, she said, shooing me away. I don't want you getting under my feet.

But you said!

Not now.

Well, when?

Later. As soon as I can. Now go and play.

She was hot and harassed, but she managed a smile.

Go!

I barely flinched at the little flames licking the bottom of the pot.

Outside I heard a gang of the neighbourhood children shrieking and yelling. I ran over, saw them kicking up dust, leaping and dancing like demons. One or two of them had sticks and were beating the ground with them, their screams getting more excited, high-pitched, as they stamped and screeched. I pushed through and saw what they were doing. They had tipped out a nest of baby crows and the boys ran and jumped and struck, chasing them, trying to stamp on them or hit them with the sticks.

I was excited and horrified all at once. There was a huge exhilaration in the game, in the hitting and beating and striking out, trying to crush and kill, and the crows were carrion, they were vermin, to be rid of them was good. But I could feel the panic and terror of the tiny birds as they fluttered and scurried, tried to escape. I felt it in my stomach, an agitation, discomfort, and maybe torturing the birds was a sin. I was suddenly hot, felt the prickle of tears. I pushed through the crowd of boys and ran back to the house.

My mother had said she would tell me, as soon as she could. But now she was sitting on the porch, talking to a neighbour whose husband was ill.

These things are sent to try us, said my mother.

What's for us will not go by us, said the woman.

They were sipping tea. They could talk like this for hours.

He was fine in the morning, said the woman. Then in the afternoon he took a turn for the worse.

14

It's often the way of it.

My mother looked over to me.

I haven't forgotten, she said. I'll talk to you soon. Now go and play a little longer.

Soon. A little longer. The whole morning could pass by and they would still be talking. I heard my mother tell the woman to burn the moxa herbs on her husband's spine, and to continue chanting the sutras.

Back outside I saw the gang of boys running off into the distance, whooping and brandishing their sticks in the air. There was no trace of the baby crows, then I saw a scraggy stray cat had dragged one of the tiny carcasses into the shade of a tree and was holding it down with its paws, tearing it apart with its teeth, crunching the little bones.

My mother was still talking to the woman. At least they had stood up now, but that might mean nothing. They could still take another hour to get to the door and for the woman to actually leave. It was unbearable.

My head hurts, I shouted. I have a fever.

My mother smiled, nodded at the woman.

This young man has things on his mind!

When more time had passed, and the woman had finally gone, my mother turned to me.

So, she said. Your head aches. You have a fever. Let us deal with those things first.

No! You said you would tell me!

But headache and fever are no joke, she said, and she placed her cool hand on my forehead.

The thought had been niggling at me, and now it began to grow, that she didn't have an answer after all, and she had been lying and stalling just to keep me quiet.

Tell me!

A remedy is called for, she said.

You told that woman to burn moxa and chant the sutras, I said. Is that what you're going to tell me?

You were listening, she said. You have big ears!

Tell me!

Moxa would help your headache.

But moxa meant burning, and the fear would be there again.

Not moxa!

She laughed.

You're the wisest child in the world, she said. You've found the answer all by yourself. No moxa, you only have to chant a sutra. But not just any sutra. You have to chant the Tenjin Sutra.

Tenjin. I said the name. Tenjin.

Tenjin is the deity of Kitano shrine, she said. In life he was Michizane, a scholar and poet, a great calligrapher. As a god he is Tenjin, with the power of fire and thunder. He can drive out angry ghosts and conquer the fear of hell.

Tenjin, I said again. Tenjin.

All you have to do, said my mother, is chant the sutra, every morning when you wake and every night before you sleep. It is only a few lines long, a hundred Chinese characters, but it is very powerful.

I felt a kind of fire kindle in me, in the centre of my chest, and below that, in my belly. I was excited, impatient.

Teach it to me now!

She laughed.

Come, she said, holding out her hand, and she led me out by the back door.

Where are we going?

Sanen-ji, she said.

Sanen-ji was the Pure Land temple, across the road from our house. It had a shrine room and a little sacred grove

16

dedicated to Tenjin. The place was tended by a young monk who was sweeping the steps as we came in at the gate. He bowed to my mother, then to me, and asked if he could be of help to us. My mother explained about the sutra and he smiled at me, said yes. He could not have been more different from the old monk I had heard at the other temple, Shogen-ji, who had filled my head with hellfire and damnation. This young man had a mildness and a gentleness about him, a kind of lightness. He beckoned us to follow him into the shrine room, leaving our sandals outside. We kneeled beside him on the tatami floor and he lit a stick of incense at the altar. A few flowers had been placed in an old vase in front of a painting of Tenjin, one hand raised in blessing. The expression on the face was benign, kindly, but behind him a thunderbolt emerged from a cloud, and beside him was an ox, looking up at him.

The ox is his messenger, said the monk. So the best time to pray to him is the hour of the ox, between two and three in the morning.

My mother shifted uneasily.

But, of course, said the monk, a young man like you should just meditate as early as you can, whenever you wake up.

I will wake up at two, I said. The hour of the ox.

The monk nodded approval, gave a little chuckle. Then he became serious again, reached forward and opened a drawer at the side of the shrine, drew out a scroll of paper which he unrolled and handed to me. I could only read a few of the characters, like *wind* and *fire*. But the page had an effect on me – again I felt that sensation in my chest, in my belly, and something in my forehead, a kind of tingling.

We'll chant, said the monk. Take it a line at a time. I'll chant it first, then you repeat it with me.

He folded his hands and began, his voice surprisingly deep and resonant. I folded my own hands, copied him as best I

17

could, my own small voice cracked and high but eager, and my mother joined in, a clear sweet singsong. By the time we'd gone through the whole thing two or three times I was singing out with all my heart and soul.

The monk bowed to me again and said I could keep the copy of the sutra, and from the same drawer he took out a smaller copy of the painting of Tenjin.

You should take this too, he said, for your shrine.

I carried my treasures home, overcome with excitement, and went straight to the little altar room in our house. I swept the floor and dusted the shrine. I took down the painting that hung in the alcove and replaced it with the image of Tenjin. I laid out my copy of the sutra in front of it. I emptied the ash from the incense holder and cleaned it out, lit a new stick. I pestered my mother for a few fresh flowers from the display in the front room and I put them in a vase. Then I bowed to Tenjin, and I chanted the sutra over and over till I knew the words by heart.

*

It was the middle of the night. I didn't know the exact time, but I knew it must be close to the hour of the ox. The whole house was dark and quiet as I felt my way, step by step, to the altar room where I managed to light the oil lamp, put another stick of incense in the burner. Then I kneeled on the tatami in front of the shrine, folded my hands and started to chant the sutra.

Namu Tenman Daijizai Tenjin . . .

I thought I was awake, but from time to time my eyes started to close and my head nodded forward, jerking me awake again. Then I would start the sutra all over again, from the beginning.

Namu Tenman . . .

In the flicker of the lamplight, the image of Tenjin changed, came in and out of focus. Now it was kindly, the way I had seen it before, now the expression was fierce. I invoked him to ward off demons, to keep me from the perils of hell.

Namu Tenman . . .

My legs began to ache. Outside a wind rose, shook the pine trees. There was a howl, a shriek. Something darted past, brushed against the shoji screen, scared me. But I told myself it was only a bat, and if it was anything else, anything worse, out there in the dark, Tenjin would protect me.

Namu . . .

The house itself seemed to creak and groan. Shadows shifted, wavered. Something scurried, was gone when I looked. I shivered, chanted louder.

Namu Tenman . . . *Tenjin* . . .

There was a sudden noise behind me, a rustling, a thud. I sensed a huge dark shape, looming, and a great deep voice boomed out.

What the hell are you doing?

It was my father, his robe pulled about him, his hair dishevelled, eyes staring.

I am chanting the Tenjin Sutra.

Do you know what time it is?

The hour of the ox.

He growled.

The bloody hour of the bloody ox!

It's the best time, I said.

It's the middle of the bloody night!

I bowed low, kept my head down on the tatami. I heard another rustling and smelled a faint perfume I recognised as my mother.

The boy is doing what the monk told him, she said. He's doing the right thing.

He's wasting lamp-oil, said my father. At his age this is ridiculous. You'll turn him into a useless layabout, a lazy good-for-nothing with his head full of nonsense about burning in hell.

At this rate, you'll burn in hell yourself, she said. You neglect your own devotions and now you're trying to stop the boy from following the way. You should be ashamed.

I thought my father was going to choke. The veins stood out on his thick neck. The lamplight changed his face, made him look demonic. He let out a kind of grunt and turned away, went crashing through the house, shaking the whole wooden frame of the building as he slammed shut the shoji-screen door.

My mother held me a moment, spoke calmly.

Don't be troubled, little one. You are doing what you must. This is your path. For this I bore you. Now, chant the sutra one more time, then go and get some sleep.

TENJIN

Encouraged by my mother, I persisted with my devotions. For weeks, months, I got up faithfully, every morning at the hour of the ox, while it was still dark. I bowed to Tenjin, I chanted the sutra. My father said nothing, but from time to time I caught him glaring at me then turning away. I continued, regardless. Then something happened that shook my faith.

Among the boys in the village there was a sudden fashion for a game of archery, shooting at a target with a special small-scale bow and half-size arrows. My father gave me a set, perhaps to deflect my attention from what he still saw as a waste of time, and briefly I became obsessed with the game, determined to improve.

It was summer and my brother was home from school, hanging about the house, and he watched my efforts with a mixture of irritation and amusement. Some day he would inherit the family business, run the inn, take over the way-station from my father, and already he was puffed up with the sense of himself and his place in the world.

One particular afternoon he was lolling back on the balcony, cool in the shade, as I tried again and again to hit the little pine tree that grew in the yard. The more I tried, the louder he laughed and the wilder my shots became.

Great samurai, he said, maybe you should try hitting a barn door!

I tried again, missed again, and he laughed even more.

Maybe you should pray to your Tenjin, he said. Ask him to help you out.

I picked up my arrows and strode into the house, trying to calm myself and fight down the rage. Inside it was cooler, and without my brother taunting me I thought I might have more success. I looked around the room. One set of shoji screens was decorated with a chrysanthemum flower. The circular shape of it, the petals radiating out from the centre, to my eye made a perfect target. I set myself to hitting it right in the middle, the heart of the flower. I got it in my sights, let fly and missed, the arrow skittering through the open half of the screen and into the room beyond. It was frustrating, twanging the string, seeing the arrow float harmlessly wide of its target.

I had to concentrate. One of the older boys I'd seen practising spoke mysteriously of *kyudo*, the way of the bow, as if it was a kind of meditation in itself. You have to act as if you are not acting, he said. Pull the bowstring as if you are not pulling it. Aim at the target as if there is no target.

None of this made any sense to me. It all just sounded like so much nonsense, and the boy, like my brother, was full of himself, cocksure. Nevertheless, he hit the target more often than not, so perhaps if I tried not trying, I would improve. And after all, I knew a little about discipline, I got up every morning at the hour of the ox to chant the sutra. Perhaps my brother was right, and Tenjin would help me.

I stood a moment and folded my hands, chanted the opening verse. Then I picked up the bow and breathed deep. I concentrated my gaze on the painted chrysanthemum, at the point right in the centre, the target. I remembered the older boy,

22

tried to copy the way he stood, the way he held his arm out straight, grasping the bow, the way he placed the arrow, pulled back the string. I tried to empty my mind, I asked Tenjin for help.

Now.

I released the arrow, saw it fly, higher than I'd shot it before, wide of the target and through the gap into the next room. In the room was the *tokonoma* alcove where a special scroll hung, a painting of the poet Saigyo standing under a willow tree, composing verses. My mother had very few possessions she treasured – a hair clasp, a silk kimono with a lotus pattern, a little wooden statue of Kannon, Bodhisattva of mercy, and this scroll with the painting of Saigyo.

The arrow had flown straight and true, as if guided by some malevolent spirit. It had hit the scroll, pierced the poet's left eye.

I dropped the bow and ran into the room. I pulled out the arrow and that only made things worse as the arrow tore a bigger hole, as if Saigyo's eye had been gouged out. I let out a cry then pressed my head to the ground. I asked Tenjin to protect me, to let my crime somehow go undiscovered. But my brother had heard the noise and came rushing in.

You're dead, he said.

And my father was standing in the doorway.

What is it now? he asked. And he looked where my brother was pointing. He saw the damage to the picture and he grabbed the arrow from me, picked up the bow.

Useless! he said, and he strode off.

Then I saw that my mother had come into the room, stood staring at the scroll. She said nothing, and the look in her eyes was not anger, but sadness, and that was much much worse.

*

23

That night I couldn't sleep, turned this way and that, tortured. If I hadn't picked up the bow. If I hadn't fired at the target. If I hadn't tried not to try. And the final, terrible thought, if I hadn't asked Tenjin for help. He had failed me. But I mustn't think that. Ultimately Tenjin would protect me, he would save me from hell.

I was wide awake at the hour of the ox – I hadn't slept. So I sat as usual in front of the shrine and lit a stick of incense.

There was something I had heard, a way of reading the smoke from the incense. I would ask the deity a question, and the smoke would give the answer. I folded my hands.

Great Tenjin, I sit at your feet and ask you this question. If you can save me from the burning fires of hell, make this smoke rise straight up. But if you cannot help me, make the smoke blow this way and that.

I concentrated intensely, my eyes clenched shut, my folded hands pressed tight together. Then carefully I opened my eyes and peered at the smoke. It rose in a long white line towards the ceiling, straight and unbroken. I felt sheer relief, elation. Tenjin had given me a sign. I laughed and let my hands fall to my lap, and immediately the smoke started writhing and breaking up, dispersing and drifting across the room.

The answer was clear. Tenjin could not protect me. I was damned.

*

Next morning I was miserable. There was no point in getting out of bed, no point in eating, or playing. No point in chanting the sutra. No point in anything.

My mother came to me in my room.

It was just an old painting, she said, a dusty old scroll. It can probably be patched up. And if it can't, it doesn't matter. It's not worth the misery.

It's not just the painting, I said. And I told her about asking Tenjin, and the smoke from the incense giving me my answer.

And, of course, she said, you're such a terrible, terrible sinner.

I could see she was trying not to smile, but I turned away. This was serious.

In the first place, she said, sometimes it's better if we face up to things. It's better for our karma if we take our medicine. And second, you're being very hard on Tenjin! Are you going to give up on him just like that, and believe some hocus pocus about incense smoke? Are you going to be like that smoke, at the mercy of a puff of wind, blowing you this way and that?

I felt something in my chest, a bubble bursting, and I let out a great sob.

There, she said, hugging me. There.

*

A puppet show was advertised in nearby Suwa, and my mother said she would take me.

They're performing a wonderful story, she said, about the great teacher Nisshin Shonin. I wanted to know what happened in the story, but she wouldn't tell me. She said she didn't want to spoil it for me, she would let me see it for myself.

The performance was outdoors, in a temple courtyard. It was early evening, the light beginning to fade, and lamps had been lit all around. A little stage had been set up with a simple black curtain as backdrop. I had never been to a puppet show, or any kind of theatre, so I didn't know what to expect, but I knew from my mother's quiet excitement it must be something special. The place was crowded but we had arrived early and sat near the front.

25

A group of musicians sat at the side of the stage and suddenly, with the whack of wooden clappers, they began to play, the ripple and twang of a koto, wail of a samisen, breathiness of a shakuhachi flute. Immediately the atmosphere changed. The sense of anticipation intensified and it felt as if we were in a special place. I hadn't seen the puppeteers come on stage, but suddenly they were there, dressed in black, the little puppet figures slumped in front of them.

At first I felt a slight disappointment. The puppeteers were in full view, it would be obvious they were manipulating the figures, it would be distracting, it would spoil the illusion.

Then the music changed, a rapid drumbeat, a man's voice chanting, intoning the story, and slowly, slowly, one of the puppet figures began to move. The little body straightened up, the little head raised, the little hands came together. He bowed and the little eyes blinked once, stared straight out, right at me, and I caught my breath, completely and utterly transfixed.

The everyday world fell away. None of it mattered, the courtyard, the crowd, the stage, the puppeteers, none of it was real. We had been drawn into another world where this little being was fully alive. He was Nisshin Shonin, come to life.

He told us of the true path to enlightenment, the chanting of the Lotus Sutra, and how his devotion to that path might cost him his life. He had fallen foul of the Shogun, Yoshinori, and been denounced as a heretic. Now he was to be tortured and forced to give up his faith.

Another figure loomed beside him. This was Lord Tokimune, the Shogun's henchman.

Tell me, he demanded. If you follow the teachings of the Lotus Sutra, can you bear the heat of a blazing fire?

A true devotee, said Nisshin, can enter into a raging fire without being harmed.

Indeed? said Tokimune. Let us put this to the test.

I felt the fear again, for Nisshin, for myself. My throat was dry, a sick emptiness in my stomach. The voices and the music said the torturers were piling up firewood and setting it alight. I could smell it, I could feel the heat. Nisshin was ordered to walk through the flames. He moved forward, hands folded in front of him. He wavered a moment, as if from the intense heat, then he gathered himself again. The music grew louder and through it came the chant from the sutra.

Namu Myoho Renge Kyo.

He stood, unscathed.

This is the protection of Kannon Bodhisattva, he said, and I felt a thrill, a tingling in my spine. The audience shouted their approval, applauded. I thought the show was over. But the music changed again as Tokimune stepped forward.

So you can bear a little heat, he said. But do you think this can be compared to the fires of hell?

I would not be so arrogant, said Nisshin.

We must give you a sterner test, said Tokimune. Now, kneel.

The music changed again, thud of a deeper drum, screech and wail of the flute and strings. Two more figures appeared, summoned by Tokimune. They moved awkwardly, carried between them two poles, and suspended from the poles was an iron pot, a cauldron. Tokimune explained that the cauldron was red-hot and the two men could hardly bear the heat. Nisshin was kneeling in front of them, and with difficulty they raised the pot over his head as he chanted once more.

Namu Myoho Renge Kyo.

The sky had darkened and a breeze made the lanterns flare. Steam and smoke rose from the cauldron as the two men shook from the effort of holding it up. The music grew louder still, the howling of demons, as the cauldron was placed on Nisshin's head, and he flinched and the audience gasped and I thought my heart would stop. I clung to my mother's sleeve.

27

Courage, she said.

Then we heard it, getting stronger, rising above the cacophony.

Namu Myoho Renge Kyo.

The two bearers staggered back and let the cauldron fall to the ground. Nisshin stood up, folded his hands and continued his chant.

Namu Myoho Renge Kyo.

There was a cheer and a few people at the back started chanting along with Nisshin.

Namu Myoho Renge Kyo.

More and more people joined in, and my mother was chanting, and I was too, and so was everyone else in the audience.

Namu Myoho Renge Kyo.

Namu Myoho Renge Kyo.

The voices rose together, like one great voice, into the night, and I felt lifted up, outside myself. I had tears in my eyes, and my mother wiped them with her sleeve. On the way home I told her I knew what I wanted to be. I would be like Nisshin. I would leave home and be a monk.

Yes, she said. Yes. When it's time.

WISE CRANE

Iwas fourteen and felt as if I had been practising these devotions all my young life. I got up every night, shocked myself awake with cold water, lit incense and sat chanting the sutras. It meant I began each day with a kind of strength and clarity, even if it faded as the day wore on. But lately it had been fading more and more quickly. Some little thing would jangle my nerves, make me angry, and it felt as if all the austerity was for nothing. Then that old fear of hell began to stir in me, and I was once again that frightened child, terrified of burning in the fires.

Something else was stirring too. My body was changing, and the young girls at the bathhouse looked at me differently. They would whisper to each other and giggle, glance in my direction and turn away. It filled me with confusion and a huge dumb longing. The pale little lizard between my legs would harden and redden, rear up like a dragon, and I had to hide it behind my towel as I eased into the tub, praying for it to subside.

It would leap up again in the night, this tough stubborn little dragon, when I woke from muddled dreams involving those girls from the bathhouse. I imagined when I doused myself with cold water it would hiss and steam. I could picture it, the way I could sometimes see the figures on a painted scroll, on the storyteller's *kamishibai* screen, move around with a life of their own, animated. It was another world, or another way of looking at this world. It was this world exaggerated, made fluid, and it made me laugh.

I took to making little drawings myself, using a brush and inkstone I'd found in an old box at the back of the shrine room. I'd beg scraps of rice paper from my mother – discarded wrapping paper, out-of-date bills and receipts. I'd turn them over, sketch on the blank side, practise my calligraphy. Sometimes an unintended drip or smear of ink would make an interesting shape and I'd turn it into a bird or an animal, a mountain or a twisted branch. One time an accidental swish of the brush became my mother's kimono and I quickly sketched in her round face above it with the tip of the brush. Another time a smudge looked like my father's thick eyebrows and I added the glowering eyes, the grim line of the mouth. I showed both the portraits to my mother and she laughed, said I'd got them just right. But I didn't show them to my father.

Once I doodled a shape that looked like my own body, naked, the way I saw it when I stepped out of the bath. The brush made a quick approximation of my face, then before I knew it I had drawn that little dragon between the legs, just the way I had imagined it with steam rising as if cold water had doused its fire. Again it made me laugh but then the laugh cut short, stopped. I saw the expression on the face I had drawn, a leer, demonic. I took the brush and tried to wipe out the drawing, but I only succeeded in blurring, smudging the shapes. The face was distorted now, ugly, and the dragon shape was still there, darker, more solid.

I crumpled up the paper, crushed it to a ball in my fist, looked for somewhere to throw it away. But I didn't want my mother, or even worse, my father, to find it. If I dropped it outside, I imagined the wind catching, unfurling it, blowing it into the village where one of my friends would find it. It would be passed around, pinned onto a noticeboard. The girls at the bathhouse would look at it and snigger. It might even blow all the way to Mishima where my brother was at school. He would find it and recognise it as mine.

I could tear it into tiny pieces and scatter it, but the pieces would never be small enough. Somebody might gather them up, put them together again.

This was madness, but it took hold of me. Then I realised the only thing to do with the drawing was burn it. There was a lamp burning in the shrine room and I bowed before it. I unfolded the drawing and held it carefully to the flame, catching one corner and setting it alight. But I hadn't allowed for it flaring up so quick. I had to get it outside or I'd burn down the house. I stumbled towards the door and out into the yard, shook the burning paper from my hand just as the flame reached my fingers, scorched me. My eyes smarted. My fingers stung, red. They would blister.

I tucked the hand under my armpit to numb the stinging. I stamped barefoot on the ash, on the charred remains of the page.

My father stuck his head out the window.

What is it this time?

Nothing, I said. I was just burning something. Out here. Outside.

He took in a breath, about to say something, but then stopped as if he truly, genuinely, had no idea where to begin.

*

My burned fingers nipped for days. I eased them in cold water, dabbed them dry. My mother asked what had happened. I told her I'd burned my hand on the lamp.

Testing yourself again? she asked.

I'd gone through a spell, a year or two back, of holding my hand over a candle flame, seeing how long I could bear it.

Not this time, I said. It was an accident.

But this pain, now, reminded me how little I could take, and how this was nothing, less than nothing, compared to that other, endless fire. And I knew it was the fire of desire that had brought me here, that fierce little dragon. I had read about it, and I'd seen beasts in their season, cattle in the fields, dogs in a dusty backyard, grimly coupling. My brother had taken a leering delight in telling me our mother and father had done this, that it was how we were made, how we came into the world.

I made up my mind. The only way to conquer this desire, to go beyond it, was to throw myself into the spiritual life. It was time for me to go away, to become a monk.

*

Fuji was this constant presence, this vastness, towering above the village, filling the horizon. It changed from moment to moment, day to day, season to season. It was hidden by spring mists, shimmered in summer haze, burned almost red in autumn, shone pure white in winter. But the shape of it, the form, was always there, taking the breath away, quickening the heart.

I was wandering at the edge of the village, gazing up absently at the mountain, when I heard shouts in the distance. I had forgotten the procession would be passing through – the Daimyo and his entourage, his retinue, returning from Edo. Every year he had to make this journey – to Edo and back – on pain of death and at huge expense, to declare his loyalty to the Shogun.

We heard crazy stories about the Shogun. He was known as Inu-Kubo, the Dog Shogun. He'd been born in the Year of the Dog and some rogue of a Buddhist monk had told him he'd been a dog in his last animal incarnation, before becoming human. So he'd issued an edict, *On Compassion for Living Things*, making a law that dogs should not be harmed and should be treated with respect. Anyone disobeying was liable to summary execution.

I'd heard people talk about it at the inn. If they had too much to drink they might start by criticising the Daimyo, then they'd move on to the Shogun. (Somebody would bark.) Or they'd even criticise the emperor himself. Then a friend would make a cut-throat gesture or my father would clear his throat loudly and change the subject.

I'd always loved watching the procession pass through Hara, the endless ranks of pikemen and flag-bearers, riflemen, armed samurai on horseback, ranks of foot-soldiers, priests and servants, palanquins wobbling on the shoulders of the bearers, the Daimyo himself in his elaborate *norimon*, curtained to shield him from view. There must have been a thousand men in the procession, and it took hours to pass through the village. Some of the Daimyo's retainers would stop at the inn to water their horses, and my father would take charge and be suitably deferential as they ate and drank and shouted out their orders. The critics and gossips would stay well back, emerging later to share the news they'd picked up from the footsoldiers, rumours from the capital, tales from the floating world.

I found a vantage point, back from the road, and settled to watch. The pikemen appeared first, the vanguard, all dressed in black silk, walking with their strange exaggerated slow march that was almost a kind of dance, raising the foot high then gliding forward. They did this in concentrated

33

silence, the only sounds the swish of silk, the crunch of gravel underfoot.

The lead man stepped for a moment to the side of the road, hitched up his loincloth and let out a great stream of piss, spattering in the dust. A few of the young girls from the bathhouse had been standing nearby and they jumped back, laughing.

Did you see his thing?

What a pike!

The size of it!

They laughed even louder, but the pikeman had returned to his position sombre and dignified, and resumed his slow march.

A little way behind came the Daimyo himself, carried on high, hidden inside the *norimon* with its silk curtains, its elaborate carvings, and some way further back came another *norimon*, smaller, less ornate, but still beautifully decorated. This too had its curtains closed, but just as it passed me, they opened with a swish of silk and a woman was looking out at me. Her face was the most beautiful I had ever seen, like an *ukiyo-e* painting, like the goddess Kannon herself, embodied.

I must have been staring, and I'm sure my mouth fell open so I gulped like some stupid carp surfacing. The woman smiled and the curtain fell shut. I was shaken, but I bowed and turned away, continued walking up the hill, Fuji ahead of me.

There was a haiku I had read.

Beloved Fuji –
The mist clears and reveals
Your snowy whiteness.

When I'd climbed far enough, I looked back, saw the procession still trailing into the distance, but so small, so insignificant. I imagined each and every one of that huge entourage plodding along with head down, eyes fixed on the ground, not once looking up at this. This.

I knew when I went back to the inn I would have to help clear up the mess. My father would ask where I had been and raise his eyes to heaven.

I bowed once more to the mountain, and dragging my steps I headed back down.

*

Now I made drawings of Fuji, with swift simple strokes, and I tried to draw Bodhisattva Kannon. Sometimes her face looked like my mother, sometimes like the woman who had looked out at me through the curtains of the norimon.

My restlessness increased and I went out walking every day, climbed the slopes of Mount Yanagizawa in search of a quiet place to sit, away from the everyday world. I found the perfect spot, a flat rock above a mountain stream, a sheer cliff face rising up behind. I sat for hours, totally absorbed, reciting what I knew of the sutras, looking down at the rushing stream, or up at Fuji.

One day I noticed that a configuration of the rock, viewed from a certain angle, resembled Kannon herself. The next morning I brought a chisel and a small mallet, borrowed from my father's workshop, and I set to carving the likeness into the stone, accentuating what was already there, bringing it to life. When I'd finished I stood looking at it in amazement, the Bodhisattva smiling at me. I bowed my head and chanted to her in reverence.

Enmei Jikku Kannon Gyo.

35

That afternoon there were heavy rains and I took shelter under an overhang of rock. When the rain had subsided I climbed down to head for home. The stream was swollen, the waters rushing fast, and I had to wade across, carrying the chisel and mallet, wrapped in cloth, above my head. Twice I stumbled, lost my footing and almost went under, the water reaching up to my chin. I made it to the other side, and I got home, drenched and shivering, my clothes sticking to me. But I was elated, and my mother could see it in me.

Perhaps it's time, she said.

*

My mother was Nichiren Buddhist. That was why she had loved the story of Nisshin Shonin walking through fire, saving himself by chanting the Lotus Sutra. So it was no surprise when she suggested I go to Shoin-ji, a Nichiren temple. But then she said something else that did surprise me.

And after all, she smiled, it is where your father studied as a young man.

At first I thought I had misheard, or misunderstood.

My father? I said. He studied at the temple?

For a few short years, she said, he trained for the priesthood. He was taught by his uncle, Daizui-Rojin.

My head felt cold. There was a taste like iron in my mouth.

I didn't know, I said. I had no idea.

There is much you do not know about your father, she said.

I bowed.

Where do you think that brush and inkstone came from? she said. The ones you've been using.

They were his?

His calligraphy was good, she said, though he lacked your talent for making these drawings and bringing them to life!

36

I thought of the drawing I had burned. I felt myself blush.

So you see, she said, when he gets angry at you, or loses patience, it is not a simple matter.

The drawing I had done of him, glowering.

He knows how difficult that life can be, said my mother. Perhaps he is afraid for you, and thinks you are too young.

He thinks I will fail.

She left a silence, then continued.

Perhaps in his heart he feels that he failed, and it pains him to think of such things, so he pushes them away.

My father, the businessman. My father with his brusqueness, his ferocious samurai manner, inherited from his father. My father's impatience with me, his anger at my devotions, calling it all a waste of time.

The way is not easy, said my mother. And perhaps his real work, like mine, was to bring you into the world, to provide for you. Until now.

*

Tanrei, the head priest at Shoin-ji, was old and frail. He said I might be better to follow my vocation at another temple, Daisho-ji, in the neighbouring town of Numazu. Perhaps he also thought it would be best for me to move away from home, to put some distance – even just a few miles – between myself and my parents. But he said he would accept me into the order. I would receive the tonsure and he would give me a new name.

On the appointed day I bathed and dressed in monks' robes of rough grey cloth. My head was shorn then lathered and shaved, scraped close to the scalp. The monk who used the razor had a steady hand and only once, when I twitched, he nicked the skin with the blade, just at the crown of my head. He dabbed the little bead of blood.

This one's keen, he said. He wants to open his crown chakra already.

I rubbed my head, felt the rough stubble. I was led into the meditation hall and told to kneel in front of Tanrei who sat upright on a hard wooden bench. The sharp tang of incense filled the air.

From today on, he said, Iwajiro is no more. You will leave the name behind as you leave behind your childhood. Your new name is Ekaku. Repeat it after me. Ekaku.

Ekaku.

It means Wise Crane.

Ekaku.

Go to the shrine room, he said, and chant the name one hundred and eight times. Let the sound of it fill you. Become the name. Ekaku.

Ekaku.

The monk who had shaved my head handed me a string of *juzu*, counting beads. From the length of it I knew there must be 108 beads, the sacred number. I would count them between thumb and forefinger as I chanted. I thanked him and sat in front of the shrine. Here too the smell of incense was strong. The very walls, the old wooden beams and pillars, were infused with its ancient musky scent.

I straightened my back and began to chant, my own voice as strange to me as this new name, my mantra.

Ekaku. Ekaku.

Wise Crane.

As I chanted I felt the sound resonate in my belly, my chest, my throat. Then the word lost all meaning, became pure sound.

Ekaku.

It became the cry of a bird, a white crane in flight across the evening sky.

Ekaku.

Then I was the crane, neck thrust forward, spreading my wings. I alighted on a rock, folded in on myself, and I was an old Chinese sage, looking out over a range of mountains.

Ekaku.

My finger and thumb closed on the final bead, larger than the rest. I chanted one last time.

Ekaku.

I stepped outside and into this new life.

My shaved head. The spring breeze.

*

A few weeks later my parents came to see me off on my journey. The arrangements had been made. The head priest at Daisho-ji would be expecting me. My father had given me a few coins tied in an old purse, enough to pay for my keep when I arrived. I thanked him and bowed low, pressed my forehead to the ground, stood up again and dusted myself down. My mother held me a moment, stood back and bowed to me with folded hands.

I shouldered my pack and set out walking along the Tokaido. The spring morning was bright and cold. Looking up, I saw Fuji, immense above the clouds, then they swirled and closed in again, obscuring it. I turned and looked back, saw my mother and father still standing there. I waved and my mother bowed, my father gave a nod of the head and turned away, went back inside.

Further on I stopped and put my straw *kasa* on my head. Again I looked back and could still see my mother, small and distant. Again I waved, and this time she also waved. I walked on. At a bend in the road, I turned and looked back one last time, and she was still there, a tiny figure, just distinguishable.

I thought she was waving again, and I did the same. I kept walking, and the next time I looked I could no longer see her, or the house, or the village. The world I knew had shrunk and disappeared, and now Fuji shook off its mist and cloud and loomed there, huge and serene, a great being, dreaming itself.

ONE TIME, ONE PLACE

The head priest at Daisho-ji, Sokudo Fueki, was a wiry, vigorous man, perhaps my father's age, in his forties.

So, he said, you didn't last long at Shoin-ji. Why did they throw you out?

The priest, I said, Tanrei Soden. He thought . . .

That old fart, said Sokudo. He hasn't had a thought in years. He should just write a death-verse and pack his bags, be done with it.

I was shocked at his bluntness. Then I wondered if his words were a test.

I'm sure he is a man of wisdom, I said, and a very capable priest.

Oh, you're sure, are you? said Sokudo. On the basis of what?

I . . .

He took one look at you, shaved your head, slapped a new name on you and shunted you out the door.

It was true. I'd been disappointed at the speed of my departure from Shoin-ji, with barely time to let the dust settle. But I'd assumed the old man knew what was for the best.

Your loyalty does you credit, said Sokudo. And perhaps I'm being harsh. Maybe if I get to that age I'll be content to sit on my arse waiting for enlightenment. But right now I think it would be better to die and descend into hell.

I felt the heat prickle my scalp, sweat run down my back.

41

Descend into hell.

He sensed my reaction.

Ah, he said. The fear. Well, that can be a good place to start. As good as any.

*

I was set a number of seemingly menial tasks – scrubbing the floors, sweeping the courtyard, scouring out the rice-pots in the kitchen. With long sessions of zazen – seated meditation – in between, beginning early in the morning, the work filled my time and I was glad of the routine. But right from the beginning I hankered after more.

One day Sokudo told me someone wanted to see me, a respected guest who was passing through. He led me to the shrine room and bowed to the old man seated there. I recognised him straight away – he was Kyushinbo, a wandering monk with a fearsome reputation. When I was a child he had often stayed at my parents' home on his way along the Tokaido. They were grateful to have him visit and to offer him hospitality.

Once he had told me I would achieve great things when I grew up. Remember the path is long and arduous, he told me. Shakyamuni was six years in the mountains. Bodhidharma was nine years at Shao-lin. You must persevere.

He was famous for chanting the Nembutsu and he played the shakuhachi with a wild spine-chilling energy. It was rumoured he could fly through the air and he was reputed to be over a hundred years old.

Now here he was, seated in front of me. I bowed and pressed my forehead to the floor, didn't get up till he addressed me.

So, he said, young crane. You have embarked on your journey.

42

I didn't know what to say. I nodded and stood silent.

One time alone, he said. One place alone. Remember this precept. Be one-pointed in your practice. One time, one place.

I bowed deep and he continued.

I have three pieces of advice, he said, and I stood, ready to receive his guidance.

First, do not waste food. When you have finished eating, clean your bowl by rinsing it with warm water, then drink the water from the bowl.

This made sense. It was wise, and frugal, though perhaps not the kind of instruction I was expecting.

Second, he said, never piss standing up. Always crouch down.

Yes, I said. I mean, no.

Third, he said, never piss or shit facing north.

Again I was at a loss, not knowing how to respond.

Follow these instructions rigorously, said the old man, and you will live a long healthy life.

Remember Shakyamuni, he said. Remember Bodhidharma. Persevere.

The interview was over. I bowed and backed out of the room.

Later Sokudo spoke to me.

An unexpected blessing, he said.

Yes, I said. I am sure his advice will be . . . useful.

He laughed.

Persevere.

*

More than anything I was eager to read the Lotus Sutra. The teaching of Nichiren had sustained my mother all her life. I could see her face, smiling at me. I remembered the feeling

43

at that puppet show, the tale of Nisshin Shonin walking through fire, the power and intensity of the whole audience joining in the chant. *Namu Myoho Renge Kyo.* Now I could read the sutra for myself.

I was alone in the library, the book on the table in front of me, lifted down from its special place, unwrapped. I had lit an incense stick. I kneeled in reverence and gratitude. I chanted. *Namu Myoho Renge Kyo.* Outside, a bird sang, a *hototogisu.* I bowed and opened the book, began to read.

It was hard work.

It wasn't just that the Chinese characters were difficult to read, it was the words themselves, the density and weight of the thing.

It began well enough, clearly and simply.

Thus have I heard.

Then it told of the Buddha dwelling on Mount Gridhrakuta, Vulture Peak, with a great gathering of Bhikshus, twelve thousand in all.

Their names were Ajnatakaundinya, Mahakashyapa, Uruvilvakashyapa . . .

I read with a sense of panic, fearing it would list all twelve thousand names. But it stopped after twenty or thirty, adding *. . . and other great Arhats such as these.*

I breathed easier, read on as it indicated the others in attendance – eighty thousand Bodhisattvas, thousands of Gods, Dragon Kings, Asura Kings, all with their hundreds of thousands of followers.

I read how they all walked round the Buddha, paying him homage, and he then spoke this sutra, *The Great Vehicle of Limitless Principles.* Then there fell from the heavens an endless rain of flowers – *mandarava, mahamandarava, mahamanjushaka.*

I intoned the names. I could picture the blossoms, imagine breathing in their fragrance.

44

Then Buddha emitted from between his brows a white light illuminating all the worlds. Manjushri stepped forward and spoke in verse.

> *The Buddha will speak the Dharma Flower Sutra.*
> *All of you should now understand*
> *And with one heart fold your hands and wait.*
> *The Buddha will let fall the Dharma rain*
> *To satisfy all those who seek the Way.*

It had taken me a whole afternoon to read the introduction, just to get to the point where the teaching would begin. My head ached as if held tight in an iron clamp. I chanted once more, *Namu Myoho Renge Kyo*. I bowed and closed the book.

*

Perhaps it was because I was not as accomplished in Chinese as I had thought. Perhaps it was the endless lists of names and designations, the Bodhisattvas and Arhats, the Gods and Asuras. Whatever the reason, my progress through the text was slow.

The second chapter spoke of the Buddha's Expedient Devices, the way he taught. Tricks of the trade, I thought, then stopped myself, inwardly asking the Buddha's forgiveness for such irreverence.

Expedient Devices.

He spoke at length – at great length – about the Dharma, wonderful beyond conception, profound and hard to understand. He made this clear, over and over, the difficulty of grasping the truth, even for the greatest of them.

Thousands of beings present, listening to this, bowed and took their leave.

Buddha spoke of their overweening pride, said they claimed to know what they did not know. Then he said he had shaken the tree and cleared its branches and leaves so only the trunk remained.

Those who can hear the Dharma are rare, he said.

And yet . . .

A few pages further on he said that through these *Expedient Devices* the Dharma would spread.

Even children at play, he said, who draw with a stick, or their fingernails, an image of the Buddha, will gradually accumulate merit and virtue. And if people in temples make offerings with a happy heart, or with songs and chants praise the Buddha, they have realised the Buddha Way.

I thought of my mother. I saw her face clearly.

Have no further doubts, said the Buddha. *Let your hearts be filled with joy. You know you will reach Buddhahood.*

The third chapter began with a lengthy discourse on falling into the net of doubts, fearful that the very voice of Buddha might be a demon in disguise, come to cause confusion. But the Buddha himself spoke and made all clear, dispelled the doubts, calmed the heart.

I ploughed on, through endless lines of incantation, singing the Buddha's praises, telling of a future age, after limitless aeons, a Pure Land, tranquil and prosperous and abounding with gods.

It shall have lapis lazuli for soil and trees made of seven jewels, constantly blooming and bearing fruit.

I shifted to ease the ache in my back. I sipped bitter tea from my rough clay bowl. My head was beginning to feel clamped again, tight. I read on, through more lists, more praising, more offerings, to a passage where Buddha spoke in a parable.

In a particular country there was a great elder, old and

worn, who had limitless wealth and lived in a huge house. Hundreds of people lived there as well as all manner of other creatures. There were snakes and scorpions, lizards and rats and mice; there were owls and hawks and vultures, magpies and crows. The house was swarming, overrun with packs of scavenging dogs, and corpse-devouring wolves. It was haunted by hungry ghosts and malevolent spirits, and the whole place was rotting and falling into ruin and decay.

One day, the owner of the house, the old man, went out through the open door, and he had hardly gone any distance when a fire broke out at the back of the house and quickly spread till all four sides were in flame. The beasts and birds and ghosts and demons all fought among themselves, devouring one another.

The old man suddenly realised that all his children had gone into the house, aeons ago, to play, and he rushed back inside to save them from the fire. But they were so intent on their play, their endless amusements, that they didn't hear his warnings. He told them of the fire, and the hundreds of vicious creatures surrounding them, but they carried on playing and paid him no heed. So he called out to them that he had all kinds of precious things waiting for them outside. And they gave up their games and rushed out through the door, and they gathered round him where he sat, in a clearing some distance away. And he rejoiced to see them safe, and he showered them with gifts as he had promised. He used his wealth to provide fabulous jewelled carriages, pulled by pure white oxen, and the children rode off in the four directions, unobstructed, to enjoy his gifts.

When he had told the story, the Buddha spoke.

All living beings are my children. Deeply attached to worldly pleasures, they have no wisdom at all. The Three Realms are like a burning house, terrifying and filled with suffering. Ever present are the endless woes of birth, old age, sickness and death — these are the fires that burn without end. And although I instruct my children, they do not believe or accept, because of their deep attachment to greed and desire.

He then went on to repeat the Four Noble Truths. *Existence is suffering. Its cause is desire. Suffering can be conquered. There is a Way.* And he held up the sutra itself as the purest vehicle for transcending desire, for going beyond suffering.

The Buddhas rejoice in it, and all living beings should praise it.

This very world we were living in, a burning house, collapsing all about us. I could feel the flames licking at me, hear the howls and screams of all my fellow creatures.

I chanted once more. *Namu Myoho Renge Kyo.* I stood up and went outside, felt the cool evening breeze.

*

For weeks I read the sutra every day, pored over it hour after hour. The Bodhisattvas and Arhats and countless other beings listened without end to the Buddha's sermons, his descriptions of the various worlds and the beings who inhabited them, the future Buddhas and the worlds they would create, the blessings they would bestow.

> *Turn the Dharma wheel.*
> *Beat the Dharma drum.*
> *Blow the Dharma conch.*
> *Let fall the Dharma rain.*

The parables at least were easier to read, simple tales, each with a simple point to make. Expedient Devices. To spread the teaching. *The Dharma falls on all alike, nourishing the smallest herbs and the largest trees. Each one receives what it needs.*

The tale of the young man who falls into a drunken sleep

48

while visiting a friend's house, and the friend has to leave early in the morning to go to another country, and before he goes he secretly sews a pearl into the man's clothing. And he wakes and goes out into the world, seeking wealth, trying to earn a living, not realising he carries this priceless pearl with him all along, till he meets his friend again, and his friend tells him it is there.

So with the wealth the Buddha has bestowed on us . . .

The tale of the young man who leaves his father's palace and wanders in the world, and falls into poverty, and ends up shovelling dung for twenty years till his father finds him and brings him back.

I wondered if shovelling dung for twenty years might be an easier path to enlightenment than ploughing through these scriptures.

Then I found another of those passages that made me stop, read it again. It spoke of spreading the Dharma through the sutra.

If there is one who reads and recites, receives and upholds the Sutra, or copies out even a single verse with reverence, know that this person in the past has already made offerings to tens of millions of Buddhas.

Further down the page, it took it even further.

If a good man or woman, after my extinction, can secretly explain one sentence of the Sutra to one single person, know that this person is my messenger, come to do my work.

It also made it clear that this work would not be easy.

Entering the fire at the end of the Kalpa and not being burned, that would not be difficult. But after my extinction, upholding the Sutra and preaching it to one single person, that would be difficult.

Entering the fire.

There were passages about right conduct, injunctions to monks as to how they should behave, particularly in relation to women.

49

Do not take delight in looking at young women. Do not speak with young girls, maidens or widows.

And another parable – *another* parable! – began: *The body of a woman is filthy and impure and not a fit vessel for Dharma. Thus spake the Venerable Shariputra.*

Once more I thought of my mother, the pure simplicity of her devotion.

And yet . . .

The parable continued with the story of the Dragon Girl, daughter of the Dragon King and Queen, who was clearly an exception to this general rule. She possessed a rare and precious pearl which she was able to offer to the Buddha, who accepted it.

Was that not quick? she asked, and was thus transformed into a living Buddha herself.

So, however grudging and reluctant the admission, it was there. The possibility existed.

I ground on through more lists, more expositions, more injunctions. My brain ached. Sometimes after hours of it I felt a sense of virtue, a kind of dutiful piety at forcing myself to sit there. At rare moments I went beyond that into a fleeting glimpse of something beyond, which was yet, at the same time, here and now.

> *In a quiet place*
> *he collects his thoughts*
> *dwelling peacefully*
> *unmoved and unmoving*
> *like Mount Sumeru*
> *contemplating all dharmas*
> *as having no existence*
> *like empty space . . .*

50

Then more numbing lists, more simplistic parables, and the moment would be lost.

Buddha spoke of the Bodhisattvas. If you were to count them for as many aeons as there are sands in the River Ganges, you could not count them all, your counting would have no end. There are as many Bodhisattvas as there are dust-motes in the great world, and each and every one of these Bodhisattvas was taught by the Buddha and transformed.

Propagate the Dharma. Cause it to spread and grow.

Endless, limitless, infinite numbers, to fill the mind with awe.

I began to make notes for myself, copy out short passages, exhortations that spoke to me directly.

> *Be vigorous and single-minded.*
> *Hold no doubts or regrets.*
> *Abide in patience and goodness.*

One particular Bodhisattva, Guanyin, could be invoked in times of suffering and distress.

> *In times of suffering, agony, danger and death, he is our refuge and protection.*
> *If someone is surrounded by bandits who threaten him with knives, and he invokes Guanyin, the knives will shatter into pieces.*
> *If someone is pushed into a pit of fire and invokes Guanyin, the pit will be turned into a cooling pool.*

I wrote these lines beside my other notes. I read on, finally reached the last page.

When the Buddha had spoken this sutra, all the great assembly rejoiced and received his teaching, and they made obeisance and withdrew.

51

I closed the book and sat in silence for a long time. Aeons. Kalpas. Then I returned it with reverence to its special niche in the library.

*

The priest realised I had read the whole sutra, from cover to cover.

Well, he asked, what have you learned?

I did not know what to say, so I said nothing.

Are you banging at the gates of Paradise? he asked. Ready to ascend into Nirvana?

Still I was silent.

Is this the silence of the enlightened man, or are you just dumbstruck, stupefied?

I cleared my throat.

It was not what I had expected.

Ah.

This time it was the priest who let the silence sit there. After a while he spoke again.

And what did you expect?

I do not know.

But you know it was not this.

Not this. Something more.

I thought of my mother, her eyes shining, chanting *Namu Myoho Renge Kyo*. I felt disloyal. I thought of the passage describing those who disparage the sutra, the hundreds of painful rebirths they have to endure. I felt a twinge of fear.

There are many beautiful passages, I said. Absolute jewels. But they are buried.

Hidden, he said. For you to discover.

But forgive me, they are hidden amongst so much dross, they are hard to find.

That may be the point.

Endless lists, I said, endless arguments about procedure and hierarchy, endless incantations. Then page after page of teaching through parables, simple tales of cause and effect.

It had all come out of me in a rush. I bowed.

Forgive me, I said again.

There is nothing to forgive, he said. Perhaps some day you will read it again, perhaps in another life, and it will speak to you more directly.

Perhaps, I said, not believing it for a moment, and feeling empty and bereft as though I had been cheated or had lost something precious.

TWO

FLOATING WORLD, FLOWER-PATH

By the time I was eighteen, in spite of the skimpy rations at the temple – the basic diet of rice and greens, a little fish from time to time – I had grown taller. And doing my share of the physical work – weeding and tending the garden, sweeping and cleaning, working in the kitchen – had made me strong. I liked nothing better than walking beyond the village and into the foothills, but also along the Tokaido and through the neighbouring towns, amazed at the passing show, the constant stream of people flowing to and from the capital. There were pedlars and salesmen and merchants touting their wares, quack doctors and medicine men, farmers taking their crops to market, geisha with their quick mincing steps in thick-soled clogs, samurai swaggering down the middle of the road, demanding respect, aristocrats carried in their palanquins, actors and acrobats, travelling storytellers with their portable *kamishibai* screens.

In the post-station at Ejiri, close to the temple, was a courtyard where groups of travelling players would sometimes perform. I heard that a troupe from Edo was passing through and would be presenting a drama based on the tale of the Forty-seven Ronin. I had been struggling in my meditation, and I thought it might lift my spirits to see the play, so I made my way to Ejiri in the early evening, and took my place among the audience gathering in the courtyard. There was a sizeable crowd, a few of my fellow monks among the villagers and townsfolk, the merchants and their families. A little platform had been built where the wealthier and more prominent patrons could sit and watch the performance in comfort.

As the sky darkened and the lamps were lit, I looked around me, took it all in. I remembered the puppet show I had seen with my mother, how it had opened my eyes and changed my life, and I felt an anticipation overlaid with something bittersweet I couldn't quite name, a kind of yearning for something I didn't know.

Everyone knew the story of the Forty-seven Ronin. It was based on real events that had happened only a year ago, but had already become a legend throughout the whole land.

A group of forty-seven samurai had avenged the death of their lord, Asano, by murdering the man responsible, a court official named Kira. Because they had done this out of loyalty, they were allowed a noble death themselves by committing *seppuku*.

The incident had inspired poetry and painting – I myself had seen a number of woodblock prints depicting the ronin – and plays based on the story drew huge audiences all over Japan. The government in Edo had banned any contemporary reference in the drama, so the play was set in the distant past, four hundred years ago, and all the names were changed. But the audience knew the real story that was being re-enacted. These heroes were men from their own time who had only recently walked the earth.

Because I had arrived early I had a good position, next to

the viewing platform. As I looked across I was momentarily distracted by a young girl seated at the front of the platform, very close to me. She caught my eye, then immediately looked away, flustered, and hid her face behind a paper fan, but just that glimpse of her beauty had unsettled me.

The lights around the courtyard flickered, and the drama began with the thud of a drum, the shrill wail of a flute, and for the next hour reality shimmered and wavered. We were here in this courtyard, in the post-station at Ejiri, watching seven actors move through each scene, chant their scripted lines. But at the same time, *at the same time*, we were in Edo, looking on as the forty-seven ronin waited patiently and took their revenge on the villain Kira, walked through the snow to place his head on their lord's grave, then sit in a half circle and fall on their own swords.

This floating world of theatre was a thing of magic and enchantment. As the ronin fell forward they let out a collective death-cry that sent a chill down the spine. It was terrifying and magnificent, and the crowd were so caught up in the action many of them also cried out. A group of young men who had arrived late were particularly carried away, and they climbed up at the back of the little grandstand and pushed forward for a better view.

What happened next was as strange and dreamlike as anything I had just seen on the stage. Everything seemed to slow down, as sounds and movements were heightened, intensified. I heard a cracking, straining noise and the shouts grew louder. The young girl was looking straight at me, her mouth open, confusion and alarm in her eyes. Then everything was shifting, moving, as the platform collapsed. The girl pitched forward, throwing out her arms to protect herself, and without thinking I stepped forward and caught her, cushioned her weight and broke her fall.

Her head cracked against mine and I stumbled a little but managed to step back and lift her clear as the others fell around her.

She clung to me and I held her safe. I could feel her small body shaking. I could smell her perfumed clothes, her hair, and that irrepressible little dragon reared between my legs again, roused, and I chanted the Daimoku quickly to myself, *Namu Myoho Renge Kyo*, trying to calm it down.

Then an older man was at my side, speaking to me.

I thank you for saving my daughter, he said. But now I think you can put her down.

I set the girl down on the ground, carefully, stood back and bowed, still silently chanting the Daimoku. Now I was the one who was shaken, flustered. My face burned as the girl bowed and bowed, thanking me over and over, fluttering in front of me.

Her father introduced himself as Mr Yotsugi. He asked my name, and said he was grateful to me, and if my superiors might give permission he would like to express his gratitude by offering me hospitality at his home.

The ronin who had ritually disembowelled themselves just moments before had gathered round, helping people to their feet, offering sympathy. The manager was bustling among the crowd, endlessly apologising, anxiously bowing. When he stood back to let Yotsugi-san pass he bent almost double and his apologies rose to an even higher pitch as he asked if there was anything he could do to make recompense, anything at all.

There was no harm done, said Yotsugi-san, thanks to this young man.

Then he turned to me and told me where they lived, said he hoped I would visit them soon.

I watched them go.

The girl gave a last look back at me over her shoulder. She smiled and undid me completely.

*

The whole of the next week, at odd moments, I found myself thinking about the girl. I remembered the way she had caught my eye and looked away, the fear as she had pitched forward, the feel and smell of her in my arms. I sat in zazen, I chanted the sutras, and the more I willed myself not to think of her, the more clearly her image arose in my mind.

Sentient beings are numberless. I vow to save them.

The scent of her. Jasmine and sweat.

The deluding passions are inexhaustible. I vow to extinguish them.

The sheen of her lacquer-black hair. The white nape of her neck.

The Buddha Way is supreme. I vow to enter it.

The warmth of her small thin body through the kimono.

As I left the meditation hall after a particularly difficult session, torn between trying to picture her face and trying to banish it completely, the head priest called me to one side and instructed me to wait. He stood with his back to me until everyone else had left, then he turned and fixed the full intensity of his gaze on me, fierce and withering. He must have been observing my meditation, seen every thought, every desire. I bowed deep, kept my head bent.

So, he said. This merchant, Yotsugi-san, he has a daughter.

I felt myself burn, said Yes, my voice a squawk. Even that one word felt like a confession. I didn't trust myself to say more.

Her name is Hana.

Hana. Her name. Hana. Flower.

Hana.

According to Yotsugi-san, you saved his daughter's life, or at the very least kept her from serious injury.

A faint hope. Perhaps I was not, after all, about to be damned.

He has sent a letter singing your praises and inviting you to dine with the family this evening.

I looked up. The gaze was just as fierce, unremitting – nostrils flared, an irritated twitch at the corner of the mouth. He breathed out, part snort, part sigh.

Go, he said. But do not be distracted by this young woman or her father's wealth. Stay in the Buddha-mind.

With a curt nod, a grunt, I was dismissed.

Do not be distracted. Stay in the Buddha-mind.

Her name was Hana. I spoke it, tasted it in my mouth. Hana.

A mantra.

*

I bathed and put on my cleanest clothes, the ones that smelled least of mildew and sweat. The Yotsugi home was about a mile from the temple, and I set out walking, past a row of little shops and stalls selling fruit and vegetables, pickles and dried fish, trinkets and knick-knacks, clogs and straw umbrellas, sweets made from bean paste, scrolls and paintbrushes, netsuke, incense. I loved the stink and fragrance of it all, the light of the day fading, oil-lamps lit for the evening. I felt light and buoyed up, exhilarated.

An old woman bowed, in deference to my monks' robes. I bowed lower in return. A crazy drunk laughed at me, sprayed spit, his face a toothless demon mask. I laughed right back at him, bowed again, walked on.

The way led through some narrow back streets and past a

62

stretch of open ground next to the graveyard. I was aware of a movement, turned and saw a scraggy-looking dog loping towards me. It stopped and growled, started barking at me. I looked around for a stone to throw at it, but there was nothing. Hackles raised, it came closer, barked louder. I turned and faced it down, barked back at it louder still, and it ran off, whimpering.

Ha!

I offered up a silent prayer to Kannon, for protecting me and for *not* letting me find a stone. The edict of the Dog Shogun was still in force. Compassion for living beings. I saw myself reported, arrested by some petty official, thrown in jail, sentenced and executed. A sad end to a young life, and before I'd even had the chance to know Hana. I laughed again, this time at myself.

The Yotsugi residence looked modest from the outside, a solid wooden gate, weathered and worn, bamboo fencing on either side, the family name carved on an old oak panel, and beside it a length of rope, a bell-pull. I breathed deep, gathered myself and tugged at the rope. Somewhere far inside, a temple-bell clanged. I heard the shuffle and clack of wooden geta and the door creaked open. An old servant peered out at me and when I announced my name he showed me inside, led me along a walkway to the house, told me to wait in an anteroom of polished hardwood, immaculate tatami mats on the floor. In a *tokonoma* alcove, a single chrysanthemum had been placed in a vase in front of a hanging scroll inscribed with vigorous, fluid calligraphy reading *The Flower-path*. On one wall was mounted a samurai sword in its sheath. On the wall opposite hung a magnificent kimono, sleeves spread out like wings, dyed deep pink, patterned with gold-embroidered birds. The air was filled with the scent of a rich musky perfume, a dark, spicy expensive incense. I breathed it in.

The shoji screen slid open with the barest whisper and my host stepped into the room and greeted me by name.

Welcome to my humble home, he said, and motioned me to sit.

I kneeled on the tatami, and he sat facing me on a low wooden seat.

Now, he said. Let us get to know each other.

Yotsugi-san asked all the questions. He wanted to know about my family background and I told him what I knew. He was intrigued that my father was samurai and could trace his ancestry back to a warrior clan of the Kamakura period. I told him with some pride that they had fought alongside the great Minamoto no Yoshitsune.

Excellent, he said.

I told him my father had also spent time at Shoin-ji, where my own training had begun.

And now he runs the busy way-station at Hara?

Yes, I said, and I must have registered surprise that he knew this.

Forgive me, he said. I took the liberty of making some enquiries.

I am honoured, I said, bowing.

I find it fascinating, he said, that your father's early Zen training was no barrier to his becoming a successful businessman. In fact, I am sure it prepared him well for the cut and thrust of commerce.

I heard *Zen* and *barrier*, *cut* and *thrust*, pictured a swordsman cutting down his enemies. Yoshitsune on the battlefield.

My own modest success, he said, is founded on a love of beauty.

He indicated the kimono on the wall.

I deal in these gorgeous creations, for those who can afford to pay.

64

The gold birds glittered against the deep pink silk. The shoji screen opened a fraction and Yotsugi-san gave the slightest nod towards the gap. It opened wider and a young woman stepped into the room and set down a lacquer tray bearing a teapot and two bowls, a bamboo whisk and a lidded box. Another maid followed behind with a heavier tray of dark wood, on it a small stove and an iron kettle. The two women backed out through the gap, bowing.

So, said Yotsugi-san.

I thought he was about to prepare tea for us himself. But he clapped his hands and the screen slid open once more, and kneeling there was Hana.

I'd known I would be seeing her at some point in the evening. I had struggled between anticipating it and trying not to think of it at all. But the actuality took me completely by surprise. I felt as if I'd been struck in the chest, and just for a moment I could not draw breath.

She wore a floral-patterned kimono in blues and greens, the sash a rich purple. Her hair was swept up, just so, held in place by a silver clasp and exposing the exquisite curve of her neck. I caught again a waft of her perfume, jasmine, and in behind it the smell of *her*.

Hana.

She kept her head down, not looking at me.

Tea, said her father, and she bowed, glanced up, just for an instant caught my eye, gave a quick half-smile that turned me inside out.

Tea.

Her movements were extraordinarily graceful as she placed the kettle on the stove, wiped the bowls with the *chakin* linen cloth, removed the lid from the box and scooped a little tea into each bowl, all with the deftest of movements designed to keep her sleeves out of the way but performed

with the flow of a dance or a piece of kabuki. I was mesmerised.

You are familiar with the way of tea? asked her father.

Yes, I said. No. I mean . . .

He smiled, waited.

I mean I have read about it, but never . . .

So, he said. Hana will initiate you into the mysteries.

Hana.

I imagined making a calligraphy of her name, the brushstrokes flowing into a simple drawing of a flower.

Hana.

The water in the kettle had come to the boil. She poured
a little into the first bowl, the one in front of me. Then
she whisked the tea into a bright green froth, bowed and
offered it to me, holding the bowl in both hands. I took it
clumsily, touching her fingers. Her eyes smiled, and she
made a slight rotating movement of her head, trying to
tell me something.

Then I remembered the form of the ritual, and I turned
the bowl through a quarter-circle, sipped from the side.
Nothing in my life had tasted as sweet as this bitter green tea.

She whisked up more in the other bowl, handed it to her
father who took a sip, let out a great slow sigh of satisfaction,
made a comment on the fragrance of the tea, the perfect
form of the bowl.

I knew this, I had read about it. The custom was to engage
in conversation about the tea, the bowls, the room, all of it.
But my brain was numb and unable to link with my tongue.
Hana had robbed me of language.

The bowl is beautiful, I heard myself say. The tea is delicious. The room is . . . very nice.

Hana bowed again, looked away. Was she trying to hide a
smile?

The taste of tea is the taste of Zen, said her father. It sounded like something he had read rather than composed himself, but I nodded appreciatively, grateful that he was trying to put me at ease.

I sipped more of the tea, felt a warmth in my chest, a lightness in my head.

The taste of Zen!

And it all felt suddenly ridiculous, the stiffness and formality, the strained responses, the sheer tight-arsed artifice of it. And yet. And yet. There was the lightness. It bubbled up out of me and I laughed.

Good, I said. It tastes good!

Hana held out a tray of sugared sweets. I took one shaped like a flower and popped it in my mouth, let it dissolve.

I feel I have died, I said, and awakened in the Pure Land.

Her father chuckled, nodded approval.

*

By the end of the evening I had eaten more food than I had in the previous week, all prepared by Yotsugi-san's cook. I had downed white miso soup and noodles in a golden vegetable broth, rice and tempura, four sorts of fish. Yotsugi-san had insisted I drink a cup of sake.

One for the road, he said. Let us drink to our continuing friendship.

The road, I said. Friendship.

The sake slipped down, warming, left a pleasant aftertaste. But it was deceptive. I wasn't used to it, felt the rush to my head and again I found myself laughing.

Yotsugi-san said I could stay in one of their guest rooms, return to the temple in the morning, but I said I couldn't miss the *sesshin*, which began early. The word slipped in my mouth and I pronounced it again with great deliberation. *Sesshin*.

I understand, said Yotsugi-san. But I hope, we both hope, you will visit us again soon.

I bowed, smiled directly at Hana who smiled back.

It would be a great honour, I said.

On the way back past the cemetery, the same dog came running after me, yapping and snarling.

Stupid dog! I shouted. What is *wrong* with you?

He barked louder, and this time instead of barking back at him, I just laughed and that was even more effective in driving him away.

*

The *sesshin* began at 3 a.m. with the clang of a bell. I'd had no sleep to speak of, was a little hungover from the sake, the rich food, the sheer unaccustomed intoxication of it all.

Hana.

Bleary and barely awake, head numb, I managed to fold up my bedding – the thin futon, the single rough blanket – and bundle it away. Then I joined the line to use the toilet, the pit dug in the dirt floor. Ignore the stink. Splash my face with cold water, taking particular care to wash my ears. Cup a little water in my hands to swill in my mouth. Swallow it down. Follow the others into the meditation hall. Sit on my cushion on the *tan* platform.

We sat in two rows, facing each other. Incense was lit, a thick, heavy scent.

Clang.

The bell rang, deep and resonant, beginning the session. The head priest entered the room without a sound, and we sensed it, a change in the atmosphere. Backs straightened. He walked slowly, silently, behind each row, stopping here or there to administer a sharp rap with his stick on a curved spine, hunched shoulders. He stopped for a moment right behind me and I braced myself for a blow that didn't come. I bowed with folded hands, *gassho*, and he moved on.

At the end of the hall he stopped and turned, then he told a story, by way of instruction. It was one I had heard before and I knew it was sometimes assigned as a koan, to be addressed in meditation, an insoluble problem to push the mind beyond itself, beyond thought.

The priest's voice was measured, incantatory, as if imparting some ancient wisdom.

In ancient China there was an old woman who took it upon herself to provide for a monk and support him in his practice. She had a hut built where he could meditate, and she provided a little food for him every day. This went on for twenty years, and one day she decided to test him, to find out what progress he had made. So she approached a beautiful young woman and asked her to visit the monk.

Embrace him, she said, then ask him suddenly, What now?

The girl did as she was instructed. She caressed the monk and said to him, What now?

The monk remained very serious and stern.

In the depth of winter, he said, a withered tree grows on an old rock. Nowhere is there any warmth.

The girl returned to the old woman and reported what he had said.

That rascal, said the old woman. To think I've fed and supported him for twenty years.

She went to the monk and railed at him.

You showed no concern for this girl, she said. You gave no

69

thought to her situation. By all means resist the temptation of the flesh, but show at least a little compassion.

Then she threw him out of the hut and burned it to the ground.

When the priest had finished reciting the story, he bowed.

Now, he said, meditate on this.

*

Had the priest chosen the koan particularly for me? The thought was arrogant. The truth of the story was universal. It applied to each and every monk meditating in the *zendo*. And yet.

I imagined Hana coming to me in my room, embracing me, asking me suddenly, What now?

Hana's fragrance. The curve of her neck.

A withered tree on an old rock.

The monk's reaction was wrong.

Nowhere is there any warmth.

But returning the girl's embrace would also have been wrong.

A koan.

This is wrong, the opposite is wrong. What now?

Act.

And yet.

I hadn't noticed the priest moving slowly along the row, his footsteps silent on the wooden boards. Then in an instant I was aware of him standing behind me, and in the same moment the swish of the stick, the *keisaku*, the whack between my shoulderblades jarring me awake, shaken.

Composing myself I bowed low then entered into a deep silence, and before I knew it the bell clanged again for the end of the hour, the beginning of *kinhin*, walking meditation.

70

The more experienced monks, more practised and adept at all this, seemed to unfold and stand upright in one fluid movement, push aside their cushions, stand catlike on their feet. I did as I had been instructed, rocked from side to side then slowly got to my feet and stood in line. Then again I followed instructions to the letter. Right fist closed around the thumb, placed on my chest and covered with the left palm. Elbows at right angles, arms in a straight line, body erect, eyes resting on the ground, two yards in front. Following the monks ahead, step forward with the left foot.

Breathe in, step forward, breathe out. Heel and toe, sinking into the floor with every step. Feel the stiffness in the legs begin to ease, but without being caught up in that ease. See it as incidental, by the way. Stay alert and poised. Breathe. Walk.

Clang.

It was time to return to the cushion, to another session of seated meditation. A fresh stick of incense was lit, this time a lighter scent, pine.

*

There was another koan I had read.

What was your original face, before you were born?

Once, on a full moon night, I had entered deeply into the question. Looking up at the moon I had seen there the Buddha-face shining, and for a moment I had known that face as my own.

Now I found myself revisiting the koan, asking the question. *What was your original face?* I sat on the cushion on the hard floor in the shadowy hall, in a row of monks facing another row of monks. *What was your original face?*

I sought to identify with my own Buddha-nature. But the

only face I could see, with the eye of my heart, was the face of Hana. I felt as if her features were on my own face.

The head priest had encouraged me to go to the Yotsugi residence. But he had admonished me. Do not be distracted. Stay in the Buddha-mind. Had that been my test, my koan?

Once more the priest walked along, silent, behind the row. This time he passed me by without stopping. Someone's stomach rumbled, gurgled. Someone coughed. The silence deepened. Time passed.

Clang.

*

The next break was when we were allowed to eat, and after the excess of the night before I was grateful for the simplicity and formality, the frugality and restraint.

The head priest recited the threefold vow.

Sentient beings are numberless. I vow to save them.
The deluding passions are inexhaustible. I vow to extinguish them.
The Buddha Way is supreme. I vow to enter it.

A little hand-bell was rung, and each of us removed the cloth from a bowl and set of chopsticks in front of us. Two monks moved around the room and ladled out a little rice into each bowl, topped it with a few vegetables, placed next to it a small dish of pickle.

The priest chanted a verse, reminding us that all food comes to us from the labours of many, and that we should receive it with utmost gratitude and humility.

Then a lacquered bowl was passed round from hand to hand, and each of us placed in it a few grains of rice from our portion.

This was an offering for the wretched spirits, the hungry ghosts, condemned by their own greed to a miserable existence in this and every other world. I imagined them consigned to one of the deeper hells, endlessly consuming and being consumed.

The hand-bell was rung once more, and then, and only then, we ate, savouring every grain of rice, every piece of vegetable, ending with the pickle – a little *daikon* radish – to cleanse the palate.

It was permitted to eat three portions of the rice. Three times the servers came round with the pot to ladle it out and the monks would wait, hands folded. Those who had eaten enough rubbed their hands together, bowed as the servers came by. I still felt the aftertaste of last night's meal, still felt its richness bloat my stomach, so I stopped after one serving, ate the last sliver of pickle. The servers poured a little water into each bowl and we swilled it round to clean it, sipping the water, not wasting a drop. Any water left in the bowl was dripped into the same lacquered bowl, a further offering to those tortured spirits forever ravaged by hunger and thirst.

The head priest recited a prayer of gratitude for the food, and for the strength it gave, pledged to use that strength for the benefit of all sentient beings.

We bowed.

The bell clanged once more.

We stood for another round of *kinhin*, walking, then sat once more, backs straight, eyes fixed on the floor.

*

The head priest struck the bell seven times, and the sound grew and resonated, filled the room, filled our minds. Before it had completely faded, he shouted out *Mu*!

Some of the monks had been meditating on the first great

73

koan, the first barrier to be crossed, and they meditated on this syllable, this *Mu* and its meaningless meaning.

Nothing. No-thing. Emptiness.

The priest chanted it again, louder, longer.

Join me, he shouted. Chant!

And they did, tentatively at first, voices shaky and wavering, with much hawking and clearing of throats, but gradually getting louder, more confident.

Mu.

Not from the throat, the priest shouted. From the belly!

I started to join in, my own voice strange to me, getting stronger with every chant.

Mu.

It filled my head with light, radiated from my heart, growled and rumbled at the navel.

Mu.

It swelled in the room till there was nothing but the sound. Nothing but. The sound. Nothing. But the sound.

Nothing. Nothing. Nothing. Nothing.

Mu.

The bell clanged and the chanting stopped, and the silence that filled the room was profound.

*

The *sesshin* lasted six days. The same regime, long periods of sitting interspersed with walking, chanting and koan, physical labour – helping in the kitchen or sweeping the floors or digging the garden, all done in concentrated silence, and twice a day the sparse rations, the rice and vegetables served with devotion and eaten with gratitude.

Once the priest looked up as the meagre portions were dished out.

74

No work, no food, he said. Eat what you have earned.

On the last day he stopped walking the length of the room. He put aside the *keisaku* stick and bowed to us. The gesture was eloquent. It said he could do no more for us. Our realisation was our own responsibility.

We sat on as the day darkened towards evening. The priest began intoning the Heart of Wisdom Sutra. *Hannya Haramita Shingyo*. Form is emptiness. Emptiness is form.

The bell clanged one final time and the *sesshin* was over. The monks who had served the food went round the room, pouring tea into each bowl. I blew on my tea to cool it, then sipped it, savouring its green tang, sharp and bitter and good.

For a time nobody made a move to leave. Then one by one the older monks stood up and moved towards the open door, and the rest of us followed, out into the night.

Some made towards the bathhouse, joined the queue to soak in a hot tub. To ease the ache in tired legs, clenched shoulders – that too would be good. But I kept walking.

One old monk stood absolutely still in the centre of the courtyard, looking up at the night sky through the branches of an ancient pine tree. Another sat in the graveyard, back straight, eyes closed.

I walked round the courtyard, breathed the cool night air. I stopped by the gate, stood gazing at the patterns weathered into the old, dark wood with its knots and sworls, its landscapes. The big, heavy wooden bolt had been slid shut. I slid it open and stepped outside, looked up. The sky was clear, the bright stars high and far. Worlds. Worlds away. Away in that infinite vastness, but also here, in this heart of mine. Vastness and brightness. Here.

*

After the intensity of the *sesshin* a great emptiness overwhelmed me. I no longer recognised myself, but the head priest assured me this was no bad thing.

What is this self you want to recognise? he said. And who are you that wants to recognise it?

When Yotsugi-san sent another message, inviting me to visit him at his home once more, I was numbed. I did not know what to do.

The priest read Yotsugi-san's letter.

This merchant, he said, is a benefactor of the temple. He has made a substantial donation.

He turned the letter between forefinger and thumb, examined it as if it might have a secret to reveal.

However, he said, and he paused. There is the daughter.

The silence he left extended endlessly, a silence to be endured as my face burned and sweat trickled down my back.

Is the merchant simply extending his patronage? Or is he looking for a son-in-law?

Perhaps, he continued at last, you should meditate further on the koan I used during *sesshin*. The old woman burns down the monk's hut.

Embrace him, the old woman had said, then ask him, *What now?*

What now?

So it really had been directed at me. And once you became a monk, everything, *everything*, was a koan.

*

I walked the same road to the Yotsugi residence. I even saw the same dog. But everything was different. Now I knew this was my koan.

76

Yotsugi-san welcomed me warmly, asked politely how the *sesshin* had gone. I stared at him, found words.

It has been a time of great . . . *intensity*.

Intensity is good in a young man, he said. So too is . . . *lightness*.

I truly did not know what to say. My tongue was useless, a heavy clapper in the great dull bell of my skull, unable to make a sound.

Just as before, the shoji screen opened a fraction and the two young women stepped into the room, set down the teapot and bowls, the utensils of *chanoyu*, then the heavier tray with the stove, the iron kettle. Just as before, the two women backed out, bowing, like players in kabuki or noh.

The screen slid closed and I sat staring at it. I knew what came next but still I was not prepared. It opened again with a swish, and she was there, in the room, bowing and kneeling on the tatami and just as before I felt as if I had been punched in the chest and I gulped in air.

She was there in front of me, just as before, but this time the kimono was deep red silk shot through with purple.

Hana.

The smell of her, her own scent overlaid with jasmine. Sheen of glossy black hair, swept up.

She was actually there, utterly herself. Just as before.

Ekaku-san, she said, bowing again, hands folded. Welcome back to our home.

My own hands felt clumsy as I brought them together in *gassho*. My face burned, as red as her kimono.

Thank you, I heard myself say. It is a great honour to be here.

So.

Just as before.

The faintest smile lingered at the corners of her red, red

mouth as she looked down and busied herself with the tea powder and the bamboo spoon, the boiling water, the whisk.

I had no small talk whatsoever. Language had left me.

Her father intervened.

This incense is called Spring Snow, he said. I think it is particularly fine.

Particularly, I said, and could say not one word more.

The boiling water poured on the powdered leaves. The tea whisked to bright froth. The deftness of movement. I was mesmerised.

Ekaku-san was telling me, said her father, about his experience of *sesshin*. He spoke of its great . . . intensity.

Yes, I said, rallying. It was most . . . intense.

Perhaps you could tell us more, he said.

Much of it, I said, is beyond words.

As are a great many things, said Hana, handing me the bowl.

This time I made a point of taking it carefully, mindful of my great clumsy hands. But this time, it was quite deliberate, she let her fingers touch mine, held them there a moment, just long enough.

I ventured the opinion, said her father, voice droning, that intensity was admirable, but perhaps it had to be tempered by lightness.

Yes, I said, aware that I sounded idiotic, but savouring the word as much as the tea. Lightness.

I sipped.

The tea, I said, is exquisite.

Silence.

Perhaps, said Yotsugi-san eventually, your mind is still in *sesshin*.

The effects last for some time, I said.

And throughout the *sesshin* itself, is everyone silent, day and night?

78

There are long periods of silence, I said. But there is chanting from the sutras, and concentration on a koan, directed by the priest.

Ah, he said, grabbing onto the word. Koans!

Are they not very . . . difficult? said Hana, furrowing her brow.

Poison fangs and talons, said her father. A quagmire to drag you under.

He was puffed up, full of his own erudition.

I read about koans, he said, when I was a young man like you. Does a dog have the Buddha-nature?

We meditated on that, I said, and one other.

Which one?

The words were out before I could stop them.

Old-woman-burns-down-the-hut.

He frowned, as if I had contradicted him.

I'm not familiar with that one, he said. It must be more obscure.

Reluctantly I told him the story. I blushed ferociously when I spoke the line at the heart of it.

The young girl caressed him, then asked, What now?

I stared at the tatami as I said it, avoided looking at Hana. My face burned. When I reached the last line, the old woman's rant at the monk, Yotsugi-san barked out a laugh.

She told him, he said. No uncertain terms! *Nowhere is there any warmth.* Just what we were talking about earlier. Intensity without lightness.

My bones felt dense, my flesh heavy. I felt trapped in my body, desperate to flee but unable to move. And once again the thought came to me that *this* was my koan. This here and now.

*

79

I had no idea how long we had sat. We had eaten, though I had little stomach for it. When I glanced at Hana I could see she was uncomfortable on my behalf. She nodded in sympathy when she caught my eye, kept a smile on her face when her father spoke. And he saw nothing, understood nothing, just talked and laughed, drank sake, told endless anecdotes, his face a kabuki mask, his words washing over me.

When the evening was over, he gave an exaggerated bow, laughed again.

Burned down his hut!

He bade me goodnight and asked Hana to see me out. In the doorway she said she hoped I would not be put off coming to visit again. I opened my mouth to speak but no words came out. I folded my hands in *gassho* and she held them a moment in her own small hands. Lightness. Softness and warmth. She raised her right hand, touched her fingers to my lips. I couldn't breathe.

*

What now?

*

This was more intense than any koan. The world around me was dust and ash. I dreaded hearing from Yotsugi-san, I yearned to hear from him. When I thought of Hana I felt my heart being torn from my chest. I felt moments of wild exhilaration, but deep in my core I knew it was illusion, all of it, a kind of madness.

*

Shakyamuni's advice to monks in the Lotus Sutra was clear.

Do not take delight in looking at young women. Do not speak with young girls, maidens or widows.

And yet.

The sheer intensity of the feeling. The sweetness.

*

A month went by and the madness persisted. I would think I had conquered the emotion and it would overwhelm me again. I felt adrift, between two worlds.

*

The priest summoned me, kept me waiting outside his room for a time, then shouted to me to come in. I knew he could see through me, and this time I was sure he would confront me and tell me I was worthless.

I opened my mouth to speak but he raised his hand, said, No words!

He sat, straight-backed, breathed in and out slowly. I listened to the breath come and go. A thin-legged spider made its zigzag way across the tatami. I waited.

Eventually the priest spoke, a weariness in his voice.

There is a verse, he said, ascribed to the monk Shoshu Shonin who resided on Mount Shosha in Harima.

When worldly thoughts are intense, then thoughts of the Way are shallow.

When thoughts of the Way are intense, then worldly thoughts are shallow.

He wrote those words more than five centuries ago.

The priest looked at me, his gaze direct, but not unkind.

It is no small matter to attain human birth. And to arrive

at a point where you are shaking off the world, and following the Buddha-path is the result of many lifetimes of seeking and striving.

He breathed deep again, recited the Four Noble Truths.

Existence is suffering. Its cause is desire. Desire can be conquered. There is a Way.

The Way is not easy, he said. But nothing else has any meaning.

He folded his hands, bowed.

Nothing.

*

Another month, and the priest summoned me again. He had received a letter from Yotsugi-san, dealing mainly with financial matters, his donations to the temple. But he had made a point of thanking me once again and wishing me well. He was most grateful for my actions in saving his daughter from injury. He would not be offering hospitality in the near future as he and his daughter were moving to Kyoto where his wife was already in residence.

It is my understanding, said the priest, that the daughter is to be married to a young nobleman from a Kyoto family.

He paused, then handed me a small scroll, rolled up and sealed.

This was enclosed with the letter, he said. It is addressed to you.

I bowed and took the scroll outside. The seal showed a flower. I opened it and read, a poem from the Kokinshu, copied out in delicate script.

Over and over

Like endless waves,
My heart is carried away
By memories of the one
Who has stolen it.

It was stamped with the same seal, the flower, *Hana*. The paper smelled of jasmine.

MU

I threw myself into the work with even more intensity.

Beyond zazen and the reading and chanting of the sutras, the heart of the teaching was the koan study, grappling and struggling with these insoluble problems, unanswerable questions, battering against their impenetrable barriers till something gave and broke. There were two great koan collections, the Blue cliff Record and the Mumonkan, the Gateless Gate.

The head priest told us that to awaken to the meaning of a koan required intense concentration, and great doubt. He quoted master Mumon.

It's like swallowing a red-hot iron ball. You try to spew it up, but you can't.

I felt myself choke, felt that solid iron blocking my throat, and once again I was the child Iwajiro, terrified of the burning hells. Swallowing a red-hot iron ball. I felt the panic begin to rise.

The priest recited the first case from the Mumonkan.

A monk asked Joshu, Does a dog have the Buddha-nature?

I had heard the question before. Yes or No? To answer Yes was wrong. To answer No was just as wrong. What then?

Does a dog have the Buddha-nature?

Joshu answered, *Mu.* Nothing.

The nothing that opens up when you realise, fully realise, the impossibility of answering Yes or No. And yet.

Meditate on this, said the priest, till you sweat white pearls.

And then what?

Meditate and find out.

Mu.

*

Concentrate on Mu with your whole being, wrote Mumon, *without ceasing. Then your inner light will be a candle flame illuminating the whole universe.*

I meditated on *Mu* day and night. In zazen I chanted it to myself, a silent mantra. I took my brush and copied out the symbol, again and again. *Mu.*

I lived with the koan, thought about it, struggled with it.

You cannot get it by thinking, the priest said, quoting Mumon. *You cannot get it by not thinking. You cannot get it by grasping. You cannot get it by not grasping.*

I am sure this is helpful. I said. Nevertheless.

The question has to be answered, he said. According to Mumon it is the most serious question of all. Does a dog have the Buddha-nature?

He also says if you answer Yes or No, you lose your *own* Buddha-nature.

Dog! said the priest. Now you're swilling Mumon's words around in your filthy mouth and spitting them back at me.

If I'm a dog, I said, do *I* have the Buddha-nature?

Cur! he said. Jackal! You're rolling around in your own muck.

I lived with the koan. It was with me in the meditation hall and walking the streets of Hara with my begging bowl. It was with me when I ate and when I lay down on my pallet to take rest.

Mu.

I'm eating, breathing, sleeping it, I said.

Try pissing and shitting it, said the priest.

That too.

Well then.

*

I continued, determined to break through.

At times I felt I was so close, a single step away. It could be as close as my own heartbeat, my own breath. Then I would lose it, feel overwhelmed, beaten down by the sheer weight of it. I choked and gagged on that red-hot iron ball, unable to swallow it, unable to spit it out. It was stuck there, lodged in my throat, burning.

And if you do break through, said the priest, you will be like a dumb man who has had a dream. You will know but be unable to tell. Meditate on that.

Again the feeling of panic took hold. To be mute, unable to speak. To know it and have no words. *Mu.*

One morning, early, I came out of the temple gate and walked through the village, head full of the koan. A thin drizzling rain fell, and I listened to the sound it made pattering on my *kasa.* It was too early to beg from door to door, or at any of the wayside stalls or teashops, so I kept walking, head down, thinking of *Mu,* concentrating on nothing else.

Nothing. Else.

Before I knew it I had reached the end of the village and I turned to head back. A scrawny old dog wandered out from an alley, and it stopped and raised its head when it saw me. We stood and looked at each other, acknowledged each other's existence. He too had been soaked by the rain, his fur damp and bedraggled.

Well, I said. Here we are.

He sniffed the air, turned his head away.

So tell me, I said. Do you have the Buddha-nature?

Without hesitation he barked, at me, at the rain, at the day, at everything, and I threw back my head and laughed, then bowed to him three times.

Later I wrote it as a haiku.

*Does this dog
have the Buddha-nature?
Hear him bark!*

*

I recited the haiku to the priest.

So you're showing your teeth now, he said. What next? Cocking your leg against the temple gate?

But then he laughed. Hear him bark!

The next time I came to him for koan instruction, before I could sit down he asked if I had eaten.

Yes, I said, wondering why he was asking.

Very well, he said. You had better wash your bowl.

Now I recognised his question as another koan, another case from the Mumonkan, another story about Joshu. A monk comes to Joshu for instruction, and Joshu asks if he's eaten his rice-gruel. The monk says Yes. Joshu tells him to wash his bowl.

Was the priest assigning me this new koan? Was it because

I had made progress with *Mu*, or because I was making no headway at all.

Well? he asked.

Do you want me to meditate on this now?

Not at all, he said. I just wanted to know if you had eaten. That was all.

Not only have I eaten, I said, I have also washed my bowl.

Excellent, he said. Such diligence. Such discipline. Now, does a dog have the Buddha-nature?

Mu, I said.

*

I returned to painting the symbol *Mu*. I filled the whole page with it written large, in thick broad strokes. *Mu*. With the tip of a finer brush I wrote it again and again, covered the page in it like tiny bird-tracks. *Mu*. I made patterns with it, the words arranged round a central emptiness, a void.

MU MU MU MU MU
MU MU   MU MU
MU MU MU MU MU

NOTHING NOTHING NOTHING
NOTHING   NOTHING
NOTHING NOTHING NOTHING

Does a dog have the Buddha-nature? I drew the old dog I'd seen in the rain, barking out *Mu*. I remembered the dog that had barked at me the first time I'd gone to Yotsugi-san's home and taken tea with Hana.

I drew the dog, barking, barking, *Mu* emerging from his open jaws. I laughed and drew a cow, bellowing *Mu*.

Does a cow have the Buddha-nature?

Mu.

*

Whether it was the koans, or the place itself, the mind-numbing rigour, the repetitive routine, I began to feel constrained. I felt a great agitation, a need to get out on the road and walk. I needed movement, a break from the endless sitting. I asked permission from the head priest, and reluctantly he gave me leave to go.

You can keep up koan practice while walking, he said. In fact it may help you break through. He also insisted I visit other temples, make the journey a pilgrimage rather than rambling and meandering to no great purpose. As I took my leave he called out to me, Have you eaten?

Yes, I said. And I've washed my bowl.

So it's empty, he said. You can feast on nothing.

*

Walking was good, in all weathers, in wind and rain, scorching sun. I was drenched and frozen, burned and weather-beaten. It was freedom, and I could happily have walked the whole length of Japan. But I was mindful of the head priest's injunction to visit other temples, so I stopped wherever I could along the way, to lay down my staff and hang up my bag. I ate my rice and washed my bowl, but nowhere was koan study part of the practice. I made the best of it, threw myself into sessions of zazen, and reading texts. I recited the sutras, made endless prostrations. And after a few days I would move on. But everywhere I found the same listlessness, the same lack of intensity, the same quietism, the stagnation of sitting-quietly-doing-nothing.

I spoke of it to a monk I met on the road, a wild-eyed old reprobate from a village in Kyushu.

They're everywhere, he said, with their do-nothing Zen. They sit in rows, hugging themselves. They pick up some leavings from Soto, lick the leftovers from an unwashed bowl, then they dribble it from their mouths and call it wisdom.

Heaven is heaven, I said, and earth is earth.

That's the kind of stuff, he said.

Men are men, and mountains are mountains.

Ha! Next time I meet one I'll tell him, My arse is my arse!

We laughed as we walked on, along a steep, stony path.

Bring them somewhere like this, said the monk, and they can't stand or walk. They can't take a single step but cling to trees, or crouch down and grab at plants and grasses, anything to keep them rooted to the spot. They're bloodless and their eyes are dull. They are unable to move for fear of falling.

They don't value koan study, I said.

They don't even value the words of the great masters, said the monk. The written word terrifies them. And the koan terrifies them most of all. They call koan a quagmire that will suck you under, a tangle of vines that will choke you. But how can your self-nature be sucked under? How can it be choked?

The wind whipped up and blew in our faces. Heads down, we pushed on, and the monk continued his rant, shouting above the elements.

I pray for just one mad monk burning with inner fire. Let him perish in the Great Death then rise up again, flex his muscles, spit on his palms and roar out a challenge.

At this the old monk stopped and let out a great roar that turned into a throaty laugh.

Break through to kensho, he shouted, to true enlightenment. Only then can you make sense of it all. Only then can you live it.

I could have continued walking with the old monk, listening to him rave, but he said we had to go our separate ways.

Sip this poisonous wisdom if you will, he said. But your way is your way. You have poison of your own to dish out.

At a crossroads near Mishima we went in opposite directions.

Kensho is all, he called back to me. Break through! Then he waved and was gone.

TSUNAMI

I was back on the Tokaido, walking alone. It grew even colder and the wind stung. At one point I felt the ground shake, heard a deep distant rumbling, and the sky darkened and I was caught in a storm. By the time I found shelter, in a patched-up outhouse at a wayside inn, I was drenched and frozen, but grateful to have even the semblance of a roof over my head.

By the morning the worst of the storm had passed and the rain had eased to a thin soaking drizzle. There were more travellers than usual on the road, coming from the east, from beyond Izu, many of them exhausted and bedraggled. I stopped a few and asked, and the story emerged.

A huge earthquake had shaken Edo and the surrounding area. The city had burned. The quake had caused a massive tsunami, a great tidal wave that swept inland, drowning everything in its path. The upheaval, the fire and flood, had destroyed half the city and killed thousands. I bowed my head and prayed where I stood, at the side of the road, asking the Bodhisattva of Compassion to have mercy on all those souls.

I kept walking, broke my journey at a small temple set back from the road. I found myself huddled under a thatched roof with twenty or thirty refugees from the disaster. The temple had little enough in the way of food and bedding, but what they had they gave, and I helped hand out meagre rations and threadbare blankets. I shivered through another night, my old robe wrapped tight about me, staying awake and continuing to invoke the Bodhisattva, the compassionate Kannon.

One young man sat watching me, eyes wide and staring, face gaunt and drawn, a twitch at the corner of his mouth. I offered him my bowl with what was left of my own portion of broth, but he looked through me, and past me, into the abyss. His face was smeared with grime and ash, lined where tears and snot had run down. For a moment his eyes seemed to bring me into focus and he wiped his face with his hands. Then he spoke, and his voice was cold and toneless, beyond all hope, the voice of someone speaking from hell.

If I hadn't seen it with my own eyes, he said, I would not have believed it.

He rocked back and forth where he sat, pulled his thin blanket around him.

When I was a boy and learned to read, he said, I took great delight in spelling out signs and notices, the name on a shop-front, the inscription on a gravestone, directions at a crossroads. Well, there was one sign that made me smile.

His lips drew back from his teeth, a response to some far memory, but the face was a mask, the eyes dead.

It was down at the edge of the beach, he said, and it read WARNING. In Event of Earthquake Beware of Tsunami.

A harsh dry croak racked out of his throat, the pained semblance of a laugh.

Beware of tsunami! Might as well say if you're falling from a high tower, beware of the ground coming up to meet you.

A great sob shook him and he shivered. Again I handed him my bowl with the last mouthful of soup, and this time he took it, swallowed it down, nodded his thanks and handed back the bowl.

It was chance, he said. I just happened to be inland, on higher ground. I saw the whole thing, from far away, from up above.

First there was the noise, the great boom way out at sea. The earth shook and I stumbled and fell. I stood up and saw there was mud on my knees. I wiped it and smeared my hands. I stood there, and I looked out, and could make no sense of what I was seeing. In an instant everything had changed. Buildings had disappeared, toppled over. Clouds of dust and smoke rose up. Everywhere fires broke out and flared, fanned by the wind that rushed in from the sea. And that was where my eye was drawn, to the sea.

I stood in the midst of a great silence, a hush. I could see the shoreline, and the tide receding, further and further out. The beach and the mudflats were wider than they should have been, wet with a dull glisten. A few small boats were left stranded, keeled over. Here and there were people venturing out onto the sand, children running out, out, stopping to pick up something they'd found left behind by the tide. Out.

It was wrong, he said. The scene was wrong. The way the world in a dream is like the real thing but not.

The noise was different now, a distant roaring, a rush. I saw the wave, far out, as wide as the whole horizon and gathering speed as it moved towards the shore. I heard myself shout out *No!* and I started to run. I pitched forward, fell again. And the wave kept coming, a wall of water ten, fifteen, twenty feet high. It swept in over the beach, engulfed the small figures there trying to run away, it picked up the boats and carried them, it drove on like some great being, an implacable force pushing forward.

It smashed houses and temples, a hospital, a school. It washed away bridges and uprooted trees. It turned roads into rivers and rivers into lakes. The low hill I stood on became an island. The waters reached almost to my feet. I looked out across this new world and I knew everything I owned was gone, my home destroyed, my wife and daughter drowned.

He had told me all he had to tell. He had no more words. He looked at me across a great distance.

*

The young man and the other refugees lay down where they could in the cold hall and grappled with restless uneasy sleep. I found a corner and returned to my meditation, interrogating the silence, questioning the emptiness, the nothingness. *Mu.*

In a moment I was there, entering into the experience, looking through his eyes, seeing what he had seen. I felt the fear and the panic, faced that vast wall of water thundering inland. I was shaken by sheer terror, then numbed, unable to move, then running, stumbling, crying, scrambling to higher ground.

The great wave, the colossal destruction and loss of life. This too was a koan, beyond comprehension. This too.

Existence is suffering, said the Buddha. The First Noble Truth.

We come from nothing and to nothing we return.

The great ocean, the wide world, the vast universe itself, are no more than drops of dew on the Buddha's feet.

And yet.

And yet.

Sentient beings are numberless. I vow to save them all.

Before dawn I was on the road, walking, meditating.

At the next temple I once more laid down my staff and hung up my bag. I once more joined in the reading of texts, the chanting of sutras, the endless prostrations. I ate my rice and washed my bowl.

After a week I set out walking again, back to Daisho-ji.

Well? said the head priest, Sokudo, on my return. What now?

I had nothing to say.

CLEAR SEVERITY

After the tsunami my restlessness grew worse. I had glimpsed another kind of hell, not fire but water. This was how it ended, in cataclysm, all-engulfing. I left Daisho-ji, walked again, not settling, for weeks and months as the seasons changed, and on the way back I spent time in Shimizu village, cloistered away at the monks' training hall in Zenso-ji.

Again the regime was based on long hours of study, chanting, meditation. The head priest, Sen'ei Soen, was austere and scholarly, thin-lipped, sunken-cheeked. One day he delivered a sermon on koans from the Mumonkan, the Gateless Gate. He pointed out that the master Ganto referred to in one of the stories was Ganto Zenkatsu, or Yantou Quanhuo, the great Chinese teacher of Zen who was known as Clear Severity.

I was thrilled by the very sound of his name and by the story the priest told about Ganto challenging his own master's realisation, then laughing out loud and applauding the master's next lecture, saying the master had realised the last truth.

The priest quoted a verse.

> *If you understand the first truth,*
> *You should understand the last truth.*
> *The first and the last – are they not the same?*

If I'd had the courage I would have stood up and laughed, and applauded the priest's sermon. But it would have been empty, just a performance, and the thought of it made me burn with embarrassment. This was how far I was from any kind of realisation, first or last. But I came away from the lecture fired up, determined to find out more about Ganto. I went straight to the library and found a book on his life and teachings. I blew the dust from the book. The pages smelled pleasantly musty and damp, and faintly of ancient incense. I settled in a corner of the shrine room to read it straight through.

Ganto came to life as I read. He had indeed been a powerful character and a great teacher. He had lived the Zen life to the full, in absolute totality.

Clear Severity.

There was story with the title *Ganto's Axe*. Ganto's own master, Tokusan, had asked him to test the realisation of two monks. They've been meditating here for years, said Tokusan. Go and challenge them.

Ganto picked up an axe and went to the hut where the two monks were meditating.

If you say a word, he told them, I will cut off your heads. If you don't say a word I will cut off your heads.

He raised the axe, ready to strike. The two monks continued meditating as if he hadn't spoken, as if he didn't exist.

You are true Zen students, said Ganto, and he threw down the axe. Then he reported back to Tokusan.

I see your side of it, said Tokusan, but what about their side?

Old Tozan might let them in, said Ganto, but not you.

I had encountered Tozan's words, his koans, before. *How can we avoid heat and cold? Go where it is neither hot nor cold.*

Ganto's axe. The blade flashing.

98

The light in the room was beginning to fade. I had sat the whole afternoon, lost in the book. I had missed a session of zazen. I had missed the dishing out of rice and pickle. I suddenly shivered, felt the autumn chill in my bones. *Go where it is neither hot nor cold.* I lit a lamp and pulled my robe tighter about me, huddled over the book and read on through the evening and into the night.

It was clear that Ganto was the greatest of masters. The commentary called him a dragon of a man and said a teacher of his calibre only appeared every five hundred years. I could see him, like Nisshin Shonin walking through fire, braving hell itself.

I read the book to the very end, taking strength and sustenance from every word. But on the last page was a passage that drained the life out of me. It described Ganto's death. It said a gang of bandits had attacked the monastery where he was meditating. They had ransacked the place and found nothing worth stealing, then they had turned on Ganto and brutally murdered him, stabbed him again and again. It was said his death-cry was so loud it could be heard ten miles away.

I slumped and let the book fall to the floor. I stared at it lying there on the frayed tatami. I heard footsteps and the head priest was standing in the doorway, glaring at me. His voice boomed out.

What are you doing here?

He meant *here*, in the library, but I heard his question as much more. What was I doing here? Why was I wasting my time?

I didn't answer.

You missed two sessions of zazen, he said. You neglected your practice. Instead you sit here dreaming, using up lamp-oil.

This was the way my father had spoken to me when I was a child, meditating on Tenjin. Wasting lamp-oil. Wasting my time.

99

The priest snuffed out the lamp and the darkness closed in.

*

For three days and three nights I was in torment. I ate nothing. I couldn't sleep. The story of Ganto had pitched me into despair. If a master of that calibre could be brutally slain by common bandits, and howl in his death-agony, if even he was powerless against the forces of darkness, then what hope was there for the rest of us?

One way or another. In event of earthquake, beware of tsunami.

What was the point of this life of austerity, the endless sitting in zazen, the grappling with insoluble koans? It had all become empty, meaningless.

Did a dog have the Buddha-nature?

Who cared?

Now the teachings were abhorrent to me. The sutras and the images turned my stomach. I was sick to death of Zen and all its trappings.

By day I walked around numbed, as in a dream, the world a grey place inhabited by ghosts. At night, not sleeping, I turned this way and that, imagined the demons coming closer, ready to drag me down into hell. I imagined I saw Ganto's face, contorted, heard his final cry echoing, the sound of utter desolation and defeat.

If you say a word I will cut off your heads. If you don't say a word I will cut off your heads.

I couldn't go on. I would have to leave.

But what then?

Go home and face my mother's disappointment, my father's disdain? Better to throw myself in the river. But that would

100

take me straight to the deepest hell, reborn among the *gaki*, the hungry ghosts.

I couldn't go on. I had to go on. Life itself was a vicious koan I couldn't solve.

If you say a word. If you don't say a word.

I found myself sitting on the hard ground, in the farthest corner of the temple, leaning against an old mud wall, legs stretched out in front of me. I had no memory of walking there. I sat, looking at nothing, staring into the void. Mindless, I picked up a stick, scratched a mark in the dirt. I made a rough version of the ideogram *Mu*. I rubbed it out with my hand in the dust. I leaned forward again with the stick. Three lines made a shape like Fuji.

I remembered my brush and inkstone. I had brought them with me to the temple, but I had barely touched them in all the time I had been here.

Again I rubbed out what I had drawn, wiped out Fuji with a stroke. I stood up, shaky, unsteady on my feet. I went to the kitchen and begged a bowl of rice, ate it too quickly and staggered outside, threw it up. Then I sipped some water and brought that up too. Retching and aching I looked down at my vomit, spattered in the dust. Eyes watering, I saw worlds, sparkling landscapes in the random patterns. Then I blinked and they disappeared.

I felt weak but purged. I cleaned up the mess. I made my way back to my sleeping quarters, found the inkstone and brush among my few belongings, wrapped in an old cloth. I would start painting again. If I couldn't be a monk, I would be an artist, a poet. If hell awaited me, so be it. Let me not waste this short life in fear of it, unable to live.

THE WILD HORSE
OF MINO

I walked endlessly, along the Tokaido, on mountain paths. I followed rivers and streams, the edge of the ocean. I slept wherever I found myself, wherever I could lay my head, in the cheapest inns, in barns and outhouses, in wayside temples, anywhere I could beg lodging for the night. In six-tatami rooms, in no-tatami rooms, on loose straw and bare hard floors, in the company of thieves and vagabonds, prostitutes who called me monk-boy and asked me to keep them warm.

The young girl caressed him, then asked, What now?
The monk answered, Nowhere is there any warmth.

Once, on a cold cold night, I lay huddled in the corner of a tiny bare room, unable to sleep. In the dark I heard others come in to the room and I realised it was two young women, like me unable to afford more than this meanest of shelters on worn tatami behind thin walls. I heard them whispering and giggling as they settled down, and they called out *Goodnight* to me, their singsong voices chiming together, then more whispering, another tinkle of laughter.

I chanted the Daimoku to myself, fell asleep and dreamed

of Hana, the feel and smell of her in my arms. Then waking, and not Hana. The scent was wrong, a faint sweetness drowned out by mildew and camphor and sweat. Not Hana but the warmth. One of the two young women, here beside me. Falling into nothing, into a little death, then waking again, the two women gone. Had I dreamed this too? The cold room.

The endpoint of desire was its own cessation. For a brief moment there was no desire. Then the whole cycle began again, neverending.

What now?

I walked on, through the coldest winter. I carried my brush and inkstone in my old canvas bag. I made verses in my head, wrote them down when I could.

> *Not the other shore but this one,*
> *Battered, battered by endless waves.*
> *Useless this lifelong struggle.*
> *Useless standing here, useless to move on.*

I descended, not into hell but into bleakness, a place of desolation and emptiness, a dreariness of spirit. I still wore my monk's robe, but I was between two worlds, belonging to neither, estranged from both.

*

I had heard tell of a master named Bao Rojin who lived in the south of Mino province. He was famed for his teaching of calligraphy and verse. His knowledge of the Chinese poets, especially from the T'ang dynasty, was said to be unparalleled. These were the very poets I wanted to emulate – Li Po, Han Yiu, Tu Fu – and I was anxious to meet this master Bao. But he also had a reputation as hard and ruthless, intolerant of fools. He was said to be brutal with his students, whatever their rank or background. He would cut them down, challenge every assumption, every opinion, leave them shaken to the core. He was known as the Wild Horse of Mino.

In the spring I found out a few monks were planning to go and visit him as part of a pilgrimage, and I arranged to travel with them. There were thirteen of us in all, making our way along the Tokaido. Throughout the group there was a sense of anticipation, but trepidation too at the prospect of encountering the formidable Bao face to face. There was banter and back-chat among the monks, who recounted tales they had heard.

This Bao is six feet tall, and just as wide.

When he roars, the birds for miles around take flight.

The beasts run for cover.

He wields a staff as tall as himself.

He uses it to knock sense into his students.

I heard he knocked a few unconscious.

Broke their bones.

I heard one student died.

I couldn't help myself, I added my tuppenceworth.

I heard he actually, physically, bit someone's head off and spat it into a ditch.

A few of the others laughed at that, but one or two of them looked at me sideways, wondering what kind of madman they had in their midst.

*

104

If I'd thought our old temple was run-down and poverty-stricken, it was palatial compared to Zuiun-ji where Bao lived. Zuiun-ji was a few miles from Ogaki Castle, well back from the road at the end of a dirt track, on the edge of a tiny village. Remote and ramshackle, it looked as if it might collapse into the dust at any moment. We arrived towards evening and the monk who greeted us said we were welcome to stay, but we would have to provide our own food, even our own firewood. They could offer a roof over our heads, nothing more, except for the teaching of master Bao, which was priceless.

I'd brought a few coins with me, a meagre amount I'd begged to pay my way. Each of us chipped in, gave what he could, and we made a donation towards our keep. We were given a small bowl of rice apiece, cold water to wash it down, and shown to our quarters, a rickety outhouse with torn, patched shoji screen walls, the tatami mats on the floor worn and frayed to almost nothing. Master Bao, we were told, would see us in the morning.

At nightfall we stretched out as best we could on the hard floor, huddled in our travelling clothes, our packs beneath our heads.

This is hellish, said one monk.

Hell would be better, said another. At least it would be warm.

To travel all that way, said a third. For this.

This Bao better be good.

He will be, I said. I'm sure of it.

And I was. I felt it in my bones as I lay back, looking up at the stars through a ragged hole in the roof.

*

I slept little, woke as usual at the hour of the ox. I heard a scratching, a scrabbling in the corner, the noise of a mouse or a rat. I sat up and the noise stopped. The room was full of the stink of the monks, the sleeping bodies, like so many animals crammed in a stall. One or two of them snored, grunted. The one next to me shouted out in his sleep *Have mercy!*

I laughed at that, got up and made my way carefully to the screen door, eased it open and stepped outside.

The night air was sharp and cold. I breathed it in. A pale half-moon was just visible through a smear of cloud.

I was startled by a gruff voice behind me.

Moon viewing?

The man was not tall but gave an impression of power, solid strength, like a warrior or a wrestler. I couldn't see him clearly in the half-light, but I knew by his bearing it must be Bao.

Wrong time, he said. Wrong season.

I said nothing.

Cat got your tongue? he said.

No, I said.

A man of silence, then. You think you understand Zen?

No, I said. I mean, yes. I mean.

Ha! he said. A man who knows his own mind!

I'm here to learn, I said, the words sounding pathetic even as I spoke them.

Well then, he said. Take it from me. Wrong time, wrong season. And who ever heard of moon viewing without some sake?

True, I said.

He laughed.

Of course it is! Now, why are you prowling around in the middle of the night? Seeking enlightenment or just feeling troubled?

Maybe both, I said.

Both equally useless, he said. Now what's your name?

Ekaku, I said, and I bowed low.

Ekaku, he repeated, and gave a slight nod in return. Well, Wise Crane, I am Bao Rojin, the master of this magnificent temple, this heaven-on-earth.

Yes, I said, and I bowed even lower.

And it's me you've come here to see, you and your cronies?

Yes.

Well, who knows? Perhaps I'll be able to knock some sense into you. Or knock some sense out of you.

Once more I bowed and he turned to go, stopped.

Do you know the poetry of Li Po?

A little.

Drinking under the moon, he said, and he recited.

> *Out among the flowers with my jug of wine,*
> *Drinking alone, I raise my cup to the moon.*
> *The moon, myself, my shadow, make three.*

The verse thrilled me, but before I could tell him, he was gone, with a grunt and a wave of the hand. But I felt his teaching had begun.

*

Next morning, we each had more water, another bowl of rice, this time flavoured with a little pickled plum. The monks were grumbling.

What possessed us to come here?

If we don't freeze to death we'll starve.

The first poem I write will be my own epitaph.

Suddenly Bao was standing in the doorway, filling the space.

107

He looked even more solid and formidable. His voice boomed out.

So you think you're ready to write your death-verse?

The monk who'd spoken grovelled and bowed low.

I'll give you a death-verse, said Bao. It was written by Mumon Gensen three hundred years ago.

The wheel of life rolls on.
Every day is the right day.
Reciting a poem at your death
Is adding frost to snow.

The monk stayed down, his head pressed to the floor.

When you've learned to live, said Bao, then you're ready to die. He fixed his gaze on me, fierce.

What do you think, Wise Crane?

I was caught off guard, mind numbed. Adding frost to snow.

Well? said Bao.

I . . .

Ha! Eloquent as ever.

He turned and was gone, and the monks were staring at me.

You know him?

Only since this morning.

So what was that about?

Eloquent as ever! said the monk who had grovelled, now standing up, composing himself.

Incredibly, I was sensing resentment, just because the master had addressed me, left me flummoxed and dumbstruck.

I . . .

Bao appeared again in the doorway.

Still in full flow? he said. So, have you lot come here to learn, or to sit around eating rice and drinking water?

This time we followed him out the door and across to a little courtyard beside the *zendo*. He sat on the ground and indicated we should do the same, form a half-circle in front of him.

Every poem you write, he said, could be your death-verse. Every day could be your last. This was what Basho taught his followers. Have you read Basho?

Nobody spoke.

He's only ten years dead, Bao continued. So his poetry may not have reached you in the spiritual backwaters of Edo or Kyoto or Kamakura. Whereas here, in the very heart of the civilised world . . .

He gestured with a sweep of the hand, took in the shabby, dilapidated buildings.

Or you might say, here in the middle of nowhere . . .

He paused.

. . . great poets are valued.

He fixed each of us, in turn, with his gaze as he spoke.

And now that I have told you the name of Basho, you must read his poems, as you must read Li Po, and Tu Fu and the other immortals. Then you must forget them, and write. Basho himself said, *Learn of the willow from the willow, learn of the pine from the pine.* Poetry is what is happening here, right now, in this moment.

A dog barked. I could smell wood smoke. A crow flapped onto the roof.

Now, said Bao. Let us begin with zazen.

The monk who had spoken before made to stand up.

And where are you going? said Bao.

I thought we were going into the *zendo*, said the monk, to meditate.

Here, said Bao. Sit.

The monk apologised, sat back down again on the hard ground.

Back straight, said Bao. Mind empty. Here.

We sat, and time passed. I moved beyond numbness and ache to a kind of dogged acceptance of numbness and ache, and time passing.

Finally Bao opened his eyes and spoke again.

Since Basho is our master for today, he said, I shall tell you one more of his poems. This one was his actual death-verse, the last words he wrote, three days before he died at the age of fifty.

He took in a slow, deep breath, intoned the poem with great reverence, as if chanting a sutra.

Sick on a journey –
my dreams go wandering
across a withered moor.

He opened his eyes, looked out at us.

If you ever in your lives write one poem as fine as that, he said, you may feel your existence has not been entirely worthless.

He got to his feet, the session over, dismissed us with another wave of the hand.

I was unsettled, felt two things simultaneously, a kind of quiet exhilaration centred in my chest and a niggling irritation around the navel.

As we started to move away, Bao spoke to me directly.

Wise Crane, he said. Can you give us a haiku?

Once again he had caught me off guard. But I concentrated, came out with three lines.

Sitting doing nothing
hearing the old crow caw –
where is the poetry in this?

He glared at me.

It's full of arrogance, he said. And it stinks of Zen. And where is the poetry in that?

I couldn't answer.

But, he said. But. It's a beginning.

He chuckled.

The old crow!

He threw back his head and laughed.

I like it!

*

The next day Bao repeated the same pattern, and the next, and the next. He didn't dwell on technicalities, the arid study of verse-forms for their own sake. Instead he would just recite a poem, let it do its work. Learn of the poem from the poem. He identified completely with what he read. He was Li Po, intoxicated under the moon, or Tu Fu, pensive in the morning rain, or Basho, setting out on his last journey. Direct seeing, said Bao. Enter into the life of things.

After that first morning, he didn't single me out again. Every day he challenged someone else to write a haiku, or a tanka, or a poem in the Chinese style, and every day his comments were cutting, dismissive.

Effete, he said. Pallid. Worthy of some third-rate concubine in the emperor's court.

Too elaborate, he said. Finger-pointing-at-the-moon. If the finger wears fancy jewelled rings, that's all you see, you don't look at the moon at all.

111

Too arid. Too intellectual. No heart.

Too abstract. There's no poetry without things.

Infantile. A four-year-old could write better poetry.

Hell, I could shit better poetry.

When he taught us calligraphy it was the same. We sat in zazen, then he carefully unrolled a scroll, prepared his inkstone with a little water, dipped a thick brush in the mix, all the time asking us to watch and learn. Without hesitation, with a few quick strokes, he made the syllable for *Mu*, nothing. Then he asked each of us to do the same, and again his criticisms were withering.

Too controlled, he said. Tight arsed. Constipated.

Too formless, he said. Might as well be pigeon-droppings spattered on the page.

When he looked at my effort, he grunted.

Not good, he said. Not bad. That's something, I suppose. Something and nothing. Something in nothing!

He laughed at what we assumed was some esoteric joke. As he moved away he chuckled again, turned and shouted back at us.

Mu!

*

It continued for a few days. He would recite a poem, trail the words down a scroll and always his calligraphy had the same effortless grace. Then without stopping, as a kind of continuation, with a few deft strokes of the brush he would illustrate the poem, draw a bird on a branch, a spray of blossom, an old poet looking at the moon.

We tried again, but apart from the occasional word of encouragement, his comments continued to be scathing. The other monks grew dispirited. They griped and complained about Bao and his harsh words, about the miserable state of the place, about the starvation rations, the bugs and rats. They decided to leave.

For all the severity of his methods, I knew Bao was a great teacher and I would travel far before finding another even approaching his calibre. I told the other monks I would not be leaving with them. I would stay and take my chances with Bao.

Next morning I watched them go, a silent straggled line of black-clad figures, heading out of the temple and down through the village. Again I heard Bao's voice, behind me.

So, Ekaku, he said, Wise Crane. The other birds are flying away!

I decided to stay, I said.

Fine, said Bao. Let's see if we can make a poet of you.

The place felt empty without my travelling companions. Because of the poverty of the place, the austerity, there were only a few resident monks. One of them was a young man called Onbazan, a few years older than me. He seemed to be Bao's close disciple and was a fine poet in his own right.

Bao would never tell you this himself, he said, but he thinks highly of you. Otherwise he would have driven you away with the rest and said good riddance.

*

For a few days the weather was good – clear blue skies, no rain or mist. Bao took himself off into town, to Ogaki.

When it's clear like this, said Onbazan, the villagers call it a Bao sky, because they see him heading into Ogaki, to enjoy himself.

Enjoy himself?

Onbazan laughed.

Don't ask!

113

While Bao was away, Onbazan worked with me on linked verse. We decided to write a hundred lines between us, alternating. We gave ourselves a time limit – two sticks of incense. It was something he had learned from Bao – we would finish the poem in the time it took the sticks to burn down, a little over an hour.

Onbazan wrote the first line.

Two sticks of incense, a hundred lines of verse.

An hour later I wrote the last line.

The incense stick burns down – a heap of ash, the fragrance.

Onbazan nodded his approval.

There are good and bad lines, he said. But we got there. That last line is perfect, a little gem of a haiku in its own right.

Bao was in good humour when he returned in the evening, more relaxed than I'd seen him. It was clear he'd had a flask or three of sake.

Linked verse, he said. This is good. The important thing is, the connection from poem to poem should be subtle, not too obvious. It's like sitting next to a woman, when you're not so close that you're touching, but close enough to smell her perfume.

I was startled by the image, by the sensuality of it, and by Bao grinning at me. Then Onbazan pointed out my last line, about the ash burning down. Bao read it out loud.

A good death-verse, he said. Keep it up your sleeve till the time comes.

The incense stick burns down –
a heap of ash,
the fragrance.

*

114

Over the next month there were a few clear days, under a Bao sky, and the master would head off into Ogaki. At first I took Onbazan's advice and didn't ask. But then my curiosity got the better of me, and I pestered him to tell me.

Very well, he said at last. Master Bao has a friend in Ogaki, a nun by the name of Jukei.

I stared at him.

Do you mean . . . ?

Yes, he said. It's all unspoken, but yes. Definitely yes.

My face must have registered shock, amusement, confusion all at once.

Onbazan laughed.

Way of the world, he said.

Later I sat down with my ink and brushes, a blank scroll, and tried to empty my mind. Once again the image that came to me was my beloved Mount Fuji, rising out of the mist above Hara. With the ink thin, the strokes fluid, I sketched the familiar shape in three swift lines. Then I sat and looked at it, took it in. That poem I loved came back to me.

> *Beloved Fuji –*
> *The mist clears and reveals*
> *Your snowy whiteness.*

I remembered the day I had seen the Daimyo's procession, when I'd glimpsed the face of that beautiful woman passing by, like a vision. I thought of Hana. I dipped the tip of the brush in the ink, wrote haiku of my own.

> *Miss Fuji,*
> *Cast aside your hazy robe*
> *And show me your snowy skin.*

115

I looked at what I'd written, what I'd drawn, and it was complete. I felt a quiet excitement and with it a kind of gratitude, and I bowed to the work I'd made.

That night Bao sat staring at the scroll for some time. Eventually he spoke.

Wise Crane, he said. I don't know how much I can teach you. Learn to write by writing. Learn to draw by drawing.

He bowed and handed the scroll back to me, then he poured me a little sake, lit a tobacco pipe and passed it to me, and it felt like a kind of recognition, an initiation. But in spite of Bao's implied praise, the sense of satisfaction was immediately replaced by a kind of emptiness.

The next morning I sat with Onbazan and he told me about something he'd just been reading, the story of a Zen master, Kaisen Shoki.

Along with a hundred other monks, Kaisen was taken prisoner by a samurai warrior, Oda Nobunaga, who accused them of consorting with his enemies. The monks were herded into a courtyard and dry branches were piled up all around them and set alight, a pyre to burn them alive.

As the flames rose, one monk asked Kaisen, Since we cannot escape the passing of all things in this world, where shall we find the everlasting?

Kaisen replied, It is here, right before your eyes, in this very place.

The monk asked, What place is this, before my eyes?

As the flames licked around him and caught the hem of his garment, Kaisen said, If you have conquered your ego, coolness will rise even from the fire.

Then the flames consumed him.

Coolness will rise even from the fire.

When I heard these words I couldn't breathe. To attain that poise, even in the face of the all-consuming fire. The very thought of it left me shaken and humbled. Becoming a poet was all very well, but even if I surpassed the greatest poets, Li Po and Tu Fu, it would not save me from the fire or grant me that poise in the face of it. I felt the old despondency begin to descend. I wandered outside, and there, stacked on the verandah, were hundreds of dusty old books – scriptures and manuals of instruction – left out to be aired. When I saw them I felt an immediate calmness, a surge of inexplicable joy, dispelling the black mood. I lit a stick of incense, made three deep bows and chanted.

Buddhas in the ten directions, gods who guard the Dharma, I place my trust in you. Guide me and show me the way I should follow.

I closed my eyes and reached into the pile of books, settled on one and lifted it up, breathed in its musty smell. I pressed it to my forehead, felt an intense reverence. I opened my eyes and they filled with tears when I saw what I had chosen, or what had been chosen for me. It was a great classic of Zen teaching – *Spurring Students through the Zen Barrier*. I opened it at random and read.

As you travel in your search for wisdom, yield not to fatigue. Be oblivious of day and night. Have no fear of heat or cold. Do not let your thoughts scatter aimlessly. Do not look left or right, forward or backward, up or down. Walk on.

Again I pressed the book to my forehead, overcome with gratitude.

*

I was grateful to Bao for his teaching, but it was time to move on. I was ready to settle again in a community of monks, resume the rigours of intense practice. Poverty and chastity would be my friends, and nothing would deflect me from my

117

purpose. Bao said I could keep the book I had plucked from the pile, and I kept it close by me constantly, read and re-read it as I prepared to resume my life of pilgrimage.

One morning, when Bao had headed off once more to Ogaki, and Onbazan had gone into the village for supplies, I looked up from the book and was surprised to see a slight figure, a young monk, heading up the steep path to the temple. I was even more surprised when he approached and addressed me by name.

You are Nagasawa Iwajiro, he asked, known as Ekaku?

I am.

The young man bowed and handed me a letter.

This is from your father, he said.

He stood, deferential, and I knew before I read one word that the letter contained bad news. I unfolded the paper, read the columns of careful script, announcing, in formal language, that my mother had died suddenly after a short illness. My father had stamped it with his seal, in red, and signed it. *Your father, Nagasawa Genzaemon.*

I could picture him seated at his desk, writing it, back straight, the brush gripped firmly in his hand. I read the words again, and again, till they ceased to have any meaning. The characters separated, came adrift, dissolved into their constituent images and floated on the page, disconnected.

I read Mother. Illness. Death.

A kneeling woman, with two dots for breasts. I drew it as a child, learning to write.

A sickbed and a thin frail figure lying in it.

Death a skull and a heap of bones.

I looked up and was surprised to see the young man still standing there.

Forgive me, I said. This is a poor hovel, but I have a few coins left.

118

No, he said, bowing. No. Your father paid me to bring the message and to take back a reply on my return.

I was touched, and bowed to him deeply. He waited while I fetched a small scroll of paper and my brush and ink.

What to say that would have any meaning?

At the top of the page, thinking of Hara, I drew Fuji, just three brushstrokes. Then I wrote one word. *Sorrow.* Underneath I drew a crane in flight and signed it. *Your son, Ekaku.*

I handed the scroll to the messenger, thanked him, watched him go. Somewhere a *hototogisu* called, its cry piercing and sharp. Before I knew it I was shaken with sobs, and tears were pouring down my face.

*

What did this mean, that my mother was no more? That form no longer existed. I would never see her again, that good woman who had borne me, loved me, protected me. She was gone, dissolved into nothing.

I sat up all night in zazen, mind clear and cold.

At first I struggled to see her face, to bring it into focus. Then it was there, so vivid and alive she might have been in the room. She smiled the way she did when she held me and hushed me and kept the fires of hell at bay, when she wiped the tears away after we'd cried at the story of Nisshin Shonin, when she waved goodbye to me that last time as I set out on the path to enlightenment.

The last time.

I chanted the Daimoku in her honour.

Namu Myoho Renge Kyo.

She had absolute faith in the sutra. But could it be that even she, for all her goodness and kindness, her simple faith and devotion, had to descend into hell?

119

Her face changed, showed pain and suffering, and I wanted to tell her as she had once told me that it was fine, it was just a dream and everything would be all right.

By the end of the night the way was clear. I had already decided to return to the Zen path, now my commitment to it would be absolute. If my mother should be suffering in the deepest hell, I would go there and find her.

I chanted from the Four Great Vows.

Sentient beings are numberless. I vow to save them all.

My mother's face was calm again, eyes closed, then she faded and was gone. The rats scuttled behind the torn shoji screens. I lit another stick of incense, sat like a stone as the dark night lightened to cold grey.

In the early morning I packed my belongings, such as they were, the few clothes I wasn't wearing, a blanket and begging bowl, a spare pair of straw sandals, wooden geta for walking in the mud and rain. I also packed my brushes and inkstone, half a dozen of my drawings, rolled up tight, and the most precious thing I now owned, the copy of the *Zen Barrier* book Bao had said I could keep.

In return I gave Bao the drawing I had done of Fuji, with the haiku about her snowy skin. For Onbazan I had written out the haiku about the incense burning down, above it a swirl like smoke.

They had come out to see me off. Onbazan was sad to see me go, and even Bao, in his gruff way, seemed sorry I was leaving.

The place won't stink quite so much of Zen once you've gone, he said. But I'm sure you'll be back to teach us a thing or two after you've shaken up all those gods and Buddhas.

I bowed three times, pressed my forehead to the hard earth.

120

Then I stood up and slung my pack over my shoulders. The weight of it felt good. I gave one last bow and was on my way again, back on the Zen road.

THREE

WIND AND RAIN

Months passed, years. I travelled where the wind blew me, walked from province to province, from temple to temple. If I fell in with a group of monks on a pilgrimage, I would join them. If I heard of a Dharma talk being given by some eminent priest in a remote corner of the country, I would make my way there, no matter how far. I passed through towns and villages, mingled with the crowds along the Tokaido, walked on alone over hills and through valleys, across desolate moorland. I scrambled up steep slopes, along narrow paths. I waded through marshland, crossed shallow streams.

At times I barely noticed the countryside I walked through, so fierce was my concentration on the teachings in the book I carried with me. I challenged myself with one koan after another, spurred myself through the Zen barrier.

At one temple, Hofuku-ji in Horado, the head monk Nanzen seemed to see something in me. Like Bao, he wrote poetry, but his disposition was altogether milder, more scholarly. He asked to read my verses and see my calligraphy, and he nodded his approval. He wrote a poem for the New Year.

> *Old Man South shakes the sword of wisdom.*
> *Without this chilling winter, no spring.*
> *The New Year welcomes peace, prosperity, long life.*

I wrote a response, in the same style.

> *He shakes the sword, a handful of frost.*
> *His chamber is flooded with light.*
> *He burns incense to welcome the New Year.*

He laughed, his old eyes crinkled, and he thanked me for the poem. After a few weeks he said my progress was remarkable, and after some months he made me the third-ranking monk among the sixty or so who lived at the temple. I was grateful for his gentle encouragement, but the following summer I felt the need to challenge myself again. With the old monk's blessing, I shouldered my pack, got back out walking in the wind and the rain.

*

I was looking for a place where a monk might find time for solitary retreat, and yet feed himself with the offerings placed in his begging bowl. Nanzen had recommended I try Shoju-ji, near Matsuyama Castle in Iyo province.

The climate is good, he had said, and the land around the castle is fertile.

So the people are prosperous, I'd said.

Indeed.

Perfect for an eager young monk with an empty purse.

The journey was long, and I had to cross the Inland Sea to Shikoku by ferry. The castle was visible from some distance away, the surrounding farmland flat and green. I had stopped at a few more temples on the way, listening to more words, words, words. By the time I reached Shoju-ji, my reputation had preceded me. Somehow Nanzen had passed on a message to the head monk, telling him of my intensity and of my prowess in poetry and calligraphy.

So he summoned me to his quarters, looked at me long and hard. He didn't have the ferocity of Bao or the gentleness of Nanzen. I guessed he had settled comfortably into his role as head of the temple and had long since given up testing himself too rigorously.

We are fortunate here, he said at last, in having the protection and patronage of the castle. The Daimyo, the lord of Matsuyama, is eager to gain merit by supporting us.

I see, I said, eyes down, noncommittal.

He looked at me even more intently, not sure, perhaps, if I was being ironic. Then he explained that the Daimyo's chief minister was a man of great learning and culture, with a particular interest in painting and calligraphy.

He has invited a small party from the temple to visit him at his residence, and it would be advantageous if you were part of that group.

I let his words settle, fell to thinking about Hana and the visits to her father's home, the luxury of it. The scent of jasmine.

Well?

I breathed in, bowed.

It would be an honour.

*

Our host was a high-ranking military officer, a formidable warrior with the high shaved forehead, the swept-back hair, of the samurai. We were served tea and small sugared cakes that sparkled on the palate. They were so delicious I had to stop myself from shovelling them into my mouth and crunching every last one. There was much small talk about the weather and the seasons and the lushness of the rice harvest. Then our host gave a small sign, a raise of the hand, and everything was cleared away, and an old servant brought out a collection of hanging scrolls, one after another, each one more beautiful than the last.

The head monk nodded his appreciation, expressed his gratitude to the minister, who said he had a question about one of the scrolls.

I am unable to understand the Chinese characters, said the minister. Perhaps someone can help me decipher the text?

The head monk cleared his throat, picked up the scroll, held it at arm's length, turned it this way and that then admitted he was baffled.

With respect, he said, the characters are badly formed and it's impossible to make sense of them.

The other monks in our party also peered at the scroll, admitted defeat. Then one of them nodded in my direction.

Perhaps our young friend here can bring his wisdom to bear.

The head monk grinned.

Yes, he said. Wise Crane. Perhaps you would deign to come down from your perch above the clouds and enlighten us.

I took the scroll, looked closely at the inscription. It was indeed illegible.

A scroll and a scrawl, I said.

The general smiled.

I asked if I might have brush and ink, a piece of paper. Again the general had only to raise his hand and they appeared before me. I folded back my sleeve, took the brush and very carefully wrote the Chinese characters for *Old mother-in-law*, held it up for everyone to read.

It's a title for the scroll, I said.

We can read the characters, said the head monk. But what are they supposed to mean?

Words can have more than one meaning, I said. These characters can also mean *Difficult to read.*

The minister threw back his head and laughed.

My mother-in-law is definitely difficult to read!

It's the way you tell them, Ekaku, said one of the other monks.

The minister laughed again, louder.

Take my mother-in-law, he said. Please!

He called for sake to be poured, then he said he had something really special to show us, and he brought out an elaborate wooden box wrapped in the finest silk brocade. Carefully, almost reverently, he unwrapped the box, opened the lid and lifted out another scroll, held it up for our admiration.

The other pieces had been impressive, but this was truly breathtaking. The artwork and calligraphy were by the great master Daigu Sochiku. The composition was exquisite, the verse striking.

Is it wind that moves, or mind?

But more than form or content, it was the energy, the sheer vigour of the brushstrokes that raised the work to another level. Something palpable and powerful flowed from it, struck the viewer like a blow to the heart.

For the rest of the evening I was speechless. Back at the temple I went immediately to the dormitory and gathered up the few paintings of my own I had carried with me on my travels, rolled up in my backpack. I also took the notebooks in which I had copied out poems and some pieces of calligraphy I had collected and kept. I bundled up the lot and carried it out to the old graveyard. I piled it up on the ground, in front of one of the ancient, weathered tombstones, and I set fire to it all, stood and watched as it burned away to nothing.

FIRE AND BRIMSTONE

I had been away from Hara, and from Shoin-ji, for a long time. On my return I visited my father and found him distracted, distant. He had settled for growing old and he found it difficult to talk about my mother. His features would clench, his mouth a grimace, as he spoke her name. Then he would gather himself, comment on the fact that I was looking thin and weather-beaten.

He mentioned my brother two or three times, said he was prosperous and had made a success of his life. Yozaemon had married and had two children, a boy and a girl. He lived in Numazu where he had his own business, brewing *shoyu*, and every week he came here to Hara to help with the running of the way-station.

I wish him well, I said. My own road is different.

My father told me if I went to Shoin-ji I would find the old place much reduced.

Times are hard, I said.

Yes, he said. Well.

We had little to say to each other, and our meeting left me unsettled. But I stepped outside and great Fuji still stood there, a constant, an eternal presence, overlooking the town. As I gazed up at it, my heart filled to bursting.

*

Much reduced. How my father had described it, and exactly how it seemed to me now. It felt physically smaller, somehow shrunk in on itself, and one or two of the old buildings looked ready to collapse. I reported to the head priest, who had also aged and shrunk, and he gave me a slight bow, a mere nod of the head.

Wise Crane, we had heard rumours of your return.

Hara is a small place, I said, bowing low.

Too small for you, he asked, or not small enough?

Small enough and big enough, I said.

And how long will you stay with us?

Long enough, I said.

He gave a throaty chuckle that turned into a cough and he hawked and spat.

Still coughing up Zen, I said. Thank you.

Rascal, he said.

There was a shout from behind me and I turned to see Kakuzaemon, the cook, brandishing a ladle at me.

Another bloody mouth to feed!

Never mind, I said. You can just poison off a few of the others to make room for me.

Rogue, he said.

It was good to be home, to feel welcome.

*

I settled to the routine of the place, sat long hours in the cold meditation hall, chanted the sutras, grappled with the koans. I tramped the streets of Hara with my begging bowl to contribute my tuppenceworth to the subsistence. I did my share of sweeping and cleaning. I even helped patch a few gaps in the torn shoji screens to keep out the freezing draughts that blew in. There were three or four older monks I remembered

131

from before, grim and dogged, resigned. The younger ones, half a dozen of them, were decent, serious-minded, intent on breaking through. Occasionally I would see a glimmer of devilment in their eyes, but already they had that gaunt, haunted look of the acolyte as they worried away at the dry bone of Zen. And I felt a kinship with every one of them. We were in this together. Sentient beings were numberless. We had vowed to save them all.

*

The old man appeared in the village, crazy or drunk or both. He'd been thrown out of the inn, was barred from the teahouse, the bathhouse, the noodle shop, for railing at the customers, telling them the end was nigh. The gates of hell would open wide, and all would be consumed in fire and brimstone.

Finally he came to the temple, stood at the gate bellowing.

Call yourselves holy men? Can you face the fires of hell? Heed my words or you'll perish and burn!

The monks wanted to chase him away, drive him off, but I came out to meet him, bowed to him with folded hands. It was a cold day, a thin dusting of snow lay on the ground. I told him we didn't have much but he was welcome to come in and have some rice, a bowl of tea. He stopped his rant, stared at me.

Ah, he said. At last, someone who sees.

He was wild-eyed, his grey hair dishevelled, sticking up this way and that. His padded coat had a plum blossom pattern on the sleeve. It might once have been expensive but was old and worn, shabby. His manner, his delivery, had something of the preacher, something oracular, but also something theatrical, something of the floating world. I looked at

132

him hard and for a moment saw his face as a demon-mask from kabuki.

In the kitchen he wolfed down the rice, slurped the tea. The cook glared at him, clattered an iron pot on the stove.

So you've come to warn us, I said, about hellfire and brimstone.

It's coming, he said. Very soon.

How do you know this? I asked.

I can smell it in the air, he said. And I can see the signs.

What signs?

The snakes are leaving their holes, he said, and slithering down the mountain slopes. Dogs and cats are running mad. The birds are leaving their nests. Wells are drying up. Frogs and toads are leaping out of the ponds.

Basho's haiku in reverse, I said.

What?

The old pond. Frog jumps *out*. Ha!

He looked at me as if *I* were the madman. He slurped more tea and wiped his mouth with his sleeve.

You have eyes, he said. Look and see.

He bowed and took his leave. I thought I could smell a faint trace of sulphur in the air. I had smelled it before when plumes of smoke and steam rose up from Fuji.

*

Over the next few weeks I saw the signs for myself, just as the old man had described. A snake wriggled across the footpath right in front of me. A dog chased its own tail. A cat screeched and its hair stood on end. The smell of sulphur grew stronger, rank, catching at the back of the throat.

Then in the middle of the night I felt the first tremor, a rumbling as if from deep underground, and the temple buildings shook. I had been seated in zazen and I thought either this was the mightiest satori or the old man's prophecy was coming to pass.

I struggled to my feet, legs stiff, and went outside where a few of the monks had gathered. Fuji's crater was a red glow, flames and smoke rising from its rim, and slow rivers of fire flowed down its slopes.

Never in living memory had Fuji erupted. There were accounts in old books – ancient drawings showed fire and rock and smoke thrown into the air, the scene infernal. Now it was happening again. In the grey winter half-light the mountain seemed to loom closer. Its cap of snow was completely gone, melted in the heat. Fire flared through the covering of dense black cloud. The brimstone smell was now a stench, choking.

Word came that the villagers were already leaving their homes, gathering up what little they could carry and heading inland. The head priest gave orders that the monks should do the same. Every man should rescue a sacred book or arte-fact – a scroll, a small statue, an incense holder, a bell. I bowed and returned to the meditation hall, resumed my zazen.

I sat on, aware of the noise and commotion outside and around me, but untouched by it. Finally the priest came in and stood in front of me, cleared his throat loudly to get my attention.

So, Wise Crane, he said. Is this really wise after all? Do you want your wings to be singed?

It's a cold winter, I said. The fires of hell will warm me up nicely.

You think you are Nisshin Shonin, he asked, and can walk through the fires unscathed?

I'll chant the Daimoku for my mother, I said. She had great faith in it.

Surprisingly, he had nothing to say to that. He bowed then gave a rough grunt that might have been a blessing or dismissal, and he left me to my fate. But before I faced that fate, there was one thing I had to do.

In mentioning my mother, I had invoked her presence. I had seen her face before me, as clear as if she were alive. The look in her eyes was one of deep compassion and concern, not only for me, but also, I realised, for my father. I had to make sure he was moved to a safe place, and I hurried along the road to the family home at the post-station. The whole way I was bumped and jostled by fleeing families desperate to escape. Many carried their belongings in huge packs on their backs, or dragged them in handcarts along the rutted road. Children howled and dogs barked and the mountain grumbled and threatened and groaned. As I stepped into the courtyard my father was being led out by the family servant Shichibei and a stocky man I recognised as my brother. I bowed to all three of them in turn.

Iwajiro, said my brother. I hardly recognised you. A scarecrow has more meat on its bones.

My name is Ekaku, I said, and I bowed to him again.

Will you come with us? said my father. We are going to Numazu.

I have to stay here, I said, at Shoin-ji.

For a moment I saw a look of hopelessness in my father's eyes, then resignation.

Shichibei nodded, as if he understood, and he took my father by the arm.

The ground beneath us shook.

Right, said my brother. We have to go. Now.

I chanted the Daimoku quietly.

Well, said my brother. Are you coming or not?

I have work to do, I said. Sentient beings are numberless.

135

And you have vowed to save them all. Of course you have. But will you achieve that by sacrificing yourself?

Perhaps that is what it takes, I said, and I nodded to my father, told him he should go and I would be fine and all would be well and I would see him again soon. I watched them go, into the crowds, and I pushed my way in the opposite direction, against the tide, back along the road to Shoin-ji.

*

I was alone. Everyone else had gone. The place was deserted, like a ghost town, like an abandoned ship found drifting at sea. I sat in the *zendo* and meditated through the night as the rumbling and booming grew louder and the walls of the temple shuddered and groaned, trembled as if the buildings might tumble around me. The screens rattled and shook, the pillars and beams seemed to tip and shift, the very ground beneath me felt as if it might ripple and open up.

The gates of hell will open wide and all will be consumed.

I saw the madman's face, vividly before me, then it changed to the face of the old monk who had terrified me when I was a child, leading me down through the Eight Burning Hells.

The hells that descended in order of severity, down and down, ever deeper.

Heating Hell. Intense Heating Hell. Hell of Ultimate Torment.

I would face what I had to face. I straightened my back, chanted louder. *Namu Myoho Renge Kyo.*

Nisshin bearing the cauldron of red-hot iron.

My mother's cool hand on my forehead.

Namu Myoho Renge Kyo.

The heat rose up my spine, spread through me. My body was soaked with sweat. Outside it must be freezing. In here I burned.

As the darkness lightened towards another grey dawn, there was a sudden thunderous explosion, louder than anything I'd ever heard. It shook my whole being, tore the screens from the windows and doors, and a searing wind blew through the room.

In a dream I stepped outside, looked towards Fuji. Flame and smoke leaped from its peak in a great column, and above it hung a gathering mass of dark cloud, deepening and billowing, like a huge expanding mushroom. The smoke and mist obscured everything except that blazing fire surging upward and forks of lightning shooting down from the heavens. The air was thick with acrid smoke and cinders and soot. Around me sparks were descending on some of the wooden buildings, setting them alight.

I wondered if I had died during the night and was now a wandering spirit, stumbling across the outskirts of hell on my way to the great gate that led ever down to the deepest depths. I heard a voice, my own, chanting the Daimoku once more.

Namu Myoho Renge Kyo.

I woke to myself, here in this moment, in *this* world, catching breath as everything burned.

*

For days that thick pall of mist and cloud blotted out the sun. In the dense fog it was impossible to see more than a few yards in any direction. I drank water from the rain barrel, gritty with cinders and ash. I ate a few raw vegetables, dried out and stringy, left behind in the kitchen. I sat in zazen for hours and days, mind clear.

Eventually gaps appeared in the mist. The fog swirled. There was a heavy downpour of rain and the landscape reappeared, beaten down and grey. I heard voices outside in the courtyard. The head priest was the first to appear in the doorway.

137

So, Wise Crane, he said. Have you been sitting there the whole time?

More or less, I said.

More or less sitting, he said, or more or less the whole time?

Both, I said. Neither.

Rascal! He said. Pretending to do zazen and warming yourself at the fires of hell.

I stretched and yawned.

At least I've had a good sleep, I said, without being disturbed by all this prattling about satori.

He grunted and the cook came in behind him.

Still here?

Where else would I be?

I bet you've eaten every scrap of food.

Every last morsel, I said. I feasted on withered radishes and rotten cabbage.

Dog! he said, and made as if to cuff me, but changed his mind.

Behind it all I could tell they were both happy to see me, relieved at not discovering my miserable corpse reduced to ash.

*

After a few days a message came from my brother in Numazu to say my father was well and would return home in due course. Word had reached them that I had not been incinerated and was still on earth, for which they were grateful and offered up thanks. I replied by sending a little drawing of this stubborn monk, intent on meditating as Fuji, in the distance, threw off fire and smoke.

Through the winter and into spring, on days when there wasn't rain or snow or sleet, everyone pitched in to repair

138

damage to the temple buildings. We patched things up as best we could, and some of the villagers, when they'd rebuilt their own flimsy homes, came to help us with the work.

I bowed to them in gratitude. They too were future Buddhas.

Sentient beings are numberless. I vow to save them all.

It felt like some kind of miracle that the temple hadn't been completely destroyed. And I too had come through the fire unscathed. I threw myself into my meditation with even greater intensity. I grappled with the koans once more, locked horns with Joshu's *Mu*. My head was a battering ram. The koan was a solid oak door.

RETURN TO MINO

Word came to me that my old poetry teacher Bao had fallen sick. His only disciple Onbazan had been forced to return home to look after his own parents, leaving Bao alone at Zuiun-ji. I thought a change of scene might do me good, a change of air. I could help Bao and help myself at the same time. I set out once more on the road to Mino.

This time I travelled alone, not caught up in a gaggle of monks, and I covered the miles more quickly. As I walked I chanted the sutras, wrestled with the koan. *Mu.*

It was late in the day when I arrived at Ogaki. I walked on through the town, remembering it like something I had once dreamed, and headed out along the dirt track towards Zuiun-ji.

The temple looked even more dilapidated, had deteriorated even further, as if it might collapse completely at any moment and disappear into the dust.

As I approached the gate, swinging open on its hinges, a figure came out and I saw it was a nun, head down, moving briskly. I bowed as she passed, and she hesitated as if about to stop and speak, but she merely nodded and hurried on.

The place felt deserted, as if not a soul lived here. Three

crows perched on a sagging roof, cawed and cawed as I passed. I approached what had been Bao's living quarters, a ramshackle hut, and heard coughing from inside. I called out a greeting and his voice wheezed.

Who's there?

I stood in the doorway and bowed. The room smelled fetid, gaseous.

It's like an animal's den, I said, where some old creature has crawled in to die.

Kaku! he shouted. Is that you?

I folded my hands and bowed.

I thought I recognised the smell, he said. The stink of Zen!

It smells of worse than that in here, I said.

You're as bad as Jukei, he said. She wants me to drag myself into the sunlight so she can clean this place out, then drag me back in to rest.

Jukei, the nun who lived in Ogaki, the one he visited on a blue sky day.

You must have passed her on your way in, he said.

I believe I did.

There was a silence, and he was suddenly awkward.

She looks out for me, he said. Makes sure I eat a little broth every day. Brews up some foul-smelling herbs to purge my innards.

I'd heard you were at death's door, I said. But I can see you're in good hands.

Yes, he said quietly. But I'm glad to see you.

*

Jukei returned next morning and Bao formally introduced us. She was younger than Bao, I guessed, by a few years, her face weathered and worn, but eyes bright, alert.

141

He always said you would return one day, she said, bowing to me. Said you could teach him a thing or two.

So this illness was a ruse, I said, a rumour he spread to get me back.

Don't flatter yourself, he said.

Jukei and I helped him outside, sat him down with his back to a tree, a blanket wrapped around him. She made a little miso soup with *daikon*, and we sat supping it under the tree. Then she set about cleaning his room, vigorously sweeping and dusting with total concentration, and she lit a stick of incense and chanted a sutra. Then she brewed his concoction of herbs, poured it into a bowl for him to drink. He was right about the stink – it smelled of swamp gas and rotting vegetation. But he held his nose and swallowed the brew, screwed up his face and shuddered.

You see? he said. She's poisoning me!

So I can inherit this pigsty, she said.

They were like an old married couple, and for all they niggled and jibed at each other, what they had was real and deep. He would probably not have survived without her looking after him, and this too was the Buddha's compassion.

As it happened, she had work to do in Ogaki, and the timing of my visit could not have been better. She gave me strict instructions about making him rest, and preparing his soup, and how much of the toxic herb-mix to boil in the pot for his remedy.

You will stay till he is well, she said.

Yes, I said. I promise.

And you, she said to Bao. Don't be troublesome.

And just for a moment I saw it all in her eyes, her suffering, the depth of her concern for him. She bowed to us both and headed off down the path, not stopping or looking back.

A good woman, I said, when she'd gone.

Much good it does her, he said. Stuck with an old waster like me.

Perhaps she's paying off some ancient karmic debt, I said.

She must have done something *really* bad, he said, and he laughed, and it brought on another coughing fit. He hawked and spat, and I helped him back into his room, now clean and smelling of the pine incense Jukei had lit. Mindful of her instruction, I insisted he lie down and rest and he let out a great sigh, lay back and immediately fell asleep. I sat for a while then went outside and wandered round the temple grounds.

Just there was where I had first met him. I'd stepped outside, restless, in the middle of the night, moon-viewing. He'd challenged me and shaken me up, and he'd quoted Li Po. *Out among the flowers with my jug of wine* . . . And Basho. *Sick on a journey* . . .

It was only a few short years since I'd been here. They'd called Bao the Wild Horse of Mino. Now here he was, ailing, seeing out his days. Time and decay.

Over there was the verandah where those precious books had been piled up to dry. I had reached in, praying for guidance, chanced on that musty old moth-eaten volume that was to change my life. *Spurring Students through the Zen Barrier*. I still carried my own tattered copy everywhere I went.

Walk On.

Through the night I sat up and meditated in the corner of Bao's room. I felt the need to be on hand while he slept. Once or twice he grew restless, groaned aloud or called out in his sleep. Once he shouted, *Is this all? Is there no more?* Later he cried *No!* in a loud voice. And towards dawn he called Jukei's name as if it were a mantra or a prayer.

At first light he sat up and stared at me, confused.

Wise Crane, he said. Is that you? What are you doing here?

I told him I was meditating, and Kannon was looking after

143

him, and all would be well. That seemed to reassure him and he lay down again, slept far into the morning.

*

Over the next week, the days fell into a pattern, a routine. I made the soup three times a day, flavoured it with a little ginger. That was enough to sustain us. I mixed his foul medicine morning and night, and although he protested and made a fuss and grimaced when he drank it, he always swallowed it down.

Jukei could only visit twice in that week, and couldn't stay long. When she came she brought a few vegetables, a little rice and pickle to add to the rations.

Thank you for looking after him, she said, with great seriousness.

In the afternoons Bao would recite poetry to me, and I could see the old fire was still there. As he chanted the words of Li Po and Tu Fu and Basho, his eyes blazed.

For my part, I told him of my travels all over Japan, the teachers I had met, the rogues and madmen. He was particularly taken with my account of Fuji erupting.

And you sat there, meditating? he said.

I did.

He shook his head.

You have a gift for storytelling.

I vow to use it well.

I hope you have continued to write verse.

From time to time, I said, when the mood takes me.

You had the makings of a great poet, he said, and a great artist.

Perhaps, I said. But the most important thing is breaking through, penetrating the Zen Barrier.

And can poetry and painting help achieve that?

They can express it in some measure, I said, for others. Beyond that . . . I do not know.

I chose the way of poetry, he said. For better or worse.

Expedient means, I said. Whatever drives you.

Wise Crane, he said. You are well named! I hope many will receive your wisdom. And I hope you will not give up verse altogether. I still have the haiku you wrote when you were here, the one about Miss Fuji and her snowy skin. Now that's poetry!

I reached into my bag and brought out an old notebook I carried with me, full of my scribbles and sketches, drops of poison drool that dribbled out of me. I found the poem I was looking for, tore out the page and handed it to him, and he read it through.

> *Looking up – Mount Washizu,*
> *Vulture Peak.*
> *Looking down –*
> *fishing boats*
> *along the Shigehishi shore.*

Ah, he said, and he nodded. Yes.

Please keep it, I said. I have another copy on a painting of the mountain, the boats, the shoreline.

Thank you, he said, and he touched the page to his forehead. I shall keep this along with Miss Fuji and your poem about the incense burning down.

I am honoured, I said.

So you should be.

*

145

At night while Bao slept I still kept watch over him. I would doze and sleep for an hour or two, but the night hours were an opportunity for me to meditate intensely.

I had sat unmoving, entering into great stillness, profound silence. Suddenly I was aware of an oval-shaped light, the size of a cat's head, appearing just in front of me. Then it expanded and surrounded me, and before I knew it I was rising up into the air, flying. I moved rapidly and somehow I could make out the countryside far below, the outline of Toba castle, in the distance the shoreline of Ise and the Kii peninsula.

I knew I had to put a stop to this and I let out a loud cry, and immediately I was back in the room, seated in zazen. Bao had sat up and was asking why I had shouted out.

I knew some demon had tested me, but I also knew it had used the power of my own mind. I would have to be on my guard.

*

Gradually Bao regained his strength and was able to walk around the temple grounds. When Jukei saw this she was overjoyed, thanking me and praising Kannon for her compassion. But I could see a sadness in her eyes which I couldn't understand.

You see, she said to Bao. Now you are well, brother Ekaku has fulfilled his promise. He will leave us and be on his way.

Then I saw that Bao had understood, and his eyes too looked sad.

The next morning I gave Bao a little drawing I had made of Kannon, smiling benignly, above a verse I had inscribed.

Her expedient wisdom
extends in all directions.

146

There is nowhere
that Kannon is not.

Bao and Jukei walked with me to the gate and said goodbye,
and I saw both of them had tears in their eyes.

SHOJU ROJIN

I had heard that the priest Shotetsu, renowned for his scholarship, was giving lectures at Eigan-ji temple in Takada and I set off walking. It was good to be back on the road, in my old robe, my straw *kasa*, my bag slung over my shoulder.

Shotatsu's theme was *The Eye of Men and Gods* and his lectures were spread over several days. There were two hundred monks crowded into the main hall and I sat attentive, back straight, ready to learn. But the priest was a disappointment. He droned on endlessly about matters that were abstract and theoretical, minute and tedious points of doctrine. I grew irritated and restless, felt I was wasting my time.

I wandered around the temple grounds and beyond, and found an ancient shrine that had been built by the local clan. The building was small and dilapidated, smelled of dust and mould. But the walls were solid and the roof was intact. It felt abandoned, as if no one ever came there, and that suited me perfectly. I cleared a space in the corner, resumed my meditation on *Mu*, my interrogation of nothingness.

For seven days and nights I sat there, only leaving when I remembered I had to eat or drink, piss or shit. When I did come out I looked around in amazement. I sat in the dining room, shovelling a handful of rice into my mouth. Or I looked at my fellow-monks as if in a dream. I even went back once or twice to the lecture hall, heard the priest still droning incomprehensibly. None of it had any meaning or substance. My own being was surrounded by a white haze, and what passed for the real world was transparent, shimmering, crystalline. This must be some kind of satori, an answer to the koan, the realisation of *Mu*. But I knew intrinsically it was not enough. There must be more and I had to push on. I went back to the shrine and sat.

I sat for three more days and nights, not moving. The breath came and went of itself. I was here, in this shrine, but I was moving beyond it all. Then, as light began to break on the tenth day, a temple-bell sounded, far off, the faintest echo. But as I listened, the sound grew and swelled as if it had clanged inside my head. It resonated, endless, as if the universe itself were a great bell, ringing, ringing.

This, I knew, was the great realisation, the great emptiness, wonderful, marvellous.

I let out a roar and I thought of Ganto, the great shout he let out at his death. I saw I had misunderstood the story, and I shouted his name.

Ganto! Ganto! You were right! You were *right!*

Two or three monks were walking nearby in the temple grounds. They came rushing towards me, thinking I was dying.

Ganto! I shouted again. He was right to cry out! His murder by those bandits was neither here nor there. He was letting it all go. He was stepping into *this*.

I thought they would see the light shining out from me, but they looked fearful for their own lives, as if I might attack them. I laughed and brushed past them, ran into the temple compound looking for Shotatsu, the expert on all things Zen. Surely he would understand the depth of my realisation.

He had just come out of the lecture hall after giving his final discourse. A few monks stood around, obsequious, waiting to ask him questions. I stood right in front of him.

Look, I said. See for yourself. I have crossed the barrier and stepped through.

He peered at me, uncertain and afraid.

Indeed, he said. I am glad your time here has been well spent.

I could see in his eyes he had no idea. He was unable to grasp the reality. He was useless, full to the brim with his own thoughts, and he had nothing to say to me.

*

I was scheduled to stay a few more days at Eigan-ji and I saw the place with fresh eyes. I returned several times to the little shrine and looked at it with great fondness. Here I had broken through into this vast emptiness. I took my place once more at morning zazen, the same but not the same.

We were divided into groups for study of points raised in the lectures. Shotatsu put me in charge of one group.

In the light of your great realisation, he said, and he smiled. But I knew in my heart my realisation was true. I imagined nobody had come close to this state in three hundred years. As if to test me, he assigned a new arrival to the group, a monk with a fearsome reputation. By all accounts the monk made everyone uncomfortable, had a habit of glaring at anyone who expressed an opinion, challenging them to back it up.

So you're dumping this worthless character on me? I said.

Nobody else can deal with him, said the priest. The only thing he'll respect is physical strength and brute force.

Fine, I said. Send him to me.

The monk came in and looked around him. He was over six feet tall, an impressive presence. We sat facing each other and he waited to hear what I had to say.

I'm Ekaku from Hara, I said, and I have a fearsome temper. If you cause trouble I'll throw you out, send you back where you came from.

I understand, he said. My name is Sokaku. I come from Shinano province.

He bowed and touched his forehead to the floor. When he straightened up I bowed in return.

I can see you have gained some insight, he said. The other monks are tiger-feed. The world will chew them up and spit them out. As for the priest, he's just licking drool from the lips of dead masters.

I laughed and invited him to join us. He went to the back of the room and began sweeping the floor.

During the discussions he stared straight ahead. Occasionally he would grunt or snort, throw back his head and laugh.

Tiger-feed, he said to me afterwards. Drool from the lips of the dead. You should keep your own counsel. Or learn from a true master.

Like you? I asked.

Like my teacher, he said. Shoju Rojin. If you like I can take you to meet him. Perhaps he will appreciate your realisation.

Sokaku was water in the desert, rainfall after a long drought. If Shoju Rojin could produce a disciple like this, he was worth meeting. We left before dawn next morning, quietly and without taking leave, set out on the road to Shoju's hermitage in Iiyama.

*

151

On the way Sokaku told me more about his teacher. He was in a line of descent from the great masters Gudo Toshoku and Shido Munan. He was their Dharma-heir and his teaching was rigorous. He accepted few students, and even fewer survived his methods.

But you have survived, I said.

I have been in his poisonous clutches for many years.

And you think I am ready?

Perhaps, he said. It's a refining fire. You'd be heated in his furnace and battered on his anvil. Do *you* think you're ready?

I am anxious to meet him.

Of course, said Sokaku, he may just bite your head off and send *you* back where you came from.

Are you trying to tell me something?

I am telling you the way is not easy. Remember Bodhidharma himself left home at the age of six and sat at the feet of his master for twenty years before he understood the teaching.

As we walked along I composed a poem, expressing the realisation I had experienced.

*

A bell rings in vast emptiness.
This very moment
there's nothing to be sought.
Nirvana is right here.

*

We arrived at the village towards evening, a scatter of houses at the foot of Iiyama Castle. The castle walls were silhouetted, stark and gloomy against the sky. I could smell wood smoke but the single street was empty, except for a miserable skinny dog that barked halfhearted, as we passed. We pressed on through the woods, along a rough track. The hermitage was no more than a few wooden buildings huddled together in a clearing. An old man was chopping wood. He was stooped and bent, and I took him for an elderly monk who'd been given this menial task. But he straightened up as we approached and Sokaku prostrated before him, touched his forehead to the ground. Then he stood up again, hands folded, head still bowed.

Sensei, he said to the master. This is the monk Ekaku from Hara who has travelled with me from Eigan-ji. He has attained some measure of enlightenment and is eager to learn from you.

The master wiped the sweat from his brow with the back of his hand. He was thin but had a wiriness, a sinewy strength. The lines across his forehead were deep furrows, above his eyebrows a deeper knot at the chakra, the third eye.

He turned his gaze on me, looked fully at me, and through me. I opened my mouth to speak but he raised a hand and stopped me, rendered me dumb. Then he grunted and walked away.

I'm glad I came all this way, I said to Sokaku.

You have a lot further still to travel.

Either he is arrogant, I said, or I am useless.

For all my bravado, I had been shaken. Just by raising one hand this old man had reduced me to silence, my mind numb and cold like iron.

Come, said Sokaku, and he led me to the kitchen where a sullen monk was cleaning up and reluctantly served us some rice gruel. A single ladleful into each of our bowls. Sokaku bowed and thanked him and I did the same, then we rinsed the bowls, drank the water.

There were only four other monks visiting the place, hoping for instruction. I found a corner in the dormitory, lay down to rest my bones for an hour or two. I dreamed I had descended into one of the burning hells where I was stretched out on a slab of red-hot metal and master Shoju raised an iron mallet, ready to pound me into nothing.

*

At first light we sat outside on the hard ground and the master sat before us.

Zen? He said, as if someone had asked a question. Don't talk to me about Zen!

He cleared his throat, spat in the dust, continued.

Zen has been in decline for centuries. By the Ming Dynasty it had withered away to almost nothing. Sure, there's some of its pure poison left here in Japan. But where to find it?

His eyes glazed and he looked beyond us, into the distance.

Looking for stars in the midday sky, he said, then he brought us into focus again, glared at us.

And you, he said, you stinking bunch of useless reprobates, you stubble-headed halfwits. You're deaf and blind and couldn't stumble over it in your dreams. You couldn't even imagine it. You wouldn't recognise it if it came up and bit you.

He waved a hand, dismissive.

Useless, he said. Inert and lumpen. Look at you all! Sacks of rice draped in black robes.

He closed his eyes and took in a long, deep breath, let it out again slowly. Then he told a story.

There is a great barrier which has to be crossed. Only if you cross it can you continue on the Way. And the barrier is manned by a row of ferocious guardians who are there to interrogate you and determine if you're fit to continue.

154

A man approaches the barrier and explains he is a wheel-wright.

Show us, they say. And he sits and makes a wheel. He shows it to the guardians and they examine it, turn it, let him pass.

Another man comes up to the barrier, says he is an artist.

Show us, they say. And the man takes brush and ink, paints a picture. They let him through.

Next comes a young girl who says she is a singer.

Sing for us, they say, and she does, a sweet folksong that melts their hard hearts, and they let her through.

Then comes a priest of the Pure Land sect. He folds his hands and chants the Nembutsu with great power. *Namu Amida Butsu.* They bow and let him through.

Another figure approaches the barrier, a man in a black robe. He tells the guardians he is a Zen monk and one of them asks him, What is Zen?

He stands there dazed and dumbstruck, unable to utter a single word. He sweats like ten pigs and his robe is drenched. He smells like a pile of dung and is just about as articulate.

The guardians observe his pitiful response and don't let him pass. They dismiss him as a fake, a charlatan, a rogue. They send him packing, let him wither away in the darkness, outside the barrier.

Shoju closed his eyes again, then opened them and glowered at us, spoke quietly but with an intensity that seared.

And you, he said. All of you. Is this to be your fate? In some unimaginable future. When you're dripping with realisation and have temples and followers of your own, perhaps you'll accept an invitation from a rich parishioner to go and eat at his home.

For a moment I remembered visiting the home of Yotsugi-san

155

when I wasn't much more than a boy. I saw Hana's face, smelled her perfume. My face burned.

I can see it, said Shoju, continuing. You're lolling back on thick cushions, eating and drinking your fill, accepting it all as your due. Then someone, innocently, asks about some obscure aspect of Zen, asks you to explain it to them. And of course, you can't. You're so lost in the mire of your own delusion you can't say a word. Your heart thuds, you break out in a fetid sweat. Like the monk in the story you have nothing to say and your misery casts a black shadow over the whole room.

He punched the palm of his hand with his fist, made us jump.

It's a disgrace! he shouted. The shame of it is unthinkable!

We bowed our heads.

If you want to avoid such a fate, he said, work hard. Concentrate. Otherwise you're dead men, bound for hell.

He grunted, indicated we should go. The session was over. But as I bowed and turned away he spoke to me directly.

You, he said. Wise Crane from Hara. Do you think you are an exception? Do you think you are above all this?

No, I said.

Well, you should, he said. Call yourself a monk? And he shook his fist in my face, let out a harsh bark of a laugh.

*

Sokaku used his influence to get me an interview with the master next morning. I felt I hadn't done myself justice, and I wanted to speak to him face to face.

Well? said the master, glaring at me as soon as I came into his room.

I bowed and handed him the poem I had written on my realisation. A bell rings in vast emptiness. He snatched it from me with his left hand and glanced at it, held it away from him at arm's length.

So this is what you've learned, he said. Then he raised his right hand. Now show me what you see.

I entered into the spirit of the exchange.

If I had anything to show you, I said, I'd vomit it up right this minute. I'd throw it up all over you.

And leave me to clean up the mess, he said.

I pretended to gag as if being sick.

What about Joshu's *Mu*? said the master, changing tack. What do you make of that?

There's nowhere to grasp it, I said. Nowhere at all.

He leaned across quickly and grabbed my nose.

I've got a pretty good grip of it, he said, and he twisted my nose so hard the pain brought tears to my eyes and I cried out. I sweated and shook and the master let go, roared with laughter.

Cave-dweller! he shouted in my face. Zen corpse!

My pride was shattered, my self-esteem ground in the dust.

Are you satisfied with yourself like this? he asked.

How else should I be? I said.

When Nansen was about to die, he said, a monk asked him where he would be in a hundred years. What reply did Nansen spew up?

I knew the story, had meditated on it.

A water buffalo at the foot of the hill.

And when the monk asked if he could join him, what further poison did he spit out?

He told him to eat grass.

So, said Shoju. Where did Nansen go when he died?

I stood up and covered my ears with my hands, stumbled towards the door.

The master shouted after me. Honourable monk!
I stopped and turned back.
Cave-dweller! he shouted. Zen corpse!

*

This was how it was, how it continued between us. He challenged me with koans, with lines from the scriptures, demanded I answer now, now, now! And whatever I said he dismissed as nonsense, brushed me aside.

You're down at the bottom of a deep pit, he said. I'm shouting down at you but you can't hear, and you can't drag yourself up out of the depths.

When I opened my mouth to say a word he shouted me down. Zen corpse! Cave-dweller!

I kept silent and he challenged me again, with a verse from the Blue Cliff Record.

North, South, East, West, we head for home. In the middle of the night, the same snowy peaks, row after row.

Now, he said, where's the Zen in these lines? What's the truth of it?

I opened my mouth to speak.

Say something, he said. Anything! Show me you understand!

I hesitated and he grabbed me by the throat, then he pushed me back and started punching me in the chest. I raised my hands to defend myself but I couldn't bring myself to hit back, strike the master. He had clearly become insane. I tried to back away and he caught me with one mighty blow to the head that knocked me to the floor and I rolled off the verandah to the ground below. I must have lain there unconscious for some time. When I opened my eyes I was drenched in sweat and the master was looking down at me, roaring with laughter.

158

Well? he said. I'm still shouting down at you. Have you started to wake up?

I scrambled back onto the verandah, kneeled down and prostrated myself before him. Something had broken in me. I saw he was right about my realisation.

Again he shouted. Cave-dwelling Zen corpse!

You're right, I said.

And what use is that?

*

The next day, late in the afternoon, the master sent me out with the other monks to beg from door to door. I was still dazed from the master's battering, the fall to the ground, the descent into oblivion. I had resumed my meditation on the koans, grappled once more with Joshu's *Mu* as I tramped the streets of the village, my wooden sandals sclaffing, caked in mud.

I was so lost in myself, in relentlessly questioning, that I lost all sense of where I was and what I was doing. I only realised I had stopped in front of a house and stood there, ox-like, unmoving, when I heard an old woman shouting at me from the open doorway.

Moron! she shouted. Imbecile! Are you deaf as well as stupid!

I stared at her, not understanding anything.

Aren't you listening? she shouted. I told you to go some-where else!

Then she picked up a bamboo broom, raised it above her head.

I told you, she shouted. Go!

And she brought the broom crashing down on my head, and for the second time in as many days I was knocked to the ground.

159

But it was as if she had dislodged some final obstacle, made everything clear.

I stood up and bowed to her.

She was right. I hadn't been listening. I had to go somewhere else. And yet it was right here. It was wonderful!

Idiot! she shouted, and she slammed the door.

Somewhere else. Right here.

This time the realisation was different. There was no strutting arrogance, no puffed-up sense of my own great spiritual attainment. This old woman had awakened me with her broom-handle Zen. Beyond all duality there was only this. Only this.

I threw back my head and laughed.

Nearing the temple gate I composed myself once more, put on a serious face. But the master saw through me. As I entered the compound he hurried straight towards me and stopped right in front of me.

So! he said. You got what you went begging for.

Nothing but hammer-blows, I said, from the goddess Kwan-Yin in human form.

Just what you deserved! he said, and he cuffed me lightly on the shoulder. Then he fixed me with his gaze, intense and piercing, and he nodded.

This time you have crossed the barrier, he said. You have stepped through.

And ridiculously, for someone who had just gone beyond, I felt tears welling up in my eyes.

This too, I said to the master. This too.

*

That night in a dream I saw again the old woman who had cracked the bamboo broom on my thick skull, and in the dream I bowed to her once more, and I thanked her for her blessings.

It is I who have to thank you, she said. And all at once her face was my mother's face, smiling at me. I was overcome with joy. And it was my mother's voice speaking to me.

Because of your efforts, she said, I will move to a higher realm beyond all suffering.

Her face was shining, radiant, and I woke up laughing, a faint scent of jasmine in the air.

*

For a time after that, Shoju directed me to meditation on the Five Ranks, the Apparent and the Real.

Read Tozan's verses on the subject, nothing else. Don't get bogged down in third-rate commentaries or you'll be dragged back down into that old Zen hole.

I had read the verses in passing, but I hadn't spent any time with them. They were a key text in Soto Zen, and Shoju was often scathing about monks from that school. Quietists, he'd call them, slumped in the torpor of their do-nothing Zen. But he made me copy out the verses, replacing the koans as the focus of my practice.

I sat with the words through long hours, day and night, tried to penetrate the heart of them. I memorised the verses, chanted them till they lost all linear meaning, became like mantras, or sutras, the words pointing always beyond the form.

The Apparent within the Real.
The Real within the Apparent.
I moved on.
Coming from within the Real.
Arrival at Mutual Integration.

161

I had battled with the first four verses, the way I had struggled with Joshu's *Mu*, with the same intensity. The master seemed satisfied with my effort, but when he asked me to explain what I had learned, I bumbled about the reciprocal penetration of the Apparent and the Real.

He laughed. Is that it? That's your understanding? No more than that? It may as well be some useless old piece of temple furniture, to be discarded and thrown out.

I said nothing.

Why are there five verses, he asked, and not just four?

I recited the title of the fifth verse.

Oneness realised.

And that's it?

Again I said nothing.

He looked at me kindly, with none of the old ferocity.

You can't expect to understand it all at once.

*

A few days later I was walking along behind the master, and we followed a path along the edge of a steep cliff. Without warning he stopped and grabbed me by the shoulders as if to push me over.

The Buddha's Flower-Sermon, he said. What is that about?

By holding up a flower, I said, he sought to transmit the teachings.

The treasure of the Dharma, said the master, the pure mind of Nirvana, the gate of emptiness. How could these be transmitted?

He held up a flower, I said. Mahakashapa saw and understood.

How could that be? said the master, shaking me.

I broke free of his grasp and hit him a sharp slap. He

162

stepped back and laughed and we carried on walking by the cliff-edge.

*

The master had long since stopped calling me Cave Dweller and Zen Corpse.

One evening he called me to his quarters and offered me tea, bitter green froth in a cracked bowl. He poured it without any ceremony, slurped tea from his own bowl, also cracked and unglazed, and he told me a story.

Near the master's hermitage at Narasawa there once lived a woodcutter who came on a little wolf cub lost in the mountains. He took the creature home with him and looked after it, feeding it and rearing it like a domestic pet. He grew very attached to the animal and it became devoted to him and would follow him everywhere like a dog.

One day he was cutting down a huge tree when it skewed out of control and fell in the wrong direction. It landed on the cub and crushed it to death. He buried its body and returned home distraught. That same night, from every direction, wolves descended on the woodsman's village. They gathered in packs, eyes burning, jaws slavering. They howled as they ran through the streets and they took their revenge on humankind, dragging away babies and young children and tearing them to pieces.

The village was under siege, families trapped inside their homes with the doors and windows bolted and barred. Nobody even dared to step outside. They waited and they prayed.

News of the terror reached Shoju, and he recalled the courage of his predecessors, facing fire and sword. He took strength from the tales and resolved to put his own meditation to the test.

At midnight he went to the cemetery where the greatest

numbers of wolves were gathered, and he sat down on a grave, vowing to sit in zazen for seven nights. He sat as the wolves circled around him, black shapes, like creatures from hell. Gradually they closed in on him, sniffing the air, growling. Then the largest of them broke from the pack and ran straight towards him, picked up its stride and leapt over his head, landed behind him with a snarl. One of the others did the same, then another, and another, all charging towards him and only at the last moment breaking stride, leaping over him.

For all his mastery of Zen, he was terrified. He grew icy cold, in his guts, in his liver, in the marrow of his bones. His body shook and the breath choked in his throat. But through the fear he sat, unwavering in his purpose. The wolves nudged and butted and probed him. They sniffed at his head, at his throat. They nuzzled their snouts into his face, his groin.

He could smell them, their matted fur and rank breath, the stink of blood from the carcasses they'd torn apart with their fangs and claws.

But still he sat, back straight, hour after hour, night after night. Every breath might be his last. At any moment those great jaws might rip out his throat, tear the flesh from his bones and devour him. Knowing this, his concentration on every breath, every moment, was total.

By the seventh night he felt an immense inner strength, and with it a kind of joy. The biggest wolf approached him again, the leader of the pack. It glared right into his eyes then cuffed his chest with its massive paw. Shoju bowed to the creature then opened his throat in a howl of his own which became a great roar of laughter. When he opened his eyes he saw all the wolves slinking out of the cemetery. They left the village and never returned.

It was a good story. I would carry it with me when I left the place, a charm against darkness.

I had been at Shoju's hermitage for nine months that felt like a lifetime, or more. But the old restlessness was on me again and I felt it was time to leave. Shoju said nothing, but on the day of my departure he walked with me along the rough track through the woods as far as the village. We stopped, still saying nothing. The same mangy dog, or one very much like it, still slouched along the street, repeating its feeble bark.

A lifetime.

I had hoped you might stay, said Shoju at last. You could be my Dharma-heir and succeed me at the hermitage.

But you have Sokaku, I said. Surely he will be your heir.

He doesn't have the strength, he said. He hasn't learned how to conserve his vital energy.

That's something I too am still learning, I said.

But you will, he said. I can see it. And by the time you are my age you will be a very great teacher indeed.

I waited, half expecting a rebuke, a parting remark to wither me. But his expression was serious, a sadness in his eyes.

I bowed and I too felt deeply moved.

I would direct you to continue meditation on the Five Ranks, he said. The Apparent and the Real. You will find the verses invaluable for post-enlightenment practice.

I bowed again and he continued.

Concentrate on producing one or two good monks. More than that will be difficult. If you can produce two real successors, the old winds of Zen will blow once more throughout the land.

He held my hand in both of his and looked in my eyes for a long time, then he nodded and stepped back, motioned me to go.

I forced myself to walk away and he called after me.

Honourable Monk!

I turned and he raised his hand in benediction, farewell.
He turned away, and the dog barked, and I walked on.

FOUR

THE ZEN ROAD

The months I'd spent with Shoju had deepened my sense of purpose. I headed out, spent more than a year walking from one temple to another, covering hundreds of miles in all weathers. On the open road I was scorched by the sun and drenched by the rain. The wind battered me and the cold cut me to the bone. I listened to sermons and lectures, on the Diamond Sutra, on the True School, on the koans in the Blue Cliff Record. And for every glimmer of insight hidden in all these words, I endured endless disappointment. Shoju had railed against Do-nothing Zen and its practitioners. He said they would do anything for their enlightenment except work for it. Sacks of rice draped in black robes. Stinking stubble-headed halfwits. Now I met them by the hundred, hypocrites and reprobates, every one of them a waste of time, a waste of space.

Shoju had directed me to Tozan's verses on the Five Ranks, a Soto text to which these nothing-ists would pay lip service but stay slumped in their own inaction. I had kept my copy of the verses and carried them with me on my journey, and at each stage as I meditated on them I could hear old Shoju's voice cajoling, challenging.

Read Tozan's verses. Don't get dragged down into that old Zen hole.

*

169

In the middle of the night, in a ramshackle hut, I ignored the cold and meditated on *The Apparent within the Real*, the subject of the first verse.

> *Middle of the night, no moon.*
> *When we meet, no recognition.*
> *My heart still clings*
> *To days long gone.*

I sat, back straight, through the same watch of the night, immersed myself in the words. I saw scenes from my life as if enacted on a stage, like a moving *kamishibai* screen. My mother's face. The moon emerging from clouds. Hana smiling at me. Shoju laughing.

Is that it?

The world of things, evanescent, and beyond it, what? The middle of the night. The cold. This dilapidated hut. This.

*

At a remote temple, the priest asked me what I was reading and he dismissed it as an old broken vessel, told me not to waste my time. I gratefully accepted a bowl of rancid rice gruel from the kitchen then found a quiet spot in the temple grounds and resumed my meditation, concentrating on *The Real within the Apparent*, the second verse.

> *A sleepy-eyed old woman*
> *Sees a face in an ancient mirror.*
> *So muddled, she can't recognise*
> *Her own reflection.*

170

Unsettled, not knowing myself. Whose was that old face staring back at me, cackling? A withered old crone. Could this too be me?

This too.

The rice gruel churned in my stomach, and I racked and heaved and threw up the little I'd eaten, kept retching up nothing but acrid bile. I gathered myself and stumbled on, shivering as the sweat dried on my skin.

This too.

*

Walking, endlessly, one foot after the other. Drenched by the rain and chilled by the wind. The dirt path beneath my feet turning to mud. My old straw sandals falling apart, leaking. But concentrating with every step, the third verse, *Coming from within the Real.*

One step. Another.

> *Within this nothingness,*
> *A path leads away*
> *From the dust of the world.*
> *Naming is taboo, but walk on.*
> *Surpass the ancient one.*

Discomfort. Suppressing rage at the stupidity of existence. Naming is taboo. Ordinary folk had once been executed just for uttering the emperor's name, for speaking it or writing it down. Misery inflicted on misery in the name of power, and the power itself illusory. How to make sense? Keep walking. Go beyond. The dust of the world? Shake it off. Cross the barrier. Sit with the ancients. Transcend.

In pain I walked on, struggling, struggling.

171

Seated by a mountain stream as a whole day passed, concentrating on Tozan's fourth verse, *Arrival at Mutual Integration*. Rush of water. Stones in the bed of the clear stream.

> *The master swordsman*
> *Is a lotus blooming in fire.*
> *The spirit within him*
> *Soars to Heaven.*

Glint of steel. Blades clashing. Mind challenging mind. Cutting down ignorance. The sword and the swordsman as one. In the heart of the fire, the lotus, its petals of flame. Rising, rising, soaring free.

After long sitting, painfully getting to my feet, almost falling over as I stood up, aching in body, clear in mind.

The absolute singularity of every thing.

In a temple in Kyoto I'd seen a Chinese painting, maybe five hundred years old. *Tozan crossing the Stream*. Staff in hand, robe hitched up, wading across a river, intent and purposeful, his face calm.

Making my way back down, unsteady but sure, I composed a verse of my own.

> *Beneath the mountain*
> *the rushing stream flows*
> *without end.*
> *This is Zen mind.*
> *Satori is not far.*

I would write it down wherever I stopped for the night.

Before dawn I was back on the road, heading for the next temple. As I walked along I clearly saw old Shoju Rojin's face in the random shapes of the clouds, in the rough bark of a tree, in the pattern worn on an old clay wall, and I heard his voice in my head, unmistakable.

Is that it?

This was what he had asked me, questioning my understanding. He had guided me through the first four verses, the first four ranks, the stages of enlightenment. Then, as if it were an afterthought, he'd said, *Why are there five verses and not just four?*

I'd answered feebly with the title of the fifth verse, *Oneness Realised.* I set to meditating on it once more.

> *Who dares to equal him?*
> *All men want to leave the ordinary life.*
> *But after everything he comes back to sit*
> *Among the dust and ashes.*

It seemed to me that the distance between this level and the one before was so narrow, the gap so thin, that it should just be a matter of stepping through. Tozan crossing the stream.

I saw Shoju's face again, the way he had looked at me, compassionate, not judging.

You can't expect to understand it all at once.

*

Through the worst of winter I tramped the roads, the trails, the mountain paths, exhausting myself mentally and physically.

I grew thin from the walking and the lack of food. My feet were cut and blistered. My lungs were congested and at night I coughed and choked, unable to rest. But worse than all that, I grew sick at heart.

The great Zen teachers of old were like the dragons of legend – one drop of water and they achieved everlasting transformation, total liberation. Bodhisattvas of the past had gone beyond limitation by entering true emptiness.

What, then, was wrong with me? I had experienced these moments of awakening, of kensho. I knew discrimination. I had grasped the secrets.

And yet.

I was unable to integrate my realisation into my everyday life. I had to transcend attachment, even attachment to wisdom. Otherwise I was like a doctor who knew all the theory of medicine but was unable to cure an actual disease. If I couldn't help myself how could I help even one other sentient being?

I saw old Shoju's face again, heard the words of Tozan's final verse.

> *All men want to leave*
> *The ordinary life.*
> *But after everything he comes back to sit*
> *Among the dust and ashes.*

Jaw set, eyes wide open, I spurred myself forward.

*

One clear morning in early spring, as I approached yet another temple to hear yet another talk, I heard a voice I recognised calling my name.

Ekaku! Ekaku!

174

I turned and saw my Dharma-brother Sokaku, from Shoju's hermitage.

Sokaku! I said. You see, even our names rhyme.

We sound like a pair of old crows, he said, cawing at each other.

Kaku! I laughed. It's good to see you.

No more the Zen corpse, he said.

After all my wanderings, I said, I'm a corpse-that-walks.

Now that you mention it, he said, there's not much flesh on those bones.

And you've been pounded away to nothing by old Shoju's hammer-blows!

He drew himself up to his full height. He was still an impressive figure, but I could see that the years of study with Shoju had tired him out.

The master often asks for news of you, he said.

I will always be grateful to him, I said. He pushed and cajoled me through the barrier.

And what then? Sokaku asked.

Endless journeying, I said, in wind and rain.

We left a silence between us, comfortable. Then I asked if he might do me a great favour.

Ask, he said.

I drew in a deep breath.

The master instructed me in the Five Ranks of Tozan.

Sokaku smiled, said simply, Yes.

I am sure he imparted the same teaching to you.

Again Sokaku smiled, said, Indeed.

I had difficulty with Tozan's final verse, I said. And the master asked me why there were five verses and not just four.

And he said you can't expect to understand it all at once. Yes!

Sokaku laughed, said, This was the master's koan.

I waited a moment, continued. And he taught you, he guided you through all five ranks. He transmitted the teaching directly to you.

Again he drew himself up, stood tall, filled his lungs with air. Then he laughed again and bowed to me.

You can see right through me! he said. What do I have to hide?

I met his gaze, stared into his eyes.

You can transmit the teaching to me, I said, just as you received it, directly.

For a moment he looked uncertain.

It is not easy.

We were passing an inn, not far from the temple gates. I stopped.

Perhaps some sake would make it easier!

We stepped inside where a group of other monks had settled themselves. Mindful that there was no sake allowed in the temple grounds, they had stopped to fortify themselves for the session ahead. They raised their flasks and drank a toast, *Sakasaraba!* Farewell to sake!

This is their mantra, I said to Sokaku, and their pledge of renunciation.

Let me renounce sake, he said, but not yet!

I fetched a flask and filled a cup to the brim, placed it in front of Sokaku.

Liquid *prajna*, I said. Pure wisdom.

He raised the cup to his lips, but before he could take a sip I grabbed his wrist and held firm.

You can drink after you give me the secret of the Five Ranks.

No, he said. Let go of my hand.

I gripped even tighter.

If you drink all that sake, I said, you'll be in no fit state to teach me anything.

176

His brow furrowed, but he could see the truth in what I was saying. Reluctantly he set down his cup.

Very well, he said, and he straightened his back, composed himself, took in a long deep breath.

Let us begin.

The other monks were still being boisterous, but one of them had been listening to our exchange and saw what was happening. He hushed the others, told them to pay attention, but they continued laughing and knocking back their drinks.

Sokaku ignored them, began to speak.

You have to view it differently, he said. The Four Ranks, completely transformed, become Five.

I let out a shout, stopped him.

Not one word more! I see it! I understand.

And I did. Not the words themselves, but the wisdom embedded in them. Everything was clear, translucent. And for a moment I saw old Shoju's features on Sokaku's face.

Who dares to equal him? I quoted. *The current of ordinary life. He comes back to sit among the dust and ashes.*

Sokaku was about to continue, to remonstrate with me about my interruption, but something in my manner stopped him dead.

It's like looking at the palm of my own hand, I said, holding up my hand, flexing the fingers, laughing.

What happened? asked the monk at the other table, the one who had wanted to hear.

The rhinoceros of doubt just fell down dead, I said.

I don't get it, said the monk. I don't understand.

Don't worry, I said. You can get it from me.

I turned to Sokaku.

Now you can drink your sake!

*

177

Next morning I sat with Sokaku in the lecture hall, listening to a treatise on discrimination. Sokaku was hungover, his face grey.

That one sake became four, he said, then five.

Like the Five Ranks, I said. Four became five!

The lecture was a blur, he said. I slept through most of it.

You didn't miss much.

He groaned, then looked at me hard.

Yesterday your understanding seemed genuine and profound.

It was, I said. It was a moment of true kensho, a real awakening.

It's not to be taken lightly, he said.

I know that, I said. For all the joy I felt, it's a serious matter. Direct pointing at the ultimate. The interpenetration of the Apparent and the Real.

As I said the words I heard old Shoju challenge me again, asking *Is that it?* And this time I could answer, *Yes, that's it!*

I shook Sokaku's hand and thanked him, and he looked deeply moved.

The Gates of Dharma are manifold, I said. I vow to enter them all.

ZEN SICKNESS

The awakening had done nothing to improve my physical condition. In fact my illness grew steadily worse on the long trek back to Shoin-ji.

No physician could help me – none of their drugs and potions did the slightest good, in fact, if anything, they made me feel worse. And the monks and priests I asked were useless, spewing out banalities about letting nature take its course, or telling me to ignore the body and its suffering as so much illusion.

Some illusion!

I was in constant pain. My chest burned, my lungs felt dried out, scorched and seared, so at times I couldn't breathe. I was drenched in sweat, my head was on fire, but at the same time my feet and legs froze as if immersed in snow and ice. There was a roaring in my head, like the rushing of a mountain stream.

The slightest effort left me exhausted, burned out, drained. I shrank from daylight, but darkness and shade depressed me. Yet somehow that old dragon between my legs found the strength to spurt his fire in the night and lose even more energy, dissipate chi. I was saddened too to find the old temple, like me, beginning to run down, slide into dilapidation.

Late one afternoon I sat on the verandah outside my room, watching the light change towards evening but taking no joy

179

in it. Breathing was painful, sitting was painful, just being was painful.

I heard a voice near me, high and reedy, cracked.

So, you are suffering. What are you going to do about it?

I turned and saw a wizened old man, his face leathery and lined, grimy and weathered as if from many months on the road.

I was just passing through, he said, and I heard about your sickness. Again I ask, what are you going to do?

Nobody can help me, I said. The problem is my own.

The old man spat.

Such arrogance, he said. You may indeed be beyond help. But then again, perhaps you have been seeking advice from fools who know nothing.

Are you saying you can help?

He laughed. I cannot cure you, if that is what you are asking. But I can direct you to someone older and wiser who may be able to guide you, if you seek him out.

I was shaken with a spasm of coughing, spat up a gob of bright red blood.

Who is this man? I asked when I had recovered. And where can I find him?

His name is Master Hakuyu. He lives in the mountains of Shirakawa, in Kyoto. He is almost four hundred years old.

I was shaken with coughing again, spat another bright red flower in the dust. When I wiped my eyes with my sleeve and turned to speak to my visitor, he was gone. I struggled painfully to my feet and shuffled to the gate, but he was nowhere.

*

That night was the worst yet. The pain and misery were almost beyond endurance. I didn't have the strength to sit

180

upright, but when I lay down I coughed and retched all the more. I choked on my own thick acrid spit. I sat up again. I burned and I froze. When I did drift for a moment into sleep, I was beset by monsters and demons, creatures of fire and ice, preparing to devour me. I was losing the will to go on. Then in the midst of it all, towards dawn, I saw the old man's face again, and he was telling me without words that I knew what I had to do.

*

The journey was hell and it almost killed me. Aching in every bone, every nerve, every sinew, I dragged my sagging carcass for mile after mile, by sheer force of will made it to Kyoto. Then I headed north past the hills at Kurodani and on to the village of Shirakawa where I stopped for the night at a little ryokan. In the tiny room I dropped my pack in the corner and collapsed on the floor, lay there wrapped in a single rough blanket, sweating and shivering the whole long night.

At dawn I managed to sit up and chant the Daimoku, felt a great heat spread out from my navel and through my chest. I had a strong sense I should get out on the road early, and it was as if some unseen hand was helping me to my feet, shouldering my pack and pushing me out the door.

The old landlord and his wife were alarmed. They were lighting a fire in the kitchen, wanted me to stay and eat something, perhaps reconsider my plan altogether until I was well. But although I had eaten little I had no appetite for food. Not even the smell of the *tororojiru* she was preparing could tempt me. Usually just the sound of the mountain yams being ground to pulp with mortar and pestle had me drooling. But not today.

181

I must be sick indeed, I said, if I cannot eat this wonderful food.

The old woman nodded, appreciating the compliment, but still appeared concerned for my health.

Perhaps you are fasting? said the old man.

Yes, I said, grateful to him for offering the excuse. That is the truth of it. I am on a pilgrimage.

And what is your destination? he asked.

I am looking for the great Master Hakuyu.

Ah, said the old man.

Yes, said his wife.

You know him? I asked.

He never leaves his cave, said the man. But we hear stories from monks who go to visit him.

They say he has lived there for three hundred years, said the woman.

Some say longer, said her husband. Five hundred, a thousand.

And you believe this? I asked.

Who knows? said the old man. Anything is possible.

What else do the monks say?

Some say he is a man of great wisdom, said the old man. Others say he is a madman who talks nothing but gibberish.

Well then, I said, I will have to find out for myself. That's if I'm capable of judging. Perhaps I'm the madman, for dragging myself all this way through wind and weather!

The old woman's concern showed once more in her eyes.

Perhaps later you will feel like eating, she said, and she spooned out some of the *tororojiru*, now cooling, into a bowl. The she drained off the broth, scooped a good portion of the noodles and yams into a bamboo bowl with a tight lid. Then she wrapped it in cloth and handed it to me, bowing deep.

I am touched by your kindness, I said, taking the wrapped

bowl and placing it carefully in my pack. This was my favourite dish as a child. My mother used to make it for me specially, and I have never lost my fondness for it. I am sure from the look and smell of it, this is as good as I've ever tasted.

She waved my words away, fussed with her apron, but her eyes twinkled.

I thanked them once more and walked as steadily as I could out to the edge of the village. I passed two monks, one young, one old, and asked if they knew the way to Hakuyu's cave. The young one said he'd heard stories of Hakuyu but that was all they were, just stories, and he doubted if Hakuyu even existed.

The older monk apologised for his young friend.

He's an idiot, he said. He knows nothing. Of course Hakuyu exists, but whether you'll find him is another matter. And if you do, who knows if he'll speak to you? And if he does, will his words make any sense?

I'll take a chance, I said.

He nodded and pointed up into the mountains.

You see that stream, he said, up above the treeline?

I could just make it out, a thin line.

That's the grandly named Shirakawa River, said the monk. His cave is up there.

Have you been there? I asked. Have you sought him out?

He shook his head.

Without going out of the door, he said, quoting Lao Tsu, you can know the Way of Heaven.

So, I said, doing-nothing is best?

The further you travel, he said, completing the quote, the less you know.

In that case, I said, I shall continue my travels till I un-know everything.

He laughed and bowed.

If we find your bones by the roadside next spring, is there anyone we should notify?

Notify heaven and earth, I said. Notify the four winds.

Good luck in your quest, he said, and we went our separate ways.

*

Useless, I said to myself as I walked on. Idle talk. A waste of time. Zen banter on the road to hell.

The wind whipped up from the north, cold and stinging, made my eyes water. The ground underfoot was rough and uneven, the narrow road became a path, the path a track up through the woods, the track fading to almost nothing.

I stopped, listened.

Up ahead I could hear running water and I made my way towards it, pushed through the tangle of branches that snagged and clawed at my old robe, and I came at last to the stream I had seen from down below, the Shirakawa River. I slumped down on a rock, my breathing shallow and quick, lungs burning, blood thudding in my head. I concentrated on slowing the breath, then I kneeled by the stream, cupped ice-cold water in my hands and drank. The shock of it revived me but made me shiver, even though my body was still on fire. Shaking, I sat back down on the rock, looked around and took my bearings.

Sound of the water. Wind in the trees.

The way ahead was on and up.

One foot. The other.

On.

Up.

I kept going, one foot, the other, every step hurting, struggling to draw breath. The stream disappeared, and now there

184

was not even the semblance of a path. I stopped, surrounded by trees and dense undergrowth, no way forward, nowhere to go. Well, said an irritating Zen voice in my head, you must go nowhere.

Again I listened, to nothing. Faint rustle of leaves in the forest. Harsh cry of a shrike. Then suddenly, in the silence beyond, came the unmistakable sound of an axe blade on wood, the sharp hack of it, thud and cut. It rang in my head like that temple-bell at Eigan-ji, the sound of nothing, and that nothing falling away. Somebody was there, a woodcutter chopping down a tree.

Thwack.

I made my way deeper into the woods, towards the sound.

Thwack.

The sound was closer, louder, then it suddenly stopped and for a moment I was lost, then I stumbled a few more steps and into a clearing where the woodsman stood, axe in hand, eyes glinting as he fixed me with his gaze.

Well? he said.

Whether it was the exhaustion, or the sickness, some fevered hallucination, I thought the man looked familiar. I felt I knew his face, the skin weathered, the eyes clear.

Well? he said again as I stared at him, trying to remember, to place him.

I am looking for Master Hakuyu, I said. I have lost my way.

It is an arduous climb, he said, especially for someone as sick as you.

I know, I said. I don't know what madness possessed me.

But you've come this far, he said. You may as well continue.

He beckoned me to the other side of the clearing, pointed further up the mountain.

Up there, he said. Do you see?

185

I shaded my eyes with my hand, peered up in the direction he was pointing. But all I could see were the bare mountain peaks, now clear, now hidden in cloud and mist.

I see nothing, I said.

He let out a long-suffering sigh of exasperation.

Look again, he said.

Again the swirl of mist and cloud, the mountains emerging.

There, he said, pointing once more. And just for a moment I saw a glimpse, a tiny patch of yellow.

Something catching the light, I said.

He nodded. That's the entrance to Hakuyu's cave. If you keep climbing, you'll get there while it's still light.

I knew in the mountains distances were deceptive. I knew it was further than it looked. I closed my eyes and breathed deep, folded my hands in *gassho*, offering gratitude. But when I opened my eyes again, to thank my guide, he was gone. I looked around the clearing, called out Hello? But there was no sign of him. He had taken his axe and disappeared.

And this too was familiar, reminded me of something else. And I suddenly remembered where I had seen the woodcutter before. He was the old man who had come to the temple and first told me about Hakuyu. He was the same man, I was sure of it, but different. Somehow, impossibly, he was younger, and that was why I hadn't recognised him. I shivered, sweat drying in the cold air. I shouldered my pack again, started climbing towards that flash of light, that glimmer of gold.

*

Underfoot it grew more treacherous. Scree and tree-roots and matted undergrowth gave way to mud or loose sliding soil over bare rock. I found myself caught up in twisted vines, my

186

straw sandals soaked through, and I constantly lost my footing. The air grew thin, the chill mist clung to my clothes and I had to negotiate patches of snow and ice. I burned and froze. Once more I was racked by coughing and spat up red, red, bright against the snow.

I had joked about my bones being found by the roadside. Notify the four winds. Up here I might never be found. Keen-eyed vultures would pick the bones clean. Wind and rain would bleach them and in time they'd dissolve into the earth.

I looked up, and a gust of wind swirled the mist, and I saw that glint of gold, so close now, just up ahead. One last effort, to haul and drag myself up over jagged rocks, and at last I stood, breath rasping, limbs shaking, my body one long ache, covered in grime and thick greasy sweat, in front of Hakuyu's cave. The patch of colour I'd seen was a simple bamboo blind, yellowed with age, and painted on it was the outline of a dragon, and the dragon's eye was a dot of gold. That was what had led me all this way.

I had to compose myself before entering the cave. I sat on a rock, looked across the incredible vista spreading out below. Mountains rose out of the mist and cloud, like islands in a vast sea. Down there was the everyday world with all its suffering and misery. Up here was another realm entirely, beyond it all, pure and clear, silent, inhabiting its own light.

Perhaps I had in fact died and ascended to the Pure Land, abandoned my body somewhere down there on the rough slopes. But no. I moved my fingers in front of my face. I was still here, in this flesh and bone.

Here.

I straightened my back and breathed in and out, counted a hundred breaths. Then I did my best to wipe the dust and grime from my robes, from my skin. I approached the cave. I stopped and bowed low. Then tentative, apprehensive, I pushed aside the blind and peered inside.

*

My eyes adjusted to the dimness, and I saw the cave was small, just a few feet square. It smelled musky, of old incense. There was a single low table on which three scrolls were laid out, and behind it sat the master himself, cross-legged on a rush mat. He sat, motionless, his back perfectly straight, his eyes closed in meditation. I knelt before him, my legs aching, and I waited, and observed him more closely. He wore a big baggy jacket of coarse cloth. His hair was long and thick, flecked here and there with white and grey. His face was serene and surprisingly youthful and healthy-looking, his complexion weathered red-brown and shiny like the skin of a Chinese date. The overall impression was one of great inner strength.

I glanced at the three scrolls, recognised them as the Doctrine of the Mean, the Diamond Sutra and the Tao te Ching. Confucius, Buddha, Lao Tsu. Three traditions brought together, in a tiny cave, high above a mountain stream, miles from any monastery or temple.

I looked up from the scrolls to the master's face and he opened his eyes, stared at me with a fierce intensity and at the same time an acceptance, a benign inquisitiveness. He was not at all surprised to see me there.

You have come a long way, he said, to see this old man.

Again I had the same sense of familiarity, of recognition. The master looked like the woodcutter who had directed me here, like the old man who had set me on my journey. Now he seemed even younger, but as I looked at him, his features

188

seemed to change and I saw something ancient in him, something timeless.

My vision suddenly blurred and I rubbed my eyes.

Forgive me, I said, I am tired.

The way is demanding, he said, and arduous. It is hardly surprising you have grown weary.

I bowed, felt ludicrously close to tears.

He sniffed the air and turned his gaze towards my backpack.

If you don't mind my asking, he said, is that *tororojiru* I can smell?

Yes, I said. The innkeeper's wife insisted I take it. Was that really just this morning? It seems a long time ago.

Some days are longer than others, he said, and he sniffed again.

Please, I said, would you like some?

His eyes twinkled.

It has been a favourite of mine since my childhood, he said. And that was definitely a very long time ago!

They say you are hundreds of years old.

Ah, well. They say a good deal more than their prayers.

Yes!

Now, *tororojiru*?

Of course, I said. And I took the bowl from my pack, unwrapped it and handed it to him, an offering.

Please.

Thank you, he said, and he took it from me, touching the bowl to his forehead. I noticed his fingernails were almost an inch long. He slurped up a mouthful of the food, ate it slowly and with great concentration.

It is delicious, he said. But I am indeed very very old, and I eat but little. He handed the bowl back to me. Please finish it.

The taste of the food made me realise I was hungry, and I wolfed it down.

189

I thought as much, said Hakuyu. You haven't eaten all day.

I drank from the mountain stream, I said.

Not enough. For the quest you need to keep your body strong.

He picked up an old unglazed earthenware jug, poured a little water into my bowl, a little more into a simple tea-bowl of his own.

Drink.

I sipped and felt immediately refreshed, as if I had quaffed some rare elixir, some magic potion from a fairytale.

Ice-cold, I said.

It's from the stream, he said. Meltwater from the snow.

I set down the bowl.

I have forgotten my manners, I said. I haven't even introduced myself. My name is Ekaku.

Yes, he said. And you are suffering from Zen sickness.

*

I told him of my symptoms, in detail, left nothing out. He sat for a time, not speaking, concentrating on me with the full intensity of that gaze.

You are a great seeker, he said, an important priest, and you come all the way up here to ask my advice?

I was led here, I said. I was directed.

I was about to ask him about the two men who resembled him, but he cut me short.

What can you learn from me? he asked. I'm an old man – a very old man. I live up here in the mountains with the wild deer and other creatures. I barely survive. I get by on nuts and berries and bitter mountain fruits. Most days I am half dead. What use am I to you?

I was suddenly cold and weary, felt once again close to tears. I begged him to help me.

190

He looked at me again with that intense concentration, then he reached across and grasped my hand, took my pulse at the wrist. His thin bony fingers were strong, those long nails were hard talons.

He checked the pulses at nine other points, along the main meridians, in my hands and feet, along the neck and spine, on the top of my head. At every point I felt a burning heat from his hands.

At length he looked at me with great seriousness and gravity.

I am sorry to have to tell you this, he said, but you are very sick indeed. I said it was Zen sickness, and this is the worst case I have ever seen. You have driven yourself far too hard in your meditation, and reduced yourself to this state. No amount of medical treatment will set you right, whether it be acupuncture, moxibustion or herbs and drugs. Even if these treatments were administered by the greatest physicians who ever lived, by P'ien Ch'iao or Ts'ang Kung or Hua T'o, there would be no hope of recovery. Even these great healers would only stand back with folded arms and look on.

I must have looked crestfallen at his words. I felt chilled and desolate, empty of all hope.

But there is a cure, he said. When you fall to the ground, when you hit rock bottom, it is from there that you have to raise yourself up. It was meditation that made you sick, it is meditation that will restore you to health. You have to master the art of *naikan* – introspective meditation. This is the only way.

Is this what you can teach me? I asked. I could hear the eagerness and desperation in my voice.

He smiled.

I know a little, he said. I learned a few techniques a long time ago. If you are serious I can pass them on to you.

I controlled the emotion I felt welling up.

I would be eternally grateful, I said, and I kneeled and touched my forehead to the floor.

You are determined, he said. That is good. With that spirit you will make progress. It is hard work, but the results can be remarkable. It can restore health and strength and guarantee long life.

I am ready, I said.

I don't doubt it. But I have to insist you keep the teaching secret. If you pass it on without due regard, you will suffer terribly. And I too will be greatly harmed.

You can trust me, I said.

I am sure of it, he said. That is why you are here.

I felt a lifting of the spirit, and almost immediately a great weariness, a difficulty in even sitting upright.

It is late, he said, and your journey has been long. What you need now is rest.

I began to protest but he silenced me just by raising his hand. He gave me an old threadbare blanket and indicated I should stretch out in the corner of the cave, said we would start the teaching at first light. I lay down, let go, aware of him sitting upright in the middle of the room, poised and silent and absolutely still, returning to the meditation I had interrupted with my arrival.

*

The master was still sitting when I woke, the first grey light of day creeping into the cave. He opened his eyes and was immediately, fully awake. He stood up and stretched, beckoned me to follow him outside, showed me a sheltered spot where I might piss and shit. I said I had eaten and drunk so little the day before I had no need.

So you're already empty, he said. That's good! And I suppose

192

that delicious *tororojiru* is still being digested in your gut. Like the Buddha's teachings.

He led me up above the cave to a cleft in the rock where a little spring trickled out. It must be the source of the stream, that disappeared underground before re-emerging further down. He cupped the running water in his hands, drank from it, then splashed his face, told me to do the same. Again I felt refreshed, awakened.

We sat down in front of the cave, breathed deep and looked out over that wonderful vista, that realm of mountain and cloud, and he began speaking, instructing me, in a slow measured voice.

He began by telling a story, making an analogy.

Sustaining life-energy means looking after your body. It is very much like ruling a country. A wise ruler concerns himself with the common people and their wellbeing. A foolish ruler thinks only of the wealthy upper classes and their pastimes and diversions. When a ruler becomes caught up in his own greed and self-interest, his ministers usurp power for themselves, the petty officials under them seek only to feather their own nests, and not one of them gives a moment's thought to the abject poverty and suffering of ordinary folk. The people go hungry and sick, their faces gaunt and pale. Famine and starvation are rife throughout the land, and the streets of the cities are strewn with rotting corpses. The wise and the good retreat from it all and hide themselves away. The people burn and rage, provincial lords rebel and the country's enemies mass along its borders, ready to attack. In time the whole country is overthrown and ceases to exist.

But a wise ruler pays attention to the common good. His ministers and officials work tirelessly, mindful of the hardships and struggles of ordinary people. The farmers produce an abundance of food, the wise and the good serve the ruler, the provincial lords show respect. There are no enemies at the gate, no sounds of battle in the air, and the country grows strong.

I gazed out over the cloudscape, imagined the unimaginable, this perfect, peaceful world.

It is very much the same, he continued, with the human body. A wise man who has attained wellbeing takes care of the vital energies down below. When the lower body is filled with this energy, there is no place for the seven misfortunes of anger and joy, pleasure and grief, love and hate and their cause, desire. There is nowhere for the four evils to enter, born of heat and cold, wind and water. There is no need for the bitterness of potions, the jab of the needle, the burn of moxa. The heart and mind are vigorous and healthy.

He took in a long slow breath held it a moment, let it flow out unobstructed.

On the other hand, he said, the foolish man allows the vital energies to rise up unchecked into his upper body where they damage his organs and his senses.

He was talking about me now, about this miserable state I was in. I bowed, listened attentively as he emphasised his next words.

This is why Chuang Tzu said an ordinary man breathes from his throat, a wise man breathes from his heels.

I would write the words down, in a notebook, like a poem or an aphorism.

> *An ordinary man breathes from his throat.*
> *A wise man breathes from his heels.*

As if understanding my thoughts, the way I was receiving the teaching, Hakuyo uttered further aphorisms, left space around them so I could let them resonate, commit them to memory.

Energy in the lower organs, the breath is long.
Energy in the higher organs, the breath is short.

That was from Hsu Chun. Then came a distillation from Shang Yang.

The upper body cool, the lower body warm.
This is the art of sustaining life.

He left another silence, allowing me to absorb the words, then he explained it in terms of two hexagrams from the I Ching.

The state of sickness and decay, when the vital energies are weak, is represented by the hexagram that shows five yin lines below and one yang line above. This is known as Splitting Apart. It is like the ninth month of the year when everything drains of colour, and the leaves and flowers wither and die.

Once more he left a silence, let me imagine the scene.

The state of harmony, he continued, when the vital energies are in balance, is represented by the hexagram known as Earth and Heaven at Peace, three yang lines below and three yin lines above. In terms of the seasons, this corresponds to the first month when the ten thousand things are filled with the vital energy of creation and burst into blossom.

I felt an expansion in my chest as I breathed.

The ten thousand things are filled
With the vital energy of creation
And burst into blossom.

And you, he said, turning his gaze on me, Ekaku, Wise Crane, this is what you have to achieve in your meditation. Your illness arises from letting your heart-fire rush upward. This is against

195

the natural flow. The energy has to be directed downward, otherwise you will never regain your health and composure.

For a moment I was assailed by the thought that this might happen, that I would never recover my strength.

Hakuyu smiled, reading me.

Fear not, he said. You are a great sage, unborn as the heavens and the earth, as infinite as space. You just have to realise this truth.

I bowed with folded hands.

Now, he said, before we proceed, let us eat a little simple food, to sustain ourselves.

*

He brought two bowls of berries and nuts, and we ate in silence, then drank more cold water from the pure spring above the cave. Again I felt refreshed, had no need of more.

So, he said. Where were we?

Awakening, I said. Realising the truth.

Yes, he said, and is this not what you have been seeking? You probably think I am an old Taoist spouting a philosophy that has nothing to do with Buddhism. But what I am teaching you is pure Zen. One day you will realise this and smile.

I did smile, and he laughed.

You see, he said. You have realised it already. Now you have to realise that you realise it!

He straightened his back again, took in another long deep breath.

You are reduced to this state of illness by false contemplation, that is to say, contemplation that is diverse and diffused. The way to cure you, then, is through true contemplation, which is, in effect, noncontemplation.

Once more he was speaking in aphorisms, sutras.

196

True contemplation is noncontemplation.

He let the words resonate, settle.

In noncontemplation, he said, you are beyond all discrimination, beyond all conscious thought, in pure undefiled meditation. So, no foolish talk of giving up your study of Zen. The Buddha himself taught that we should cure all illness by drawing the heart-energy into the soles of the feet. Consider that.

I sat, absorbed in his words, and he gave me simple advice on meditation practice.

Go to a room where you won't be disturbed. Sit on a mat and keep your back straight. Close your eyes and contain the vital energy within your heart. When your breathing would not disturb a feather, count three hundred breaths. In time your ears will not hear and your eyes will not see. Heat and cold will no longer disturb you. The poisonous stings of scorpions and bees will cause you no harm. Eventually you will no longer breathe in or out. Your breath will flow from all the pores of your body, rise upward like mist, like clouds. All your ailments will vanish, and you will see with perfect clarity, like a blind man whose sight has been restored.

He opened his eyes wide, stared at me.

Once you reach the age of 360, you should have made some real progress towards becoming a true person!

He chuckled to himself.

What you have to do, Ekaku, is cut down on words. Devote yourself in silence to sustaining the primal energy.

To improve your sight, keep your eyes closed.
To improve your hearing, avoid sounds.
To sustain primal energy, remain silent.

So, he said. Now.

And the rest of his teaching he transmitted in silence, directly through meditation.

*

I wanted to thank him but I had no words. I bowed. He nodded.

When I was a young man, he said, I fell prey to the same illness as you, but I was in a much worse state. I suffered ten times as much as you. The doctors wrote me off and said I wouldn't survive. I prayed to the deities of heaven and earth for their help, and, miraculously, they responded with their guidance and protection. Within a month of practising introspection, I was cured of my ailments, and since then, through all these years, I've never known a day's illness. I became carefree, like a crazy hermit. I lost all sense of time, never knowing what day it was, or even what year. I had no interest in worldly pursuits or desires. I left Kyoto and went to live in the mountains of Wakasa, wandering here and there. That was my life for thirty years. Now I look back and it has no more substance than the fleeting world dreamed by Lu-sheng. Do you know that story?

I had heard the tale, but wanted to hear it recounted by Hakuyu. I asked him to continue.

There was once a young man named Lu-sheng, he said, who set off towards the capital to make his way in the world and find fame and fortune. On his way to the city he stopped at an inn to eat and rest. While he waited for his food to be prepared, he stretched out and fell asleep. And he dreamed that he did indeed find success and was rewarded with promotions to higher and higher ranks, till eventually he was appointed Prime Minister with jurisdiction over the whole land. He awoke from the dream with the smell of

198

food in his nostrils. Perhaps it was some of that delicious *tororojiru*! But he realised that he had just dreamed a whole life for himself, and he saw that actually living such a life would be as fleeting and empty and meaningless as his dream. So he returned home and pursued the life of contemplation.

For a moment Hakuyu was lost in his own contemplation, a faint smile at the corners of his mouth. Then, as if remembering I was there, he turned his gaze on me once more.

So, he said. Now I live here all alone in this isolated spot. I live from moment to moment. My needs are few. I have some scraps of worn clothing to wrap around my old bones. I have that one threadbare blanket you borrowed last night. But even in the depth of the coldest winter night, when the wind cuts through the thin layers of cotton and I should freeze to death, I do not. And even during the dark months when there are no fruits or berries to gather, and there's no grain for me to eat, and I should starve to death, I do not. And it is all due to this introspection, this contemplation.

His bright eyes burned.

Young sage, he said, I have just given you a secret that you will never use up in this lifetime. What more can I teach you?

Nothing? I said.

Nothing.

*

As I took my leave of Master Hakuyu I thanked him once more, and he said there was no need.

Practise the meditation, he said. That's all.

The time I had been here was short, fleeting – an evening, a night, a day – yet it felt as if it might have been a whole lifetime. As I picked my way slowly down over the rocks, I

199

could feel the chill of evening, see the light start to fade on the distant peaks, the clouds, the tops of trees far below. I stopped to gaze at it all and felt a huge emotion swell in my chest. Infinite vastness. No sound but the wind blowing.

I suddenly remembered losing my way on the ascent, hearing the woodcutter's axe, recognising in him the old man who had sent me on this quest, recognising both of them in Hakuyu himself.

Breaking the silence came the sound of wooden geta, quick choppy steps clip-clopping behind me. I turned and there was the Master, heading towards me over the stony ground, moving effortlessly as if strolling through some Zen garden. He waved when he saw me turn, and he quickened his pace. When he reached me he was perfectly relaxed, his breathing easy.

It's easy to lose your way on these mountain trails, he said. I'll lead you down to where it's easier.

I bowed in gratitude, and he strode off ahead of me down the ragged path, his clogs sclaffing, a thin stick for a staff in his right hand. Every so often he looked over his shoulder and laughed.

All right? he called out to me.

Never been better.

When we reached the stream, the Shirakawa River, he stopped and said if I followed it down I would easily reach the village before nightfall.

There was a silence, and for a moment I thought I saw a sadness in his eyes.

There was something I wanted to ask, I said, but I forgot.

Ah, he said. Questioning already!

I told him about the old man, and the woodcutter, and I asked him straight out if he himself was both of them.

He looked amused.

What do you think? he asked.

Yes, I said. I think you were.

Like some old Taoist shape-shifter?

Perhaps.

Who knows? he said. Maybe they were emanations I sent out to fetch you. But then again, are we not all one?

He laughed, and my vision blurred, and for an instant I was looking at the old man, then the woodcutter, then an ancient Chinese sage. Then it was once more Hakuyu's leathery face smiling at me.

I bowed low, hands folded in gratitude one last time.

He nodded and turned away with a wave, and I stood watching as he made his way, light on his feet, back to his own realm above the clouds. When he finally disappeared from sight I picked up my pack and continued my descent to the world below.

MOUNT IWATAKI

My wandering continued, brought me back to Hofuku-ji where I paid my respects once more to Nanzen. He was happy to see me again, though I didn't have many new poems to show him. He said he often spoke of me and still expected me to achieve great things.

An old priest named Sokai lived in the neighbourhood, another shiftless advocate of do-nothing Zen. From time to time he slithered into the temple and regaled the monks with a lecture or a sermon. One day I heard him tell the story of master Muso who once decided to spend the whole summer in solitary retreat, in a hut in the mountains, eating nothing but a single dried persimmon every day. With rigorous austerity, he would concentrate entirely on his meditation.

Muso had just arrived at his retreat, on Mount Kentoku, when he was approached by a young boy in monk's robes who offered to be his attendant for the whole time he was there. Muso explained he would be living on one dried persimmon a day and he could not feed the boy. The boy said, Just give me half a persimmon a day. That's all I ask.

The master thought the boy would soon tire of the regime. He would last a day or two then run off. So he agreed to let him stay.

The monks listening to the story chuckled in anticipation and settled down to hear the rest of the tale.

One month went by, said Sokai. Two months. The young monk never tired, he was never bothered by the lack of food. He swept and cleaned, he fetched water. If he wasn't working at his chores he was reading, or chanting the sutras. Muso was grateful and deeply impressed. On the last day of the retreat he summoned the young man to thank him and offer him a gift, the only thing he had, the surplice he was wearing round his shoulders. The young man bowed as if he had received a priceless gift from the gods. He raised the surplice three times with great devotion and draped it over his own shoulders. He said he would go on ahead to the village at the foot of the mountain and arrange for food to be prepared for the master. He touched his forehead to the ground, then sped off down the mountain path.

Muso was weak and frail after his months of austerity and privation, and his legs shook as he made his way, step by step, leaning on a stick, down the steep path. It was almost noon when he reached the village, and a man came out of the first house and bowed down in veneration. The young monk had told him to expect the master, and it would be a great honour to offer him food after his long months of effort.

Where is the monk? asked Muso as he stepped into the house.

He was here just a moment ago, said the man. Let me go and find him.

Just then one of the villagers came running up and said he had seen something miraculous. He had been passing a shrine across the road when a young monk came flying out through the screen doors, without opening them, then soared away into the distance and disappeared over the mountains. What he had seen was not humanly possible.

They all hurried over to the shrine, pushed open the door and peered inside. Muso saw a small statue of Jizo Bodhisattva, and draped round its shoulders was the damask surplice he had given the young monk. When he looked closer he saw that the face of the statue was the young monk's face. It was unmistakable. They were one and the same.

Word spread through the village, and beyond, and people started converging on the shrine. It became a place of pilgrimage, and the story was passed on, from generation to generation, that Jizo Bodhisattva himself had taken incarnation to help Master Muso.

When Sokai had finished his story there were appreciative noises from the monks, a spatter of applause. A few of the simpering idiots even had tears in their eyes at this wondrous tale of divine intervention. But the story had caught my imagination for a different reason altogether. What inspired me was the intensity of Muso's resolve and determination, his deep faith and devotion.

That was what I was after, and if Muso could achieve it, so could I.

*

I took my leave of Nanzen and set off alone with no particular destination in mind, determined only to find some remote spot where I might meditate in complete seclusion with total intensity, a spot where I might follow the injunction, to wither away with the mountain trees and grasses.

Initially I headed towards Mount Kokei, for no reason at all. I walked for miles across desolate moorland, bleak and barren, step after step, exhausted in body and mind. What demon had taken possession of me, driving me on like this, further into the wilderness? Then I saw in the distance a small wayside temple. Perhaps the monks would offer me some tea and a little rice to sustain me on my journey. As it happened, the head monk was Chin Shuso, someone I had met before on my travels, and we both laughed, delighted at the coincidence.

No such thing, he said. We were destined to meet again.

I told him of my quest, and he asked, Why Mount Kokei? I told him I had no idea.

It's certainly very beautiful, he said. But if it's not to your liking, or you can't find what you're looking for, don't hesitate to come back here. I know of a place not too far away that may be just right.

I thanked him and headed on my way, and as I left he called out after me.

Don't forget, what you're looking for may be right here.

*

I spent the next week wandering in the mountains of Kokei, and it was like some heavenly realm, some sanctified place described by the ancient sages and poets. The sheer beauty of the landscape made the heart soar, magnificent mountains rising out of lush forest, thick green foliage. In a setting like this it was impossible not to feel serenity and calm.

I had brought a little tub of cooked rice with me, and I ate a handful every day. I drank water from clear mountain streams. I walked for miles, searching for some sanctuary, some small hermitage where I might cut myself off from all distraction, spend months in solitude like Master Muso. But I found nothing. The travellers I passed on the remote paths were few, and nobody could help me. Heavy-hearted and disconsolate, I made my way back to the temple of my friend Chin.

I was sure you would return, he said. Your search was like looking for the stars in the midday sky.

An expression used by Shoju Rojin, I said.

In any case, he continued, perhaps Mount Kokei is just too beautiful, too perfect, and that in itself might have been a distraction.

Perhaps, I said. Now, you said you knew of somewhere that might be just right.

He nodded, eager, his eyes twinkling.

There's an old layman by the name of Tokugen. He's a devotee of the Pure Land. He's well-to-do and he's a good friend to the temple, a real benefactor who is always happy to help us out.

Such people are jewels, I said.

He has actually built a little hermitage that is lying empty. I took the liberty of telling him about you and your quest.

And he didn't drive you away with blows?

On the contrary, he is eager to meet you and would be honoured if you would take up residence. It's almost as if the place has been waiting for you.

Perhaps because of my exhaustion, for a moment I was quite overcome. I bowed deep, thanked my old friend.

It's a few miles north of here, he said, on Mount Iwataki.

Iwataki, I said. I like the sound of it.

Iwataki.

*

We set out early next morning and made good time on the road.

Distances are always less when you're in good company, I said.

Old Tokugen-san was waiting to meet us at the road's end, grinning and nodding and bowing to us with folded hands, eager as a young acolyte whose master has given him some task to perform.

206

This is true devotion, I said, and I saw him wipe his eyes with his sleeve.

When he'd recovered he offered us tea, then said the path up to the hermitage was steep and long, and he wouldn't be able to take me there himself.

My old legs, he explained.

But his son would show me the way. He was waiting and would leave as soon as I was ready.

I am ready now, I said. As ready as I'll ever be.

Chin had to return to his duties at the temple, so he and Tokugen-san said their farewells to me, and I set off following the young man along the path to Iwataki. He carried my few possessions slung over his shoulder, and a wooden five-bushel bucket of uncooked rice. This would be my sustenance, my equivalent of Muso's half-a-persimmon-a-day. I wondered for a moment if the young man might likewise be Jizo Bodhisattva in disguise, but it seemed unlikely. He was awkward and shy, and this made him almost sullen, as if he were showing me the way under sufferance. He made no conversation and I didn't torture him by asking him any questions. But my gratitude to him was genuine. When we reached the hermitage he set down the bucket of rice and immediately gathered firewood for later, and he took another bucket and fetched water from a stream.

I remembered a haiku I'd read, and I recited it to him.

> *Drawing water,*
> *Fetching wood –*
> *Miracles.*

He managed a smile at that, then he bowed and headed back down the path, leaving me alone.

*

Chin had called the place the perfect retreat. Quiet as *samadhi*, he'd said, far above the noise and dust of the everyday world. And he was right. All around was deep silence, only broken now and then by the whirr of a cricket, the ripple of notes that was a skylark's song, far off.

The hut was small, six-tatami, but it was clean and dry as if it had just been dusted and swept out. No doubt my young guide had been sent up the day before to get the place ready. Pinned to the wall was a single piece of calligraphy, my old friend *Mu*. The form had a certain harmony to it but lacked boldness, the lines shaky here and there as if drawn by an old man. I suspected it was the work of my benefactor Tokugen-san, and bowed to it in respect.

In one corner of the room was a rolled-up futon with a meditation cushion and a thin blanket that looked new. Beside it on a low table of rough unvarnished wood sat a jug and two unglazed bowls, a simple iron incense holder and a bundle of incense sticks. I lit one and the scent of pine filled the space. I sat on the cushion, made three deep bows, straightened my back and sat in zazen till the daylight began to fade.

A mist had descended when I went outside. I stared into it, watching the world disappear, then I went back inside, closed the door and bolted it shut, and sat once more on the cushion. I chanted the Daimoku a hundred times then entered again into the silence of meditation.

*

I had no idea how long I had been sitting. There was no way of knowing how much time had passed, and the darkness was deep. I opened my eyes and looked out, I closed my eyes and looked in, and there was no difference, other than the pressure of the air against my eyeballs. Then I heard what sounded

208

like slow, heavy footsteps outside, approaching the hut. They stopped outside the door, and my first thought was that my benefactor had sent his son with supplies. Perhaps he didn't want to disturb me and would simply leave whatever it was outside. But that made no sense. There was nothing I needed, and it was the middle of the night.

I listened, and the footsteps started again, moving round the outside of the hut, and every footfall thudded on the ground. It might be some traveller who had wandered off the track, lost. But what would anyone be doing halfway up the mountain in the pitch dark? It might be an animal, a deer or a mountain goat, but they would be light on their feet, they wouldn't make a noise like this, this, this.

I breathed deep and chanted the Daimoku, low.

Namu Myoho Renge Kyo.

The noise stopped. I paused in my chanting, and the footsteps started up again, louder and heavier, like stamping on the ground, and circling the hut, the rhythm getting quicker, like running, round and round, and I sensed a demonic presence, out there, round and round, circling, building up the energy of its hostile force, surrounding me, closing me in.

I seemed to hear a voice, rough and croaking like the call of a crow, and it spoke my name.

Ekaku. Ekaku.

I felt a deep coldness enter into me, spread from my hands and feet, up through my arms and legs, along my spine to my skull. I felt numb and immobile, encased in ice.

Then all at once, though still I could see nothing in the dark, I sensed that the being, whatever it was, was inside the hut and stood looming over me, filling the space.

I concentrated all my energy, chanted louder, faster.

Namu Myoho Renge Kyo.

I generated heat, radiating out from my navel, the lower

209

tanden, the cinnabar field. My temperature rose, and from freezing I began to burn. The heat filled the little room, made it an oven, and I thought I might actually, physically catch fire and burn the hut to ashes, perish in the conflagration and be dragged down to hell. The great hostile presence was still there, and although the darkness was still impenetrable, I seemed to discern a form, a huge figure taking shape. And just for an instant, perhaps in the light from my third eye, I saw it standing there, massive, eight or nine feet tall, its head almost touching the ceiling. Its face was contorted, its eyes bulging, a vicious beak where its nose should be. I had seen faces like this on masks depicting *yamabushi* hung outside mountain temples to ward off evil spirits.

In the moment I saw it, I named it, called out *Yamabushi!* Then I let out a great roar, and the darkness closed in again, and a great wind swirled round the room and the creature was gone. In the silence I could hear the thud-thud of a drum, and I realised it was my own heartbeat. I was drenched in my sweat, my old robes stuck to my back. I gulped in air and I slumped forward, lost consciousness completely.

*

When I woke at first light my body was one long ache. My arms and legs were stiff, my neck and shoulders clenched so tight I found it hard to straighten up and turn my head. When I managed at last, painfully, to untangle and stand up, I noticed that the door was still bolted from the inside. So either I'd dreamed the whole thing or the creature had indeed been from the other worlds.

Outside, the morning was clear, the mist lifting. I shivered and rubbed my hands together, walked round the hut stamping my feet to get the energy flowing again, the blood circulating in my veins. I realised I was retracing the creature's steps, felt a chill again as I remembered it croaking my name.

Ekaku. Ekaku.

I continued walking, seven times round. Then I stopped and bowed to the mountain, let out another roar.

Ha!

I scooped out a handful of rice from the bucket, cooked it up into a thin gruel and ate it slowly, sitting cross-legged, looking down over the treetops.

Welcome to Mount Iwataki.

I washed my bowl and left it upside-down to dry. I went back inside and sat on my cushion in the centre of the room. I straightened my spine and began my meditation once more.

*

The creature never came back after that first night. Perhaps it was a warrior-spirit, a guardian of the mountain come to test me. Whatever it was, it left me alone. If anything, the encounter strengthened my resolve, my determination to deepen my meditation. And, as if to encourage me, I remembered stories of the great masters and the trials they had faced.

*

Master Gudo, angered by some rebuke from his teacher, striding off into the mountains and seating himself on a rock, vowing to sit there as long as it took, see it through or perish. His clothes irritated him so he stripped naked and sat on, undeterred by the swarms of mosquitoes that gathered in clouds and covered every inch of his body. All night he sat through the pain as they fed on him, piercing his skin and

211

drinking his blood. Then suddenly body and mind fell away and he moved beyond it all into the great liberation. At dawn he opened his eyes and saw the thousands of insect bodies, bloated and red, covering him like a garment. Calmly he brushed them off and they lay on the ground all around him, a crimson carpet. Overcome with joy, he stamped his feet and waved his arms in a wild ecstatic dance, then he put on his clothes and made his way back down the mountain. The same teacher who had admonished him took one look and bowed to him, said without doubt he had attained the Buddha-Dharma.

*

Myocho Daishi practising austerities on the banks of the Kamo River in Kyoto. He would seat himself in zazen every night on a cushion of reeds, in the neighbourhood of Shijo Bridge, one of the worst areas for marauding gangs of hooligans. These young men would swagger through the district, testing out their swords on any hapless beggars or vagrants they came across, cutting them down without mercy. One night a group of them saw Myocho seated in meditation and they thought he would make an ideal target. The leader would strike him down with his long sword and the others would follow up with their short swords and hack him to pieces, leave his body for the crows and the jackals.

They surrounded the master who sat still and unmoving as if unaware of their presence. The leader stepped forward and raised his sword to strike the first blow. Still Myocho sat, back straight, intent on his meditation, unflinching. The leader stopped and looked long and hard at this silent figure seated before him. Then he sheathed his sword and folded his hands. He said if they killed this holy man it would be an unimaginable sin and they would be dragged down into Black Line Hell where they themselves would be endlessly butchered and cut into smaller and smaller pieces for all eternity. Hearing these words, the rest of the gang lowered their swords and fled into the night.

*

A poem Myocho wrote, later in his life.

> *Difficulties still attack me,*
> *One after another.*
> *They let me see*
> *If my mind has truly*
> *Cast off the world.*

*

This story of Myocho had inspired my own teacher, Shoju Rojin. I still felt a frisson of fear when I thought of old Shoju, the ferocity and ruthlessness of his teaching, the actual physical blows he struck me, trying to knock some Zen-sense into my thick head. But in a quieter moment, over a bowl of tea, he had told me his story about facing down the wolves that had terrorised his village.

*

When I thought of these great men and what they had faced, Master Gudo with his cloak of mosquitoes, Myocho Daishi confronting the swordsmen, Shoju Rojin and the wolves, it put my own small battle against the mountain-demon into some kind of perspective. But I also felt that these men had admitted me to their company and were guiding me. They stood behind me in solidarity – I could almost see them there, in the clearing beside my hermitage – and I was overcome with gratitude.

*

How long did I stay on Mount Iwataki? I knew it was weeks, then months, by the changing seasons, the turning of the year. But time had lost all meaning – now it was day, now it was night. By day I recited the sutras, at night I sat in meditation. Every morning I cooked up a handful of rice gruel and that was my food for the day. But not once did I feel pangs of hunger – I understood how Muso had survived, even flourished, on his half-persimmon a day. I felt a great energy and vigour coursing through me. In meditation I experienced countless awakenings, great and small, moments of satori that filled me with ecstasy. Time and again I roared with laughter, jumped up and danced around for sheer crazy joy. I laughed till I fell over, lay there clutching my belly till the fit subsided. Then I struggled to my feet only for another wave of laughter to shake me till I was once more helpless, in tears, rolling on the ground, laughing, laughing, laughing.

I emerged from one of these interludes and became aware of a figure standing a few yards away. I recognised him as my benefactor's son, the young man who had guided me up here those weeks and months ago. He had visited again in between times – once or twice I was aware the rice in the bucket had been replenished, though he had never made himself known. I assumed he had come and gone quietly when I was in zazen, or during the hour or two each night that I slept.

Seeing him now, I felt nothing but gratitude for this service he had done me, and I bowed and told him so, thanking him. But I was still buoyed up by the meditation, and the laughter kept bubbling up out of me.

Forgive me for disturbing you, he said.

Not at all, I said, the words absurd and clumsy in my mouth. I would have to rediscover the art of conversation, and that too seemed wonderfully funny.

Too many words, I said, not quite explaining.

I'm sorry, he said. I . . .

I composed myself.

It is you who must forgive me, I said. You have a message for me?

You have a visitor.

I looked round, expecting to see someone behind him on the path.

Not here, he said. At the foot of the hill. He is old. He could not make the final climb. His name is Shichibei-san.

The only Shichibei I knew was my father's servant. He had seemed old to me even when I was a child.

What is he doing here? I asked. So far from home?

He would not say.

All the way back down the hill I was trying to prepare myself, not just for meeting people and relearning speech, but for the old man's message. It could only be grave news to have brought him all this way. I remembered the messenger my father had sent to me at Bao's temple, to tell me my mother had died. The call of the *hototogisu* had undone me, made me cry like a child.

Now, most likely, it was my father's turn to go, and I would be expected to come down from my retreat and set things in order. But that was ludicrous. The best thing I could do for my father, and for all of humanity, was to stay in the mountains and continue my meditation. Set things in order! I laughed and

215

the young man ahead of me glanced back over his shoulder, alarmed. I realised how I must look to him, dishevelled, a wild-eyed madman, and I pulled myself together again. Pulled myself together! And I put on a serious face for the rest of the descent.

Old Shichibei stood up and bowed as I approached. He had indeed aged, but he had a wiry strength about him and his eyes crinkled as he greeted me.

The months on my own had stripped away the niceties, the need for excessive formality.

What news? I asked, straight out.

Your father sent me, said Shichibei.

My father? So he's not . . . ?

Your father is alive and well, he said. Although . . .

Why has he sent you?

Sometimes in his old age, said Shichibei, a man begins to worry about things he has done, and even more about things he has not done. He can be troubled by a sense of duties not honoured, responsibilities unfulfilled.

I had forgotten this in my time on the mountain, this circuitousness of discourse. I really had forgotten.

My old benefactor and host appeared behind Shichibei.

Tokugen-san, I said, bowing to him.

It is a joy to see you again, he said, and an honour. But please, forgive me. I have been remiss in my duty. Please, step inside and be seated, and I will bring some tea.

Now there were two of them fussing and bumbling around, and there would be the business with the bowls and the poetic smalltalk about the season, and it might be well past nightfall by the time the conversation meandered back to the point of Shichibei's visit.

I surrendered to the process, sat down and made a favourable remark about the bowls, admiring their shape, the way they felt in the hand, the rough unfinished quality of the glaze.

216

When we had sipped our tea and recited haiku and set the universe to rights, Tokugen-san called his son to clear the things away, and he bowed and took his leave.

There was silence for a few moments.

So, I said breaking it.

Yes, said Shichibei.

My father, I said.

Yes.

*

Shichibei had said my father was alive and well, but he had qualified it with that *Although* . . . Now he told me the whole story, the reason he was here, and at first it made no sense. He said my father had grown increasingly troubled. He looked haggard from lack of sleep and had taken to getting up in the middle of the night, wandering aimlessly from room to room, sometimes going outside where Shichibei had found him once or twice, staring in the direction of Fuji and muttering to himself.

It's all falling into ruin and decay, he would say. *It's disintegrating into nothing.* Then he would say *Ekaku is the only one who can make a difference, the only one who can save it.*

What is he talking about? I asked. The world? The universe? That's too big a job for me!

The temple, said Shichibei. He's talking about Shoin-ji.

Shoin-ji? I said. The place was run-down even when I was there. So I can well imagine the state it's in now.

With respect, said Shichibei, bowing, I don't think you can. It's utterly derelict. The walls have cracked and crumbled, and the roofs have caved in. There's nothing to keep out the rain, and even indoors you have to wear a hat or carry an umbrella. The straw matting on the floors has rotted away

217

and all the sacred books and scrolls have been damaged. *Soon,* said your father, *it will disappear completely. The earth will swallow it up and a field of wild barley will grow in its place.*

As he spoke my father's words old Shichibei's voice choked with emotion. I gave him a moment or two to recover before continuing.

But why is this bothering him? I asked. Why Shoin-ji? Why now?

He mentioned the family connection, said Shichibei. He said the temple had been restored by his uncle, Daizui-Rojin. Your father was taught by him there as a young man.

Yes, I said.

Again there was a silence. I thought Shichibei had something more he wanted to say but was struggling with it.

What else? I asked.

He hesitated then came out with it, almost apologetic.

He also mentioned your mother.

It was like a lamp being lit, throwing light into a dark corner.

Ah, I said. Yes.

*

Shichibei would stay the night. Tokugen treated him as an honoured guest. I said I would return to my hermitage and meditate till the way forward became clear.

But clarity eluded me as I sat through the hours of darkness. I had grown used to this life of freedom, the nights spent in contemplation, the days reciting the sutras. I felt strong in myself and at peace with the world, and there were those moments of unbridled ecstasy that shook me to the core.

Now this.

I saw my father's face, the way I remembered him from

218

my childhood, his anger at me, his impatience, dismissing me as useless. My mother telling him he had neglected his own devotions and was trying to stop me following the way.

My mother.

When he gets angry at you, she had said, *it is not a simple matter.*

My father's brush and inkstone. He had once been a young man, studying at Shoin-ji.

My father old and fearful, regretting what he had done and not done.

Falling into ruin and decay. Disintegrating into nothing.

He was close to death. He was afraid.

And yet.

I had made my own way here, through hardship and sickness. I had found this place where I could do my spiritual work, unhindered by the pressures of the world below with its madness and striving, its turmoil and trouble and endless demands.

A verse from the Analects came to me.

> *Do not enter a state that is in danger.*
> *Do not remain in a state that is falling apart.*

This was the advice Confucius himself was giving me.

But my father was my father, and by ignoring his wishes at the end of his life I would be plunging him deeper into suffering.

All night I grappled with these opposites.

In the deepest sense, the best thing I could do for my father would be to continue with my meditation. He would benefit from that, as would all of humanity.

But he was not all of humanity. He was this one particular old man, beset by fear and doubt. By this one act of surrender I could alleviate his suffering directly.

219

My father.

My connection to him was karmic. Without him I would not be here. Without him I would not be *here*.

And yet.

I battled anger and frustration. I chanted the Daimoku.

Namu Myoho Renge Kyo.

I saw my mother's face.

Namu Myoho Renge Kyo.

My mother. Her simple goodness. Her unshakable faith in the Lotus Sutra.

In a quiet place he collects his thoughts . . .

The verses came back to me.

Contemplating all Dharmas as having no existence, like empty space . . .

And yet.

Turn the Dharma wheel. Beat the Dharma drum . . .

The situation itself was a koan. Both extremes were right, but whatever I decided was wrong. Does a dog have the Buddha-nature?

Poison fangs and talons of the Dharma cave.

I entered into emptiness, concentrated once more on *Mu. Mu.*

I sat on, heart open, mind clear. Towards dawn I saw there was a middle way, a compromise.

I would go back to Shoin-ji and put up with the squalor and the poverty and the misery of existing there for as long as my father was still alive on this earth. When he passed away I would once more be free to follow my own path, to go where I pleased. I could return here to the hermitage or go where the four winds blew me.

I stepped out into the cold morning light and bowed to the four directions, gave thanks to Mount Iwataki for its hospitality to me. In the rice bucket there was one last handful of rice.

That too seemed like a sign. I would not ask my host to replenish the supply. I cooked it up into gruel as I did every morning and I supped it from my bowl, seated outside on the ground, looking out into the mist and clouds.

With my handful of belongings in a bag slung on my back, I headed down to take my leave of Tokugen-san and offer him my heartfelt gratitude, and thank his son, and Chin who had found this place for me, and I would tell Shichibei I would be returning with him to see my father.

Setting things in order.

As I left the mountain I sensed that yamabushi mountain-demon who had welcomed me on my first night was following me down. I even fancied I heard him call my name, *Ekaku* . . . *Ekaku* . . . and I felt he was sorry to see me go.

SHOIN-JI

My father had aged almost beyond recognition, shrivelled in on himself, his skin paper-thin. There was a hesitation, an uncertainty in his movements, a look of confusion in his eyes. But when he realised it was me coming in the door with old Shichibei, his back straightened and his eyes gleamed.

Iwajiro, he said, using my childhood name. My son.

Father, I said, bowing low, and I found there were tears in my own eyes.

Look at you, he said. You are skin and bone!

I survive on little, I said. But I am strong.

Yes, he said. I can see.

Shichibei had told me my brother had taken over the running of the inn, the way-station. He still lived in Numazu, but visited often, balanced the books, employed a manager to run the place and keep it in profit.

Yosaemon . . . said my father, then he stopped and seemed to have lost what he was going to say.

Your brother . . . he began again, concentrating.

Yes, I said. He is a good man, a good son.

Yes, said my father. But he doesn't care about Shoin-ji.

It's understandable, I said. He has other responsibilities.

The old place is disintegrating, he said. It is sinking into the ground and soon it will be no more.

It would be a great loss, I said.

It was founded by my uncle, Daizui Rojin. I studied there as a young man.

I know, I said. My mother told me this.

He looked confused, turned as if to speak to someone, then back at me remembering.

Yes, he said. Your mother.

I will go to Shoin-ji tomorrow, I said. I will do what I can.

His old eyes lit up, as if a great burden had been lifted from him.

*

I stayed the night in my old room, so small now, little more than an alcove, as small as my hut on Mount Iwataki. The futon had been rolled out and a stick of incense lit in the corner. Hung on the wall were a few of my early drawings and attempts at calligraphy, as well as the paper print I'd been given depicting Tenjin, the thunderbolt behind his head. Beside that was the scroll painting of the poet Saigyo, the one that had belonged to my mother, the one I had pierced with an arrow. I remembered the shame I had felt at that, my mother's kindness. I looked closely at the painting and saw it had been repaired. My father must have seen to that, and again I felt moved, more than I would have expected. Beside the scroll was a little statue that had also been my mother's, a wooden image of Kannon.

For a moment I was that child, the boy Iwajiro, and at the same time I was this man, in my thirties, the monk Ekaku, looking back at it all like something I had dreamed.

I sat straight-backed in zazen through the night. When I lay down briefly to take rest I caught for a moment the scent

223

of my mother, the cotton of her kimono infused with the fragrance of jasmine.

*

I knew there was no point in hesitation or delay. If this was my karma I had to embrace it.

My father was too frail to make even the short journey with me to Shoin-ji. Just as he had done all those years ago, he gave me a little money, coins in an old purse. If the temple was as run-down as they said, the money would not go far. But it was a start. Just as my younger self had done, I kneeled and pressed my forehead to the ground, thanking him.

No, he said, this time it is I who have to thank you.

Shichibei walked with me to the road-end.

This is a good thing you are doing, he said.

Good, bad, who knows? I said. It is the thing to do.

It is the right thing, he said. I know it.

He turned back and I was once more alone, on my way. When I'd left here the first time, no more than a child, Fuji had appeared, shining above the clouds. Today the mountain stayed resolutely hidden in mist.

*

It was worse than I had imagined. The gate hung by a single hinge and when I pushed it, it came away completely and crashed to the ground, raising dust. I stepped inside.

Entering the Gateless Gate.

I called out, Hello! Is anybody there? But there was no reply. A torn shoji-screen flapped in the wind.

I peered into what had been the meditation hall and it was unrecognisable. The shrine area had been cleared, gutted, sat empty. The only incense was the tang of cat-piss. The roof was almost gone, the straw mats on the floor damp and rotted black, spattered here and there with birdshit.

Disintegrating into nothing, my father had said. *Only Kaku can save it.*

I stood in the open courtyard not knowing where to begin.

A rat went skittering across in front of me, into one of the storerooms. I followed it in but it disappeared. This room too was empty, and the one next to it, and the monks' sleeping quarters. Then I went to what had been the library and was surprised to find the door intact and bolted shut.

There was a movement at the edge of my vision, something pale, and I turned, saw a skinny white cat slip out from a dark corner. We looked at each other, both surprised, and I bowed to the creature.

You are clearly the senior resident here, I said to the cat, far superior to brother rat who just ran off and ignored me.

The cat arched its back and watched me, sideways.

I assume you are the head priest, I said. I am the monk Ekaku, at your service. I am charged by my father with the task of restoring this place to its former glory and beyond.

The cat flicked its tail and gave a long mournful miaow.

I bowed again.

Namu Myoho Renge Kyo to you too!

But as I looked around I felt the chill of regret in my guts, an old familiar misery. I had given up my hermitage for this. But what my father had asked of me was impossible. It was another living koan to be faced down.

Mu.

The locked door of the library was intriguing. It was a challenge. Perhaps there were still books inside, artefacts the monks had left behind. I went in search of something I could use to break open the lock, and I found myself in the kitchen. At first glance it looked as derelict as the rest, but I noticed the old stove in the corner hadn't been damaged or dismantled, and a few pots and pans hung from hooks in the roof beam. I brushed against them and they clanked together like dull bells.

I felt a sensation like cold water between my shoulderblades and trickling down my spine, a sense that someone was behind me, watching. I turned and there was nobody, but the feeling persisted and I turned this way and that, expecting somebody to step out of the shadows.

Maybe it was the unhappy spirit of some dried-up old monk who had spent his days here, contemplating nothing, only to end up among the *gaki*, the hungry ghosts.

I thought of the mountain-demon, the *yamabushi* who had stamped round my hermitage and loomed over me in the dark. It might be that the temple too had its own protective demon come to welcome me.

I breathed deep, counted the breaths. In for one, hold for four, out for two.

Hanging from the rafter was a big wooden paddle for stirring rice. I lifted it down, weighed it in my hand, laid it out on the tabletop. I picked up a bamboo pole, put it down again. Then I saw an old iron ladle, and it felt just right, solid and heavy. I carried it back through to the library door, wedged it into the gap and tried to prise it open.

I heard a noise behind me, and before I could turn I was struck across the back. I dropped the ladle and staggered forward, lost my footing and fell to my knees. Another blow cracked the top of my head, but I managed to turn and look at my attacker, stared straight into his eyes, wild and glaring. I recognised him.

Kakuzaemon, I said.

The old cook, heavy rice paddle in his hands, peered at me, confused.

I thought you were Daikoku descending from the higher worlds, I said, ready to batter me with your mallet and knock some wisdom into me.

His mouth hung open and he gawped like a carp. He threw down the paddle and folded his hands, bowed.

Ekaku-san, he said. Sensei. Forgive me. He got down on his knees and touched his head to the floor.

Come on, I said. Get up. There's no harm done. And I'm glad there's still somebody here to look after the place.

They knew you were coming, he said, but not yet. Not for a few days.

They?

The abbot of Seiken-ji and other senior priests.

Of course, they have jurisdiction over this place.

They have a plan, said the old man, to install you as the resident priest here.

Ah.

They're going to hold a ceremony, make it official.

I laughed. They can call me Hunger-and-Cold, the Master of Poverty-Temple!

I indicated the library door with its lock. Now, I take it there's something in here that's worth protecting?

Very little, said Kakuzaemon, and he brought out a rusty old key from the folds of his threadbare robe.

We can work with very little, I said.

The door creaked and swung open and I stepped inside. The room smelled of damp and mould and rot.

Creditors had to be paid, said Kakuzaemon. The artefacts and furnishings were sold or pawned. A few were taken to Seiken-ji.

For safekeeping, I said.

He nodded, chuckled.

On a table in the centre of the room were a few books, wrapped in cloth and covered with a blanket. Among them was the Lotus Sutra. I picked it up, touched it to my forehead.

A good start, I said, feeling the weight of the book in my hand, smelling its mustiness.

There was a noise from outside, like somebody coming in at the ruined main gate.

More looters and pillagers? I said. Local hooligans? Or the abbot himself come to welcome me?

Most likely it's Teki. He's been out begging and foraging for food.

A young monk appeared in the doorway.

Teki-san, said Kakuzaemon. This is Ekaku-Sensei, come to restore the temple.

The monk was carrying a sack over his shoulder. He dropped it to the ground, bowed so his head was lower than his waist, then he straightened up, nodded towards the sack, lying there.

Rice, he explained. And yesterday I got some old *shoyu* that was going to be thrown out.

Ah, I said. So I have two gods of fortune come to greet me here – Daikoku with his mallet and Hotei with his sack.

Kakuzaemon said he would do what he could in the kitchen and Teki went to help him. I wandered around, looked in a few of the other rooms and everywhere was the same, the ceilings falling in, the screens torn, the floors rotting. Eventually I found an old broken palanquin that had been dragged indoors. I thought if I climbed inside it and wrapped myself in a blanket, it would offer at least a little shelter through the long hours of zazen and grappling with koans.

The white cat padded by, watched me with a kind of detached curiosity.

You see, I said to him. I have found my meditation seat and my shrine.

He yawned and headed off towards the kitchen.

After a while I followed him through. Old Kakuzaemon was peering into a heavy iron pot on top of the stove. Teki sat waiting, vacant. The cat feigned disinterest, disdain. It was like a little scene from a theatre performance, a drawing for a woodblock print. Interior with old cook, young monk and temple cat. All three of them looked up at me as I came in.

I could smell the rice, the rich earthiness of it, slightly burnt, catching the throat, and behind it something else, faintly rotten.

My nose must have twitched. Perhaps I made a slight grimace of distaste.

The *shoyu* was rancid, said Teki. That is why they were throwing it out.

I nodded, looked into the pot. The old man had cooked the rice first, then let it cool and added the *shoyu* mixed with water. It lay on the surface, a thin scummy discolouration flecked with white. The whiteness writhed and broke up.

Maggots, I said.

I was planning to scoop them out before we ate, said the old man.

Probably a good idea.

We eat what we can get, he said.

Indeed, I said. Nevertheless . . .

I chuckled and the old man looked relieved. He ladled the maggoty scum into a bowl, went outside to pour it onto the ground.

He didn't want to kill them, said Teki. He'll want them to hatch out.

I grunted, gruff and noncommittal, bowed to Kakuzaemon when he came back in. He dished out some of the food into three bowls, I offered up a prayer of gratitude and we ate, and I only found the one maggot, fished it out wriggling with my chopstick and set it to one side, bowed again and thanked the old man.

When we'd eaten I looked earnestly at both men, saw how worn and haggard they looked, thin and gaunt from this hard life, the struggle and lack of food.

I am grateful to you both, I said. I have no way of making things any easier. Our only assets here are the moonlight and the sound of the wind.

*

I climbed into the palanquin and they helped me get wedged in, seated upright, wrapped around with an old futon so I wouldn't fall over during the night. They said they would see me the next morning and they bowed and took their leave.

Somewhere in the small hours, the thin time between worlds, great Jizo Bodhisattva came to me in a dream or a vision. He sat in the full lotus and his form was vast, infinite, filling all of space to the further limits of the universe. I had a question to ask him, and he told me to ask it, and I managed to put it into words. How do I attain full realisation and manifest it in my everyday life?

The Bodhisattva replied, It is like sitting inside a dense thicket of razor-sharp thorns.

I woke with my veins like ice, the hairs still standing on the back of my neck.

*

Does the cat have a name? I asked young Teki.

230

He had returned from another afternoon of begging, brought more rice, a few limp vegetables, even a small piece of dried fish. Perhaps it was the smell of the fish that interested the cat and he tangled himself around Teki's legs, purring.

No, said Teki. We just call him Cat.

I laughed. That certainly keeps it simple!

Teki bent over and stroked the cat behind the ears. The purring grew louder.

We should call him Nansen, I said.

Nansen.

You know the story, I said, and the koan?

I have heard it, he said. But he looked wary, a little afraid.

I told the story again anyway, to remind him.

Two monks were quarrelling over a cat. They both claimed to own it. Nansen grabbed the cat and drew his sword. He said if either of them could say one good word the cat would be saved. They said nothing and he cut the cat in two.

Teki looked shocked. He picked up the cat purring at his feet and held it to him, protective.

Later, I said, Nansen mentioned the incident to Joshu, who took off his sandals, put them on his head and walked out of the room. Nansen laughed and said if Joshu had been there he would have saved the cat.

Teki was tense, stared at the floor.

It's a difficult story to understand, I said.

There was a silence, both of us listening to the purring of the cat.

May I be bold enough to make a suggestion? he said at last, and he bowed deep, uncertain.

Of course, I said.

He hesitated, then came out with it in a rush.

Perhaps we could call the cat Joshu.

231

I laughed so loudly, a sudden percussive bark, the cat squirmed free and ran away.

That's a very good idea, I said. Joshu it is.

He smiled and nodded, and I saw again how gaunt he was, and I felt a huge gratitude towards him for this life he had chosen.

These koans are not easy, I said. Have you heard of master Ta-hui?

He shook his head. No.

Ta-hui lived a long time ago, I said. Hundreds of years. But he knew the importance of the koan. He said quiet sitting on its own is lifeless and empty. It's mere escapism, hiding from reality.

Teki bowed, looked solemn, receiving my instruction.

He said the words life and death should be written on your forehead.

Teki touched his own forehead with his fingertips.

He said you should feel as if you owe a huge amount of money to someone and he is right outside, hammering on your door, demanding payment *NOW!*

He jumped, startled, and I told him more of what Ta-hui had taught.

Meditate with your head on fire, with urgency. But don't be in too much of a hurry.

It's like a musician tuning the strings of a koto or a samisen. Not too tight but not too slack.

Or it's like looking after a cow. (Or a cat, I added.) Don't neglect it, but don't fuss over it too much.

I left another silence, let some time pass.

Do you understand? I asked after a while.

Teki kneeled and bowed, pressing his head to the old worn tatami.

Ta-hui taught that we all have the Buddha-mind, I said. We just have to realise it.

The cat reappeared in the doorway, inquisitive.

Come in, I said. You're safe enough here. And I held up my hands to show they were empty. No sword.

*

The ceremony was concocted to coincide with a feast day that fell on the anniversary of the death of my first teacher Tanrei Soden. The connection was spurious – the old man had taught me for no time at all before sending me away. But he had shaved my head and given me the name Ekaku. So for that much I was grateful, and for the abbot at Seiken-ji it was as good an excuse as any.

The formalities were basic, minimal. The chanting of a sutra, the handing over of an embroidered robe which I wore over my old moth-eaten jacket, a few formulaic exchanges and vows, and I was installed as abbot of the wonderful ruin of Shoin-ji. I made my way back with the robe stuffed into my pack along with a little hand-bell, an iron incense-holder and a bundle of good quality pine incense sticks, each one good for two hours of zazen, and a precious tattered copy of the Blue Cliff Record restored to our library.

Word gradually spread that I had returned, and little by little there were offers of help. A carpenter from the village, or a passing monk from Seiken-ji, would pitch in with a few hours' work. A hole in the roof would be repaired, a blackened tatami mat replaced, a torn shoji screen papered over. The place was far from wind-and-water tight, and when it rained I still wore my straw hat and wooden sandals indoors. But I reclaimed a small room, set back from the main courtyard, and with the repairs it stayed comparatively dry. At night I still sat trussed up in the palanquin, grappling with the koans, their poison fangs and talons.

In another dream or vision my father came to me. He draped the embroidered robe over my shoulders, then he handed me a scroll with dense black calligraphy on it, a message I couldn't read.

When I climbed out of the palanquin at first light and straightened out my aching limbs, the old servant Shichibei was standing outside, waiting. Without one word being spoken, I knew my father had passed over.

*

Again I sat in meditation, saw my father's face, contorted in a grimace of pain, the corners of his mouth drawn down like a demon-mask. Then I felt my own face twist into the same expression, and the pain tore at my heart and I called out. The pain subsided and my features realigned, and I stared out with all the grim seriousness of the Bodhidharma confronting the void. I saw the calligraphy my father had given me in the dream, and it came into focus, the single character *shi*.

Death.

I found my father's old brush and inkstone that I'd made my own, took them from their wrapping of oiled cloth. I wet the stone, softened the tip of the brush with my teeth. I unrolled a single sheet of rough paper, weighed it down with stones at each corner to hold it in place. Then I wrote the character, filled the whole page with it, the lines thick and dense, and underneath I made an inscription in smaller letters, like a haiku.

> *DEATH*
> *a one-word*
> *koan*

When I'd come here to Shoin-ji I had resolved to endure it as long as my father was on earth. Now I was free to go my own way. I could go back to the hermitage at Mount Iwataki, I could make another pilgrimage, find another spot.

I unrolled a second piece of paper, held it down with stones.

Again I took up my father's brush.

Teki and Kakuzaemon stood watching, anxious. The cat passed by, not caring.

Mind empty, I wrote a tanka.

Good and bad, both
fade away to nothing.
Here now in this place
no need to go seeking
another mountain.

I held up the scroll and read out the poem. The young man laughed then stopped himself, bowed. The old man cackled, shook his head and wiped his eyes, shouted out.

Ha!

FIVE

HIDDEN-IN-WHITENESS

Basho had written that days and months were travellers on eternity's road, and travellers too were the passing years. How long had I been at Shoin-ji? Years passed by, wind-blown clouds.

My regime of long hours seated in zazen through the night, propped up, staring down the darkness and the vicious koans, had to be balanced by days of walking in the hills around Hara, great Fuji in the background, changeless, ever changing, always different, always the same. I would still walk miles to hear some discourse on the Dharma, listen to an illuminating talk, take part in a memorial ceremony or a recitation of the sutras.

Young Teki usually came with me on these trips, eager to help me, to beg for alms and forage for food. He also thought he might protect me from bandits and brigands.

What would they steal? I asked him. This old begging bowl? The dust from my feet? Or would they try to squeeze the enlightenment out of me and run away with it?

They might harm you, he said, so earnestly I felt my hard old heart soften, and I fell to thinking about Ganto, murdered by robbers in his own temple, letting out his great death-roar.

How to understand birth and death? I said to Teki. Everything changes, everything dies. At your final moment, what will *you* say?

239

He had no idea how to answer.

Very well, I said. There's a wonderful tanka poem by Daito.

> *When you see with the ear*
> *And hear with the eye*
> *There is no doubt —*
> *The way the rain drips*
> *From the eaves, just so.*

Meditate on this, I said, and we walked on in silence. Our way took us along a narrow trail, and I recalled old Shoju challenging my own realisation, battering away at my consciousness. He had grabbed me and shouted into my face, so close I smelled his rank breath, felt the spray of his spit.

Where did Nansen go when he died?

And now, right here, years later, striding along this narrow path, my own disciple trailing in my wake, I stepped into a deeper understanding of it. I saw with the ears and heard with the eyes, the way Shoju had done.

I stopped so abruptly young Teki stumbled into me and started to apologise. But I startled him by beating the ground with my staff and shouting out, ecstatic.

Where did Nansen go? Where indeed? Where do any of us go? We're all here!

Teki stared at me, dazed and uncomprehending as I roared with laughter, beat the ground again.

Here! I shouted. *Here!*

*

In spite of my obvious craziness, and the nonsense I spewed out by way of teaching, *because* of my craziness and the nonsense I spewed out, my reputation grew. Individually, and in groups of two or three, monks would make their way to Shoin-ji, or stop off on their way along the Tokaido, in the hope of sitting at my feet to receive instruction.

At first I was gracious and welcomed them all. It was good that the old place was beginning to live again. There was still much work to be done by way of repair; it was still dilapidated, and there was never enough food to go round. But the visiting monks understood all this. They came for the teaching, and nothing else. I repeated to them the name I had adopted on my arrival.

I am Hunger-and-Cold, I said. The Master of Poverty-Temple. Welcome.

I gave lectures to small groups. *Breaking Through Form*, and *Precious Lessons of the Zen School*. I instructed them in zazen and in koan practice. One or two showed a flair for calligraphy, and I gave them verses to copy out, tried to instil in them the sense of discipline and freedom, both essential.

Then one morning I emerged from my quarters after a long meditation, blinked my eyes in the dawn light, and blinked them again, not sure if what I was seeing was real or imagined.

I looked again and there they sat, twenty monks – I counted them – seated on the ground in two rows. I counted them again. Twenty monks.

Who are you? I asked, with a certain gruffness. Where have you come from?

We are monks from Rinzai temples throughout Japan, said one of them, seated in the middle of the front row. We met in Myoshin-ji where we heard tales of your teaching. We want to stay here and study with you.

He bowed where he sat and touched his forehead to the cold ground, kept it there, and the others did the same.

Twenty monks.

241

Impossible! I shouted, and they tensed and straightened their backs but kept their eyes downcast as I continued ranting.

Do you think this is a children's school and you can all just crowd into the classroom? You think I can just teach a mob all at once? Or should I throw the teaching at you by the handful and see where it sticks?

We are eager to learn from you, said the spokesman. We are willing to do whatever it takes.

Well then, I said. My first instruction to you is to listen to what I am telling you. And what I am telling you is that this is impossible. You cannot stay here and I will not teach you.

The spokesman motioned to the others to stand up, and he led them to the gate where they stopped and regrouped. He seemed to be discussing the matter with them, but he spoke in a low voice and they were too far away for me to hear.

Did I not make myself clear? I shouted. You should leave.

Once again they all bowed, but then they continued their conversation.

Apart from anything else, I said, there is no food for you here. If you stay you will starve.

We understand, said the spokesman, and he led them out through the gate and down into the village, a ragged pack, black-robed, straggling along the road.

Old Kakuzaemon stuck his head out of the kitchen.

Too many mouths to feed, he said. Just as well you sent them packing.

But later, towards evening, they returned, each of them carrying a small quantity of food – a few vegetables, a cupful of rice.

We begged from door to door, said the leader. There's enough here for all of us, including you and the few resident monks and helpers.

242

Locusts, said Kakuzaemon, reappearing from the kitchen. They've stripped the village bare, picked up every last grain of rice.

But he supervised the delivery of the supplies into his kitchen.

I said it would be inhospitable not to feed the visiting monks. They had come a long way, and now they had provided their own food. But that would be an end of it. They would leave after they had eaten. Once more they all bowed, heads bobbing.

The dining room was packed, and as usual we sat in silence, broken only by Kakuzaemon crashing around, dishing out the food, from time to time cursing under his breath.

I ate a meagre amount, even less than usual, not wishing to take what the monks had begged for themselves. But I thanked them and took my leave, wishing them a safe return to Kyoto, and I returned to my room, resumed my chanting and zazen, my study of the sutras.

Next morning the twenty monks were seated once more on the ground in front of my quarters. They sat in their two rows, backs straight, awaiting instruction. This time I ignored them completely, walked straight past without saying a word.

*

They stayed for three days and nights, eating only the food they had begged for themselves. I continued to ignore them, acted as if they did not exist. One or two of the younger ones looked as if they might keel over from sheer exhaustion.

Eventually, on the fourth day, I stopped in front of the leader.

Very well, I said. You have showed one-pointed determination, and at least that is a start. You are anxious to receive

243

this poisonous teaching I dish out, so come to the meeting hall and I will deliver a Dharma lecture.

They were overjoyed and piled into the hall. I gave a talk entitled *Swampland Flowers*, on the letters of Zen master Ta Hui.

Ta Hui's master had challenged him. *This Dharma is everywhere equal without high or low. So why is Yun Chu Mountain high and Pao Fang Mountain low?* Ta Hui answered, *This Dharma is everywhere equal, without high or low.*

His teaching was for everyone, I said, monk and layman alike, without high or low.

When I had finished my lecture, I bowed and left the hall, told Kakuzaemon to do what he could to give them one last mouthful of food before they left. He grumbled but managed to boil up some watery gruel, slop it into their bowls.

We are grateful for this, said the leader, as we are for the teaching.

One kind of slop followed by another, I said. Slurp it down before it gets cold.

He thanked me again, then the monks lined up one last time and bowed in unison before heading back on the road.

The next day the leader returned, alone.

The group can manage without me, he said. I need more of that Dharma-gruel.

His name was Gedatsu and I accepted him as my student.

*

As the months passed by, there was a steady trickle of pilgrims making their way to Shoin-ji, seeking the place out, looking for instruction. A few tough monks were willing to stay, ready to endure the poverty and the regime. Our numbers grew from two, to six, to thirteen. The sleeping quarters were barely big enough, and the latest arrivals bedded down where they could find space in Hara, in any old hovel – a run-down hut, an abandoned cottage – anywhere with the semblance of a roof and walls. The food they managed to beg supplemented the meagre rations and old Kakuzaemon continued to grumble as he doled it out, greens and gruel, gruel and greens, picking out the maggots from the rancid *shoyu*.

The monks endured. They sat in zazen, studied the scriptures, listened to my lectures, and one by one I battered them with koan practice. I led them through the winter retreat, drove them on.

*

Not for the first time I questioned what I was doing. What could I give these monks? What did I know? Could I really teach them, the way Shoju had taught me? Zen corpses. The cold deepened. They sat like stone.

By accepting them as disciples I was engaging with their karma, taking on their suffering as my own. Shoju had faced down wolves. Master Gudo had endured the bites of a thousand mosquitoes, draining his blood.

Alone in my quarters, I longed for Mount Iwataki and the solitude I had known there. Snow fell and the wind blew it in through a gap in the shoji screen. I made a poem but didn't write it down.

> *How cold it is –*
> *I can't even sweep*
> *the snow from the floor.*

I recalled another poem I had written, alone on a winter journey.

If only I could
make you hear it —
sound of the snow falling
late at night,
the old temple
deep in the forest.

I addressed the words to myself, and suddenly I revisited the satori, relived it, entered into the stillness and silence at the heart of it. The snow fell endlessly, into itself.

*

Emerging from an intensive *sesshin*, I gazed up at great Fuji, completely covered in snow, and above it the full moon, a shining pearl. All my life I had looked at this mountain towering above Hara, above the world of things. I had seen it erupt and burn, throw rock and smoke and fire into the air, and yet it remained, changed but unchanging. Now as I gazed up at it once more I felt an identification, I felt myself expand into its whiteness, felt it in the depths of my own heart.

I had painted this mountain a thousand times, in a thousand different aspects. I had inscribed the paintings with poems.

Miss Fuji,
Cast aside your hazy robe
And show me your snowy skin.

I laughed now when I remembered the poem, the audacity of it. How young I was when I wrote it! That old rascal Bao had encouraged me. The mountain hidden in mist, clearing to reveal its true form, pure whiteness. Like Dogen's poem, white heron in the snow, hidden but still itself. Still itself.

246

I understood with sudden and absolute clarity what I had to do.

I had been the child Iwajiro, and the monk Ekaku. Renewal was constant, and now another cycle was about to begin. I would take a new name, accepting the role of master. I would call myself Hakuin, Hidden-in-Whiteness.

When the old priest had shaved my head and named me Ekaku, I had chanted it out loud a hundred and eight times. Now I did the same with this new name I had chosen.

Hakuin. Hakuin.

Hidden-in-Whiteness.

Hakuin.

I inhabited the name, stepped into it.

Hakuin.

I bowed to the reality behind it all.

Hakuin.

*

I sat late one night, revisiting the Lotus Sutra, recalling my mother's love for it, her pure simple faith in its power. I remembered my own arrogant dismissal of it as teaching through parables, basic tales of cause and effect.

I had read it at Daisho-ji, and the head priest had said perhaps one day I might view it differently, read it with fresh eyes. Perhaps in another life, he said, it might speak to me more directly. Perhaps, I had said, not really believing it. Perhaps.

Turn the Dharma wheel.
Beat the Dharma drum.
Blow the Dharma conch.
Let fall the Dharma rain.

I saw my younger self, sitting as I sat now, the book open before me. My younger self, forehead wrinkled in concentration as the Chinese characters danced on the page and resolutely refused to give up their deeper meaning. Now here I was, reading the same words and finding them familiar, like old friends.

The Dharma falls on all alike, nourishing the smallest herbs and the largest trees. Each one receives what it needs.

My mother's voice, chanting, *Namu Myoho Renge Kyo*. The audience at the puppet show. Nisshin walking through fire.

Entering the fire at the end of the Kalpa and not being burned, that would not be difficult. But after my extinction, upholding the Sutra and preaching it to one single person, that would be difficult.

I sat, straight-backed, chanting the words, being energised by them.

> *Be vigorous and single-minded.*
> *Hold no doubts or regrets.*
> *Abide in patience and goodness.*

I saw myself sitting there, the same self, the same no-self I had always been. This self had been terrified awake as a child by the fear of hellfire and damnation. This self had heard his mother chant the Daimoku. This self had battled demons and sat unflinching as great Fuji erupted. He had learned from great masters who had hit him and cajoled him and cured him of his sickness and laughed in his face. He had sat in caves and walked on mountain trails, known hundreds of satoris, great and small. Kannon in the form of an old woman had cracked his skull with a broom. A temple-bell had rung in his head and reverberated through all time and space.

I saw myself sitting there, this place, this time, back where I had started. One time, one place.

I turned the page, read once more a verse I had once learned by heart.

> *In a quiet place*
> *he collects his thoughts*
> *dwelling peacefully*
> *unmoved and unmoving*
> *like Mount Sumeru*
> *contemplating all dharmas*
> *as having no existence*
> *like empty space . . .*

I breathed it all in, breathed it all out. In this moment, *in this moment*, I was limitless. That little self had died to itself and gone beyond, and still beyond, boundless in all directions.

A great light pierced deep into my heart, reflected out on all things as if from a bright and dazzling mirror. I looked at that brightness inside, saw through it into a clear pool, bottomless, without end. Brighter than the sun, this pure light shone on everything, mountains, rivers, the great earth, the vast sky, and I saw in all of it my own face, my own being.

At that moment a single cricket began creaking and chirruping outside in the temple grounds, and that simple sound shattered all barriers. Everything I had ever known fell away, a husk to be sloughed off in a great final realisation subsuming all others.

I understood the freedom Shoju had known, and I stepped into it.

I let out a great shout of joy and tears poured down my face, unrestrained.

I closed the book and placed it reverently back on the shelf. I sat a while longer, absorbing what had happened. I took my brush and with one stroke drew a cricket in the corner of the page, and beneath it I wrote a haiku.

> *Beyond it all*
> *I just sit here as if*
> *I just sit here.*

Beyond it all. As if. Here.

BEATING THE
DHARMA DRUM

One cold autumn day, grey rain falling steadily, a messenger brought the news that Shoju Rojin had died, or as he would have put it, left the body. At first I felt a kind of detachment. Is that so? He had decided to leave, to move on. Like the Chinese master with his precious tea-bowl, used every day although it might break at any time. The bowl was already broken. We were all of us already dead.

The message had been sent by Sokaku, still residing at Shoju's hermitage. The calligraphy was a little weak, uneven. He must have been shaken by Shoju's death, would have found it difficult to write about it.

Shoju had known it was his time to go, had sat cross-legged in zazen. Sokaku said he had sat a long time, as if unwilling or unable to compose his *jisei*, his death-verse. Finally he had dictated it, and Sokaku had written it down.

> *Facing death at last*
> *It is hard to utter*
> *The final word.*
> *So I'll say it*
> *Without saying it.*

251

Nothing more.
Nothing more.

Then he had hummed an old song to himself, looked round the room and laughed, and in an instant he was gone.

I read the message again, lingering on the poem. I set down the scroll, stood up and walked to the gate. The rain still fell, soaking me, and Fuji was completely obliterated in the mist, as if it were not there, as if it had never been. I walked a little further, composed a verse of my own, a haiku.

> *I can't see you*
> *But I know you're there –*
> *Fuji in the mist.*

I gathered the monks and held a simple memorial ceremony for Shoju, chanted a sutra, told a few stories about him knocking me senseless, breaking my head to let the light in. Then as I sat alone, remembering him and what he had taught me, I realised the enormity of it, the true vastness of his consciousness. And for a moment I was overwhelmed, wondering why I had never returned to visit him after those few months of intense training. I felt a sudden tightness in my chest as if my heart were being ripped out of me, and my tears flowed.

That night I saw him in a dream, his face so familiar, staring at me with unmitigated ferocity. Then he laughed and shouted, What now?

*

What now?

*

252

When I had stepped into that great realisation, the great enlightenment, beyond all thought, I had seen what the Lotus Sutra had been telling me all along, from the first time my mother chanted a single verse to me when I was a child, from the great doubt arising in me at the age of fifteen. It had always been there. In the beginning was the end.

The attainment of Buddha-mind was in turning the Wheel of the Four Great Vows, striving to put them into practice. Intensify and deepen your own experience, and at the same time, *at the same time*, work to help others still mired in illusion and ignorance.

*

Propagate the Dharma. Cause it to spread and grow.

*

I had been on earth more than forty years. But somehow I knew I was only halfway through this life. The road ahead of me was long. The work had barely begun.

*

Word had continued to spread about my poisonous teaching, and I received invitations to go and lecture about this or that aspect of the Dharma. I had to spend time replying in the most fulsome and effusive manner, expressing gratitude but turning them down.

What did they expect? I asked. They wanted a thorough-bred stallion, not a clumsy stumbling jackass. They wanted the song of a heavenly phoenix, and what they'd get would be the croaking of an old crow. They wanted a man of great learning and superior virtue, and I was a bumpkin struggling to maintain this little temple, impoverished and barely able to survive. More to the point, I added, what did I have to say about the subject matter, the particular sutra, the text in question? If I took the book and squeezed it, would it pour out its meaning? Would it ooze out drop by drop? The Vimalakirti Sutra and its wonderful teaching on nonduality? The Bodhidharma's *Breaking Through Form*? I searched my heart and mind and felt unable to utter one word that would contribute to the deeper understanding of these great works.

I sweated over the replies, I wept as I tortured myself in saying no. I begged forgiveness and expressed the hope, no, the certainty, that there were many scholar-priests who would be far better suited to the task of giving lectures. I remained, their most humble servant, the monk Hakuin, known as Hunger-and-Cold, the Master of Poverty-Temple.

Then something changed. I had given informal talks to the monks at Shoin-ji, like that mob of twenty who had turned up insisting on instruction. My outpourings on Ta Hui's *Swampland Flowers* had satisfied them and bamboozled them – a bone for them to gnaw. I saw the possibilities and gave a few more talks as the mood took me. Then two other monks asked if I would talk on a particular theme – *In Praise of the True School*. I agreed, and so it continued. I awakened to the power of the word, pure and simple.

I was not a professor of Zen, I lived and breathed it. I was Hakuin, Hidden-in-Whiteness, and from that place I could speak, and those who had ears would hear.

*

What now?

*

Turn the Dharma wheel. Beat the Dharma drum.

*

The monks planned another series of talks for me. As soon as I agreed, they began spreading the word far and wide. They were sure an audience of a hundred or two would come to Shoin-ji to hear what I had to say, and they started right away on making the place ready. For months they worked, long days of hard labour, often in shifts, and through the nights. They shored up walls, replaced sagging beams, patched shoji-screen windows and doors, made roofs watertight. The place rang to the rhythmic thud and drumtap of hammering, wood on wood, repetitive, mantric. They chanted over it, through it.

They reopened an old blocked-up well, sunk the shaft deeper and tapped into the water level. They laughed and cheered as they brought up the first bucket of well-water.

Their spirit was remarkable, indomitable, and in between shifts they still took it in turns to beg for food round the village, stocking up what they could in readiness for the visitors who would, they were sure, be coming to hear the talks.

The talks were scheduled for spring, and nearer the time I went to spend a few days at the home of Ishii Gentoku, the physician, to rest and prepare myself. The first time I had met the doctor, I recognised something in him, and he in me. Our paths had been destined to cross.

He said my resting was so powerful that my snores shook his house to their very foundations. He said I slept coiled like

255

some great overfed snake and my snoring stirred up clouds of dust.

I laughed. I felt invigorated, and a few days before the first talk Shoju Rojin appeared to me once more in a dream, shaking his fist at me then laughing in my face. I stepped out into the spring sunshine and composed another poem.

> *The spring wind blows east*
> *over India, China, Japan.*
> *Branches burst into flower.*
> *In all that riot of colour and form*
> *I see my old master's ugly face.*

*

Two of the younger monks, Jun and Ko, had come from Shoin-ji to check that my preparation was going well. They had been instrumental in setting up the talks and were anxious that they should be a success.

I was resting when they arrived, and Gentoku said they were alarmed to hear me, as he put it, snoring up a storm. When I woke they approached me, tentatively, humbly, respectfully, and suggested, tentatively, humbly, respectfully, that I should dictate some Dharma talks which they would write down and take back to Shoin-ji. The talks would be a great encouragement to the body of monks labouring day and night at the temple, making it ready. I thought for a moment, put on a grave face, then smiled and nodded, said I would do it. Then I lay down again to take more rest.

Jun and Ko came back later, approached me with great purpose, like children pestering their parents to keep some promise they had made.

256

Very well, I said, yawning and stretching. Let me see what rumbles up from my bowels.

Gentoku caught my eye and smiled, then he left the room and returned with brush and ink, scrolls of paper.

So now I have no excuse, I said. Let us begin.

I took a deep breath and launched into my discourse, and Ko wrote down every word. It poured out of me, five lines, ten, twenty; one sheet of paper, five, ten. We continued for hours, through the evening and on into the night. I spewed out the words, Ko transcribed and Jun corrected, made sense of it. Gentoku listened and plied us with tea and rice cakes, brought more paper and ink. By the early morning there were no less than fifty sheets covered in writing. I stopped and clapped my hands.

So, I said. I think that should be enough.

Gentoku announced grandly that up until now the three finest examples of Zen writing, for teaching the Dharma, were the works of Wan-an, Ta-hui and Fo-yen.

But I can truthfully declare, he said (declaring it), with the utmost sincerity, before heaven and earth, that none of these great teachers, without exception, ever created such an endless tangle of vines and branches as you have produced today.

I bowed, and we looked at each other and laughed.

*

Back at Shoin-ji I gathered all the monks together in the evening, and we sat in a circle drinking tea, and I thanked them all most humbly for the work they had done in restoring the fabric of the old place. As the light faded we lit the lamps. Ko and Jun brought out the sheets of paper, the pages of my Dharma talks, edited and neatly written out. Their pride in it was touching, and I nodded, gave them permission to read a few extracts out loud. The other monks fell silent, and two hours later they were still listening, rapt. When the session was over, a number of the monks thanked me, and Jun said he and Ko had discussed the matter and thought it essential that the talks be published. I told them it would be better to bring the manuscripts outside and light a fire with them in the courtyard.

They looked at each other, and Jun clutched the papers and ran from the room. Ko bowed and apologised and ran after him.

Next morning they asked if they could speak to me and I said they could have a few minutes. They sat in silence, awkward.

Well? I said.

Forgive us, said Jun.

What nonsense is this? I said.

The manuscript, said Ko. Your Dharma talks.

Ah, I said. You have taken ownership of them.

We have put them somewhere safe, said Jun.

You have found somewhere safe on this earth? That is a miracle.

I was not making it easy for them, nor did I intend to.

Jun took a deep breath, summoned up his courage.

The Dharma talks should be published, he said, in a rush. They would be of great benefit to all who study Zen.

You speak about them as if they are the Lotus Sutra, I said. Or the Blue Cliff Record. But they are just my foolish ramblings. Your pestering was an emetic and this was what I spewed up. I was half awake, incoherent. What did Layman Gentoku call them? An endless tangle of vines and branches?

With respect, said Ko, the monks who listened to these words last night were moved and inspired.

They were exhausted, I said. Months of hard labour had

reduced them to a state of simpering idiocy and robbed them of all discrimination.

Forgive me, said Jun, again steeling himself to speak. It felt . . . true.

There was something happening in the room, I said, with this particular group of monks. This time, this place. There was a willingness and a receptivity. The seeds had been planted and watered. Beyond that I am not yet willing to go.

I stood up, ending the meeting, and they bowed deep, foreheads to the floor. They looked disappointed, but not completely crushed.

*

The monks had been right about the numbers attending my public lectures. There were close to two hundred at each one, all of them listening attentively, and many queuing up afterwards to offer me their thanks.

When it was all over, Jun and Ko approached me again, this time accompanied by an older monk, Chu, and my physician-friend Layman Gentoku.

A delegation, I said. Why am I apprehensive?

We all wanted to pay our respects, said Chu, bowing. The lectures were magnificent.

I spit out my poison, I said. They lap it up.

You are spreading the Dharma, he said.

That is the work, I said simply.

Chu seemed to hesitate a moment, then ploughed ahead with what he had to say.

It would seem to be a good time to spread it even further. These young men were discussing with me the possibility of publishing your Dharma talks. They have the manuscript.

259

In a safe place, I said. Unless it has been eaten by moths. And if the moths have eaten my words, would it enlighten them? Does a moth have the Buddha-nature?

Nobody answered.

You know my master was Shoju Rojin, I said. And he was the dharma-heir of the great Shido Munan.

They all nodded, bowed.

There is a story I have often heard repeated. It has become a kind of parable. If it concerned anyone but Shoju, I would have taken it as no more than that, a tale to be told, a point to be made. But Shoju himself told me the story, and I know it to be true.

When Shoju was a young monk, Munan was impressed with his understanding of Zen. I am old, he said to Shoju, and I want you to succeed me and carry on my work. Shoju said he was grateful and honoured. Then Munan said he had something precious to give him, something that would help him immensely, and he held out an old book of Zen writings. It was no ordinary book. It had been handed down from generation to generation, from one great master to another.

It embodies their accumulated wisdom, he said. Each of them added something to it, and I too have added my notes and comments.

But Shoju was reluctant. If this book is so precious to you, he said, you should keep it. I have received your Zen without any writings, and I am more than satisfied with that.

I understand, said Munan. Nevertheless, this has been handed down for seven generations. It is a powerful symbol of the transmission. You should keep it as a reminder of what has gone before. Please accept it.

Shoju took the book from his master, weighed it in his hand. It was heavy, the binding worn, the pages musty.

It was winter and a fire was burning in an open brazier.

I have no need for possessions, said Shoju, and he shoved the book into the burning coals.

It was said that Munan had never showed anger in his life. But when he saw the book burst into flames, he shouted at Shoju in a rage.

What are you doing?

And Shoju shouted back at him.

What are you saying?

When I had finished telling the story, everyone remained silent.

A teacher's words are the dross of his teaching, I said. And writing them down reduces them even more.

Nevertheless, said Chu.

Ha! I said. Above the gate of hell is written *Nevertheless* . . . !

Nevertheless . . . said Chu, persisting.

Rascal! I said. There's a gob of phlegm in your throat. Spit it out.

I understand, he said, that if these talks are published there may be consequences which irk and vex you.

Indeed?

They may be read purely as works of literature, by scholars with no grasp of Zen. Their criticisms would be nitpicking, missing the point. This could be an irritant.

Flies buzzing round dogshit, I said.

At the other extreme, said Chu, there will be readers who do understand Zen and might feel challenged, even threatened by what they read.

How so?

When a great tree grows tall and towers over the forest, it is buffeted by high winds. And when a great man stands head and shoulders above everyone else, it may cause resentment and others may attack him.

Fools, I said. They are only making a hell for themselves.

And its name is jealousy, said Chu. And this is the second possible outcome that might displease you.

On the other hand, I said.

On the other hand, said Chu, which is another way of saying *Nevertheless*, there are disadvantages in *not* publishing.

Such as?

Now that the manuscript exists, the monks will want to read it. They will wheel and deal to get hold of it and make copies for themselves. This will take up valuable time and may lead to inaccuracies being compounded as copies-of-copies-of-copies are circulated.

I knew I should have burned it, I said.

I fear it's too late for that, said Chu. The copying has already begun.

So, I said. Publish and be criticised. Don't publish and it will be copied anyway. Damned if I do, damned if I don't.

Ta Hui once destroyed the printing blocks for the Blue Cliff Record, said Chu. We want to make printing blocks and publish your talks. There are many ways of spreading the Dharma.

This is a koan, I said. One I have to solve.

Chu bowed. The two young monks looked anxious. Gentoku smiled. I sat for a while in silence. Then I took in a deep breath, let out a great sigh.

Perhaps in the future, I said. If some scholar, some man of wisdom, were to look over the manuscript and correct it, I might reconsider.

Thank you, said Chu.

If I can help with the printing costs, said Gentoku, I would be honoured.

Your generosity is exceptional, I said. Let us wait and see.

Again he smiled, and bowed, and followed the three monks from the room.

*

The story took some time to unfold – many months – and much of it was hidden from me. Ko and Jun secretly made another copy of the manuscript, and Chu corrected it then set out on a trip to Mino with the pages rolled up and concealed in his robe.

In Mino he showed the script to the priest Joshitsu, exactly the kind of scholar I had mentioned. Chu asked the venerable Joshitsu if he would read the manuscript and make corrections, and he refused. Chu persisted, and again Joshitsu said no. A third time he asked, and the answer was the same. Finally, at the fourth time of asking, the priest said yes.

If I had known this was going on, I would have been mortified and would have put a stop to the whole sorry business. But I did not know, and the story continued.

Chu continued on his way, to Kyoto, and there, by chance – or as Chu would have it, by some kind of miracle – he happened to run into the bookseller Kinokuniya Tobei who lived in Numazu, near Shoin-ji, and had visited the temple to hear me speak. When Chu told him of his quest, Kinokuniya was excited and offered to help in any way he could. Before long he had found a publisher, the blocks had been carved and the book was being printed.

A message was brought back from Chu.

Burn incense. Press your hands in supplication and bow towards Kyoto. I will return home with this gift as if I had rescued a precious jewel from the jaws of the black dragon.

At first I did not know what he meant, then Ko and Jun explained it all, told me the whole story. They were exuberant, but I remained silent.

So it's done, I said. There's no way to stop this happening.

No, said Jun. But it's wonderful.

I nodded and motioned for them to go. Gentoku was with them, and he hung back and waited, then approached me.

So, I said. These Dharma talks I spewed out at your place will make men know me, and they will make men condemn me.

Indeed, he said, smiling. But I think perhaps you are secretly pleased that this book will carry your teaching far beyond Shoin-ji.

Perhaps, I said, and I laughed. Perhaps.

*

When I held the book in my hand I was overjoyed and deeply moved. The venerable Joshitsu had written a preface, an introduction, a few words commending the book to all who would seek to understand the Dharma. I pressed the book to my forehead then placed it on the shrine and folded my hands, chanted the Daimoku in gratitude to all who had made it possible to bring this into being.

DHARMA-THUGS

The damage had been done. With the publication of my Dharma Talks, my poison spread far and wide, as if carried on the wind. It polluted the rivers and streams, the very air, it entered minds and hearts everywhere. The numbers of monks and lay seekers beating a path to Shoin-ji to hear me speak grew into many hundreds, and the old place was overrun.

At times there were almost a thousand visitors, invading the surrounding area as far as Mishima and Numazu in search of a place to stay. They slept in barns and outhouses, abandoned temple buildings, roofless hovels. By day they crammed, uncomplaining, into the grounds at Shoin-ji just to hear me open my mouth and rant.

A handful of the resident monks worked tirelessly to make the place ready. For weeks on end they slaved and laboured, endured ten thousand hardships. They dug the rough ground and hauled away stones to clear an open area for the meetings. They sunk another well to draw water. They tended the vegetable garden with its crop of *daikon* and greens. They patched up the monks' quarters, the kitchen, the bathhouse. They extended the privy, dug more holes to receive more piss and shit.

They worked themselves to exhaustion, sweated bucketloads. Every day they would start at dawn, the dew soaking

265

into their robes, and they'd finish at night when the stars were out. Their backs ached, their hands were blistered and calloused, they could hardly stand. But the light in them burned bright, and every morning they were back out at dawn to start the work again.

Old Kakuzaemon in the kitchen complained endlessly. There wasn't even enough food for ourselves, so how could we deal with yet another flock of locusts passing through and stripping the place bare? There would be hundreds of them. How could he be expected to cope?

They'll bring their own food, I said, beg rice enough for their own needs.

And who is to cook it? he asked. This old fool, that's who. I'll be sweating in the kitchen from dawn till dusk.

I'll get some of the monks to help, I said.

Dolts, he said. Dullards. They'd only burn the rice and ruin every pot.

He was right, and could see I knew it.

My faith in you is absolute, I said. And let's see if someone can donate a bigger pot.

If you get me a big enough cauldron, he said, I'll throw *you* in there and reduce you to nothing, sweat you down to a stock.

Now that would *really* spread my poison, I said.

*

Miraculously, through hard work and grace and plain cussedness, when the crowds came, the old temple could cope. Somehow there was room for everyone, and just about enough rice to go round. For the most part, the visitors were earnest and disciplined, and grateful to be there, lapping up what I spewed out. They listened in concentrated silence. They made the best of the conditions. They queued patiently for their meagre rations, or to wash, or use the privy. They gave me hope for the future of the teachings.

But there were a few young monks, a handful only, who were clearly stopping here as a way-station on their road to hell, intent on wreaking one last round of havoc before they went. Their behaviour was demonic.

They formed themselves into a gang and swaggered about the temple grounds, trampling through the garden, shouting out to each other in loud voices.

They congregated outside the meditation hall, bantering and singing, making a racket.

They ignored admonitions from the senior monks, laughed in their faces and walked away.

They pushed over the temple-drum, lifted down the temple-bell and left it on the ground, upside down.

They swarmed over the hill behind the temple, clapping their hands and hollering, disturbing the peace.

At night they would sneak out the side gate and into the village, ending up in some teahouse or wineshop then go on the rampage looking for women.

They would roll back in the small hours, fall through a gap in the fence and wake everybody up, singing rude songs at the tops of their voices.

They were appalling in every way. But they too had come here seeking enlightenment. I waited. It got worse.

They took sharpened sticks and drove them into the ground in a dark corridor behind the monks' hall, where folk would walk into them.

In the same corridor they placed a huge water jar filled to the brim, so anyone passing through would knock it over.

I waited. They were sentient beings, of a sort. I had vowed to save them.

267

They upset Kakuzaemon by soaking the kitchen firewood so it wouldn't catch and filled the room with smoke.

Still I waited.

They split and weakened the wooden plank over the privy so it would give and crack if someone sat down. One old monk was tipped into the pit and covered in filth. He stood before me, dripping, stinking.

Enough. It was time to put a stop to this.

I let it be known I was to give a very special lecture and these young monks were invited to sit in reserved seats in the front row. I knew I was taking a chance. If they reacted badly to my rant they might disrupt the meeting entirely. They might give full rein to their purely demonic nature, run riot and burn the place to the ground. Well then, that would be karmic retribution visited on me for daring to give these talks on the Dharma.

I imagined myself heading off to the wilderness, regrouping with a few old cronies. We could gather up wood to light a fire, brew tea, talk. I could happily live like that, unburdened, carefree. Nevertheless . . .

Nevertheless, I had responsibilities to the hundreds of seekers gathered here, to keep driving them on, through the barriers, as old Shoju had done with me.

*

From time to time I'd overheard one or other of the resident monks describe me to some newcomer. They'd say I was *imposing*, or *formidable*.

So my girth had increased and I resembled Hotei with his great pot belly. But this weightiness was perceived as impressive. One monk said I combined the shambling gait of an ox with the piercing eye of a tiger. So, tiger and ox

– an intimidating combination. Let me use it now to my advantage.

When everyone had gathered in the lecture hall, and these halfwit delinquents had taken their places at the front, braying and guffawing, full of themselves to the very brim, I strode to the platform and stood for a few minutes in silence, hands folded in *gassho*. Then I began.

When Shakyamuni delivered his famous Flower-Sermon, he used no words. He simply stood in silence in front of an assembled multitude and held up a single flower. Maha Kashapa, seated in the front row . . .

(I paused for a second, fixed the row of young monks with my gaze. One or two of them squirmed).

. . . Maha Kashapa understood the teaching in an instant, and he responded by smiling. The Great One said that in that moment the transmission was direct, and immediate, and complete, and beyond words.

If I were Shakyamuni, I said, standing before you today, I too could hold up a flower and make you see. But I am not Shakyamuni and I hold no flower.

I held up my right hand, empty, open.

See.

Again I looked at the row of reprobates. One of them smirked. I continued.

Nevertheless . . . I have always cherished the belief that by dedicating my life to spreading the Dharma, and by doing so unconditionally, I would bestow this gift on all who came to me, seeking.

Hear.

Turn the Dharma wheel. Beat the Dharma drum. Blow the Dharma conch. Let fall the Dharma rain.

The Dharma rain falls on all alike, I said.

I waited, the length of three heartbeats.

However. These are dark days for the teaching. There are idle useless priests who take no responsibility for their students, sending them out into the world with no respect for the tradition.

Unlike most of you who have come here determined to learn, these students are truly unteachable. In number they may be no more than a handful, but the damage they do is incalculable. They trample roughshod on the Dharma, grinding the precepts into the dust. They tarnish the reputation of the Order, and all of us suffer. Ordinary folk lump us all together and condemn us for the actions of a few. Can you imagine how the good townsfolk of Hara regard monks after this past week? We'll be as welcome as pigs covered in shit, or scabby dogs oozing pus from their sores.

Now I glared at each of the troublemakers in turn, fixed them with my tiger-eye. Most of them looked away. The smirker tried to stare me down but couldn't hold my gaze, snorted and looked round him, scornful.

Monks like these, I said, are an abomination. They appear and reappear from generation to generation. And rarely do they live out their allotted span of years without suffering retribution. In this life they will fall foul of humanity. In the next, they will be torn apart by demons and all trace of their existence will be swept away as they are consigned to the realm of the hungry ghosts.

The smirker stood up, his face now a twisted demon-mask, a caricature. I had stationed a few of the younger, stronger monks in the row behind the troublemakers, in case the hooligans should become violent, and two of these guards also stood up, making their presence known. But they didn't have to intervene. I directed my gaze once more at the young man and I felt my own features change, as if I too were wearing a mask, and I knew I had the terrifying aspect, the fierce intensity, of the ancient masters, of Bodhidharma himself, of some guardian deity presiding over the temple, protecting it. My third eye burned, as if it might reduce the young man and his gang of Dharma-thugs to ash. And he saw it, and so did the rest of them. And without a word, without once looking back, they made their way, shaken and pale, out of the hall and across the courtyard, through the main gate onto the Tokaido, out into the wide world, never to return.

There was the beginning of a faint murmur in the hall, but I stilled it by raising my hand.

Now, I said. Let me proceed with my Dharma talk.

*

Later, outside, I saw old Kakuzaemon, scraping burned rice from the bottom of a pot.

Well? he said. Have those rascals gone for good?

For good or ill, I said.

They won't be back, then?

They won't, I said. But there will be others like them, as long as the Dharma is taught.

Why are they even tolerated? he asked.

Perhaps they thicken the plot, I said.

And he laughed and went back to the kitchen, shaking his head.

CHIKAMATSU

The Floating World, *Ukiyo*, was exactly that, another world, a world apart, separate and self-existent, alongside this, the mundane, the everyday, the real. *Ukiyo* was illusion inside illusion with its theatres and bars, teahouses and pleasure gardens, its cast of actors and musicians, artists, courtesans, geisha. Here were heaven and hell, the realms of gods and demons and hungry ghosts. And depending on how you spoke the word, *Ukiyo* could also mean the world of sorrow and suffering.

Existence is suffering. Its cause is desire.

And yet.

I had been fascinated by theatre since my childhood, the sheer magic and wonder of it. The puppet show I saw with my mother, Nisshin walking unscathed through the flames. *Namu Myoho Renge Kyo.* That had been an awakening, an early moment of kensho, and it had been brought about by the drama. Expedient means.

And that fierce old monk who had terrified me with his sermon on the fires of hell. That too was a kind of theatre, more expedient means, designed to jolt me awake. The power of the word. His third eye had blazed.

The travelling players at Ejiri, performing *The Forty-seven Ronin.* The platform had collapsed and I'd held Hana in my arms. Scent of jasmine. The floating world.

*

I was in Kyoto to deliver a lecture at Myoshin-ji, and my friend and benefactor Ishii Gentoku had accompanied me to discuss the possibility of publishing more books of my talks.

More toxic dog-spew, I said. More unpalatable venom for readers to lap up.

More of the same, he said. They can't get enough of it.

An unfathomable mystery, I said, and we laughed. We had known each other long enough, and he understood I was truly grateful to him.

When I'd given my lecture, on the Five Ranks, the Real and the Unreal, the good doctor approached me and handed me a small printed handbill. It advertised a performance at the Bunraku puppet theatre. I turned the leaflet this way and that, read the title of the play. *Love Suicides at Sonezaki.* A tragic tale of love and loss. I looked at him, quizzical, raised an eyebrow.

?

It's based on a true story, he said, about real people who lived not so long ago.

And?

It's the latest drama by Chikamatsu, he said. I thought it might be of interest.

Ah, I said, looking more closely at the leaflet. Chikamatsu.

That puppet show I had seen as a boy, *The Cauldron-Hat of Nisshin Shonin*, had been written by Chikamatsu.

I owe him a great debt, I said.

Yes, said the doctor. That was why I thought . . .

I must have told him the story, more than once. The lamplit courtyard. The little figures utterly alive. The audience chanting the Daimoku.

I have a friend who works at the theatre, said Gentoku.

273

You have friends everywhere, I said.

I understand Chikamatsu himself will attend the performance.

Indeed? I peered more closely at the handbill.

Furthermore . . . said Gentoku.

I laughed. Why am I alarmed at this *Furthermore. . .* ?

In his own way, said Gentoku, he is a student of Zen.

In his own way.

He knows of your teaching and would be honoured to meet you.

I can see it now, I said. Word will fly along the Tokaido to Hara. Hakuin has fallen. He is in the floating world of Ukiyo, consorting with actors and dancers, geisha and courtesans. He worships at the temple of Bunraku, at the feet of master Chikamatsu.

No doubt, said Gentoku. However . . .

However, I said.

*

I was more than ever the village bumpkin, awed by the big city. Even on my other visits to Kyoto, or to Edo, I had never seen so many people crowding the streets. It made the Tokaido at Hara seem like a quiet country road.

So many, I said to Gentoku, turning my head, looking this way and that, taking it all in. So many.

The air was thick with cooking smells from wayside stalls, fish and seaweed, ginger and garlic and sesame oil, scallions and *shoyu*, pickles and noodle-broth, seared tofu and burned sugar. At one point I detected the scent of *tororojiru* and my mouth watered. Live octopus floundered in a vat of water. Further along, two men, stripped to the waist, raised wooden mallets and alternated, kept up a rhythmic beat, pounding

274

rice into fleshy *mochi* to be stuffed with sweet bean paste. There was even a stall selling nothing but my favourite *konpeito* sugared sweets, heaps of them piled up in dishes on the counter, mountains of them, sparkling.

Simplicity and poverty, I told myself. Moderation in all things.

In a side street there were jugglers and acrobats. One man breathed fire, sent onlookers scattering. Another spun plates on thin bamboo sticks, balanced one on his forehead, one on each hand, one from his outstretched foot as he stood on one leg.

Gentoku laughed as I gawped, amazed. He kept having to tug at my sleeve, guide me through the crowds, down narrow alleyways towards the theatre.

Banners flapped outside the building, lanterns blazed, and as we stepped inside I was once more a child, overcome with excitement and anticipation.

*

The main stage reached out into the audience, and to the side was a smaller platform where two men sat, motionless, dressed in black robes. One played the samisen, its notes deeper than any I'd heard before. Its strings wailed and cried, a mournful overture. The other man listened, his face an impassive mask. Then he opened his mouth and began to chant, his voice an eerie, unearthly singsong, setting the scene, introducing the main characters, Tokubai, a merchant, and Ohatsu, a courtesan. The story was the tale of their doomed love. The samisen moaned.

Out of the shadows on the main stage two puppet figures appeared, the lovers, each one operated by three puppeteers, also dressed in black. At the sight of the puppets I was thrilled,

275

transfixed, just as I'd been as a boy, watching Nisshin. In the slightest movement of the hand, the head, each puppet was utterly alive. The narrator gave them voice, deep and gruff for the man, high and melodic for the woman, and as I glanced across at him, his expression changed for each character, now intense and solemn, now anxious and alarmed. Then I forgot about him, forgot he was there, and I forgot about the puppeteers, forgot I was in a theatre at all and the whole thing was artifice. The characters drew me into their own world, their own realm of being.

As the story ended, as the lovers prepared to die, they chanted the Nembutsu, invoking the compassion of Amida Buddha, asking to be born into the Pure Land. I found myself silently mouthing the words, joining in the chant. *Namu Amida Butsu.* I folded my hands and bowed my head.

Well? said Gentoku as we left the auditorium.

I looked around as if in a dream. This world, the everyday. What passed for reality, ephemeral and transient as the little puppet-play we had seen unfold.

Illusion on illusion, I said. And yet . . .

*

The doctor led me backstage where a young woman ushered us into a small room, tatami on the floor, an elegant flower arrangement in a *tokonoma* alcove, woodblock prints on the wall depicting characters from Chikamatsu's plays – a medicine pedlar, a warrior, the couple from the play that had just been performed. Seated in the corner of the room, propped up on cushions, sat Chikamatsu himself. He was old, close to seventy, gaunt and thin-shouldered, but still with a kind of aristocratic elegance, a refinement of bearing. In a deep red jacket he resembled a figure from one of the *ukiyo-e* prints, an

276

aging actor, a court poet. I could only imagine how I must look to him in my old robes of coarse grey cloth. But he was the one who bowed, called me *Sensei*, said it was an honour to meet me.

I laughed. You bow to this old bag of bones, draped in sackcloth!

Doctor Gentoku has told me a great deal about you, he said. He gave me a book of your writings.

Poison drool, I said. I can't imagine a man of your sophistication lapping it up.

It tastes of Zen, he said.

Ah, I said. Zen.

I let the word hang there, left a silence which he broke by clapping his hands, calling for tea. In an instant, it seemed, the tea had been placed before us by three young women moving as swiftly and unobtrusively as the invisible puppeteers on stage. They also left a dish of the *konpeito* I loved.

I see the good doctor has also told you of my weakness for these sweets.

Please, said Chikamatsu, indicating the dish.

I took a handful of the sweets, popped them one by one in my mouth, crunched them to sweet grit.

Exquisite, I said, as he poured the tea.

You are in Kyoto to give a lecture, he said, at Myoshin-ji. On the Unreal and the Real.

The Five Ranks, he said. I have read Tozan's verses.

Indeed? I said, remembering old Shoju driving me to understand these words, the suffering and austerity I underwent for month after month on the road, in all weathers, frozen and starving, sick, battering, battering, battering at the gates. The moment of kensho when I saw it clear. *The current of ordinary life . . . He comes back to sit among the dust and the ashes.* Now I sat here in the Floating World, eating sugared sweets.

277

It's my understanding, said Chikamatsu, that art lies in the thinnest gap between the real and the unreal.

He had honed the thought, polished the words till they shone, an aphorism.

I threw back my head and laughed.

Spew it up, I said. I'll add it to my vat of poison!

His lips formed a thin smile. He was shrewd enough to know I was paying him a backhanded compliment. His eyes were world-weary, amused, but I saw there a flickering of insight, an intense awareness of transience, of his own mortality.

We all die, I said.

And then?

Perhaps you'll be a monk in your next life.

And perhaps you'll be a playwright.

And would that be progress?

Perhaps, he said, and I laughed again.

There are those who say, I continued, that when Zen teaching is flourishing, it has little to do with art. But when the teaching is in decline, the reliance on the arts increases. So instead of monks we produce poets and painters and tea masters.

So all of this . . . He waved a languid hand, indicating the posters on the wall . . . is simply a diversion, a distraction?

Everything is illusory, I said. But some illusion leads to liberation, some just leads deeper into the mire.

And what about this illusion? He waved the hand again, towards the poster for the play we had just seen.

I was enchanted by the performance, I said. It told a timeless story of *giri* and *nijo*, duty and desire. But at the end, when the lovers chanted the Nembutsu and offered everything up, it became something more. It transcended the telling, and I must say I found it deeply affecting.

He gave the slightest bow. Thank you.

The doctor, I believe, has mentioned my own debt of gratitude to you. When I was a small boy, my mother took me to see your play on Nisshin Shonin, and it was one of the most powerful experiences of my life, a kind of awakening. So, this is what art can do.

But you won't be encouraging your followers to come and enjoy the pleasures of the Floating World?

I want to produce monks, monks, monks, not aesthetes, not geisha!

But you yourself are here.

Indeed! I said, thanks to our good friend the doctor.

Gentoku bowed, gave a little exaggerated flourish.

I have a story to tell the monks, I said, if they should ask how I could visit such a place.

I am listening, said Chikamatsu.

In ancient times, I said, there was a great king who also happened to be a spiritual seeker.

What is it they say? asked Chikamatsu. A memory of the spiritual life often haunts the throne.

I have heard the same, I said. Great seekers who just fail to attain realisation are often reborn in auspicious circumstances as an emperor, a great ruler, so they can do good in the world.

I fear they don't always succeed.

Too many distractions? I said.

Please continue, said Chikamatsu.

In the case of this particular king, I said, there was no contradiction. Although he lived in a palace, his life was disciplined and his meditation was profound. His rule was wise and benign.

But one day a young monk came to the palace to see this enlightened ruler for himself, and unfortunately the young

279

man was horrified. All he saw was luxury and opulence. He looked around at the beautiful surroundings, the servants and handmaidens, musicians and dancing girls, and he denounced the king. How can you live like this, he said, and claim to see the truth?

The king listened to his outburst, then summoned the young man to his quarters where he set him a task. He filled a small bowl with oil, right to the brim, and he handed it to the young man.

I want you to carry this the whole length of the palace and back, said the king, and return it to me without spilling a drop.

By this time the young man thought the king was quite mad. But he thought it best to humour him, so he took the bowl and set off to fulfil his task. After quite some time he returned. With tremendous effort he had managed to keep his hand steady and not spill the oil. He returned the bowl to the king who took it from him and set it down.

You have done well, said the king. You have learned how to concentrate. But as you walked through the palace, what did you see?

I saw nothing, he said. Only the bowl, and the oil in it, and my hand holding it.

You didn't drink in the opulence and beauty of your surroundings? You weren't distracted by the music or the dancing girls?

I didn't even notice them, he said.

Well then, said the king. This is how I can dwell here, in the midst of distraction, and not be distracted. My concentration on what is real is total and absolute.

The young monk understood, and returned home a little wiser.

Chikamatsu laughed and applauded.

An excellent tale, he said. It would make a wonderful puppet show. Perhaps I shall turn it into a play.

Then I will come and see it!

Once more he clapped his hands together and once more the young women were in the room and clearing away the tea things and replacing them with a wooden box, inlaid with a dragon design.

He said he would smoke a pipe and invited us to join him. Gentoku nodded and I said I would be delighted, it would be the perfect way to round off a day of indulgence. He took the clay pipes and a jar of tobacco from the box, and we lit up with a flint and sat content, wreathed in fragrant fumes.

There was a tap at the shoji screen and it slid open. A middle-aged man sat there, carrying the puppet figures of Tokubai and Ohatsu, the two lovers. I didn't recognise the man till he stepped into the room. He was the *tayu*, the narrator of the play. He had changed into a lighter-coloured *yukata*, but his features had also changed as he reinhabited his everyday self. He bowed to us, smiling.

Please, said Chikamatsu, and the man placed the puppets on a low seat opposite me, and sat down beside them.

The puppets wanted to bid you farewell, said Chikamatsu, and he nodded to the man and took the puppet Tokubai from him. They sat for a moment then the man began to chant in the singsong voice of Ohatsu, and once again his face transformed as he became the courtesan and gave voice to her emotions. My heart thudded as the little figure moved. Then the voice changed, and the *tayu* became Tokubai, and the other figure also moved. And I knew the two men were operating the puppets, but the figures were alive, conscient. The *tayu*, possessed, sang in one voice then the other, a song of parting, ending with the Nembutsu, invoking compassion. The two little figures faced me, looked at me. The little hands,

281

folded in supplication, were shaking. The little heads bowed, and it was over.

Between the real and the unreal, said Chikamatsu.

I bowed to him, and to the *tayu*, and I bowed to each of the little figures as if they were sentient beings.

SIX

IS THAT SO?

I had seen the girl a few times in the village. Her parents owned a stall at the market, selling fruit and vegetables, and the girl worked there, serving the customers. She worked with a quiet courtesy, a deference, her manner brisk and efficient. But once or twice I saw a look in her eyes, a glimmer, a spark. There was a fire in her that might illumine or consume, and no way of knowing which it would be.

She was pretty, with a natural gracefulness about her, a lightness. It was there even in the smallest of gestures, the way she weighed the vegetables on an old scale, wrapped them and handed them over, took the money, gave change. I heard her father call her Kazuko.

I had gone into the market one day with one of the young monks, Taku. He had asked with great earnestness about the aphorism *Your everyday mind is the way.* He found it difficult to understand, and I thought down there among the sights and sounds and smells of the marketplace he might catch a glimpse.

We stopped at the stall to buy vegetables – I picked out a few radishes and leeks and the girl placed them in a sack Taku had brought with him. Everything on the stall was laid out just so, the fruits and vegetables piled high. Right in the centre was a basket of persimmons, perfect and ripe. I could smell

285

their sweetness. I told Taku to choose one and he asked the girl which was the best.

She bowed to him and smiled.

They are all the best, she said.

I laughed and slapped Taku on the back.

You see, Taku, I said. This young woman has a deep understanding of Zen!

The girl laughed too, but politely, covering her mouth with her hand. There was still a faint smile in her eyes as she picked up one persimmon, cupped it in both hands and handed it to him.

This one, she said.

He took it and bowed, said Thank you, but he was flustered, as much by her smile as by my testing him. He blushed as bright as the persimmon. I would have to remind him what Shakyamuni said about women. However beautiful, they were still only bags of guts and blood and bone.

Nevertheless.

*

The next time I saw the girl was one evening near the temple. I had gone outside for a walk as it grew dark, and I saw her standing there quite still, distracted, staring into the distance.

At first I didn't recognise her and I asked who she was.

I am nobody, she said. Just a girl.

Then I saw she was the girl from the market.

I know you, I said. You taught us persimmon Zen. Every one is the best!

I am nobody, she said again. Leave me alone.

She turned away and hurried into the dusk, moving with quick short steps as the temple bell rang, its single note resonating, long.

286

It was some time later – a few days, a week. I had been absorbed in re-reading the Lotus Sutra, chanting the Daimoku, when I heard a commotion at the gate, a man's voice, rough and guttural, angry.

I stepped forward, spoke to him quietly.

Who is making this noise?

You know why I am here, he said, lips tight, jaw clenched.

You think I have magic powers? I asked him. You think I can read your mind?

You call yourself a master, he said, but you're useless.

No doubt, I said. But how does my uselessness concern you?

I could see he was controlling himself with great difficulty.

This is about my daughter, he said.

I recognised him then as the girl's father.

Ah, I said. Yes.

She is pregnant, he said. At first she refused to name the father. My wife pleaded, I threatened. The girl is stubborn, but eventually she could take no more and she blurted out the truth. She said your name.

The monks could not believe what they were hearing. They were ready to seize the man and bundle him out the door, but I raised my hand, restraining them, and let him continue.

The child is yours, he said. You must accept responsibility.

I breathed deep, from my core. I answered him, said three words.

Is that so?

*

My reputation for purity had been hard won over many years of self-discipline, ferocious austerity. Now, overnight, it had been destroyed. I had fallen. This young girl had come to me for refuge, they said, and I had taken advantage. No doubt, they said, it was not the first time. No doubt. Even some of the monks left the temple.

One morning young Taku came to me, the one I had teased about the girl's persimmon Zen.

It is unbelievable, he said.

Well then, don't believe it.

It is unthinkable.

So don't think about it.

I can't understand it.

It is not to be understood.

He looked even more perplexed.

Take it as a koan, I said. Grapple with it as you would any other, struggle with its poison fangs and talons. Conquer it and go beyond.

He looked so miserable a great roar of a laugh burst out of me. Then I bowed, recited from the Four Great Vows.

Sentient beings are numberless. I vow to save them all.

He mouthed the words, silently repeating them.

Fangs and talons, I said. Go beyond. Now, meditate.

*

Weeks passed, months. By now word had spread and my reputation was in tatters. Folk in the village would turn away if they saw me in the street, they would cross the road to avoid me. Begging for our livelihood became more difficult, but the few hardy souls who still had faith in me gave more when they could. Somehow we survived. We got through the winter, looked forward to the coming of spring. Taku didn't ask about the situation again. He grappled with it, his koan.

One clear, cold morning he came and told me the girl's

mother was at the gate, carrying a bundle. I told him to show her in.

The woman was uncomfortable, distressed at having to be here, having to enter this place.

How is your daughter? I asked.

As if you care, she said. She's as well as anyone would expect under the circumstances.

I nodded and she handed me the little bundle, wrapped in a blanket. The child began to cry.

This is your son, she said. You have to take care of him.

Again I said, Is that so?

*

The villagers who had faith in me continued to give what they could, and even some of the others found ways to help the child. There would be offerings left at the temple gate – fruit and vegetables, a cup of rice, a jug of milk. Someone left a blanket, someone else a tiny shawl. A few times I thought I saw the girl's mother setting down a basket. Once or twice I was sure it was the girl herself, her head covered, as she hurried away.

I had no experience of looking after a child, never mind a baby, but I was determined. I had to see this through. Taku and the other monks offered to help, but the responsibility was mine.

He must be a great seeker, I told Taku. He wakes every night at the hour of the ox, screaming his devotions.

And every hour after that, said Taku, through till dawn.

So you hear him? I asked. Clearly he is a little Bodhisattva, sent to awaken us.

Taku grunted.

There are worse ways, I said. The Chinese sage Tzu-ming

used to jab his own thigh with a gimlet to keep himself from falling asleep in his meditation through the long cold winter nights.

Taku looked as if the gimlet would be easier to bear. The baby wailed and thrashed around in the little basket-crib where he slept. I picked him up.

So, little Buddha, you sleep, you wake, you eat, you piss, you shit, you sleep. And one day you'll be enlightened!

The baby gurgled, laughed.

Tell me, little Buddha, I asked him, What was your face before you were born?

The baby kicked his legs, reached out his arms.

Look! I said to Taku. See how his tiny fist grabs the empty air!

Taku laughed.

He is teaching us, I said. It has to be realised here in this world. Your everyday mind is the way.

*

One morning they came back – the young girl, her head bent, tears in her eyes, her mother distraught, turning this way and that, the father straight-backed, tight-lipped, trying to hold on to some measure of dignity.

We owe you the humblest apology, he said, bowing low. She has told us the truth. The child is not yours. The real father is a young man we don't even know.

He was passing through the village, said the mother, just passing through, on his way somewhere else.

He told me he loved me, said the girl. Then he was gone.

We still don't know why she blamed you, said the mother.

The girl looked towards me, not catching my eye.

I didn't know what to do, she said. I spoke your name.

290

We have caused you untold suffering, said the father. We
have come to take the child and beg for your forgiveness.

Once more I spoke the three words, a mantra.

Is. That. So.

?

SATSU

A cousin of mine, Shoji-san, lived not far away, in Mishima. He was a merchant, made a good living trading in furniture and wood carvings. But when he could he came to the temple to meditate. One day he approached me looking anxious and fretful.

You are troubled, I said.

He nodded.

It's my daughter Satsu, he said. She's fifteen years old.

Ah, I said. Is that so?

The story of Kazuko, the young girl and her baby, had been told far and wide, had become a kind of koan.

Oh no, said Shoji. She's not in that kind of trouble.

What then?

She's been sitting with me in zazen, and I feel she may be making some progress.

But?

She lacks reverence or any kind of decorum and she shows absolutely no respect for tradition.

I remember her as a young child, I said. She was always fiery.

Last week, he said, she was sitting meditating on top of a bamboo chest. I remonstrated with her and told her there was a statue of Buddha in the chest, and she should sit somewhere else. She refused to move, and said, Can you tell me somewhere I can sit where Buddha is *not*?

I smiled, said, That sounds like true insight.

Reluctantly she moved, said Shoji, but it went from bad to worse. She sat on a copy of the Lotus Sutra.

Thus have I heard . . .

Again I told her to move, and she said, What's the difference between the Lotus Sutra and my arse?

I choked back a laugh, turned it into a cough.

Perhaps I can help.

I would be most grateful.

I took a brush and a piece of paper, copied out a poem.

> *If you can hear the voice*
> *Of a crow that doesn't caw*
> *In the dark of night,*
> *You will know your face*
> *Before you were born.*

Give her this, I said, handing the poem to Shoji, and tell me what she says.

When he'd gone I chuckled to myself. Lotus Sutra my arse!

*

The next day Shoji returned.

Well? I said.

He was uncomfortable, looked at the floor.

She read the poem, he said.

And?

He hesitated, took a deep breath, spoke all-in-a-rush.

She said, Is this old man Hakuin's work? Is this the best he can come up with?

Perhaps she would deign to come and speak to old man Hakuin, I said.

293

A few days later he brought the girl to the temple. She sat in front of me, bowed.

Well? I said.

Well what?

Her father opened his mouth to scold her, but I raised my hand, stopped him.

Tell me about yourself, I said.

What's to tell, she said. I'm fifteen years old. What do I know?

I'm sure you know a great deal.

I know I'm not much of a looker, she said. When you're fifteen there are things that become apparent, things you see with great clarity. On the other hand, I'm not hideous.

No.

And perhaps with luck and a bit of help I might actually find a husband.

Is that what you want?

Again her father opened his mouth.

She . . .

Again I silenced him, let her continue.

Here's what happened, she said. Luck and a bit of help. I thought I'd get both by praying to Kannon Bodhisattva.

You could do worse, I said.

I went in secret to the temple at Yanagizawa. Quietly I offered up prayers, recited the sutra to Kannon.

I nodded and folded my hands, recited. *Enmei Jikku Kannon Gyo.*

The girl bowed.

It is a mantra that can bring great consolation, I said, in times of adversity. It is also said to combat illness and prolong life. Do you know the story of Kao-huang?

She shook her head.

He lived in ancient China, I said. He was a pious man, but

294

he fell foul of the authorities and was sentenced to death. The night before he was due to be executed, he was meditating on Kannon. The Bodhisattva appeared before him and said if he chanted the sutra a thousand times through the night, then he would be spared and would live a long life. Kao-huang thought this was impossible but nevertheless he chanted through the whole night and completed the thousand recitations. At dawn he was taken to the prison yard. He kneeled and the executioner raised his sword. Kao-huang invoked Kannon one last time and waited for the fatal blow. But it never came. The sword mysteriously broke in two and the blade fell to the ground. Another sword was fetched and the same thing happened. They tried a third time and again the sword broke. A priest was summoned and he declared this must be the will of Heaven, and Kao-huang was set free. And of course he lived to a great age.

It's a good story, said the girl.

The sutra is very powerful, whether you're praying for long life, or looking for a husband, or seeking enlightenment.

Yes, she said. I went to the temple whenever I could, and soon I found myself completely absorbed in the devotions. I didn't want to do anything else. Thoughts of finding a husband, of praying for anything at all, just faded away. I found myself chanting the sutra constantly, when I was reading or writing, cooking or washing up, cleaning the house. I lost myself in it completely.

The girl paused, rubbed her forehead. I could sense she was not used to talking like this, so openly and seriously, about her experience.

I recalled the intensity of my own devotions as a child, getting up in the middle of the night to chant the Tenjin Sutra. My father's outrage, my mother's concern. The huge excitement and uncertainty of it all.

Go on, I said to the girl.

All of a sudden, she said, as I looked out at the temple garden I made a kind of breakthrough. I can't put it in words. But I saw things clear, as they really are. The old pine tree. The crack on the wall. A *hototogisu* singing. Myself just sitting there.

You experienced kensho, I said. An awakening.

Yes.

She said it quietly, without a trace of arrogance, but with simple wonderment. Again I remembered my own early experiences, swaggering, puffed up with pride at the great realisation I had achieved.

Child, I said. You have made a beginning. If you wish, you are more than welcome to come here with your father and meditate with me.

She bowed, then turned to her father who also bowed, and this time he didn't speak.

*

Two or three times Satsu came with her father and sat in zazen from early evening right through the night till dawn. He had long since slumped over, fallen asleep, but she sat, back straight, eyes clear.

I told her to meditate on one of the simpler koans. A monk enters the monastery and asks Joshu to teach him. Have you eaten your rice-gruel? asks Joshu. Yes, said the monk. Well then, says Joshu. Now wash your bowl.

Satsu said Thank you, went off to grapple with the problem. The next time I saw her I asked if she had made any headway.

It is clear, she said, and at the same time it is hard to see.

Searching for fire with a lighted lantern, I said.

She laughed and clapped her hands.

Use the fire to cook the rice!

I set her meditating on Joshu's *Mu*, sent her off with furrowed brow. But stage by stage she intensified her understanding of it. At one point I sat down to question her about the koan, and she asked if I would repeat what I had just said. I opened my mouth to speak and she bowed deep, said, Thank you for taking all this trouble. Then she stood up and left the room.

I laughed.

Later I saw her father.

I'll have to wake up, I said. I've just been outdone by your precocious daughter!

*

One day a monk named Rimpen came to visit. He was a pious fellow whose name meant Completely-encompassed. As it happened, I had been talking to Satsu and I allowed her to stay in the room when Rimpen arrived. She sat quietly in the corner, but I noticed him dart a glance across at her, uncomfortable.

Well, Rimpen, I said, as an opening gambit. Have you completely encompassed the great void?

Rimpen kept silent, drew a circle in the air with his finger.

That's still only about half, I said.

He looked puzzled, unable to respond.

Satsu spoke up, said, Just a moment ago it was completely encompassed.

You're right, I said, and I stared at the monk. Is there anything else?

There was something I wanted to ask, he said, gathering himself.

I am here, I said. Ask.

I read an inscription on one of your paintings, he said. *Breaking up white rock inside a poppy seed.*

Yes, I said.

I've been struggling to understand, he said. What do the words mean?

Before I could reply, Satsu jumped to her feet, picked up a teacup and threw it to the floor, smashing it to pieces.

Useless! she said, and strode out of the room.

You should listen to her, I said. And I drew a complete circle in the air with my finger.

*

Satsu continued to stamp her way through the teachings, trampling ignorance underfoot, facing down the koans. When I was convinced she had fully broken through, I presented her with a scroll inscribed with her name and a drawing of a circle. She touched the scroll to her forehead and smiled. Her eyes were piercing and clear.

TEASHOP ZEN

There was a teashop in the village run by a ferocious old woman who had gained a reputation for her understanding of Zen. I remembered my broom-handle enlightenment near Shoju's hermitage at the hands of that other old woman who had battered me senseless, stunned me awake.

Aren't you listening? she had shouted at me. Go somewhere else!

Somewhere else.

I resolved to visit this teashop in Hara, sample the old woman's tea and Zen.

It was mid-morning when I pushed in through the bamboo curtains that clacked and swished behind me. Outside it was a bright clear autumn day. In here it was dank and dimly lit, light filtering in through tattered grimy shoji screens. But the smells were good – the fresh green bitterness of *sencha*, the slight acridness of charcoal from the stove, a sharp clear pine incense. I breathed it all in.

There were no other customers and I sat myself down at a low table in the corner, legs tucked under me as if for zazen. A few minutes passed, and a few more. I cleared my throat by way of announcing my presence, in case it hadn't been noticed. A screen separated the shop from the kitchen area at the back, and from behind the screen the old woman's head suddenly appeared.

Well? she demanded, irritation in the sharpness of her voice.

She wore an old kimono, dark green with a plum blossom embroidered on the sleeve. Her head was huge, her iron-grey hair caught up in an old-fashioned topknot skewered with a chopstick.

I bowed.

Tea, I said. I would like some tea.

Right place, she said, and she disappeared again, only to pop out a moment later.

Shows you have at least half a brain, she said. Tea . . . Teashop. You could have gone to the fishmonger, or the knocking shop, or the Zen temple. No fish here. None of the other. And definitely no Zen. Just tea.

She waved a ladle at me.

And nothing fancy. No *chanoyu* frippery and nonsense. Tea. Plain and simple.

That's all I'm after, I said. Plain and simple suits me fine.

That's all right then, she said. Some of you black-robed shavepates come in here expecting Buddha-knows-what.

Tea, I said. Nothing else.

Right, she said. Tea it is.

I must have passed some first test, some initiation ceremony, as she went back once more behind the screen and I heard the pouring of water, the clattering of utensils.

More time passed. I began reciting the Lotus Sutra in my head.

Thus have I heard . . .

I got through the lists of Arhats and Bodhisattvas, on to Manjushri's prologue.

All of you should now understand
And with one heart fold your hands and wait.

The Buddha will let fall the Dharma rain
To satisfy all those who seek the Way . . .

The old woman poked her head round the screen again, shouted Tea!

She shuffled over and unceremoniously banged the lacquer-wood tray down on my table.

So!

She lifted the lid from a little clay teapot, roughglazed, and stuffed in a handful of crushed leaves, tamped them down with a bamboo spoon, poured in water from an iron kettle, spilling a little on the tray.

Wait, she said, holding up one hand, then counting on her fingers. Twenty seconds.

She counted to twenty, then one more, for luck, poured the tea into a bowl.

Now, she said. Drink!

I took the bowl in both hands, bowed, then sipped the tea. The taste was the deep green of the forest, fresh cut grass on a summer day. A rush of brightness to the brain, then something lingering, a mellowness, an aftertaste.

Well? said the old woman, wary.

Yes, I said. Yes.

She poured more boiling water onto the leaves, this time didn't bother with the twenty second wait.

Drink, she said, and I did.

Ah!

I set down the bowl and nodded, content.

Plain and simple, she said.

Plain and simple.

Reading nothing into it.

Nothing.

She squinted at me, her old eyes crinkling.

301

If I'd thought for a moment . . .

What?

She beckoned me to follow her behind the screen where she picked up an iron fire-poker, turned and brandished it in my face.

This is what I dish out to those curs and mongrels who come sniffing around for a whiff of Zen.

She prodded me in the chest with the poker.

A whack with this soon sends them packing.

I laughed and stepped back, bowed.

Thank you for the tea, I said.

*

After that I sang the old woman's praises, told the young monks her understanding of Zen was profound.

But go to her for tea, I said, and nothing else. Otherwise . . .

The first monk to try his luck came back with a black eye.

She's a monster, he said. She might have killed me.

She's helping you die the Great Death, I said.

The second monk came back rubbing his shoulder.

All I did was quote Nansen when he said to Joshu, *Everday life is the way.*

You were stinking of Zen, I said, and she smelled it.

The third monk had a bruise on his arm from raising it to ward off the blow.

Don't tell me, I said. You made some obscure remark about *chanoyu* and the Way of Tea.

I only quoted a haiku, he said, one I thought was apposite.

I shook my head.

You might as well have vomited in her kitchen.

And so it continued, as one after another they returned to Shoin-ji battered and shaken.

302

I turned the bowl, the way you do in *chanoyu*.

Foolish in the extreme.

I dropped the bowl and it smashed on the floor. Then I tried to make light of it, and said it was the bowl's time to die.

You'd have been as well grabbing a sword and committing *seppuku* there and then.

I said her tea was a little bitter, too astringent. She drove me out with blows and told me never to return.

Quite right. You have to know when to discriminate and when to go beyond discrimination.

But . . .

Enough!

The tea was so strong I wondered out loud if the leaves had come from the plant that sprang from Bodhidharma's eyelids when he threw them down after cutting them off. So he wouldn't fall asleep in meditation.

You thought she wouldn't know the story.

I suppose . . .

So you laboured it in the telling?

I . . .

Idiot! Have you ever been *awake* in meditation?

No answer.

Bodhidharma would cut off more than your eyelids if he heard you retching up his story undigested.

I didn't say a word, but I sat staring at the old woman so long, waiting for her to *do* something, that I let my tea get cold.

Useless. The old woman's fire-poker is her *kyosaku*, her wake-up stick. Perhaps I should get hold of one myself and crack a few heads with it.

Finally, after nine or ten monks had come home from the teashop battered and bruised, chastened, one young man came back to the temple unscathed and whistling an old folk song tunelessly to himself.

Well?

I was tired, he said, after an hour of reading scriptures. I just wanted tea, that was all.

Mindless, I said. You were lucky. The old woman must have been off guard. She should have split your skull with the poker, let in some light.

He looked startled, then grinned and bowed.

Nevertheless, he said.

Nevertheless.

And he went off whistling his tuneless tune like some happy Zen fool, showered with countless blessings.

TWO GOOD MONKS

I had vowed to save them all. I had taught so many, and so many had taught me. I had dished out my poison to them – monks and lay followers alike, men and women, old and young – and I'd taken it when they threw it back at me. For the lay followers I'd used whatever would work – chanting the Nembutsu or the Daimoku or invoking Kannon Bodhisattva, hard-to-pass koans, tales of cause and effect. Expedient means. For the monks it was more rigorous, zazen and koan study leading to kensho. And after awakening, working to help others, to continue transmitting the Dharma. Old Shoju Rojin had told me how difficult it would be to produce even two good monks to succeed me. I could see his weathered face, his burning eyes, as he said it to me on the day I left his hermitage.

Produce two real successors and the old winds of Zen will blow once more throughout the land.

But the years had passed, each one quicker than the one before. One day you are forty. You blink and you are fifty. It was hard to believe, but now sixty was on the horizon, and these Dharma-heirs had still not appeared.

The autumn wind blew and I wrote a tanka.

> *Last quarter, last third*
> *of my life?*

Either way, it's autumn,
shading, shading
into winter.

Then they both came, my two good monks, and they could not have been more different, one from the other.

*

Torei Enji was still in his twenties, and I knew him by reputation before he arrived at Shoin-ji, gaunt and sickly, bright-eyed. When I saw him I said, You really should have come here sooner.

He bowed and placed a gift before me, wrapped in rice paper. To my delight it was a package of *konpeito* sugared sweets.

You have clearly done research into the weaknesses of this old reprobate, I said.

Like me, Torei had been awakened to the Zen quest at the age of eight. (I still remembered that cantankerous old monk and his hellfire sermon terrifying the life out of me, scaring me awake.) Torei had become a monk at that tender age, and at sixteen he had left his home temple and travelled as far as Kyushu in search of enlightenment. He received training from Rinzai masters and experienced a kind of satori. All this he told me on that first day over a bowl of tea and some of those delicious *konpeito*.

After your satori, I said. What then?

I continued the search, he said. Satori is just the beginning.

I wish there were more who realised that, I said.

At the age of twenty I returned to my home province of Omi. I entered into a solitary retreat and sat in zazen for many days and nights. I became so exhausted I could no longer sit up straight.

306

Zen sickness, I said. I know it well.

I became desolate, he said. I let out a great cry that I was useless and no longer had the strength to follow the Way. At that I fell over, but just before my head hit the ground I experienced an enlightenment and saw things clear.

Good, I said. And then?

Enlightenment was one thing, he said. Carrying it into everyday life was something else entirely.

This wisdom too is hard earned.

I heard of your teaching from other monks who had been here.

Tiger-fodder, I said. They lapped up my poisonous drool.

They said you were rigorous, and I confess it was fear that held me back.

Fear of what?

Of ending up totally humiliated, knocked to the ground and lying flat on my back.

That was how old Shoju taught me, I said. Knocked the stuffing out of me. So what do you think? Did it work?

He bowed, said, I'm here.

And still fearful?

A little.

Again I remembered that fierce old monk who had terrified me as a child. He had said the fear was a good place to start. My mother had consoled me, said perhaps a little fear could help us do the right thing.

A little, I said.

I'm afraid my health is still not good, said Torei.

Many years ago, I said, I met an old sage who cured my Zen sickness.

How did he do that?

Like with like, I said. Hair of the dog. The cause of the sickness is also its cure. Zazen made you sick, zazen will cure you.

Torei bowed, touched his forehead to the floor.

I crunched another sweet between my teeth.

*

Torei came to me for instruction, hands folded, after many hours of zazen. I challenged him.

Suppose right now a great demon came up behind you and grabbed you in a tight grip. And the more you struggled the tighter he held. And suppose he carried you off and threw you into a blazing pit of fire. Right there and then, in that moment, would you have any way out?

He looked stunned, as if I had struck him a blow to the head.

Well? I said. Here and now. Is there any way out?

He sweated and shook, numbed, unable to move.

Too late, I said. You're burned to a crisp.

He told me later he couldn't even breathe. The universe itself felt cramped and small. The sun and moon were dark.

Every time I saw him, I asked again. Well? Do you have any way out?

He could say nothing, do nothing.

At least you're not like some of these glib young fellows who come through the door, I told him. They throw off some facile answer to cover up their ignorance. Or they try to get away with a piece of third-rate theatre. They shout or stamp their feet. But they fool nobody. They're bound for hell.

Now, I said. Do you have any way out?

*

I continued to challenge Torei, although his realisation was true, his understanding profound. I continued to challenge him *because* he was true. But he was not physically strong. I resolved to teach him *naikan*, the meditation imparted to me by the ancient Hakuyu in his cave outside Kyoto. Torei was immediately suspicious of the story.

This hermit was four hundred years old?

At least.

It's a wondrous tale, he said.

Indeed.

And he lived by the Shirakawa River?

Yes.

We sat for a time, saying nothing, till I broke the silence.

You know the old story? Night Boat on the Shirakawa River?

I have heard it told, he said. The country bumpkin who boasts to his friends about his visit to Kyoto where he'd seen all the wonderful sights of the city. Someone asks him about the Shirakawa River . . .

Which in fact is nothing more than a small stream.

. . . and he replies that it was night-time when his boat sailed on the river, so he couldn't get a clear view and was unable to describe it.

In other words, his visit to Kyoto was a fabrication, a tale he'd made up.

Idle talk.

Expedient means.

He smiled and bowed deep.

I would be honoured to learn this introspective meditation from you.

*

I began to teach Torei techniques for improving his health. I

309

told him to imagine as he sat there that a little piece of pure soft butter, sweet and fragrant, the size of a duck egg, had been placed on top of his head, on the crown chakra, the *sahasrara.* He sat, back straight, breathing deep, eyes closed, visualising.

Slowly the butter begins to melt and flow down over your head, soothing and calming. It continues to flow down, moistening, inside and out. You feel the sensation, exquisite, as it reaches your neck and shoulders, your chest and your spine, your lungs and all your internal organs, your stomach, your bowels . . .

At this, Torei seemed to flinch a moment, then he steadied himself and I continued.

It flows on down through the hips and the lower body, carrying with it all the accumulated ailments, the aches and pains, down through the legs to the soles of the feet, permeating your whole being with warmth. It is as if you are seated up to the navel in a hot bath suffused with fragrant healing herbs. Balance is restored. Body and mind are in harmony.

The ten thousand things are filled
With the vital energy of creation.

After the session Torei breathed deeply and thanked me. He had experienced a sense of wellbeing he hadn't known since he was a child. He smiled.

You know my mother was skilled in the use of herbs. So I had no difficulty in imagining those scents.

And the pure butter?

I can still smell it.

This is the power of the mind.

*

For a time Torei's health seemed to improve, but his body had been badly damaged by the long periods of austerity he'd undergone. In particular he suffered from a weakness in the stomach and bowels. (I had noticed that *flinch* during his meditation). At times he would have to interrupt his zazen and rush to the privy – a miserable ramshackle structure built over four holes dug in the ground. The atmosphere in there was rank at the best of times, but when Torei was caught short it was downright fetid. The other monks could be ruthless.

So that's what they mean by stinking of Zen.

I'd heard Torei could sit for hours at a stretch.

Did you say sit?

Smells like hell.

And stinks to high heaven.

He bore it well, but he grew weaker again. He needed rest, and some of those herbal potions his mother could brew, and better food than the Shoin-ji staple of greens, greens and more greens. Reluctantly he decided to go home for a while, to Omi, in the hope that he might regain his strength. I was sorry to see him go, and I prayed he would return.

*

The second of my two good monks was called Eboku. He was almost thirty and he came from Shimotsuke, north of Edo. Another student, Shojo Domu, arrived at the same time, riding on the back of an ox, and when Eboku saw him he threw back his head and laughed.

This layman has outdone all the monks in the temple, he said. He's caught the bull and he's riding it home!

So you know Kakuan's Ten Bulls, I said.

I've seen the pictures, said Eboku. I've read the words.

311

And where does that leave you? I asked. Have you set out on the way?

I'd like to leap to the end of the journey, he said, and live in the world.

Barefoot and bare-chested, I mix with ordinary folk.
Clothes ragged and dusty, I dwell in endless bliss.

It's easy to recite the verses, I said. But where are you? Are you searching for the bull? Have you discovered its footprints? Have you seen it for yourself?

You tell me, he said. You're the one doing the teaching.

And who are you? What do you have to say?

I am known as Eboku, he said, from Shimotsuke. I like to draw and paint, and to drink sake.

And without those, I asked, what then?

You tell me, he said again.

Layman Domu had dismounted from his ox, the actual flesh-and-blood animal, and tethered it to a post. It raised its head and bellowed long and loud.

Such wisdom, said Eboku, and he bowed to the beast, to its great understanding of Zen.

*

After that Eboku came to Shoin-ji whenever I was giving a talk and at no other time. He would sit at the back of the room, listening attentively, and leave as soon as I had finished speaking. Once I sent one of the younger monks to run after him and bring him back.

Tell him I want to speak to him, I said.

The young monk returned, flushed and out of breath.

Well? I said.

He refused to come, said the young monk.

312

Why?

He said you might want to speak to him, but he didn't want to speak to you.

I laughed.

What am I to do with this vagabond?

He refused to live in the temple compound, preferring to stay on his own in a simple hut some miles away. The communal life held no appeal for him. But in time he began to linger after the meetings. He still didn't speak, but I could tell by his manner that he would not object if I spoke to him. I had heard he was fond of playing *Go* and I invited him to join me in a game. He said he would beat me easily. I showed him a drawing I had done of myself as Hotei, playing the game. In my drawing there were no counters and no markings on the board, and Hotei was grinning, contented. Eboku laughed and sat down opposite me, cross-legged, ready to start.

He played with a skill and calculation that seemed at odds with the freedom and spontaneity he valued so highly. For my part I went at it with gusto, banging down the counters without pausing to think or keep track of the moves. My tactic unnerved him and I won as many games as I lost. He bowed, realising my teaching had begun.

I took my brush and inkstone and added a little haiku to the scroll, by way of commentary.

No markings on the board
His hand is empty
He makes his move.

*

By this time Torei had returned to Shoin-ji, a little healthier but still not strong. I was overjoyed to see him and immediately appointed him my personal attendant, to the great disgust of some of the older monks.

He's hardly been here five minutes.

Just in the door.

And there he is at the master's right hand.

He's no more than a boy.

No substance.

A puff of wind would blow him away.

He still stinks of Zen.

And the rest.

I overheard a group of them, outside my room, cutting Torei to shreds with their words. Without opening the shoji screen I roared at them, told them they were the ones who stank, and I knew who they were, and if they continued their niggling and backbiting I would personally kick their arses and send the lot of them packing. They fell silent, moved away from my door.

The same useless halfwits were even more critical of Eboku.

He's a layabout and a drunkard.

The bastard son of some nobleman in Edo.

That would make sense.

The arrogance of the man.

I doubt he's read a scripture in his life.

Wouldn't recognise a koan if it headbutted him in the face.

This time I didn't even waste words on them. I just let out a roar that scattered them. Next time I saw them, huddled outside the meditation hall, I glared at them, gave them my tiger-eye, and that dispersed them even more quickly.

I continued to instruct Eboku through the game of *Go* and in direct, individual teaching, challenging him, facing him down. Torei, as my assistant, was the only other person who knew about these sessions, and he kept the information to himself.

The two men were utter opposites, and they skirted round each other with a wariness that grew into a grudging respect. In Eboku's presence, Torei would be even more formal and procedural, precise to the point of fastidiousness. Eboku for his part would exaggerate his own quirks. He would swear loudly, make a point of swigging sake from a flask, then belch as he recited a verse from one of the sutras.

The truth of it was more complicated. One evening I showed them some of each other's brushwork, and neither could conceal their astonished surprise.

Eboku's drawings were the model of classical restraint, traditional in composition, skilled in execution. Even when painting a subject like Kanzan and Jittoku, the crazy Zen hermits, they were rendered with precision, a delicacy and elegance that was quite unexpected.

Even more unexpected was the breathtaking vigour of Torei's paintings. They manifested a freedom and boldness I had rarely encountered, a briskness and confidence, a sureness of touch. With broad strokes and a fluidity of line, he imbued the work with dynamic energy, pure chi.

Where Eboku's calligraphy was neat, compositionally correct, Torei's lettering spilled all over the page, flowed from the drawing itself, extended its meaning.

Now, I said. Who is the traditionalist? Who is the wild man? Who upholds the rules? Who is burning the temple to the ground?

They both laughed, and from then on they saw each other with fresh eyes.

*

When I had driven Eboku through the Zen barriers, when he had attained experience of kensho, he agreed it was time to assume an appropriate name. After much thought he decided on the name Suio because it contained the character *sui*, meaning drunk.

Why would you choose such a name? asked one of the older monks, one of the crew who had continually criticised him.

My love for sake is endless, he said. My thirst is unquench-able.

It is inappropriate, said the monk, not quite suppressing his irritation.

What does the master say? asked Eboku, turning to me, a smile twitching at the corner of his mouth.

I thought for a moment, wrote another character, also pronounced *sui*, but which meant accomplished.

Eboku laughed.

Does this meet with your approval? I asked the older monk, and he nodded, growled.

Again Eboku laughed.

Suio it is, he said.

*

Suio had no time for formal teaching and had no intention of ever becoming a teacher himself.

I would rather descend into hell, he said.

For a true teacher, I said, that's exactly what is required.

So I was surprised to hear that a monk had come to visit him in his retreat, seeking guidance. Not only that, but Suio had told him to meditate on the *Mu* koan and the monk had come to him for instruction a number of times over three years. Now it was almost time for the monk to return to his home in Ryukyu, in the far south.

And is he enlightened? I asked Suio.

It seems not. He regrets having to return across the water and show his face back home.

So what have you advised him?

I told him not to be discouraged but to continue his meditation for seven more days.

A week went by and I asked Suio for news.

No change, said Suio. He still makes no progress.

And what did you tell him?

To try for seven days more.

Another week went by and I asked the same question. Is he enlightened?

Not yet, said Suio. I told him many great masters had achieved satori by meditating for twenty-one days.

So he's giving it another week?

Yes.

A third week passed.

Well? I asked Suio, but I could tell by his expression there was still no change.

He is ready to give up and go home, said Suio.

Give him one final instruction, I said. Tell him to meditate for three more days.

And then?

If he doesn't attain enlightenment, he should just kill himself.

Suio laughed, then looked worried.

Three days later he returned.

So, I said. What about your monk from Ryukyu?

He meditated for three days, like a man who was going to die.

317

And?

He was awakened. He has gone home with a shining face.

I laughed.

See what a fine teacher you would make!

*

Once again Torei had to return to his home in Omi, this time because his mother was ill. By the time she had recovered and he had come back to Shoin-ji, his own health was once more in decline. Now his lungs were badly affected, and deep breathing was difficult.

The local doctor was my good friend Ishii Gentoku. He attended meditations at Shoin-ji as a lay brother, and he was generous with his time when it came to treating the monks. He examined Torei, prescribed a few herbs, treated him with moxibustion, but the diagnosis was not good.

It's a very bad case of what *you* would call Zen sickness, he said. A physician might say he'd had tuberculosis, or pleurisy.

These are the forms of Zen sickness, I said. These are its outer names.

Torei shivered, coughed, spat up blood. I continued to teach him the techniques of *naikan* introspection, and he rallied a little. But the poverty at Shoin-ji, the lack of nourishing food, had weakened him considerably. Going home again was out of the question, so reluctantly he agreed to go to Kyoto, to the mother-temple Myoshin-ji. I gave him an old coat of mine that had once been warm but was now threadbare and moth-eaten. He wrapped it round his thin shoulders, set off on the journey we both thought might be his last.

*

Suio had not visited Shoin-ji for months. He had gone to a remote spot, to Kumano, to meditate alone, far from any distractions. When he finally showed up again, his face had the smug inwardness of do-nothing Zen. I railed at him.

So the noise and bustle around here were unbearable. You couldn't take it and you ran off into the mountains to commune with rocks and streams. You went looking for peace. Well, where did that get you?

I wanted to jolt him out of it, but I don't think I'd ever directed my anger at him so powerfully, and for the first time I saw him flinch.

Take yourself out through the gate, I said, and walk along the Tokaido. Look, really look, at the streams of people passing by, at the farmers and labourers, the merchants and pedlars. Look at the donkeys and packhorses, carrying their loads. Look at the samurai and the travelling players, the fishwives and courtesans. Go in and out of the inns and teahouses, the public baths. Walk along between the great rows of pine trees, look across the rice fields to Fuji. Walk to Numazu, or on to Shinagawa, or all the way to Edo itself. Watch the endless traffic, the great hordes of people crossing every bridge, going in and out of the great temples. It is endless, it never stops, the bustle and movement, the teeming life. And all of this, all of it, is the great body of the Buddha.

For once Suio had nothing to say for himself.

*

As it happened, the following week a Korean delegation came along the Tokaido on the way to Edo, passing through Hara and right past the temple gates. They would be here to promote trade, and at the head of the little procession was a troupe

319

of performers, musicians and dancers, jugglers and acrobats, led by three horsemen showing off their skills. They wore bright tunics, and their routine was breathtaking. On horseback, and without saddles, they spun and leaped and balanced, did tricks that seemed impossible. One stood on his head. A second bent right over backwards, body, arms and legs forming an arch. The third stood upright, riding two horses at once, one foot on the back of each. Then they rode round in circles, jumped on and off, changed places. It was dizzying, and the crowd lining the road applauded and cheered, and the monks joined in.

You see? I said to Suio. Are they not magnificent?

He gave a half smile, grudging, reluctant.

Later I did a painting of the three horsemen, tried to capture their movement, their sheer life-energy.

Underneath I wrote a poem.

> *Korean acrobats horse-riding bareback,*
> *as one, galloping round and round.*
> *See them bend and twist, leap*
> *on and off, on and off.*

I handed the painting to Suio.

Buddha-body, I said. Buddha-mind.

He bowed, grateful.

*

I had heard rumours that Torei was preparing to die, and was writing a book he might leave behind for others following the Zen path, to pass on the little he thought he had learned. A visitor from Kyoto brought me a parcel, beautifully wrapped in handmade paper. It was Torei's book, *The Undying Lamp of Zen*.

He had written an inscription, dedicating the book to me and thanking me for communicating the teaching and enabling him to break through and face death with equanimity. On the title page he had written, *Great Faith, Great Doubt, Great Determination.*

I lit the lamp in my room and settled to read the book through the night.

At dawn I put the book aside with a deep sense of humility. This disciple of mine had written a work of great power and simplicity. It would open the gates of Zen for many generations to come. I remembered old Shoju's words to me. *The old winds of Zen will blow once more throughout the land.*

I stepped outside in the early morning light and stretched my old limbs, heard my very bones creak and crack. Then I went back inside and wrote a letter expressing my gratitude and pride. I inscribed a poem and drew a carp, swimming through the words.

A golden carp swims through the weeds of Omi's great waters.
He overcomes all obstacles and passes through the Dragon Gate.
Now he is free to play in the poison waves of Buddha-ocean.
Performing true charity, he gives not a drop to others.

I entrusted the scroll to a young monk who was leaving for Kyoto that very day and who would deliver it to Torei at Myoshin-ji.

*

In the next letter I received from Torei, he was elated. His writing of the book, and my response to it, had broken down further barriers. He had stepped into a profound satori.

With your help, he wrote, I have grasped the marvellous realisation you inhabit every day.

321

He intensified his meditation, and miraculously his health began to improve. Again he returned to Shoin-ji, again I welcomed him with great joy.

I had been discussing him with those senior monks who had been so eager to dismiss him. I had shown them Torei's book, *The Undying Lamp*, so they might understand the depth of his understanding. Still they refused to recognise his worth, and I lost patience, shouted at them.

Fools! If you cannot recognise this man's worth from his writings, how can you begin to understand the scriptures? How can you value what is written about the ancients and the great masters? Can you not grasp the power of the word?

Not one of them made a reply, and a few days later I presented Torei with the gold-brocade robe I had been given on my installation as abbot at Shoin-ji. I was hoping to appoint him as my successor, but he was reluctant.

I am grateful for this gift, he said. But I am not ready to teach, and I cannot succeed you at Shoin-ji.

That is your decision to make, I said, and only yours.

But some time later I approached him again with another scheme. There was a run-down temple, Muryo-ji, in the nearby village of Hina. I mentioned that the temple was in an advanced state of decay, worse even than Shoin-ji when I first arrived. Unless someone were to take over as head priest, temporarily at least, then Muryo-ji would simply cease to exist.

However small the temple, I said, however dilapidated, it is a centre for spreading the Dharma, and its disappearance would be a great loss.

I let the idea settle, hang in the air.

And you want me to go there, he said at last.

That is indeed a thought, I said, as if it had not occurred to me.

I left him to ponder the matter, and he grappled with it as if it were the fiercest most poisonous koan. After a night of intense zazen he came to me, haggard and wretched, dark lines under his eyes.

This was not what I had in mind, he said, when I left my home and followed the Zen path. My aim was to pursue enlightenment at all costs, and I still have much to learn in terms of my own training.

I left a silence.

On the other hand, I said.

On the other hand, he said. You are asking me to do this, and if I don't, the temple will disappear into nothing.

This is true, I said. But the decision is still yours to make, and only yours.

There was another silence, longer. It began to rain, and we listened to the steady drip, drip, drip on the leaky roof.

Finally Torei spoke. I will do it, he said. But, with respect, I will insist on a number of conditions.

That is your privilege, I said.

First, he said, the position at Muryo-ji is self-existent and sufficient. It is not a stepping-stone to succeeding you here at Shoin-ji, and you will not try to persuade me otherwise.

Agreed, I said.

Second, at Muryo-ji all decisions concerning the running of the place will be made by me and me alone. Nobody else will interfere.

He looked at me pointedly and repeated, *Nobody*.

Of course, I said. That goes without saying.

He allowed himself the faintest smile at that, continued to his third point.

I have always vowed to be free, he said, and not to be tied down to any one place.

I understand, I said.

323

So, if I choose, I can move on at any time, and hand over the running of Muryo-ji to someone else.

I see no problem with any of these conditions, I said.

Good.

Then I am talking to the new head priest at Muryo-ji.

So it would appear, he said, as if he had been tricked and couldn't quite believe it had happened.

Have a cup of tea, I said, and I poured it, whisked the bright green brew to a froth.

*

In time I was forced, as I knew I would be, to renege on the first of my promises to Torei. I asked him to consider becoming my successor at Shoin-ji.

It was as if I had challenged him with the most difficult, most vicious, most poisonous of koans. He became agitated, distraught. For a few days he would avert his gaze when he met me, rush off on some pretext so he didn't have to talk. Eventually I collared him, asked if he had made his decision. He said he would give it one more night of intense zazen so he could proceed with a clear mind.

In the morning he stood before me, looking worse than ever, his shoulders clenched, his eyes sunk deep in their sockets.

Well? I said.

It is not a simple matter, he said.

I am growing older by the minute, I said, even as we stand here.

So, before I decide, he said, I would first like to make a short visit to the shrine at Mount Akiba, to pray for your continued health and long life.

I knew he was simply delaying, giving himself more time, but I agreed to his request.

If that is what you wish, I said. And your concern for my welfare is touching.

The shrine was in Totomi province, not a great distance away. He would be back in a few days and I could press him for a decision. But a week went by, then two weeks, and there was no sign of Torei and no word from him. I stood at the gate one day, looking into the far distance, perhaps hoping I would see him on the road. And there was a figure approaching, someone in monk's robes, definitely heading this way. But as the figure drew closer, I realised it was Suio.

Showing up for your tuppenceworth of instruction? I said.

I'm sorry if you were expecting somebody else, he said. I'm just who I am. No more but no less.

Rascal! I said, and he bowed and walked past me, went in through the gate. But then he stopped and turned back, facing me.

If you are looking for Torei, he said, there is something perhaps I should tell you.

Indeed?

He happened to speak to me before he left, and he was in great turmoil about your request.

Yes.

He felt there was nothing he could do but run away and go into hiding.

I see. So he's not in Totomi?

I heard a rumour he had gone to Kyoto and was in retreat at the mother temple.

Myoshin-ji.

That's the rumour, for what it's worth.

We stood for a few moments in silence. The breeze blew. Fuji appeared from mist and haze, disappeared again, reappeared.

Oh well, I said. If Torei won't take over the running of this place, I'll have to ask you.

325

Suio threw back his head and laughed so hard he was in tears and had to wipe his face with his sleeve.

Abbot Suio! he said, and the very thought started him laughing again.

*

A few days later the nun Esho-ni came to visit me at Shoin-ji. She had on occasion taken instruction from Torei, and he had stopped to visit her on his way to Kyoto.

His heart was heavy, she said, but he exhorted me to continue my practice and fulfil the Four Great Vows. He also copied out a poem he had written.

She unrolled a small piece of paper, smoothed it out and placed it before me. I read the poem, in Torei's unmistakable script.

Leaving myself behind,
In what world will I see again
The floating island of Hara?

I thanked Esho-ni for her thoughtfulness in coming to see me and letting me read the poem. When she'd gone, I wrote it out on another sheet of paper, added a drawing with a few strokes of the brush, Fuji in the distance, Hara like an island floating in the mist.

I sent it to Torei in Kyoto, adding the words he himself had inscribed in his copy of *The Undying Lamp.*
Great Faith. Great Doubt. Great Determination.

326

SEVEN

OHASHI

Among the increasing number of lay followers who came to Shoin-ji to listen to my outpourings of venomous wisdom was a middle-aged businessman, Layman Isso. He had married late, and I knew nothing about his wife. Then one day he asked if she could come with him to hear my teachings.

Of course, I said. By all means.

She is an extraordinary woman, he said, and her story is a remarkable one.

I assumed he was just besotted with her, but the following week he brought her to the temple, and it was clear she was indeed out of the ordinary. Her name was Ohashi and she was perhaps in her thirties, classically beautiful in a way that would still turn men's heads, even dressed as she was in plain simple robes. But more than that, there was an inwardness, a seriousness about her. It seemed to me she had known great sadness, great struggle, had won through to an acceptance and a gratitude at finding herself here.

One evening, after I had given a brief talk on the Blue Cliff Record, I noticed her sitting very still, deep in meditation. I asked her and her husband to stay behind and join me for tea, and I asked if she would mind telling me her story.

She composed herself, glanced at her husband who nodded

329

encouragement. Then she began, slowly at first, a little uncertain.

My father was a high official serving the Daimyo of Kofu, she said. We lived comfortably in splendid surroundings. We had servants attending to our every need. Then our circumstances changed.

She paused a moment, her voice wavering.

That is the nature of circumstances, I said, pouring her more tea. She sipped it and continued.

My father was forced to leave the Daimyo's service. It was over a trifling matter, but a matter of honour. So he had to go.

Of course.

He was forced to live as a ronin, a masterless samurai. We went to Kyoto where we knew nobody. We had nowhere permanent to stay and moved from place to place.

This is how we live on earth, I said.

Our money ran out, she said. My mother and father grew haggard and thin. My mother fell ill. I couldn't bear to watch her fade away. Then I realised there was something I could do.

Once again she paused. Again I filled her cup but she stared at it, lost in remembering.

I was young, she continued at last. I understood men found me beautiful. I said they could sell me into service as a courtesan.

Her husband Isso cleared his throat, shifted on his cushion. Ohashi glanced across at him, gave a faint smile, continued.

My mother said she would rather starve to death. She said any parents who did such a thing to their child were worse than animals. My father remained silent. His mouth was a grim, straight line. His silence filled the room. It was difficult to breathe. Eventually I spoke again. I said any child who watched her parents starve was less than human. I said I would do this thing, it would only be for a short time, till our fortunes changed and we could be together again as a family.

My mother wept and said it was contrary to the Buddha's law. From somewhere, born of desperation, I found the right words and grew eloquent. I said the Buddha spoke of Expedient Means, used to spread his wisdom. This course of action would simply be expedient, a necessity in the short term, and perhaps this too would be a kind of wisdom.

My father left the room then, his face set, an angry mask. I heard him let out a great roar of rage and pain and some piece of furniture clattered to the ground. When he came back in, his expression was blank, desolate.

You are right, he said. There is no other way.

A week later I was handed over to the madam in a Kyoto teahouse, to begin my training.

She looked at the tea in her bowl going cold. The light in the room was fading, and one of the young monks approached and asked if he should light the lamp. I thanked him and asked if he might also bring more hot water to replenish the tea. This he did, with a brisk efficiency, then he bowed and removed himself.

I waited till Ohashi seemed ready to resume her tale, nodded to her.

This is a story of great sacrifice, I said. Such a thing is rare in one so young.

She bowed.

Necessity, she said. Expediency.

A kind of wisdom.

At first, she said, I convinced myself it was not so bad. The madam, in her way, was kind. She did not ask me to . . . *be* . . . with many men. And she was very selective, chose only men who would be gentle and considerate.

331

Again Isso-san tensed and shifted on his cushion, cleared his throat loudly. Again she glanced across at him, reassuring.

And of course, she said, I received an education. I learned to play the koto, I studied poetry and calligraphy . . .

She plays beautifully, said Isso. Her calligraphy is fluid and expressive. Her waka poetry is sublime.

She smiled at him.

You are too kind.

So it was all very . . . refined, I said.

Yes.

But still . . .

Yes, she said. Still.

Her face was half in shadow, the lamplight flickering in the room. But I could see the deep sadness in her eyes, the set of her mouth. She spoke quietly.

It was a kind of hell, she said, however comfortable. I had no freedom, no life of my own. I had been cast out of paradise, and the worst of it was remembering my former happiness. I grew wretched and fell ill. The madam sent for the finest doctors she knew. Some of them were her customers! But none of them could help me.

Some illnesses are beyond cure, I said.

This was a sickness of the heart, she said. Born of despair.

So how did you conquer it? I asked.

She smiled.

One of my . . . patrons . . . was a young man from a noble family who had studied with a Zen master.

Not one of those do-nothing layabouts, I hope.

She looked confused.

I have no idea, she said.

Forgive me, I said. I was just launching into a familiar rant! Now, please, continue.

He said there was a cure, and its name was detachment. I

332

simply had to detach myself from my seeing, hearing, feeling and knowing.

Simply, I said.

He said, Concentrate your full attention on only two questions. Who is it that sees? Who is it that hears? If you can do this in the midst of your everyday activities, whatever they may be, then your inborn Buddha-nature will come to the fore. This is the only way to go beyond and free yourself from this world of suffering.

Sound advice, I said, but not such a simple matter to put into practice.

I did my best, she said, and it definitely helped. But I felt so far away from realisation, and I longed to meet a true master who could teach me.

Not easy in your situation, I said.

One night, she said, a few years ago, the whole city was battered by terrible storms. There were twenty-eight lightning strikes reported in Kyoto alone, she said. And since my childhood I had been terrified of lightning.

Her eyes grew wide as she remembered it. I nodded, recalling my own fear of hellfire.

I retreated to my room, she said, and closed all the windows and doors. I straightened my back and sat in meditation, confronting those questions. Who is it that sees? Who is it that hears? All of a sudden there was a flash of light and a deafening crash. A huge bolt of lightning had struck a tree in the garden and shaken the whole house. I completely lost consciousness and fell into a swoon.

She closed her eyes, shuddered as the memory overwhelmed her. Then she opened her eyes and looked out again, as if from somewhere else, and her voice grew quiet and calm.

When I came back to this world, she said, my seeing and hearing had completely changed.

Who is it that sees? Who is it that hears?

I had been jolted awake, she said. The world was a different place.

And yet it was the same place, I said. It was the seeing that was different.

Yes! she said, grateful that I understood.

An experience of kensho, I said.

This was what I thought, she said. But there was nobody I could ask. Now more than ever I wanted to meet a master who could help me. But my situation was still impossible. Then another customer had compassion for my plight. He offered to marry me.

Let me take you away from all this . . .

Yes. The madam agreed, in exchange for a substantial fee. I left the pleasure quarter for good, a free woman.

But this was not your present husband, I said, indicating my friend Layman Isso.

No, she said. This was my first husband, a kindly man with a good heart. He died two years ago and I met Isso-san and remarried. And now Isso-san has brought me here to sit at your feet.

Expedient Means, I said. The Buddha and his box of tricks.

*

From then on, Ohashi accompanied her husband every time he came to meditate or to hear my Dharma talks. One day they stopped and bowed to me as I was crossing the courtyard.

My wife is grateful to you, said Isso.

For what? I said. For spewing out more words? Pouring water into the ocean?

For accepting me, said Ohashi.

Sentient beings are numberless, I said.

334

And some masters think women are more difficult to save. Is that so? I said.

She smiled, said, Even the Buddha himself was reluctant to accept women as disciples.

It was his own son who persuaded him, said Isso. It was his own wife he accepted.

And what do you think, Isso-san? Was the Buddha right to change his mind?

That sounds to me like an insoluble koan, he said. Whatever way I answer will be wrong.

You have learned wisdom from your wife, I said.

Again she bowed, and I was moved to put something into words.

I owe much to my own mother, I said. I try to see her in every woman I meet. I try to see in all women the Bodhisattva Kannon herself.

I had never expressed this thought before. But as I spoke the words I knew them to be true.

In the coming months, Ohashi far surpassed her husband in meditation. One day they approached me and asked if she could be ordained as a nun.

I have played my role, said Isso.

Ohashi bowed to him in gratitude.

This too, I said.

Her head would be shaved, she would put on the robes and enter the imperial Hokyo-ji convent in Kyoto. She would adopt the name Erin.

*

The following year I received a visit from Layman Isso. He too had moved to Kyoto where he had business interests, and he kept contact with his wife. He brought a message from her to say the convent was not what she had expected, and if I should ever happen to be in Kyoto, perhaps I might visit Hokyo-ji and deliver a Dharma lecture.

As it happened, my next expedition was to western Honshu on the Inland Sea, where I gave a series of lectures. On the long journey back to Shoin-ji I stopped for a time in Kyoto at the great Myoshin-ji monastery to which our little temple was affiliated. I was made welcome and invited to give more talks, and I received a letter from the abbess at Hokyo-ji inviting me to visit the convent. Nuns from the other imperial convent, Kosho-in, would be in attendance. I accepted, wondering if Erin had been instrumental in my being invited.

The two abbesses were sisters, young princesses from the imperial household. They were both in their twenties and had been appointed as part of their own training, to ground them in Buddhist principles and deepen their understanding. They were the embodiment of charm and grace and refinement, but they were worlds away from the simplicity and rigour of convent life. They wore elegant silk kimonos, ate lavish meals prepared by their own cooks. They were surrounded by luxury and the temple chores were performed by a host of servants.

I recalled old Shoju admonishing us about monks who wallowed in luxury, lolling back on thick cushions, eating and drinking their fill, accepting it all as their due, lost in the mire of their own delusion.

Out of courtesy and deference I said nothing. But I resolved to compose a letter to the princesses on my return to Shoin-ji. As I was leaving the compound I saw Erin, standing back. She made three deep bows and I nodded to her and smiled.

*

336

In the letter I thanked the princesses for their hospitality, but said I had to make a few observations. I referred them to stories of great Zen figures, especially women, who had led lives of exemplary simplicity and frugality. I reminded them of the virtue of poverty. I humbly suggested they wear home-spun robes and eat only small amounts of plain food. I also suggested they send their servants back to the palace and perform the temple chores themselves.

The next time Layman Isso visited Shoin-ji, he said my letter was the talk of the capital.

To admonish the daughters of the emperor, he said. It is unheard of!

Perhaps the emperor will throw me in prison and cut out my tongue. But then again, I'm just a bumpkin from a small village. I don't know any better.

*

One night Erin appeared to me in a dream. She bowed to me as she had that last time I'd seen her, in Kyoto. Three bows. I hadn't heard from her in some time, and Layman Isso had been caught up in his work and unable to visit Shoin-ji. The day after my dream I saw him standing at the back of the room when I'd finished giving my lecture, and I knew without asking what he had come to tell me.

Erin had suffered a recurrence of the illness she had suffered as a young woman. This time nothing could help, not even the introspection I had taught her.

Perhaps that gave her those few precious years, I said.

I am sure of it, said Isso, a choke in his voice.

Those early years were difficult, I said, and full of suffering. But they led her to you, to this life.

I am grateful, he said, and so was she. It was her wish that

337

her ashes be buried here at Shoin-ji. And I would ask that you make an offering of incense on her behalf.

I would be honoured, I said.

On the appointed day I approached the shrine, ready to make my offering, and I noticed there was no mortuary tablet in Erin's name. Instead there was a small votive statue of Bodhisattva Kannon. I turned to Layman Isso who was standing with folded hands.

I brought the statue, he said, to be dedicated in her name. Erin studied the Dharma in a woman's form. She gained enlightenment in a woman's form. She spread the teaching in a woman's form. For me she was an incarnation of Kannon herself.

I nodded and lit the incense, bowed and chanted to the Bodhisattva.

Enmei Jikku Kannon Gyo.

Isso joined me and his wavering voice grew strong as the incense smoke rose.

Enmei Jikku Kannon Gyo.

The little statue glowed as if alive.

THE SOUND OF
ONE HAND

I had kept contact with Torei in Kyoto, bombarded him with letters, reminders that I had chosen him as my Dharma-heir and he deserved that accolade, but repeating that I would put no more pressure on him to take over at Shoin-ji. In time he believed me, and we made peace. We came to an arrangement about the running of Muryo-ji, and when he was not there, or in Kyoto, he would visit me at Shoin-ji. I even asked if he would consider writing my biography, and he said it would be an honour.

One evening I sat with him and Suio and a handful of other monks. I had been driving their koan practice, pushing them to meditate further on *Mu*, enter into its nothing and go beyond. Now I drew the symbol for death – *Shi* – as I had when my father died, repeated the inscription I had written at that time.

> *Death*
> *a one-word*
> *koan.*

I instructed them to meditate on this, as they would on any other koan.

To see into your own nature, I said, you must enter into this *death*, into the word itself and the reality behind it. Whether walking or standing, sitting or lying down, not caught up in action, not lost in contemplation, simply address this koan.

I placed the drawing in front of them, left a silence, then I continued.

When you are dead and your body has been burned, reduced to ash, what then? Where are *you*, the main character, the principal actor in this drama?

Again I sat in silence, let them look at the drawing.

Death, I said. The very word is ugly to us and fills us with fear. Yet if you concentrate on it fully, with your whole being, you will be filled with a kind of joy. If you penetrate this koan, it becomes the key to unlock the Buddha realm, beyond birth and death.

A sudden heavy shower of rain began to fall, and the wind drove it hard against the shoji screens.

A warrior who has not faced this koan, I continued, will be weak and feeble on the battlefield, cowardly and fearful, unable to act. But master the koan, go beyond your own death, and your actions will be resolute. Your consciousness will be firm as a great rock, solid as a mountain range, vast as the sea.

The wind drove the rain even harder, battered the screens.

You die, I said, and your body is burned. What then?

*

Over the next week I saw them, day and night, meditating on the koan. Torei made his own brush-drawing of *Shi* – vigorously executed in half a dozen bold strokes – and he lost himself in contemplation of that, the word itself, the symbol. Suio took to sitting in the graveyard, under the pines, confronting the reality of his own death.

340

I didn't have to summon them to come and sit before me. They came willingly, Torei first, then Suio.

Well? I said to Torei.

He unrolled a scroll with his latest version of *Shi*. The lines were still fluid and strong but he had thinned the ink, so the character itself looked translucent, as if written on water, in air.

Shining through, I said. What then?

He took the paper and tore it in half, threw the pieces aside.

Ah! I said, nodding. And then?

He took the pieces and tore them again, then again.

Ever smaller, I said. And after that?

I'll burn them, he said.

And the ash?

Blown by the wind, he said. Dissolved in the rain.

And what remains?

Who is asking? He said. Who wants to know?

I took one of the small pieces of paper. Beside me was an iron incense holder, blackened with soot. I rubbed my finger in it, drew *Shi* on the scrap of paper and handed it back to Torei. He took it reverently, touched it to his forehead, then tore it in half, threw the pieces aside.

There's no end to it, he said.

I laughed. So clear up this mess and get on with your practice.

*

Suio looked haggard, dark lines under his staring eyes.

What's this? I said. You look like something the cat dragged in.

We die, he said.

Yes, I said.

341

I knew this before, he said. But not . . .

Not in your bones. Not with every living breath.

I could see it. The quality of that *knowing* had deepened in him.

We die, he said.

We die, I said. And knowing this, how do we live?

Knowing this, we live.

We live.

*

I continued to drive the monks through koan practice. Both Suio and Torei had gained strength from their meditation on *Shi*. Now I urged them deeper into the heart of *Mu*.

Where is this nothing? Where does it reside?

One winter evening I had spoken to them in turn, Torei then Suio. I had coaxed and cajoled them, pushed them further. Now I sat alone, far into the night, questioning, as the lamp burned low. I saw their faces before me, earnest, intent on breaking through. I saw myself, just as earnest, determined to pass on what I thought I'd understood. A great laugh burst out of me.

Old fart! I shouted, in the empty room, and I clapped my hands.

My head was suddenly a huge cavern, and the sound of my handclap seemed to echo and fill the space. I looked at my hands, held in front of me. I folded them in *gassho*, then looked at them again, separate, and a question formulated itself, took words.

When you clap your hands together, it makes this sharp sound, distinctive and unmistakable.

I clapped my hands again, listened.

But what is the sound of just one hand?

342

Sekishu no onjo.

I raised my right hand in front of me, palm facing out.

What do we hear in the empty valley? The echo of the soundless sound.

*

Next morning I sat again in front of Torei and Suio and half a dozen others.

So, I said. I have a new koan for you.

They straightened their backs, sat attentive. I continued.

Sound is made by striking two things together.

I raised both my hands, then swiftly brought them together in a sharp slap. One monk twitched, startled. The others folded their hands, waited. I clapped my hands again, harder, and the sound was louder.

Two hands clapping, I said.

I raised the right hand only.

But what is this sound, the sound of one hand?

I sat for some time in silence, the hand raised, then spoke again.

It is not an outer sound. It cannot be heard with the ear.

I left another silence, hand still raised.

In fact it is beyond all hearing, distinct from all perception.

Further silence.

Beyond all difference, all discrimination.

Outside the wind blew, a crow called.

Meditate on this koan, I said. The sound of one hand. Proceed with it. Enter into it. Do not give up. Whatever you are doing, walking or standing, sitting or lying down. The sound of one hand. Eventually you will reach the place where reason is exhausted and there are no more words. *The phoenix will escape the golden net. The crane will fly free.*

343

Outside, the wind blowing, the crow calling.

Enter into this soundless sound and see through all the worlds, your own world here and now, and all the realms of heaven and hell. Enter into vast perfection, vast emptiness.

I raised my right hand again, palm out.

Abhaya Mudra. The gesture made by Shakyamuni Buddha on attaining enlightenment.

One hand.

Listen.

*

Once again I picked up my brush, did a drawing of Hotei seated on a meditation cushion – a great sack stuffed with all his wealth, the blessings of good fortune he bestowed on mankind. His hand raised in benediction, he smiled his mischievous, knowing inner smile. Behind him I drew a spray of plum blossom in a bamboo vase, and down the left-hand margin of the painting I wrote an inscription.

> *You think you understand anything?*
> *Unless you hear the sound of one hand*
> *It's all just nonsense.*
> *May as well stretch a skin*
> *Over a wooden koto.*

I found the image strangely satisfying and it made me smile, I imagined, with the same smile I had drawn on Hotei's face. Skin on a koto. Animal hide stretched taut over the beautiful paulownia wood, making the instrument impossible to play. The thought of it would cause anguish, that great ball of discomfort in the chest, rising into the throat, a good koan doing its work.

Ha!
I continued with another verse.

> *You think you just have to dig in the ground*
> *To unearth ingots of pure gold?*
> *You'll have to work hard to hear*
> *The sound of one hand.*

The drawings continued to flow. A monkey hanging from a branch over a pool of water, reaching out with his free hand, trying to grab the moon reflected there.

> *The monkey tries to grasp*
> *the moon in the water,*
> *again and again until*
> *death grabs him.*

> *If only he'd let go of the branch,*
> *dive into the deep pool,*
> *the world itself would shine,*
> *dazzling, clear.*

I sat a while longer, made another drawing, playful. It showed a smaller monkey, a character, hand cupped behind his ear as if straining to hear some far-off sound.

> *Is he listening*
> *to the cuckoo?*
> *The monkey holding up*
> *one hand.*

I set down the brush, smiled, listened.

I watched them struggle with the koan – grapple with it, grab it by the throat, laugh at it, smile and approach it sideways, turn their back on it, rage at it, ignore it and hope it would go away. If any of them caught my eye, in the meditation hall, on their way out to beg, looking up, mindless, from some seemingly menial task, I would raise my right hand, glower or smile, and say nothing.

They sweated over it, they ground their teeth and clenched their fists. But the fact that it was new to them, a fresh challenge, an unexplored path, meant they made fast progress, and one by one they broke through the barrier, experienced kensho, heard the soundless sound.

And after the Sound of One Hand, I said, what then?

I came up with my own answer, challenged them further.

Go beyond, I said. Put a stop to all sounds.

Vast emptiness. Vast silence.

Stop. All. Sounds.

One of the younger monks looked stunned. He had come this far, made headway with the koan, experienced his first kensho. Now this. This.

There's nothing else, I said, but to keep going. Your life is as short as the span of an insect that's born at dawn and dies at dusk. But even if you lived like one of the immortals, for a hundred thousand seasons, it would all be just froth and foam, the flickering of illusory flowers. Your days are like wild horses galloping by, just glimpsed through a crack in the wall.

The young monk straightened his back, grimly determined, his mouth a tight line.

For fear of hell, I said, you gave up the outer life. Looking for certainty in the world of transience is like trusting a blind donkey to lead you. You gave up comfort and security. You turned away from human love, from affection and family life. For what?

I left a pause in which he didn't answer.

I had asked myself these self-same questions as a young man.

For this, I said. To be here. Now, concentrate. Put a stop to all sounds.

*

It is like the ocean, I said. The further you enter in, the deeper it gets.

It is like the mountain. The further you climb, the higher it gets.

*

Continue. Go on.

*

Silence at the heart of sound. Sound in the depths of silence. And beyond both?

*

Again they broke through, one by one, in their own time. They entered the gateless gate, heard the soundless sound. I could see it in them, in their eyes. I could hear it in the way they spoke. They rang true.

For each one who crossed the barrier and achieved kensho I made a drawing, a priest's staff carved from a single sturdy branch, a Zen teacher's whisk wrapped round it, a smaller branch entwined round its base. The whole staff in the process of changing into a dragon, its head at the top. A moment of transformation. Underneath I wrote *Hearing the Sound of One Hand. Putting a Stop to All Sounds.* And trailing down the scroll I wrote lines from the *Hekiganroku* with a declaration from master Ummon.

> *My staff has transformed itself into a dragon*
> *And swallowed up the whole great universe.*
> *Where are mountains, rivers, the world itself?*

Each drawing was unique. Each dragon had a life and a character of its own.

To remind you, I said to each monk as I handed over the scroll. Now roar!

*

In time I drove some of my lay students through this twofold koan. Sound of One Hand. A Stop to All Sounds. It turned them inside out more quickly, more effectively, than Joshu's *Mu*. And to each of them also I gave the Dragon Staff Scroll as a kind of certificate of graduation. Without exception they received it with profound gratitude, often moved to tears.

But once I was visited by an old priest who had travelled from another temple. He had heard about the scrolls and came to Shoin-ji to take me to task.

You're heading straight for hell, he said, for the sin of unremitting flattery. You're debasing the Dharma, devaluing the teaching.

Great enlightened being, I said, do tell me more.

Your pieces of paper are worthless he said. You might as well wipe your arse on them and hand them out to these gullible fools.

Don't hold back, I said. Rain down your hammer-blows on me!

You make light of it, said the priest, his voice squeaking higher, his face reddening. But some of these idiots think by earning this useless certificate they have attained enlightenment. They give up their practice and go back to wallowing in ignorance.

And how do you know this?

I have ears, he said. I can hear.

Hear what? I said. Rumour? Gossip? Better to hear the Sound of One Hand. Better to Put a Stop to all Sounds.

Are you trying to offer me your spurious wisdom?

No point, I said. Pouring water into a bowl that's full to the brim. You're full of yourself, full to bursting. No room for a single drop of my venom.

He glared at me, eyes vicious.

You exploit these people, he said. You take their money and fob them off with a piece of paper.

Now it was my turn to glare, tiger-eyed. I left a silence the length of three long breaths. Then I spoke again.

Each and every Dragon Staff Scroll was issued on merit. These men and women may be lay followers, but their realisation was genuine and hard earned. They sweated white beads. They persevered and broke through.

Most convenient, said the priest.

Many lay followers make donations to Shoin-ji, I said. Survival would be even more difficult without them. But not all those who pay receive the scroll. And not all who receive the scroll have paid. Attaining kensho is not easy, and I would never diminish the experience in the way you suggest. I give the scrolls only to those who have crossed the barrier and gained insight.

He snorted, clearly unwilling to be convinced. He wiped his nose with the back of his hand.

349

Mind you, I said, in your case I might make an exception. If you hand me a sheet of paper, I'll gladly wipe my arse on it as an acknowledgement of your great spiritual attainment.

He stood up to go, neck muscles tensed as he constrained himself to make the slightest, most perfunctory bow.

Everything I've heard about you is true, he said.

It's been an honour to meet you too, I said. I look forward to seeing you again in hell.

*

When the priest had gone I chuckled to myself. Arse-wipe! Then I thought I could make a story of the incident, tell a tale that might reach some of those very lay followers he had been talking about. The Buddha's message had to spread ever wider. Beat the Dharma drum.

I would give the story a supernatural element, make it an otherworldly tale of spirit possession, a message from the beyond.

A bitter twisted old priest condemns the practice of issuing Dragon Staff certificates to mark attainment of kensho. He has harsh words for the monk responsible – let's call him Hakuin.

A young man named Yukichi is praying at the local Inari shrine and is possessed by the presiding Shinto deity.

A crowd gathers to hear as the young man beats a drum. He wails in the singsong incantatory voice of the spirit that speaks through him.

He says the monk – yes, we'll call him Hakuin – is absolutely right to do what he's doing. The certificates he has issued are thoroughly merited and issued personally by Hakuin to each student who has attained kensho. Far from

350

encouraging laziness and complacency, becoming an end in themselves, they inspire the students to continue, to work even harder.

Let the dragon continue to roar.

Let all sentient beings be enlightened.

I read the story to a few of the monks.

Another tale from the Night Boat? asked Torei.

Another, I said.

*

I told more tales, alongside my formal lectures. I made more drawings, wrote more poems and songs. And this too was teaching. All of it. Direct transmission. Expedient means.

*

I drew an iron grindstone from the tea ceremony, and on its rim a tiny ant.

> *Endlessly circling the rim of a grindstone,*
> *The tiny ant goes round and round.*
> *Round and round without rest.*
> *We're born, we die. Then what?*
> *For liberation we have to hear*
> *The sound of one hand.*

*

A long thin bridge, a single log, spanning a ravine, and three spindly figures crossing it, blind men with their canes, edging forward.

Blind men crossing a chasm — that's us.
Our lives, this fleeting world, a log bridge.
How to cross to the other side?

*

An old monkey-trainer, laughing as he makes a little monkey dance to the beat of a drum, played by another smiling figure in the foreground. The trainer holds the monkey by a string and carries a thin stick to beat time.

> *He tames his monkey-mind*
> *And makes it dance.*
> *Monkey and master linked together*
> *In the void, in all the worlds.*

*

Two white foxes, dressed, like the monkey, in trousers and smocks, up on two legs, and like the monkey, dancing, playing. They look knowing. Are they the guardians of Inari shrine?

> *White foxes — are you*
> *full of yourselves,*
> *bewitching us?*

*

Pilgrims making a circuit of thirty-three temples, many of them determined to leave their mark in passing, write their name on a wall, scrawl an aphorism, some observation. The same urge in me, perhaps, that has me write this, leave these drawings, these scribbles. I was here. I existed. I passed through.

In this drawing two pilgrims are in front of an official notice, high on the wall. One has climbed on the other's back so he can reach up to write something on the notice. The one reaching up has a sash on his back. *Bodhisattva Kannon Official Tour.*

The notice reads, *Absolutely No Graffiti. By Order.* Across it, the pilgrim has written, *So sorry!*

*

This too.

*

The Seven Gods of Good Fortune. I've drawn them celebrating New Year, enjoying the festivities. Daikoku with his mallet is pounding grain – a good harvest, prosperity.

Shoki with his long beard is dancing. Hotei beats a big drum. At the back is Fukurokuju with his elongated head bumping the edge of the frame. He's playing a smaller hand-drum, as is Jurojen, and Benzaiten blows on a bamboo flute. Ebisu is reading a manuscript, chanting a verse from the noh play on Shoki in his role as demon-slayer.

The mice that inhabit some of my other drawings are here too, dressed as monks and priests, courtiers and street entertainers. They dance attendance on Daikoku, gathering round him. Behind him is a banner with another inscription.

> *Without extravagance, no greed.*
> *Without laziness, no poverty.*
> *Be loyal and devoted*
> *And I'll give you all I have.*

On his hat is written *Ju*, the symbol for longevity.

The blessings of all the gods, showering down.

It's one great party, on the good ship *Long Life*.

*

Long Life.

I painted the symbol, larger, in the centre of another scroll.

JU

The very form of it held a power. Gazing intently at the word, or chanting it out loud, was an invocation of all that is benign, all that the gods bestow on true followers of the Buddha-way. In itself it is a spell against the dark, a magic amulet.

JU

The sage Liao-fu drank the waters of a sacred spring and lived to be 150 years old.

I could see Torei raise a quizzical eyebrow at that, but say nothing.

In Liao-fu's honour, the character *Ju* was carved in the wall of the cliff above the spring. It was written large, then surrounded by 100 smaller versions of the same character.

I did the same with my scroll. Around the symbol I had painted I wrote it 100 times more, each time subtly different.

Always different, always the same.

The finished scroll was a mandala. It directly invoked the power of the word.

JU

Developing the theme, I quickly made another painting with 100 more versions of *Ju*, but in the centre I placed a drawing of Fukurokuju with his great elongated head, a brush in his hand as if he himself had just painted the hundred versions.

354

Underneath I added a verse in which the god praised the efficacy of the painting, saying it was the equal of the Lotus Sutra. He indicated also that he had been specially commissioned to do the painting by Old Man Hakuin.

Arrogance? Sacrilege?

Fukurokuju's smile.

JU

After the gods, the demons. After heaven, hell.

I made a scroll depicting one hundred demons, conjured them from my imagination, from childhood nightmares, from drawings I'd seen by other artists, generation after generation invoking the same tormented beings, facing them down. There were creatures I recognised, remembered from my own encounters with the other worlds – ghosts and spirits and goblins and ghouls. The huge demon that had entered my room on Mount Iwataki and croaked out my name. *Ekaku . . . Ekaku . . .*

I drew him the way I remembered, fierce and threatening. I gave him a long beaklike nose and bulging eyes, named him Tengu.

I drew horned devils and *gaki*, hungry ghosts. I drew a tall fearsome goblin with one staring eye in the centre of his forehead. In front of him I drew a blind man with a stick squaring up to him.

> *Growl away, one-eyed goblin.*
> *You don't scare me.*
> *I have no eyes at all,*
> *I can see beyond seeing.*
> *You're the one who should be afraid!*

Laugh at them and send them packing. That was the way to deal with these creatures of the night. By the time I'd finished

355

painting, the scroll was covered with them, fighting for space, crowding each other out. The way it would be in hell.

*

I took another sheet of paper, drew Shoki the demon-slayer preparing to make a huge pot of soup. The ingredients are four demons he's grinding down to make miso for the broth. The demons look up at him in torment, but he's relentless, grinding, grinding, using a mortar and pestle. A small boy, Shoki's son, helps by holding the bowl steady. He's grinning, eager to taste the concoction.

> *By far the best miso —*
> *I can't wait to try*
> *this demon-soup!*

*

Another image of Shoki, almost identical, looking down, not into a grinding-bowl, or a cooking pot, but into a pool, and startled to see his own face looking back at him. The last demon he has to face.

PRECIOUS
MIRROR CAVE

O ut along the Izu peninsula was a cave that had
gained a reputation as a sacred place, a shrine where
pilgrims – those who had eyes to see – could behold
a miraculous vision. There were some who saw nothing, or
dismissed what they saw as a trick of the light, a chance
formation of rock worn down by the waves. But for others,
what they saw was transformative, a glimpse into the Pure
Land.

The stories went back more than a century, to an old
fisherman who lived in the small village of Teishi. He was
miserable in his work, forced to kill thousands of fish, each
one a sentient being. He knew he was nearing the end of his
life, and he felt he was piling up terrible karma, day after day,
and would be punished for it in this world or the next.

He started chanting the Nembutsu, invoking the compassion
of Amida Buddha. Whatever his sins, Amida would forgive
him and protect him from harm. He chanted the Nembutsu
night and day, with great intensity and devotion. He focused
on it with total concentration to the exclusion of all else. It
was more important to him than eating or sleeping. There
were days when he even forgot to look after his nets or cast
them on the water. The Nembutsu was everything and he

357

chanted it constantly, on dry land, in his boat close to the shore or far out on the ocean. He chanted at dawn, at noon, at twilight, in the dark night.

Namu Amida Butsu.

Namu Amida Butsu.

This was his real work.

One evening as the light began to fade he was returning to shore and saw in the distance a strange glow playing on the surface of the water. He steered his boat towards it and saw that it seemed to be coming from a cave, almost hidden, at the foot of a sheer cliff. By the time he got close to it, the glow had disappeared and the dark had closed in. He could barely see into the mouth of the cave, and the rise and swell of the waves carried him dangerously close to the cliff. At high tide, he could see, the waters would flood in and completely fill the cave. He resolved to come back in daylight when the tide was low.

A few days later he returned to the spot and negotiated the entrance to the cave, using his oar as a pole against the rock walls, easing his boat inside. Although outside the sun was high in the sky, in the cave it was dark, and the darkness deepened the further in he went, until it was total, all engulfing. He couldn't see the boat, not his own body, not his hand in front of his face, not the tip of his own nose. He could see nothing. He shivered and his legs shook. He lost all sense of direction. In the midst of the void he folded his hands and chanted.

Namu Amida Butsu.

Namu Amida Butsu.

His mind grew calm, empty. A great stillness pervaded him. He opened his eyes and saw that the walls of the cave were glowing with a soft light, a wonderful radiance, and he seemed to breathe in a rare and subtle fragrance. As he gazed and continued to chant, there in the heart of the

358

light three figures took shape, the form of Amida Buddha flanked by his attendant Bodhisattvas. The fisherman lost all bodily consciousness, felt suffused with light, became nothing but light itself.

When he returned to his everyday self, inhabited his body once more, there were tears streaming down his face. He sensed that hours had passed and he heard the waves crashing into the cave. He knew if he didn't move quickly, the waters would block his exit and swamp the boat. He bowed farewell to the three holy figures and again used his oar to pole his way out, through the cave-mouth to the open sea, all the time still chanting the Nembutsu.

When he returned to shore, the villagers saw he had changed. He inhabited a great stillness and an inner light shone from his face. He told them of the vision he had been granted, and from that day on, the cave became a place of pilgrimage.

*

I had heard this story as a child growing up in Hara. The Izu peninsula was not far away, and tall tales were common currency along the Tokaido, told and retold in the inns and way-stations. Some small incident would be told as a story, then become a parable, grow into legend or myth. The Fisherman and the Cave was one such story, and I had heard many first-hand accounts from pilgrims who had gone to the place and seen the light for themselves.

One particularly bumptious layman had recently visited Shoin-ji and told us of his own experience. He was eager to quote a great priest who said, A man of great faith sees a great Buddha. A man of little faith sees a little Buddha. A man of no faith sees nothing at all.

And what did you see? I asked the layman.

Ah, he said, and he cast his glance downwards with an air of humility and self-effacement. There were some, he said, who were clearly struggling, peering into the darkness and rubbing their eyes, then looking around them with barely disguised scorn.

The layman mimicked the seekers he described, rubbing his own eyes, looking bemused. Someone chuckled.

There were others, he said, who clearly saw something, but it was small and indistinct, barely discernible.

He indicated the size of the pathetic vision, a few inches high.

And you? I asked again. What did you see?

Once more he cast his gaze down to the ground, then he straightened up and puffed out his chest.

The three figures, he said. The Buddha and his two celestial attendants. Twenty, no, thirty feet high, radiating golden light.

His eyes shone as he grew intoxicated by his own words.

I could hear heavenly music, the like of which I'd never heard. The air was filled with a fragrance I'd never known.

He dabbed his eyes with his sleeve, sniffed loudly.

It was wonderful, he said. Glorious.

Indeed, I said. Perhaps I should visit this wondrous cave myself and gain a glimpse of the Pure Land.

You must, he said. You must.

*

As it happened, I had occasion to visit Izu a few weeks later. I was delivering a Dharma talk on the Unreal and the Real, and I took the opportunity to slip away and travel by boat to Teishi on the southern tip of the peninsula. This was where the old fisherman had lived and I put up for the night at a cheap inn. It was winter and only a handful of pilgrims had arrived in the village, ready to visit the cave at the first low tide. There were four of us, waiting on the shore in the morning – two middle-aged businessmen, a young monk and myself, this old reprobate on his endless journey.

The older of the businessmen had travelled from Kyoto. He was shrivelled and thin, shivered in the cold even though he was wrapped in layers of clothes. The doctors had told him he didn't have long to live, and he had come here in expectation of seeing the shining form of Amida Buddha, praying to him for mercy and whatever grace he might bestow.

The other businessman was dismissive. He lived not far away, in Numazu, and he'd heard so many stories about the cave that he'd come to examine the phenomenon, settle an argument or two.

As far as I'm concerned, he said, it's all illusion. The figures are some stunted rock formation, weathered by the sea. They just happen to resemble the Buddha and the Bodhisattvas. It's pure chance, and folk are so desperate and gullible they see what they want to see.

And what about the light? said the sick man.

Phosphorescence, said the other. Something in the seawater on the walls of the cave. You see it out at sea sometimes, way down in the deep.

The sick man looked around, desperate, caught the young monk's eye.

You, he said. You believe.

The monk was counting his prayer beads between finger and thumb, silently chanting the Nembutsu. He replied without pausing.

I expect nothing. This is a holy place. I come to pay my respects.

And you? said the sick man, turning to me.

The Buddha gives to each of us according to our needs, I said. Let us see what we shall see.

At that, the boatman appeared, a solid, stocky man, perhaps in his forties. His manner was gruff, businesslike, but not unkind. He helped each of us, in turn, into the boat, and pushed off. He made no small talk but concentrated fully on rowing, his stroke measured and rhythmic as we cleaved through the waves.

Offshore it was even colder. The wind scythed, cut to the bone. I wrapped my old robe tighter about me, pulled my hood up over my head and practised the *naikan* introspection that had saved me all these years. I felt the warmth in the navel centre drawn up to the chest and spread through my whole being. I felt compassion for the sick man, was sorry I could not teach him this. He huddled in the stern of the boat, wrapped in his layers, shivering.

The other man, the doubter, clenched his teeth against the cold, stared straight ahead. The young monk kept his eyes closed, telling his beads, chanting his prayer. The boatman rowed.

The journey only took half an hour, perhaps less. The boatman steered us into the mouth of the cave – it was maybe twenty feet across, the cliffs towering above. We were carried in on a sudden surge, turned a bend and were engulfed by the darkness. It was total and it closed us in. Not a glimmer of light penetrated. We sat in the heart of the void.

I could hear the lapping of the waves against the boat, the young monk chanting the Nembutsu.

Now, said the boatman. Wait.

The waves lapped. The monk chanted.

Faintly, faintly, a light began to spread at the far end of the cave, and silhouetted against it I could see the three figures, just as they had been described. I couldn't make out the faces, but the shapes, the configuration, were unmistakable. Amida Buddha flanked by the two Bodhisattvas. I heard the sick man moan, the other man let out a gasp, and the young monk continued to chant. *Namu Amida Butsu.*

I joined him, folding my hands in *gassho.*

Namu Amida Butsu.

The others added their voices, and the boatman joined in.

Namu Amida Butsu.

Namu Amida Butsu.

Above the dank salty smell of the cave I could sense a subtle fragrance, like jasmine. Then the sick man let out a howl of pain, and the light faded, and we were back once more in the dark.

On the journey back to shore the businessman was chattering, ecstatic.

I can't believe it, he said. I saw it. It was real. It was larger than life.

The boatman laughed.

Another satisfied customer!

And you, said the businessman, turning to the young monk. Your chanting certainly worked!

It was there, said the monk. Small and indistinct, but definitely there.

And you? he asked me, eager.

Yes, I said. I saw.

He looked at the sick man, didn't ask. But after a time the sick man spoke, his voice desolate.

I saw nothing, he said. I saw the darkness. I saw my own death.

*

I was troubled by the fact that the faces of the Buddha and his attendants had been indistinct and I hadn't been able to see them clearly. Perhaps I had been distracted by my companions, by their anxiety and need, their arrogance and desperation. Perhaps the fault was my own and in spite of all my introspection I was simply not receptive. Whatever the truth of it, I resolved to visit the cave again.

I'd meditated at the hour of the ox, and it was still dark when I made my way from the inn down to the shore. The cold had teeth, the wind off the sea was vicious, and my feet in their old straw sandals slipped and sank into the shifting shingle at every step, grit between my toes. The only light was a faint glow from the boatman's hut – a patchwork construction that looked as if it might be swept away by wind and wave at any moment. I stood in front of the door, and before I could announce my presence, the boatman called out a greeting and invited me to enter. I stepped inside and bowed to him, and he stood up and bowed in return.

Sensei, he said. I am honoured by your visit.

It was warm after the cold outside, and my numbed hands and feet began to thaw. The room was dim and smoky, from the little oil lamp sputtering, from the soot-blacked iron stove in the corner, burning wood, from the boatman's bamboo pipe which he had just laid aside. And in amongst the thick mix of smells was a tang of cooked fish, the redolence of old incense.

Please, said the boatman, and he cleared space for me to sit on the tatami.

I sat cross-legged and looked round the room. Against the far wall was a little shrine, lit by a single candle, and in its flickering light I saw three standing figures, the Buddha and his two attendants, exactly as they appeared in the cave. I drew breath in amazement, bowed to the figures.

An old friend of mine carved these from driftwood, after he'd been to the cave. The robes and the features I painted myself.

A wonderful likeness, I said, and I bowed again.

I thought perhaps . . . he began, then faltered, uncertain.

You thought what?

There are many people who cannot make the journey to the cave, he said. They may be too old, or infirm, or the tides may be too high at the time they are here. I thought if they were to see these figures, they might at least feel something of Amida's presence.

I was suddenly, deeply moved by this act of compassion, the man's understanding and single-mindedness.

The Buddha is here, he said, just as much as he is in the cave. Those who have eyes, let them see.

We sat for a moment in silence, and I gazed at the little images, the three figures in the flickering candlelight, and they seemed alive. I nodded to the boatman and smiled, bowed. He brought out a little flask and two small ceramic cups, asked if I would like a little sake to warm me against the cold. I thanked him, said yes. He poured and I sipped, felt the slight burn of it in my throat, the warmth spreading in my chest.

Perhaps not as powerful as *naikan* meditation, I said. But a good quick short-term remedy.

Sakasaraba! he said, raising his own cup. He swigged the sake, then picked up the pipe he'd set down. He caught my glance, asked if I would also like a smoke. Again I thanked him, said yes.

Purely medicinal, he said. Fortification on a cold winter morning.

He took down another pipe from a rack, filled it and handed it to me, lit it with a taper then lit his own. We sat puffing away, content.

This too, I said.

Like two old Chinese sages.

Han-Shan and Shih-Te.

The sweet fragrant smoke filled the little hut.

Nevertheless, I said. I would like to visit the cave once more.

He nodded, said simply, Yes.

An hour later, the sky still not light, I sat in the back of the boat as it pulled out from shore. The wind whipped even harder, freezing, drove icy spray into our faces. Again I wrapped my old frayed robe tight about me, entered into *naikan*, generating warmth. When we reached the cave, the sun had still not risen over the horizon. Seabirds screeched and shrieked above the cliff face. The boatman held steady against the tide, negotiated the entrance to the cave, caught the swell and we were inside. This time the darkness was even deeper than before, dark within dark, intense and palpable. I could feel it on my skin, then in an instant there was no barrier, no distinction between myself and the dark. I inhabited it. The darkness was in me. I *was* the dark.

Then it happened, as it had before. It began with the faintest glimmer of light, barely discernible, then little by little it spread along the far wall. The boat creaked and rocked, and the boatman chanted, *Namu Amida Butsu*. The light increased and the figures took shape, stood before us. Another surge carried us closer and they loomed above, the height of a man or larger. I heard my own voice joining in the chant. *Namu Amida Butsu*. The faces grew clear, distinct, the two Bodhisattvas serene, inward, the Buddha radiant, all compassion. He smiled down at me and tears of gratitude were flowing down my face. They tasted sweet.

*

Back in the boatman's hut, he gave me a little cooked rice and pickle, a bowl of miso soup. I told him he was offering a great service to the Buddha, both in taking pilgrims to the cave and in setting up his little shrine.

I feel I have a duty, he said. And perhaps I can alleviate my past karma.

You are continuing the work of the fisherman who first discovered the cave.

There are those who think I *am* the fisherman, he said, and that I'm three hundred years old!

Like a master I met called Hakuyu, I said. But that's another story.

A tall tale, he said.

Perhaps.

He nodded, his eyes crinkled in mirth, and we sat for a time in companionable silence. Then I said I had a humble suggestion to make.

The cave has become known as Amida Cave, I said, and that is a good name, a fine name.

But you have a better idea.

Everyone who visits the cave sees what they see, depending on their faith, their spiritual development, their past karma. It's as if they are standing in front of a bright mirror that reflects back at them everything they are. I would give it a new name. I would call it the Precious Mirror Cave.

I recognised the look on his face, startled, as if he had been shocked awake, a moment of kensho. He folded his hands and bowed, repeated the words, quietly.

Precious Mirror Cave.

We sat a while longer, and I looked again at the features he'd painted on the little carved figures. I said he was clearly an artist, and I asked if he could spare a piece of paper, lend me a brush, an inkstone. He brought them out from an old wooden box under the shrine.

I unrolled the sheet of paper, moistened the inkstone, chewed the brush to soften it. I breathed in, and on the outbreath made a few quick strokes, outlined the three figures, the Buddha flanked by the Bodhisattvas. A few more strokes and the figures were complete, their faces compassionate, benign. Above the figures I inscribed a poem.

> *See just who you are*
> *In Amida's Precious*
> *Mirror Cave.*

The boatman smiled and nodded, deeply moved. I asked for another piece of paper, and this time I drew the outline of his boat and a figure seated in it. And I wrote another poem, the words drifting round the shape of the boat.

> *Steering his boat*
> *where it wants to go —*
> *Hotei out at sea.*

This time the boatman laughed and clapped his hands. Then we bowed to each other and chanted the Nembutsu one last time, and I took my leave and headed back to Shoin-ji.

ILLUSION AND PLAY

I added the story of the Precious Mirror Cave to my repertoire. One evening at Shoin-ji I told it to a few of the monks. I embellished it here and there in the telling, made it vivid and real.

Torei wrote down my words, asked if it was another tall tale.

You set out for the cave before dawn, he said, while it was still dark. Is this Night Boat on the Izu Peninsula? Night Boat in the Precious Mirror Cave?

Go there and see for yourself, I said. Then you'll know.

Later I took out my father's old inkstone and brush, unrolled a scroll of paper. I drew a rowing boat with no oars, Hotei lolling back in it, content, gazing up at the full moon emerging from a swirl of cloud. Above his head I wrote a poem, the words floating beneath the moon.

> *Here and now I'm Hotei,*
> *hands clasped behind my head,*
> *out in a boat, moon-viewing.*

*

Of all the gods I loved Hotei best. Now I saw him clearly. He stood in front of me, grinning, patting his fat belly. He shouldered his bag, wandered the city streets and remote villages, he played children's games, he sat in meditation. I drew him over and over again, and each time I drew him, his face more and more resembled my own.

*

Hotei carrying a great huge mallet over his shoulder, but hurrying along, his face calm.

> *This hammer's so heavy.*
> *Won't it kill me?*
> *Not at all!*

*

Hotei balancing a plate on the end of a long stick held between his teeth, at the same time juggling four balls.

> *Keep it all in the air!*
> *Keep it moving!*
> *Don't let it drop!*

*

Hotei looking up at a leather ball he's just kicked high in the air.

> *What's it all about?*
> *Just playing kickball.*
> *Boot it as high as you can!*

*

I spread the drawings around me on the tatami. Hotei the

370

boatman took me back to the boatman's hut in Teishi. I lit a pipe, savoured the sweet tarry smoke filling my lungs, spreading its mellow warmth.

Torei called from outside the door, announcing his presence, asking if he could come in. I knocked out the pipe in a little iron bowl, hid it behind me, waved away the smoke as best I could.

Exquisite incense, said Torei after he'd bowed.

Medicinal, I said. A comforting warmth.

Naikan in a pipe.

I nodded.

Just so.

These are new drawings, he said.

I'm becoming Hotei, I said. Or Hotei's becoming me.

They're excellent, he said, nodding.

Rascal! I said. You think you'll flatter your way to the Pure Land?

I'd fail at the first barrier, he said.

The doodlings of a madman, I said, looking at the drawings. But for all that, I suppose they're not bad.

I looked at the last one, Hotei booting the ball in the air, and I laughed.

Not bad at all!

Torei placed a sheaf of paper at my feet.

I wrote out your story again, he said, the one about the cave. I made a fair copy so it can be circulated. It really is a marvellous tale.

Told by the same madman, I said.

You should publish a collection of them, he said. Tales from the Night Boat.

Illusion on illusion, I said. But if they dupe one human being into wakefulness, they may just be worth the paper they're printed on.

I looked at the title page, Torei's fluid, cursive script. *Precious Mirror Cave.*

It's good, I said. Thank you. I'll copy it out in my own crude handwriting to be made into printers' blocks. Then we'll send it out to do its insidious work.

Torei bowed.

I'll inscribe it, I said. Written on the Day of One Great Vehicle, under the Full Moon of Suchness, in the Village of Tranquility, Incomprehensible District, by the Priest Flowers of Emptiness.

Disciple of High Priest Lighting-Flash-Morning-Dew, said Torei.

Of Dream-Vision Temple, on Self-Realisation Mountain.

Approved by Absolute Purity, Disciple of Perfect Unity.

Abbot of the Great Temple of Dedicating-Body-And-Soul to the Dharma.

Ha! Let anyone try arguing with that!

*

When Torei had gone, I looked again at the manuscript, the drawings scattered around me. Illusion on Illusion. Expedient devices. Beating the Dharma drum. This was the path I had chosen, and I would follow it till I breathed my last.

*

The boatman was a true man of Zen, selfless, plying his boat to the Buddha cave, carrying anyone who asked, man or woman, layman or monk, child or old crone, madman or saint. He didn't judge anyone, just took them to the place where they could see for themselves. And if that wasn't enough, he had made the shrine for those too old or fearful, too frail to make the journey.

I saw more clearly the nature of my own work, this post-satori practice.

I would walk the length and breadth of Japan, wherever I was invited, to preach the Dharma, continue my outpouring, my endless effluent. Torei would sweep up my leavings from the floor, shape them into books. Those who have ears, let them hear. Those who have the stomach for it, let them wolf it down.

I'd pour out other writings, make poems, crack jokes, tell tall tales. Cock and bull, shaggy dog. I'd mimic street songs, echo voices from the Floating World. Whatever it took.

*

I made more paintings of Hotei. Hotei as Hakuin. Hakuin as Hotei. Saint and madman. Holy fool. Sage and child. I worked on them – work that was play – through days and nights, barely sleeping, forgetting to eat.

*

Hotei walking with his bag slung over his shoulder.

*

Hotei sitting on his bag, meditating.

*

Hotei opening his bag with his mouth. (Hotei *eating* his bag!)

> *Nothing else for it –*
> *I'll eat this*
> *and have a cup of tea.*

373

*

Hotei's bag, left on the ground, just the bag, nothing else.

Where's he gone, this god,
this future Buddha?
He's nowhere to be found.
All he's left behind,
his old cloth bag.

*

Hotei concealed *inside* his bag, just his face visible as he peers out, grinning, at two little mice, sumo-wrestling. The tiny mice grappling, one lifting the other by the belt, the tiny mouse-referee looking on, ensuring fair play.

Here we are then —
the Great Sumo Contest
for mice!

*

Hotei flying high in the air, his bag inflated, a kite attached to a long string pulled by five tiny figures, straining to raise the kite higher and higher in the wind.

Heave away!
There goes Hotei
High as a kite!

*

Seen all together, the drawings of Hotei had even more of an energy. They told a story, *kamishibai* images to be shown on a screen. I looked at them, spread around me, and I laughed. It was the middle of the night and the wavering flame of the oil lamp made the images dance and flicker, as if the figures had a life of their own, were moving in their own world.

I stretched my old bones and rubbed my tired eyes. I filled a pipe and lit it with a taper from the lamp. I drew the smoke deep into my lungs, held, exhaled.

Ah!

Torei never remonstrated with me about the smoking. Exquisite incense. *Naikan* in a pipe. But he disapproved. It showed in the slight tightening of his upper lip, even as he joked. He was concerned for my welfare, and he was right. Old fool that I was. Tobacco and sugared sweets would be the death of me. And yet. Perhaps over the course of a long life, a little respite, a little ease, was permissible.

I finished the pipe and knocked out the ash in an iron dish. Then I took up the brush again, made a quick sketch of Hotei popping a sugared sweet in his mouth. I drew him again, massively content, with a pipe in his hand, blowing out a stream of smoke. Then as if the smoke itself had taken form, I saw in it the homely female figure of Ofuku, all things to all men. Serving girl in a teahouse, dispensing Zen, compassionate courtesan challenging orthodoxy, breaking barriers. I drew her like Hotei, smiling, and on the sleeve of her kimono I drew a plum blossom, a sign that she followed the life of the spirit. She was the prostitute Yamamba in the old noh play, attaining wisdom, helping others.

I thought of the remarkable young women I had known. Hana who had turned my head. Kazuko who had accused me. Satsu who had challenged me. Ohashi and her life of sacrifice.

With great care and great lightness of touch I added a few lines to the face, made my Ofuku the embodiment of happiness.

I set down my brush, clapped my hands and laughed.

*

Now Ofuku herself became the subject of my paintings. Ofuku grinding tea, surrounded by the paraphernalia of *chanoyu*. Ofuku whisking the tea in a bowl. Ofuku pouring the tea.

Hana, a lifetime ago, her movements deft and measured as she made the tea for me, the bright green froth. Our fingers touching as she handed me the bowl. The taste of Zen.

Once more I drew the plum blossom on Ofuku's sleeve, and I added the symbol *Ju* for long life. Happiness and long life, the life of the spirit. She poured more than tea. She bestowed wisdom and compassion, profound understanding. Her face shone with an inner light, the eyes twinkling.

> *She has time on her hands –*
> *she's grinding the finest tea*
> *just for you!*

*

Another image came to me, unbidden, and I was once more the mischievous child who had first picked up the brush, drawn that unruly dragon leaping between my legs. I smiled as I thought of him, the anguish he'd gone through. Now I found myself drawing the worldliest of men, wearing an elaborate robe. But he was down on his knees, a grimace on his face, the robe hoisted up to his waist, his arse sticking out. And behind him, also kneeling, was Ofuku, applying moxibustion.

Here's the cure
for your haemorrhoids —
a little fire!

Purification. Curing like with like. Fire with fire.

*

In that noh play, *Yamamba*, a famous courtesan meets a wise
old woman in the mountains, and they learn from each other.
I sketched the two figures. The courtesan became Ofuku. The
old woman's face looked remarkably like my own. Underneath
I wrote, *Ofuku meets Granny Mind-Master*.

It made me smile and I saw what I had to write. It would
have the quality of a sutra, instructional. It would bring in koans
and quote scripture. But the form of it would be like a street
song, earthy and knockabout. Those that had ears, let them hear.

*

On another trip to Kyoto, for another Dharma talk at
Myoshin-ji, I had once more accompanied the good doctor,
Ishii Gentoku, on a walk through the Floating World, the
realm of illusion and play. Just being there, he said, was a
tonic, a respite from worldly care, and he prescribed the visit
as an antidote to the harshness of life at Shoin-ji.

There was no puppet show this time, no meeting with
Chikamatsu who had passed on to the other shore. But we
did see another truly remarkable performance, by the great
kabuki actor Ichikawa Danjuro. He played an old medicine-
seller, the kind of character I'd seen often on the Tokaido,
peddling their remedies, hawking their wares. And Ichikawa
was thrilling, like the real thing but more so. A tall man, he

ruled the stage, splendid in a jacket of orange and black, trimmed with lucky coins and decorated with bright streamers. In one hand he carried a fan, in the other a bag containing *uiro*, a miracle medicine, guaranteed to cure all ills.

Diarrhoea? Constipation? *Uiro* is what you need. Marital troubles? Headaches? Hangover? Bad breath? *Uiro* will do the trick.

He mimicked the high singsong register of the actual street-sellers and added something entirely his own, musical, incantatory, mesmerising. The words poured out of him, rhythmic and fast-flowing, rhyming and punning and tongue-twisting, never missing a beat. He soared and he carried the audience with him, and they laughed and cheered and thundered their applause at him, a wave of sheer gratitude.

Gentoku had seen the glint in my eye, asked if this was how I would be peddling Zen. I'd laughed and said I could see it, I'd package my poison in a pill.

Step right up! Try Hakuin's snake-oil. It may stink of Zen, but just hold your nose. Take the potion and swallow it down. Better than *uiro* for effects that last. Unique Become-a-Buddha Formula. Enlightenment guaranteed!

*

I spread the word to the monks and a few lay followers that I would give a special Dharma talk at Shoin-ji, and on the appointed evening the lecture hall was full.

I began by announcing that the title of my presentation was *Old Granny Mind-Master and her Tea-Grinding Song*. Some of the younger monks chuckled in anticipation. Most of the older ones straightened their backs, looked straight ahead. The lay followers glanced around, bemused and uncertain.

It's really a talk for two voices, I explained, so I'll channel two characters and let them speak through me.

I breathed in, held, breathed out the voice of Ofuku, high-pitched and lilting.

> *I'm Ofuku – and no jokes, please!*
> *No need for that kind of sleaze.*
> *Never mind the grubby piss-take.*
> *Yes, I'm from the red light district.*
> *But not your ordinary hooker –*
> *fat face, big nose, I'm quite a looker.*
> *It doesn't matter what you say,*
> *I'm beautiful in my own way.*
> *They say my looks are Heaven's blessing.*
> *Well, Heaven's curse must be quite something!*
> *But I get love letters by the score*
> *and passing fancies even more.*
> *Don't take me for a one-night stand,*
> *some flirty, flighty bird-in-the-hand.*
> *A man-eater, is that what you think?*
> *I'll slay you with a nod and a wink.*
> *But listen to this, you can't go wrong.*
> *Hear Old Granny's tea-grinding song.*
> *With men of taste I'll sing it well.*
> *The rest of you can go to hell!*
> *You think I'm talking through my fanny?*
> *Here's the wisdom of Old Granny.*

There was laughter at that, as I knew there would be. But I cut across it, spoke in the other voice, the wail of an old crone.

> *Heaven's blessings, darkness and light,*
> *heat and cold, day and night.*
> *The winds will blow, the trees will bend,*
> *until time comes to an end.*

379

For all the blessings we're in debt,
something we must not forget
from life to life — remember that,
or you're no better than dog or cat.

I had them. Their attention was total, and I could sense there was something chilling about this cracked old voice coming out of my mouth.

Mind Master is what matters most —
without it you're a hungry ghost,
an empty house fallen to ruin,
with snakes and vermin overrun.
Without it great sages are nothing special,
the finest palace is just a hovel.
Meditation's a waste of time,
preaching's so much slobber and slime.
But living it, now that's the thing,
beyond all joy and suffering.
And who's in touch with this infinite chi?
Granny Mind-Master, that's me!

I spoke again as Ofuku.

Granny Mind-Master, how old are you?

I replied as Old Granny.

Old as the Void, I swear it's true.
Old Man Space could die any day.
But me? I'm really here to stay.

Again I was Ofuku. I could feel my face change back again.

380

Granny Mind-Master, where do you live?

Then Granny was replying, getting into full flow, spewing out philosophy, rattling off one koan after another.

> *That information I'll gladly give.*
> *I live in a shack in the Cinnabar Field*
> *where all life's ailments can be healed.*
> *It's just south of the navel centre.*
> *Go there, knock the door and enter.*
> *It's right beside the ocean of chi.*
> *Dive in and feel the energy.*
> *I know these koans through and through –*
> *The poisonous fangs of Joshu's Mu.*
> *Where do you go when you die?*
> *Stop that boat from sailing by.*
> *Scramble down the mountain trail*
> *in less than no time, do not fail.*
> *What's the colour of the wind?*
> *What's the sound of just one hand?*
> *I burned that monk's hut to the ground.*
> *His realisation was far from sound.*
> *(Live by the Dharma, embrace right action,*
> *but show at least a little compassion!)*
> *Jump the barriers, now, don't wait –*
> *the carp fly over the dragon gate*
> *the foxes leap Inari shrine.*
> *Fly high, you'll transcend space and time.*

Granny took a breath. Ofuku got in a quick response.

> *And after satori, Old Lady, what then?*
> *Do you just sit back and wallow in Zen?*

381

Granny wound up, concluded with a flourish.

> *Enlightenment is just the start –*
> *to pass it on's the hardest part.*
> *Even Yamamba the prostitute knew*
> *what was what, she saw it true.*
> *She saw it and she understood –*
> *preaching the Dharma's the greatest good.*
> *Find a true teacher, know his worth.*
> *Establish the Buddha-life on earth.*
> *Keep going, keep going, you have to try.*
> *And now Old Granny bids you goodbye.*

I bowed, first as Ofuku then as Granny. There was a slight uncertainty in the audience / congregation. Then they also bowed, and some applauded and one or two laughed. Suio looked irritated and left without saying a word. Torei said if he could have the text he would copy it out. Gentoku said he would make arrangements for publication.

I've already done the drawings, I said. I just need to add a few more verses to make the manuscript more substantial.

More weighty, said Gentoku.

Then I can thump folk on the head with it if they don't understand.

Whatever it takes, said Gentoku, bowing low.

STONE GARDEN

E ver since my childhood, looking up at great Fuji from Hara, I had taken inspiration from contemplating mountains. I drew strength from them, identified with their unshakable nature, rock-solid, grounded.

> *The winds blow —*
> *the mountain*
> *is unmoved.*

Even after Fuji had erupted, thrown fire and rock from its core, it had settled once more, secure in its own nature, the ground of its being. This was how we should be.

Because of this I had a weakness for stone gardens – a flat expanse of raked white sand or gravel, broken by a single well-placed rock. In the absence of real towering peaks, these scaled-down mountains could quicken the heart. Reducing it even further, I even loved bonsan and suiseki, the miniature landscape, the tiny rock garden laid out on a tray. I had collected a few of these over the years, and when I was sick at heart, it was a great solace to me, a great delight, to lose myself in these little worlds and to write about them.

I was born with a great love of rocks and streams —
In this little stone I see a huge mountain.
No one can climb this tiny peak.
No mountain on earth can surpass it.

The good doctor Ishii Gentoku diagnosed this obsession as a chronic illness, a form of desire that would eventually lead me to hell. Nevertheless, on the basis of treating like with like, he gave me the most wonderful gift – he made provision for an actual stone garden to be created at Shoin-ji.

From the moment he told me of his plan, I was as excited as a schoolboy on a feast-day, a young man anticipating a meeting with his love. I was anxious and eager, slept even less than usual, waking every night at the hour of the ox.

The ground was cleared and rolled flat, covered with pure white sand. But that was just the beginning. Doctor Ishii had arranged for a massive spirit-rock to be transported from the village of Hina at the very base of Mount Fuji. This was a huge task, an unimaginable undertaking that would require a whole squad of labourers. The rock would be hauled and dragged down to the riverside and loaded onto a great raft to be floated to the ocean, then towed by a bigger boat along the coast to the beach near Hara, and from there, somehow, it would be grappled and manhandled the short distance to Shoin-ji.

I was numbed at the thought of it, the enormity, the actuality, and more than once I told the good doctor it was too much and he should abandon his plan. But somehow he didn't quite believe I was being sincere.

In any case, he said, think of the merit I shall accumulate, the good karma.

Ah yes, I said. So, karmically, I am doing you a huge favour!

Indeed, he said, his eyes twinkling, and he bowed.

384

The night before the rock was due to arrive I didn't sleep at all. Well before dawn I was moving around the compound, calling out instructions. I browbeat the cook, the venerable Kakuzaemon, to get on with boiling up a huge pot of rice. It steamed and hissed on the stove, its lid clattering. I rounded up the youngest, strongest monks to be ready for the task ahead.

It was still dark as I paced up and down, anxious for the safety of the crew and their precious cargo. The mountain streams were swift and cold, their currents treacherous. The spirit-rock was no ordinary lump of stone. The river-gods would covet it for their own watery kingdom. They would try to capsize the raft at every turn. I invoked the protection of the mountain-gods and of Shakyamuni Buddha.

I marshalled my troops – the crew who had woven the bamboo ropes stood ready, there were lookouts stationed at every vantage point with instructions to call me as soon as the raft was sighted. I had barely sat down again to meditate, breathing deep to calm my excitement, when I heard shouts from outside.

One of the lookouts called out first – he was young and his eyesight was keen.

The raft! The magic rock!

I clattered in my wooden sandals down to the beach where everyone had gathered, shouting and cheering like the crowd at a country fair. The roars got louder with every surge that brought the raft closer to shore. I felt my own heart thud in my chest and I laughed with sheer exhilaration. The raftsmen were unharmed, the rock was safe. Shakyamuni and the mountain-gods had prevailed. What I didn't realise was that the hardest part of the work was still to come.

The weight of the rock was immense and pressed down on the raft that rode low in the water, buffeted this way and that by the tide. Steering was almost impossible and at every moment the top-heavy load threatened to tip over.

The bamboo ropes were cast out and lashed to the raft, and the monks on shore struggled to hold firm, their heels sinking into the sand. The other monks waded into the water, tried to heave and shove the raft ashore, but they lost their footing, staggered and fell, floundering in the crash of the waves.

As they stood up and regained their footing, a cheer went up. Doctor Ishii had arrived with his labourers – eight or nine of them, strong as wrestlers. Dressed only in loincloths, they too waded in, and at first, like the monks, they struggled to keep their feet. Three times they tried and failed, then something came right, the rhythm of it, and they all pushed together, caught the lift of the wave, and the raft pitched forward, and the great rock toppled over onto the sand. There was another cheer and the men punched the air in triumph then slumped to their knees, exhausted, catching their breath. The cook brought food for them – rice and soup – and water to drink, and they gathered their strength again. I thanked them all, overcome with gratitude for their efforts.

Now I could take a closer look at the rock, and it was magnificent, veined and patterned, mottled with bright green moss that seemed to glow.

Well? said Doctor Ishii. What do you think?

I am speechless, I said.

He laughed.

Now that is unusual!

I have no words, I said, to thank you for this.

He bowed, then spoke to the labourers again, said there

386

was still a long way to go, the temple garden was a distance away, and as in any undertaking the last part of the journey was often the most difficult.

I had no idea how true his words would prove to be.

For half an hour the workers grappled and heaved and strained to no effect. The rock didn't move an inch. Again they slumped to their knees, half dead from the effort. They took a hard-earned break, drew breath. The sweat ran down their backs. Grey sand clung to their bare feet and legs. Once more the cook brought them water in a stone jug and they glugged it down, cup after cup. Then as if they had been commanded, they stood up and spat on their palms, rubbed them together, pumped their fists and set to once more, heaving and straining, every muscle and sinew tensed. But the rock refused to budge, implacable, sunk in the wet sand, and for the first time the men looked despondent, beaten.

To have come so far.

Now here's a real koan to be solved, I said. Can we bend solid matter to our will? And what if the stone itself doesn't want to move?

The monks waited, expecting me to say more. The other workmen stared at me, vacant. I looked at the rock, felt the life of it, its sheer solid entity and presence.

Clearly we need a miracle, I said.

Nobody spoke. The tide lapped closer to the base of the rock. The wind picked up, the sky darkened as clouds went scudding across. Then in the distance, rising above the wind and the waves, came the sound of voices, calling together in unison, rhythmic. It faded out then rose again, caught by the wind, and gradually it came closer, distinguishable as a group of men, chanting.

One . . . Two . . . Three . . . Four . . .

They came into view, a dozen of them, led by another

387

friend and benefactor Nakai Zenzo. Each of the men carried a log over the right shoulder, swung the left arm wide for balance as they moved at a slow march, and as they got closer they alternated their counting with the Daimoku, chanted to the same rhythm.

Namu Myoho Renge Kyo . . .

They stopped beside the rock and Nakai stood in front of me, bowed deep.

Perhaps we can be of assistance, he said.

I think Shakyamuni himself has sent you, I said. Once he went to the mountain, now he is having the mountain brought to us!

I stood back as Nakai organised the men. The first log was placed on the sand, right against the rock, and the others were laid side by side, forming a kind of path. Then the men gathered behind the rock and Nakai ordered them into three rows, arms round each other's shoulders, interlinked, and they leaned and pushed forward into the rock, all their strength combined as they drove forward as one. At the third push, the rock tipped and toppled with a great crash onto the logs, and they gave but held, sank a little into the sand.

Now, said Nakai, and the men pushed again, and the rock eased forward a few inches as the logs rolled under it.

Here is your miracle, said Doctor Ishii.

I laughed.

The path itself is moving!

Ishii's labourers got in front of the rock and tied the bamboo ropes round it. They formed a line, like a tug-of-war team, and they pulled as Nakai's men pushed, and little by little, inch by inch, the rock moved up the beach, and across to the temple, and into the little area of pure white sand that sat there waiting for it. With one last almighty heave, the whole workforce pushing together, the rock juddered and came to rest, not quite in the centre of the garden, but a little to one side.

Wonderful, I said. It could not be better.

A great cheer went up from the monks and labourers alike. Ishii and Nakai were grinning at each other, then Ishii turned to me.

You've worked these men so hard, he said. You'll definitely go to hell!

Well then, I said, you and I will meet there and discuss philosophy for all eternity.

The cook was ushering everyone inside to sit and eat – I could smell the rice and vegetables, the fish stock, the noodles and broth. And for a moment everything seemed to slow down, and I saw it all with the vivid clarity of a dream. I saw the tiredness in every face, the sheer effort that had gone into the task, but shining through that was a kind of joy, and once again I was overwhelmed with gratitude.

*

For the second night in a row I didn't sleep. At first light, as the monks in the meditation hall chanted the sutras, I went outside and stood in front of the rock, walked round it, looked at it from every side. From one angle it looked like an ancient dragon, the moss on its back bright emerald green, from another it was a towering mountain peak. All around it the sand had been scattered, the ground rutted and churned up, by the sheer brute physical work of heaving and dragging, cajoling it into place. I fetched my rake and a flat-bladed spade and I set about levelling the ground again, raking the sand into patterns around the rock, concentric circles, ripples spreading out. A great sense of purity entered into me, right into my bones, permeated my entire being.

I sat cross-legged in front of the rock, back straight, and entered into zazen. Now the rock had the dignity of a venerable sage, immersed in meditation, beyond all resentment and desire. The sky lightened and I sat on, rock-like, adamantine, unshakable.

EIGHT

DUST UNDER
THE PINES

Life at Shoin-ji continued from year to year, moved at its own pace, followed its own necessity. One time, one place. The little community of Hara had its own exist- ence, linked to us but separate, dreaming its own dream at the foot of Great Fuji. But along the Tokaido came news of the wider world, of politics and commerce, wealth and power. From Edo and Kyoto came rumour and gossip, tales of scandal and intrigue.

Inu-Kubo the Dog Shogun had died, murdered, they said, by his wife who then, conveniently, killed herself. The successor was a six-year-old child who only lived a few more years. I imagined the drama Chikamatsu would have made of it all, his little puppets, more than human, bringing the stories to life.

The present Shogun was Yoshimune, by all accounts wily and cultured. It was said he imported foreign books, spoke of trading with the barbarians in the even wider world, far to the West. He drove through reforms, raised taxes, brought a measure of stability and prosperity, at least for the wealthy merchants.

*

Rations at Shoin-ji were meagre at the best of times. The monks subsisted, survived, on a handful of rice a day. On good days there might be a dash of fish broth, a few drops of *shoyu* – with or without maggots – a little pickle. I watched them endure, grow thin and dried out. Their skin grew pallid, drawn taut over their bones. But their eyes shone, their will was strong, their inner fire burned.

Then everything changed for the worse. A summer of drought was followed by winter storms. The rice crop failed. Locusts blackened the fields, stripped them of anything that had managed to grow. The people went hungry and had nothing to spare.

And yet that very summer the Daimyo's procession had passed along the Tokaido, right past the temple gates, bigger and louder, brasher and more extravagant than ever. And how had he paid for this excessive display? By raising the taxes, taking an ever higher percentage of the rice crop, the little the farmers had managed to grow.

To those who have, it shall be given. From those who have not, it shall be taken away. That had a fine Zen ring to it, ironic. But the reality was bitter and wretched and bleak. People were starving, and dying.

I railed against it all in a talk to the monks and laymen. Torei wrote down what I said, kept a record. I quoted from my story of Hakuyu in his cave. Torei looked up a moment, quizzical, then continued writing.

When a ruler becomes caught up in his own greed and self-interest, his ministers usurp power for themselves, and no one gives a moment's thought to the abject poverty and suffering of ordinary folk. The people go hungry and sick. Famine and starvation are rife throughout the land.

This is what we are seeing, I said. These Daimyo live in luxury with never a thought for the poor, except to bleed them dry. It is their blood and sweat that pays for the Daimyo's indulgence, the food and drink, the vast entourage of retainers. It pays for the dancing girls and prostitutes gathered from the pleasure quarters of Kyoto, used for a time and cast aside, replaced over and over. And every time they are replaced, at greater cost, the Daimyo sends out his ruthless ministers to raise the taxes again and again.

And when there are summer droughts and winter storms, and the crops fail, the people are left with nothing. They starve and sicken and die.

I stopped for a moment, looked at the monks, themselves suffering and undernourished, but every one of them listening, attentive. Torei's brush paused, resumed when I continued.

Unless the Shogun himself intervenes, the people will rise up and rebel. They will turn on the ministers and petty officials. And who can blame them?

> *A cornered rat*
> *will bite a cat.*

And it will not end there. The uprising will continue till the government itself is overthrown.

I folded my hands and bowed to these frail, brave monks. *Sentient beings are numberless*, I chanted.

Together, as one, they gave the response. *We vow to save them all.*

*

I made a painting of Fuji for the Abbot of far-off Jisho-ji temple in Kyushu. I laid out a large sheet of paper and sketched in the shape of the mountain in three strokes, then filled in the background so the mountain stood out white and clear, dominating the landscape.

I remembered the simple drawing I had once done, the poem I had written.

> *Miss Fuji,*
> *Cast aside your hazy robe*
> *And show me your snowy skin.*

I had glimpsed that beautiful woman, a courtesan, looking out at me as she passed by in her palanquin. The Daimyo's procession. I remembered it all, the great army of retainers and attendants, the pikeman pissing in the dust.

In this new painting I drew a few figures on the lower slopes of Fuji, two of them seated, gazing up at the mountain, three of them, pilgrims, making their way along the path. The scene was one of simple devotion, tranquillity, the mountain majestic, transcendent.

Below that I drew the Daimyo's procession in all its busy intensity, snaking along the Tokaido, the tiny figures walking forward, not looking up.

I set down my brush, stood in front of the painting, taking it in, and Torei joined me.

They cannot see what is in front of them, he said. They ignore the great truth towering above them. They are caught up in worldly show, marching towards oblivion.

The Daimyo are born to great wealth, I said, and can do great good. This is because of merit from past lives. But if they forget this and misuse their power, they are bound straight for hell.

*

The news along the Tokaido was grimmer every day. Now the talk was of famine, pure and simple. Hundreds, perhaps thousands of people had perished. There were bodies in fields and forests, on riverbanks and right by the side of the road. We heard stories of old folk just walking out into the night, refusing to be a burden. And hardened though we were to *samsara*, to suffering on earth, there were tales that made us weep, of newborn babies left out in the cold to die, culled by families who could not feed one more hungry mouth.

A petty official of the Daimyo, a miserable cur in human form, passed through the village, encouraging the practice.

It was far better, he said, to abandon these excess children, leave them to freeze and starve, rather than beating them to death, crushing them with stones at birth, which was usual in some other, more barbaric provinces in the far north.

I felt a great rage when Torei told me this.

Perhaps the Shogun should order a cull of petty officials.

Perhaps, said Torei, his voice lifeless, flat.

Existence is suffering.

This too.

The monks could do little to help. They too were growing weaker, falling sick. Some of them left while they could still walk, made for Numazu where there might at least be a little food, or they headed home to be with parents who might be dying.

My own family home, the old inn, was closed and boarded up. Hara was a ghost town, overrun with rats. The good doctor Gentoku himself fell ill and took to his bed.

I ate only a mouthful of rice gruel a day, sipped a little rainwater. The skin on my belly hung slack. I no longer resembled Hotei.

On the anniversary of Bodhidharma's death, we sat in meditation, no more than twenty of us, skeletons in black robes. I was moved to compose a verse.

Great angry winds sweep the land,
Scattering demons, idle spirits.
Twenty brave men, iron-willed
Chew on nothing, savour emptiness.

The twenty became fifteen, then ten, as one by one they sickened and died.

Many of them were young, had arrived eager to learn. I had bombarded them, beaten and pummelled the teaching into them, and they had taken it, year after year, uncomplaining, heroic. Now they were dust under the pine trees. They had come from emptiness, dwelled in emptiness, returned to emptiness.

And yet.

I missed them all. Old Kakuzaemon gone. He said he would cook for us all in the great cauldron of hell. And Teki who had looked after the cat and its descendants. And Gedatsu who came back for my watery Dharma-gruel. Jun and Ko who had pushed me to publish my books.

I grieved for them, and the rest of the monks, and for all of humanity. I wept.

*

Time passed. The seasons turned. Crops grew again. The survivors got on with their lives. I looked at those gravestones in the little cemetery under the pines. I resolved to write a letter to Ikeda Tsugumasa, Daimyo of Okayama. I had heard he was a serious man, practised in meditation and the art of the brush. Among his class, perhaps he alone might listen to my words, might consider the need for reform.

I summoned Torei to my quarters, said I would dictate the letter if he would kindly write it down.

My calligraphy grows ever more illegible, I said. Thick,

clumsy strokes, one word confused with another, mistakes everywhere. I know your own style can be as slapdash as mine, but I also know you can be painstaking and meticulous when you need to be.

He bowed.

Every stroke of your brush is imbued with your life-force, your chi, he said. But it is an honour to copy your words. I shall be careful, and attentive.

And I shall be concise, I said.

I began by addressing the Daimyo with the utmost formality, showing the greatest possible respect. I expressed the profound sadness I felt on contemplating the recent famine, the loss of life on such a scale in our province and throughout Japan. I mentioned our own losses at Shoin-ji.

As a monk, I said, I had vowed to alleviate suffering, and I knew that he, as a follower of the Buddha-way, would uphold the same principle.

I paused and Torei looked up, waiting.

However . . . he said.

However comes later, I said. *But* comes later still.

I continued, expressing my sympathy for the Daimyo's own burdens, not least the necessity of having to comply with the Shogun's directive that a residence be maintained in Edo for the Daimyo's wife and family.

Where they are effectively held hostage, said Torei, to ensure the Daimyo's loyalty.

That's the truth of it, I said. But it's not always necessary to express the truth so directly. Now . . .

However?

Not yet.

I understood, I said in the letter, that this meant the Daimyo had to travel back and forth to Edo and would have to be accompanied by members of his household.

More than a thousand of them, said Torei.

Perhaps you should hand me the brush, I said, and dictate the letter yourself.

I wouldn't dream of it, he said, and he dipped the brush in the ink once more.

Well then, I said.

However?

However, I said, and I pointed out to the Daimyo that the sheer scale of the processions, the massive numbers in the entourage and retinue, could be perceived as excessive and extravagant. It is argued that it is necessary for protection, that without it the lord would be prey to brigands along the road. But I myself could not remember the last time such an attack took place. And surely ten loyal retainers, well trained, would be enough of a deterrent? If a ruler was wise and benevolent, it would be more than enough. If he put the needs of his people first, his enemies would be few.

I paused again.

But, said Torei.

But, I said. The Daimyo march along the Tokaido accompanied by an entire army, not to mention the courtiers and concubines, the dancing girls and other entertainers. And the truth of it is that the poor and needy are forced to pay for this extravagance, and the processions grow ever more lavish as the Daimyo compete with each other to put on the biggest display of wealth.

At times of great hardship, such behavior is unbearable, and the people will not bear it.

A cornered rat will bite a cat, said Torei.

Indeed, I said. Well remembered.

You said it in the talk you gave during the famine.

Yes.

Perhaps we might combine that talk with this letter. The two would reinforce each other and make a powerful statement.

Then I could send the whole thing to the Daimyo.

Do you think he will react favourably?

If his commitment to the Buddha-way is genuine.

And if it is not?

Then perhaps he will send one of his swordsmen to discuss the matter with me. My head on a pike overlooking the Tokaido – now *that* would be a powerful statement.

The image was too vivid for Torei. He could clearly envisage it as a reality, my severed head, the eyes pecked out, a grim warning to all who transgressed. His face grew pale. His hand shook and he had to set down his brush.

Nevertheless, I said. We should edit this diatribe of mine into a book.

Torei composed himself, straightened his back.

Yes.

Another portion of my poison slobber to be dished out. I shall call it *Hebi-ichigo.*

Snake-strawberries.

They are weeds, I said, and they stay close to the ground, in the dirt where they grow. They taste bitter and have the reputation of being poisonous, but they cure all manner of ailments.

Torei nodded.

I told you my mother was skilled in the use of herbal remedies, he said. She used the strawberries to cure diarrhoea and haemorrhoids, toothache and headache, pain in the joints.

Anything that ails you.

Almost.

So. *Hebi-ichigo* it is. The book shall be called *Snake-strawberries*.

And if it eases the suffering of one human being, it will have done its work.

I recited the Four Noble Truths, and Torei joined me.

Existence is suffering. Its cause is desire. Desire can be conquered, there is a way. The way is to follow the Buddha-path.

*

I went to the little graveyard, chanted a sutra for the monks we had lost. Dust under the pines. I was returning to my quarters, crossing the courtyard, when something caught my eye, a movement on the ground, something tiny and frantic in the shade. I looked closely, saw it was a cicada, struggling to cast off its skin. With great difficulty it succeeded in getting its head free, then its front and back legs – hands and feet – one after the other. Only its left wing remained caught, stuck, and no matter how hard it tried it was unable to shake off the dead husk. I was moved to pity for its predicament and I thought I could help. I leaned forward and eased it free with my fingernail, watched the cicada take a few stuttering steps. But its movement was awkward, unbalanced. The wing I had touched stayed shut tight and refused to open. My efforts to help had caused damage, and the little creature was unable to fly as it should.

And sentient beings were numberless. And I had vowed to save them all.

OPENING THE GATES

I had been seated in zazen for many hours, mind sharp and clear, beyond the body's deep ache, the dull pain in bone and sinew. Perhaps one day I would be like Daruma, the Bodhidharma, I would sit so long my legs would atrophy and fall off.

Slowly, inch by inch, I stood up and stretched my limbs, my back, my neck. I stepped outside to the raked sand of the garden, breathed in the air. It was late afternoon, shading towards evening. A cicada rasped its harsh cry and it was music. Wind stirred the pines, wafted their sharp green scent.

One of the monks, Betsu, brought me tea in an iron kettle and poured some into my favourite bowl, old and misshapen, the glaze rough and unfinished. I took the bowl and sipped the tea and it was good. Its smokiness tasted of autumn.

Betsu had stepped back, still holding the kettle, but I sensed there was something he wanted to say. I looked at him, raised my eyebrows.

Well?

He bowed, uncomfortable.

I didn't want to disturb you, he said.

But?

There is someone here to see you. He has been waiting for some time.

He wants to speak to me?

Betsu hesitated.

He insists on it.

I held out my bowl, indicated Betsu should refill it.

Who is he? I asked.

Again Betsu hesitated, mindful that my questions could be double-edged and wondering whether he should answer that the man was a living Buddha, yet to be realised.

That is what he must ask himself, he said. Who am I?

Very good, I said. But for once I was asking a simple question. Who is this fellow waiting to see me?

His name is Nobushige, said Betsu. He is a soldier, a samurai warrior.

I knew of this man. He fancied himself as an expert on Zen, a sword-wielder cutting through ignorance. That was one way of looking at it.

I sipped my tea. The sand of the garden was pure white, raked into sworls and patterns. The single rock sat in the midst of it, placed just so. A mountain above the mist. Island in a vast expanse of sea.

Time passed.

I had finished the tea. I handed the empty bowl back to Betsu, bowed to him. He bowed deeper.

I will see this idiot samurai, I said.

The man was waiting in the courtyard, just inside the temple gate. He stood with his arms folded, his expression ferocious. He was not used to being kept waiting.

Who are you? I asked, catching him off guard.

I am Nobushige, he said, and he stood to attention, bowed stiffly.

I know your name, I said. But who are you?

His hair was swept up in the samurai topknot. He wore a grey robe with his clan crest on the sleeve, Tucked into the sash around his waist were two swords, one long, one short.

He gave the impression of great strength, immense physical power. I had no doubt he was a formidable warrior. But that samurai arrogance, that rage barely held in check, might be his undoing.

The waiting had made him angry. My question had made it worse.

Well? I asked.

He composed himself, straightened his back and stood tall.

I am samurai, he said. I have fought in many battles. I guard my lord with my life.

So why have you come here to see me?

Again my brusqueness unsettled him.

I wanted to ask you a question.

Ask.

I want to know, he said, if paradise and hell really exist.

I threw back my head and laughed, and that shocked him even more.

What a useless question! Are you one of those cowards who only does the right thing out of fear? This is your morality. You do good for fear of hell and in greedy expectation of paradise.

Now he glared at me, clenched his fists.

You say you guard your lord with your life, but what kind of master would employ a beggar like you?

He snorted through his nose, as if breathing fire. His hand rested on the hilt of his long sword.

So, you have a sword, but what use is it? I am sure the blade is too dull and blunted to be able to cut off my head.

To criticise his precious sword was an insult too far. He let out a roar and drew the sword, raised it above his head, ready to strike me down.

For a moment I was in the heart of a great silence, as if I stood outside myself, separate, dispassionate, observing these

405

events unfold as they must. If this was my death, so be it. The swordblade flashed, moved slowly as if through water.

I stared Nobushige in the eye, heard my own voice, strong and unwavering.

Here open the gates of hell.

He looked as if he had been struck. And in that instant, he saw, he understood. He lowered the sword, replaced it in its sheath, and I spoke again, that same certainty in the voice, but this time more quietly.

Here open the gates of paradise.

He took in a long slow breath, held it a moment, breathed out. He bowed low from the waist.

Thank you for your teaching, he said.

It is yours, I said. Use it.

When he had gone I sat a while in the garden and sipped more tea, mind open to all of it, hell and paradise, a flashing swordblade, as the evening grew cool and the light began to fade, lingering on the raked white sand.

DAIMYO

One bright fine spring morning, Fuji shimmering in the haze, there was a commotion at the temple gate and a young monk came running, stopped in front of me and bowed.

There are visitors, he said, bobbing his head and pointing. Dignitaries . . . An entourage . . .

I looked and saw a pikeman striding in through the gate. He stopped and looked around, then turned and nodded, and a little procession followed him in, four young retainers carrying a norimon on their shoulders, and behind them two horses led by a groom and behind that four armed men, samurai, bringing up the rear, watchful and on guard. One of them carried a banner bearing the butterfly crest of the Ikeda clan. As I watched it flutter in the breeze, the pikeman stepped forward and spoke.

You are Hakuin Ekaku, master of Shoin-ji?

My head, mounted on a pike, overlooking the Tokaido.

I am, I said, bowing.

The curtains in the norimon stirred and I had a memory of that procession I'd seen long ago, the courtesan's face looking out at me.

The pikeman stood to attention.

My Lord craves an audience with you.

I am sure I can make the time, I said, and I heard what

might have been a chuckle from behind the curtain. The norimon was set down and a young nobleman stepped out. He wore a broad-sleeved *hitatare* jacket, deep red, with the same butterfly crest on the sleeve.

I am Ikeda Tsugumasa, he said, Daimyo of Okayama.

I am honoured, I said.

I have tasted your *Hebi-ichigo*, he said, your *Snake-strawberries*. And as you can see, I am still alive.

This is a miracle, I said.

And as you can see, I have taken your poison to heart and am travelling almost alone.

A few villagers, curious, were peering in at the gate. One of the samurai took a step towards them and they ran off.

I have brought you a little gift of my own, said the Daimyo, and he nodded to the pikeman who reached into the palanquin, brought out two small packages, exquisitely wrapped. The Daimyo took them from him, handed them to me.

From the scent of it, one was the finest and subtlest incense. I breathed it in, thanked him. The other package was slightly larger, but still light, and I couldn't tell what was inside. I shook it, but that gave no clue.

This may offset the bitterness of the strawberries, he said. And I knew then it was a box of my favourite *konpeito*.

Perhaps with some tea? he suggested.

Forgive me, I said, and I invited him inside.

*

The young Daimyo had indeed taken my words to heart. He was reining back the extravagances of his household, sincerely trying to simplify his own life and uphold the precepts. He had come, in all humility, to receive teaching from this old monk. When we had sipped tea and eaten a few of the

408

delicious *konpeito*, I began by instructing him to look after his health. Only then would he be able to extend his span of years and work to bring prosperity and wellbeing to his subjects.

Be moderate in what you eat and drink, I said. (Here I raised an eyebrow at the little dish before me, bearing the last few sugared sweets. The Daimyo laughed.)

Show restraint in your physical desires, I said. (I added that his concubines would not thank me if they heard this advice. Again he laughed, though perhaps less heartily.)

Nourish your life, I said. Be strong in your mind and firm in your faith. Do this by developing the power of introspection.

I then gave him instruction in *naikan*, as Hakuyu had taught me, as I had taught Torei and others.

This will help conquer illness, I said, and debilitating weakness. It will give you the strength to carry out your duties. And remember always that your noble birth at this time, in this peaceful and well-governed domain, is the result of past good karma. You have gained merit from good deeds in a previous life when you rigorously practised the disciplines. Take care in this life that you do not exhaust those blessings or fall into cause and effect and accumulate new karmic suffering. Only then will you fulfil your destiny as a great leader.

Think of the great Minamoto no Yoshiie. (An ancestor of mine fought alongside him.) He never recklessly took any life, and he recited every day a verse from the Lotus Sutra. Going into battle he had a tiny gold figure of Kannon Bodhisattva woven into his hair. Thus protected, he defeated a vast enemy army. Strong in mind, firm in faith.

In your case, I told the Daimyo, you should chant the Kannon Sutra.

Emmei Jikku Kannon Gyo.

It will cure disease and ensure long life. Join me in chanting it.

Emmei Jikku Kannon Gyo.
Emmei Jikku Kannon Gyo.

*

We had sat so long the afternoon was beginning to darken.
It had also grown cold, and I asked the monk attending to
bring us some warm sake, which I poured.

So, I said.

He bowed.

Thank you.

We sat for a time in companionable silence, watching the
light fade. I looked out across the courtyard and saw the
pikeman standing there, motionless, guarding the norimon.
The samurai were seated on the verandah, but he had had
to stay at his post.

He must be cold, I said. We have talked a long time. Perhaps
you could take him some warm sake.

The Daimyo looked confused, then he realised I was
actually asking him to do this small thing, and it mattered.
He nodded, poured sake from the flask into a cup and
carried it carefully out to the pikeman. The man looked
even more confused than his lord, then grateful as he sipped
the drink.

When the Daimyo came back in I said now he would have
to promote the man to the rank of samurai.

Is that not the case?

Yes, he said. Only samurai can receive sake in this way
from the Daimyo. And for me to pour it for him is an acknowledgement of that.

He smiled and poured a little more sake for himself, and
for me.

Sakasaraba!

410

Later, as they were preparing to leave, the pikeman stood in front of me and bowed.

Thank you, Sensei, he said. I know this was your doing. I have a family to keep, and I am grateful.

It was your own merit, I said. I was merely the instrument.

His lord called to him and he returned to his duty, led the little procession back out onto the road. The Daimyo gave me a wave of the hand then his curtain swung closed and he returned to his own world.

*

A little later, Torei approached and asked if the meeting had gone well.

As you can see, I said, I still have my head.

That in itself is a miracle, he said.

I had been pressing Torei to continue writing my biography so generations to come would be able to sup my poison, albeit in diluted form. He had been working away at it diligently, occasionally becoming exasperated at the yarns I would spin, the different versions of my story. For my early life, he had to take my word for it. At times he would be quite blunt.

Is this true, he would ask, or is it seen from the Night Boat of your imagination?

It's all true, I told him. In its own way.

Now he wanted an account of my meeting with the Daimyo. He sensed it was important and wanted to get it down while it was still fresh and comparatively unembellished, so I told him what I could, as much as could be communicated.

And you're right, I said. It is important. The Daimyo has a long way to travel but he is well intentioned and could do great good for the people. He also mentioned five or six other

411

Daimyo who might visit when they are passing along the Tokaido. So perhaps we might make sure they receive copies of my poisonous rant, my *Snake-strawberries*. Let us see if they can digest it.

He smiled, and I asked him why.

Hunger-and-Cold, he said. The Master of Poverty-Temple. And here you are advising some of the most powerful men in the land.

I laughed.

Who could have imagined it?

TALL TALES

*I*t *was a dark and wintry night . . .*
    . . . and Hunger-and-Cold, Master of Poverty-Temple, was seated with a few of his followers (Torei and Suio among them). There was something about the cold and the dark, closing in around us, the sheer depth of the midwinter night. Spirits and demons would be close at hand. It was a night for telling tales of the other worlds. I turned down the lamp a little, to save oil. The light flickered, turned us into shadows, and I began . . .

Back from the Land of the Dead.

There were seven elderly women making a pilgrimage and they came to Shoin-ji and knocked on my door. They had a terrifying tale to tell, and the oldest of them took it on herself to tell it to me.

This is a true story, she said, and it concerns my daughter. She would have been with us on this pilgrimage, but she fell ill and took to her bed. She grew weaker by the day and eventually she stopped breathing and lay lifeless. The physician pronounced her dead, but our local priest said he thought he still detected a little warmth in the centre of the chest, and he told us to delay the funeral arrangements if we could.

Ten days went by and we thought perhaps that was long enough, and we should prepare her for burial. Then suddenly

413

in the middle of the night, she came back to life and sat upright with a great cry. And this is the story she told.

*

A little time ago – I don't know how long and have no way of knowing – I was led from here by some dark hooded figures. They had no faces – beneath each hood was a featureless blank mask – and I was numb with fear as I followed them along the rim of a great valley. There was no sun or moon, only the black flames of hell rising up from the worlds below.

Screams of torment rose up from the depths, and I could see the damned were from all walks of life – aristocracy and beggars, the famous and the outcast, saints and sinners. There were even monks and nuns among them, unable to understand how they had fallen to this place, and I saw people I knew, people from my home village.

A great featureless plain extended all around, further than the eye could see, inhabited by skeletal figures burned black and wailing in pain. When we'd crossed the plain for an endless length of time we came to a huge iron gate that towered hundreds of feet in the air, and above it, in letters of flame, was written The Palace of Emma, Lord of the Dead. Inside the gate, darkness within darkness, was a dank and terrifying prison, its walls fetid and decaying, collapsing in on themselves, and locked inside, in cramped cells, were countless more beings who had once been human, thousands upon thousands of them. So many, so many. They had no tongues, they had lost the power of language, and all they could do was howl in agony and misery and rage.

I felt them drawing me down among them, into that place of desolation. Then there was a great roaring and a rush of wind, and I woke up in the mortuary, screaming myself hoarse.

414

The old woman was shaking as she came to the end of her story.

Since this happened, she said, my daughter has been terrified. She cannot sleep for fear of waking again in that terrible, terrible place and being consigned there forever.

She bowed and asked with deepest humility if I might write something she could take back to her daughter, a scroll with the sacred words, a charm against damnation.

Moved that she had made a pilgrimage to ask me, I drew the characters with a slow careful hand.

Namu Amida Butsu.

Let her chant this with devotion every day, I said, and the words will guide her through.

I thought of my own mother, her simple dedication.

I handed the scroll to the woman and tears of gratitude filled her eyes.

*

Realm of the Angry Demons.

This is a story I was told about the priest Gedatsu Shonin when he was residing at Mount Kasagi. One dark night, after he had been meditating, he sat up late in his room, reading the Lotus Sutra by the faint light of a lamp. Everyone else at the temple had fallen asleep and a great silence had descended on everything.

Suddenly there was a huge uproar outside the room, a howling and screaming and growling. The noise was terrifying, non-human, not of this world, and Gedatsu, for all his courage, felt his blood turn to ice. Trembling, his legs weak, he went to the window and tore a tiny hole in the paper screen, placed his eye to it and peered out.

What he saw almost stopped his heart with fear. He was looking into the realm of angry demons, creatures with the heads of horses or goats, tigers or wild dogs, creatures with horns, fangs, tails, claws, all snapping and tearing at each other, consumed by rage.

Gedatsu could hardly breathe. He didn't want to stand there watching. He was too afraid to run away. He thought he might fall over in a faint. Then he realised the figure of an ancient monk had appeared beside him, absorbed in meditation. His voice a croaking whisper, he asked the monk who these creatures might be.

The old monk came out of his trance and spoke in a solemn voice.

Strictly speaking, he said, it is wrong even to talk about them. But you have asked, and I must tell you. These wretched beings were once monks and priests. But because they did not possess the Mind of Enlightenment, they fell from the true path into evil ways. They are always with us, day and night, waiting for opportunities to lure others into their midst. Be resolute and do not be drawn into their world.

There was a smell of incense and the old monk rose into the air and disappeared. The noise had stopped and the hellish creatures had vanished from sight. But Gedatsu knew their realm was closer than his own heartbeat and they might reappear at any time and he had to be on his guard.

He bowed with gratitude.

*

Outside in the courtyard something screeched, something rustled.

An owl, I said. Dead leaves.

But one of the young monks asked if he could turn the lamp up just a little.

The Undying Lamp of Zen, I said, and I nodded to Torei who bowed.

Your inner lamp is lit, I said to the young monk. How brightly does that burn?

Not brightly enough, he said, suddenly grateful for the shadow.

Tend to that, I said. But then I did turn the lamp up a fraction.

Just a little, I said. Then I asked one of the older disciples, Daikyu Ebo, to tell a tale of his own, about something that had happened to him many years ago. He bowed and composed himself, began speaking in a slow measured voice, entering deep into the memory of the experience.

*

Release of a Soul in Torment.

It was in Kyoto, he said, after I had given a lecture at Tofuku-ji. As I was leaving the hall, a young woman, clearly from a wealthy family, approached me without saying a word and handed me a note. The note was a request for an immediate meeting with me, in private. My first thought was to say no, without hesitation, but the look in her eyes was one of absolute despair and desolation. They were not her own eyes, but the eyes of a soul in torment.

I consulted with a few of my fellow priests and she was allowed to join me in an anteroom and tell her story. As soon as she opened her mouth to speak, the chill of fear gripped my heart. The voice was not the voice of the young woman in front of me. It was the voice of an old crone and it shook and wavered with anguish and pain. The young woman was possessed.

I was a good woman, said the voice speaking through her, a virtuous woman, an honest trader. I sold rice and other

417

grains in the marketplace and I treated my customers fairly. In my youth I had followed the Pure Land teachings and chanted the Nembutsu with great devotion. Then in middle age I fell under the influence of a priest who taught the doctrine of the Unborn. Death is the end of everything, he said. There is no afterlife, no heaven or hell, nowhere to fall. Here and now you are a Buddha. Why then should you chant sutras or sit in zazen?

Her voice broke at this point, said Daikyu, and she found it difficult to continue.

I am so ashamed, she said at last. I listened to his advice and my life changed. I no longer sat in meditation. I no longer took inspiration from chanting the Nembutsu. I fell from grace. My life lost all meaning and before long I was cheating my customers, using false measure and selling them short.

A great sob broke from her and shook the young girl's body. When the voice continued it was mournful and desolate and came from a deep dark place.

I died, she said. And no, that was not an end of it. The priest had been wrong. I fell into this hell and have been here ever since, tortured more than anything by memory of my earlier life when my devotion was simple and true. But perhaps some vestige of my good karma remained, a tiny glimmer of light in all that darkness. From somewhere came the will to escape, and I found myself in my disembodied form seeking out this young girl and entering into her. She has understood my plight and has brought me to you for help.

*

At this point in the telling, Daikyu seemed exhausted, as if he were revisiting the episode, reliving it, and identifying once more with the woman's suffering. At times in bringing the

418

story to life, he had mimicked the woman's voice, almost as if he too had been taken over. But now he sat upright, folded his hands in *gassho*.

We conducted a ceremony of purification, he said. We burned incense and read from the sutras. I composed a verse and recited it. We made offerings of fruit and water for the liberation of all beings. When all of this was done, the woman's voiced breathed out, *Thank you!* And she fell into a trance.

When she opened her eyes again the young woman was herself once more. Her eyes shone and she said the old woman had been released to dwell in a higher realm.

*

It's a fine story, I said when Daikyu had told his tale. A false priest consigned the woman to hell, a true priest rescued her.

He bowed.

Here's a verse for you, I said.

> *And what's the vilest creature? A stinking skunk?*
> *Creeping cockroach? Slithering snake? A thieving monk!*

*

There are many tales, I said, of true priests coming to the rescue of the living and the dead.

Questioning the ghost.

There was a young man whose wife fell ill and died. With her last breath she made him promise never to marry again, and if he did so, she would return as a ghost to haunt him. He was distraught at his loss, as any young man would be. But in the fullness of time he met another woman and fell in love again, and made plans to remarry.

But a ghost took the form of his wife and came to visit him every night, claiming to be in torment at the prospect of the marriage. He was pledged to her, she said, and the vows they had made were forever.

The young man was torn apart. On the one hand he wanted to be true to his wife's memory, on the other he wanted to make a new life. And there was something else, a deep unease when the ghost appeared. Was this really the ghost of his wife? She certainly knew a great deal about him, as if she could read his thoughts.

Eventually he approached a Zen priest and told him the story.

The priest said she must be a very clever ghost, to know what he was thinking. But there is one way to test her, he said. Ask her one simple question. If she answers it correctly, she is indeed your wife and you will do what she asks. If she cannot answer, then she is a creature of your imagination and has no substance.

And what is the question?

Take a handful of soya beans and ask if she can tell you exactly how many you are holding.

The young man returned home, and the ghost appeared to him again.

Well? she asked.

You are a very clever ghost, he said, to know so much about me.

And I know you went to see that Zen master today, she said.

I did. And he told me to test you by asking one simple question.

And what might the question be?

He had brought a jar of soya beans from the kitchen and he took a handful, and held them out towards her.

How many beans am I holding?

By the time he had asked the question, there was no ghost there to answer it.

*

The young monk who had asked for more light went round the room serving tea. Suio looked up at me with an expression I had come to recognise, a look of exasperation and barely suppressed disdain.

You don't approve of my poison tales of the beyond? I asked him.

Your poison's diluted, he said. It's sickly sweet, no more than an emetic.

Spew it up, I said.

Tales to frighten children, he said. As you were frightened.

My childhood name was Iwajiro, I said, quoting myself. And I was eight years old when I first entered at the gates of hell.

Thus have I heard, he said, also quoting. But perhaps you should keep the tales for your lay followers.

Perhaps you might do well to take heed of them yourself, I said. Even great masters have been known to fall into the abyss. A fox spirit once approached Master Po-Chang and told him his sad tale. He had once been a high-ranking Shinto priest, the abbot of a great temple. At that time he had been asked whether an enlightened man could fall into cause and effect. He had replied glibly, There can be no fall for such a being. And for this alone, *for this alone*, he was condemned to be reborn as a fox for five hundred lives.

Cause and effect, said Suio. In that case I'll go to hell in my own way.

He finished the tea in his bowl, stood up and bowed, and

left the room. I sensed that he was walking straight out the gate and into the night, putting some distance between us again.

Abbot Suio . . . I said.

I have written down these stories, said Torei. I will make fair copies and add them to the rest.

Yes, I said. Who knows? Perhaps they will frighten some grown-up children into wakefulness.

But when the others had gone, and I sat alone through the watches of the night, I felt Suio's departure like a blow, a punch to the stomach.

*

I had to keep driving the older disciples. There were degrees of kensho and they had to keep going deeper, intensify the experience.

I had written a poem.

> *The sound of the rain on fallen leaves is an awakening.*
> *But how can it compare to this richness —*
> *The warm glow of sunset clouds*
> *Over fields of yellow grain?*

Ever deeper, till they died the Great Death, embraced post-satori practice.

With Suio gone, and Torei ploughing his own field, who would succeed me at Shoin-ji?

I called to mind the great Master Daito's final words of instruction, before his passing.

After all my travels, many temples flourished, with splendid images of the Buddha, and great libraries of scriptures, some written in silver and gold. They have large congregations, monks who spend all day in

422

meditation and reciting scripture, rigorously upholding the vows, eating only once a day, carrying out observances at appropriate times. But even so, even so, they do not have in their hearts the Sublime Way taught by the Buddha. When I'm gone not one of them will be my true descendant.

But if just one solitary individual, living and practising in the wilderness, under a thatched roof, subsisting on a handful of roots cooked up in an old pot, is focused utterly on understanding the self, then this is someone who meets me every day.

Would you dare look down on such a one?

Now, work on this.

Work on this.

RYUTAKU-JI

Time did not just rush past, it actually accelerated. Year by year, it moved ever faster. A child's toy, a cord fastened to the top of a pole, its other end tied to a ball, weighted. Spin the cord round the pole and every time it turns, the loop gets shorter, the ball moves quicker and quicker till it stops. Just so. The years were speeding past. I was an old man and still had made no real provision for the continuity of the teaching. My Dharma-heirs had appeared, but Torei was unwilling and Suio was downright hostile. I could see no way forward.

Then I hatched another plan, or rather it came to me unbidden, and the vehicle once more was my physician friend Ishii Gentoku.

You want to prescribe another remedy for me, I said, administer more of your poison, cure me by killing me.

We are all duty-bound, he said, to expedite your journey to hell.

The good doctor had a friend, another of my lay followers who lived a few miles away in Mishima. This man, Takahashi, was a successful trader in tea and silk and had amassed considerable wealth. He had also come to the realisation that he should invest in his future, not in a worldly sense as he had all he could ever need, but in order to gain merit and atone for past karma in his business dealings. He had bought and sold property in his time, and when a particular piece of land became available, the site of an old ruined temple, he became interested in buying it for himself.

The location was beautiful, nestling among hills on the outskirts of Mishima, and Takahashi thought he could build a house there where he could spend his later years in quiet and contemplation.

Gentoku said it was an excellent plan, but might he suggest something even better, something that would bring him lasting merit and abiding peace?

Takahashi was shrewd, and he knew the doctor of old.

What do you have in mind?

We have benefited from Master Hakuin's teaching, said Gentoku, perhaps more than we will ever know. What he needs now is a teaching monastery where many more monks can receive his curative poison.

When Gentoku reported this to me, I was enthusiastic, excited, and felt the compassion of Bodhisattva Kannon descending like rain. Finding a place for a new temple was no easy task. The government was hell-bent on restricting the building of monasteries, the spread of our poisonous teaching. They had effectively put a ban on any expansion, the development of new sites. But there was a loophole in the regulations. It was sometimes possible to buy the site of an existing temple and rebuild it. If the old temple was listed on the government register, it should be a matter of transferring the title deeds. Gentoku and Takahashi negotiated the transfer, and the payment of the fee, and the sweetening of various officials involved.

*

The place was purchased in the autumn when the hillside was a riot of bright red maple. The only buildings were a

425

run-down meeting hall, a cottage, a few dilapidated outhouses. But I saw it as it would be in years to come, a thriving monastery where generations of monks could throw themselves into the maelstrom of zazen and koan study, drive through the barriers to kensho and satori, then carry the Dharma out into the world.

I see it clearly, I said to Takahashi and Doctor Gentoku, and I could feel a choke in my voice as I spoke. Tears of gratitude were not far away. Then a fine rain began to fall, soaking my old robe.

Grace descending, I said, and I thanked them from the bottom of my heart.

*

The site is perfect, I told Torei on his return from another trip to Kyoto. It's a place of exceptional beauty, in the foothills close to Fuji, surrounded by forests. The atmosphere is one of great peace and tranquillity, and it's truly sanctified. There is a shrine to the guardian deity, Azuma Gongen, and there is an image of the Buddha carved by the great Kobo Daishi who founded the original temple on the site.

Torei remained silent and looked troubled, a small vein pulsing on the side of his head.

You are reluctant, I said, as you were with Muryo-ji.

I have already spoken to some of the other monks, he said at last. They accompanied you to look at the site, and they say it is damp and marshy, practically a quagmire, and you have to wade through mud to get to the buildings.

I was stung, partly because what he said was true.

They have no stamina, I said. They say they'll drive through the Zen barriers, batter down the gates of hell and leap beyond, but they're afraid of getting their feet wet.

426

Torei half smiled at that. If I could still rant, then he hadn't cut me to the core.

A few days later he came to me again.

Perhaps there is a solution, he said.

I am listening.

If the temple could be moved, as it were, one hill over. I understand the site is just as beautiful, but the new buildings could be constructed on solid ground. Access would be easier, so I'm told, and the drainage would be better. So.

So!

I shouted out loud and clapped my hands.

You see? A little imagination and we leap the barriers!

Torei bowed and I felt a depth of gratitude to him. He knew in my enthusiasm I hadn't been entirely honest with him about the site, and yet he had come up with this solution, to spare my feelings as much as anything else.

Thank you, I said.

*

By the following spring, an old well had been re-opened, a small meditation hall and the monks' quarters had been built on the new spot, with dormitories and a kitchen, a room that would be a library. Further up the hillside a few small shrines had been placed, and in a small inner courtyard a miniature stone garden had been laid out. The work had been done by the monks from Shoin-ji, with a great deal of help from the lay followers and some of their friends from the surrounding villages, tradesmen and artisans, carpenters and builders, labourers happy to pitch in with lifting and hauling and digging.

I took Torei to one of the shrines, high up and overlooking the whole site, the pine and maple, the bamboo groves, shade on shade of green.

427

We stood, getting our breath back after the short climb, looking out at the vista, all of it.

Well? I said.

He was silent for a while. He knew what I was asking.

Again you try to persuade me, he said.

You have made it clear you will not succeed me at Shoin-ji. And Muryo-ji was in decline. But this . . .

With a sweep of my hand, I took it all in. His breathing was serious.

It would be a completely fresh start, I said. It would be yours to run exactly as you wish. You would even have time for your own practice, for your writing, your painting. The younger monks would benefit greatly from your guidance.

A light spring breeze blew through the forest, shimmered the leaves.

Well?

He stared into the green depth.

I will need time to think, he said.

Will you go to the shrine at Mount Akiba to pray for my health?

He bowed his head.

And will I then hear you are in Kyoto?

That was wrong of me, he said. I was confused, and reluctant, and fearful.

Yes.

I am still confused, he said. I am still reluctant. But I am no longer fearful. I will answer you straight.

Good, I said. Good.

*

The next morning Torei stood before me, hands folded, and I knew he had meditated long and hard. I quoted his own words to him, from *The Undying Lamp*.

428

Great compassion is like the sky. It covers all living beings. It produces all the great teachings, pure knowledge for the sake of others.

He bowed and responded from the same work.

Great compassion makes it possible to go beyond, for the sake of others.

I continued.

Great compassion brings great blessings in the form of expedient means to teach others.

Again he responded, and we exchanged the lines.

Great compassion can remove conceit in our dealings with others.

Great compassion gives rise to benevolence towards others.

Great compassion brings detachment and bases everything on truth, for the sake of others.

Finally, I said, great compassion enables us to enter into the real. There is nowhere it cannot go for the sake of others.

I am humbled, he said, that you know my work.

I have devoured it, I said. Now I'm spewing it up, word for word.

Again he bowed.

And? I said. What now?

I'm hanging over the edge of the sheer cliff, he said. Now I have to loosen my grip and let go.

Let go, I said. Die to be reborn. It's like falling into water. If you struggle and thrash around with your arms and legs, you'll grow tired and drown. But let go, let your feet touch bottom and then you can push and rise again to the surface.

*

Now, I said. Do you have a way out?

He had been meditating on the koan, The Old Woman Burns Down the Monk's Hut.

And?

I had missed it before, he said. I hadn't seen the subtlety.

Burning down his hut? Subtle?

She would have shocked the monk into serious depression and baffled him half to death.

So what should he have done? What would *you* have done?

I'd grab the old woman, he said, and yell at her, I've been receiving your support these twenty years . . .

Before Torei could even finish what he was saying, I saw he had penetrated to the very depths of the koan. I let out a great roar that rattled his bones and stopped him dead. His chest hurt, his head was dazed.

So, I said. Now do you have a way out?

*

When Torei had run away to Kyoto rather than take over the running of Shoin-ji, he had left behind the old brocade robe I had tried to give him. Now once more I presented it to him, and once more he refused.

This filthy old rag is for your successor at Shoin-ji, he said. Not for me. I won't drape it over my stinking carcass.

Nevertheless, I said, and I pushed the robe towards him.

Nevertheless, he said, and he pushed it back.

The robe sat there between us, faded and moth-eaten, the dulled gold of the brocade catching the lamplight. I let out a great exaggerated sigh and folded up the robe. It smelled faintly of sweat and old incense. I put it away in my bag to take back to Shoin-ji.

The next day at dawn, as a cool breeze ruffled the leaves of the trees around the temple, Torei was formally installed as Abbot of the teaching monastery Ryutaku-ji. The clang of a bell. Thud of a drum. Assembled monks chanting. Incense sticks burning, for purification.

This will be a fine temple, I said.

I will do my best to make it so, said Torei.

There is no one else who could do this, I said. Your best will be more than good enough.

In Torei's eyes a lingering trepidation, but nevertheless, *nevertheless*, a look of gratitude.

BODHISATTVA OF HELL

I had always known in my bones I would live a long life on earth. This was my blessing and my curse. On into my seventies I drove myself. I still travelled, still beat the Dharma drum. When I could no longer walk great distances, some of the younger monks carried me in a palanquin from temple to temple.

Look at me, I said, like some debauched old potentate. Now I am the Daimyo of Poverty-Castle!

I refused to bow to illness, to the miseries of old age, though the Zen sickness of my youth was as nothing compared to what I experienced now. I lived in pain. But I had known from the outset this was how it would be. In taking the karma of others, I would suffer on their behalf. The sharp knives of Black Line Hell, the pain endlessly renewed.

I endured. I still wrote, still drew and painted, still poured out my poison and spread it shamelessly.

*

Now here I was, past eighty. Another year gone and this old body still barely holding together. Out of breath, eyesight fading, limbs aching, but still here. Still here.

New Year's morning, among the high peaks.
This old monk's face is wizened and thick-skinned.
Eighty-four and welcoming another year.
He owes it all to the sound of one hand.

A few months ago old Master Hakuyu came to me in a dream. Then I woke from the dream and he was sitting there in the room, exactly as I remembered him. He didn't speak, just sat in profound silence, meditating. Then he opened his eyes and smiled at me. And my eyes filled with tears.

When I looked again he was gone.

*

I told this story to some of the young monks, and one of them bowed low and apologised for having to tell me, but Master Hakuyu had passed away.

How can you say such a thing? I asked. Hakuyu was no ordinary human being. He was an immortal, walking the earth. How could he die?

That was exactly how he died, said the monk. Walking the earth. He was striding along a mountain path and came to a great ravine. He tried to leap across but fell to his death on the rocks below.

*

Hearing this I knew my own time was close at hand.

*

I had entered a cave and followed a stony path that led ever downwards. All around was darkness and yet somehow I could see the way ahead, as if I carried my own light. But with every step I took, the darkness closed behind me.

Then all at once the way was blocked by a great stone wall right in front of me, a sheer cliff stretching endlessly in every direction. I could hear the trickle of water down the rock face, though I couldn't see it. And I heard my own breathing and the beat of my heart, and beyond that, behind it all, a deeper beat like the thud of a great far-off drum.

The narrowest of cracks appeared in the rock, immediately before me and exactly my own height. As I looked, the crack widened just enough for me to step inside, the sides of the crack pressing against me. I pushed forward and it gave, again just enough, inch by inch. But still I could feel it pressing on all sides. My heartbeat and breathing grew louder, and for the first time I felt fear. Perhaps this was the gateway to the Great Crushing Hell. The rock closed me in completely, and so did the dark.

I was unable to move. My chest was constricted, but I breathed as deeply as I could, invoked the compassion of Bodhisattva Kannon. I chanted in silence, then out loud.

Enmei Jikku Kannon Gyo.

The distant thudding grew louder, seemed to vibrate through the very rock, through my bones and sinew. The pressure increased, grew tighter about me, the rock turning to clay and moulding itself around me, gripping me. I was buried here and being crushed. Still I invoked Kannon.

Enmei Jikku Kannon Gyo.

And I was pushed forward against the resistance. The noise became a loud rushing and the rock itself heaved me out through the clay. I emerged into a spacious cavern, the noise stopped, and once more I could see by my own light.

I was on my knees, hands folded in *gassho*. Ahead of me I could see a bridge over a great chasm, and on the bridge, at intervals across it, were seven figures.

At first I took them for the gods of good fortune. Then I saw that the first was a young child, and the last was an old man. And the seven figures were the same man – Hakuin – at different stages in his life. The seventh figure was kneeling as I was now, hands folded. I stood up and made my way towards the bridge, began to walk across it.

As I approached the first figure, myself as a young boy, he looked up and smiled at me. I stepped forward and replaced him. I *became* that young boy.

My childhood name was Iwajiro, and I was eight years old when I first entered at the gates of hell.

I relived the terror of seeing the flames under the iron bathtub, a cauldron to boil me alive.

My mother's cool hand on my forehead, her soft voice chanting the Daimoku. Nisshin walking through the fire, unscathed.

Namu Myoho Rengu Kyo.

I got to my feet and walked on across the bridge.

The next figure was the youth with the dragon between his legs. Once more I became him, relived his anguish and awkwardness, the desire that burned him. I took brush and inkstone and drew my world and myself in it, great Fuji a constant presence. Her snowy skin. The Daimyo's procession. The woman looking out at me through parted curtains and smiling at me. By grace I had seen her as Kannon embodied. Once more I chanted.

Enmei Jikku Kannon Gyo.

I walked on further, to the third figure on the bridge, the young monk I had been, my head shaved, walking in the spring breeze, chanting my new name.

Ekaku. Ekaku.

Wise Crane.

I had met Hana. I had caught her and saved her when she fell. Now I held her once more in my arms. I breathed in her

435

scent. Then in an instant she was gone. Butterfly in its season. Everything grew dark. Ganto's death cry shook all the worlds. There was nothing but bone and ash, desolation.

I dragged myself on, one foot after the other. Beneath the bridge was a great chasm and in the background Fuji threw up flame and molten rock.

I was felled by blows – Shoju's fist, the old woman's broom. My skull cracked open and let in light.

Spine straight, I stood tall at the arc of the bridge. I was that figure, solitary, breathing deep, but suddenly held there, encased in ice. There were hells that did not burn but freeze. I was clamped, immobile, closed in. The ice extended endlessly all around, vast emptiness and cold. Then the clear sound of a bell rang true and shattered the ice into crystal fragments, each one a perfect mirror reflecting back the light that was in me, the light that I was. Mind clear and cold, I was Hakuin, Hidden-in-Whiteness.

Hakuin.

The demons he had encountered fell back and howled. The koans he had grappled with dissolved into nothing.

Mu.

He continued on his journey, on the Zen road, back to where his head had been shaved, to Shoin-ji. He was Hunger-and-Cold, the Master of Poverty-Temple.

Beat the Dharma drum.

He sat in a circle of skeletons in monks' robes. Then they were gone, dust under the pines. But he himself survived and continued. Sentient beings were numberless. He had vowed to save them all.

He heard the sound of one hand, and put a stop to all sounds.

He walked and wrote and talked and drew.

His body became heavy again, sluggish. His health failed. His eyesight grew dim. But still he drove himself, to walk and

436

write and talk and draw, to teach, to spread the Dharma.

Everything was effort, and effort was pain, in body and heart and mind. He drew breath in pain.

He walked on, across the bridge, stopped in front of the last figure, the seventh, down on his knees, but hands still folded in *gassho*, in supplication.

I looked down at him, at myself, kneeling there.

And beyond the bridge, on the other side, my old body wrapped in a winding sheet, covered by a rush mat, ready for cremation.

I lay there, in my winding sheet, under the rush mat, and I looked out at the great cave all around.

Far below, in the abyss under the bridge, I knew the all-consuming fires were burning. But they were one. Fire of desire and fire of aspiration. Fire of destruction, fire of trans-formation. Fire of purification, fire of illumination.

They were one and the same. Emma, Yamaraj, the terrible Lord of Hell, Jizo the Bodhisattva of Compassion.

One and the same.

I had heard a cacophony of voices, howling. Then it changed and the howling became a chant, an invocation.

Enmei Jikku Kannon Gyo.

Enmei Jikku Kannon Gyo.

Now the face in the Precious Mirror, here in this place, at the end of all torment, was Kannon the merciful, the benign.

I bowed to the Great Bodhisattva of Hell.

*

I wrote that as a calligraphy, old hand shaking but brushstrokes still firm and thick and bold, the characters forming a solid column down the scroll.

I BOW TO THE GREAT BODHISATTVA OF HELL.

Let that be my epitaph, I said.

437

My condition grew worse, an overwhelming fatigue that made it difficult to move. But I wanted to deliver another Dharma lecture. Torei and the others were concerned. Finally a young nun, named after the great Erin, stepped forward and spoke up.

Perhaps, she said, bowing, your teaching can wait till you are stronger.

And when will that be? I asked. And what is a little fatigue compared to the sufferings you have undergone, the poverty and famine, the deprivation?

Again she bowed.

If you were to stop this flow of sweetness from your mouth, it would be like taking food from the hungry, like denying medicine to the sick.

I raised my hand, acknowledging the pure devotion in her words.

And if it should happen, she said, *if* it should happen that your condition deteriorated and you were to enter into Nirvana tomorrow, then without you we would not know where to turn.

Again I raised my hand and opened my mouth to speak, but no words came.

However, she continued, even if we do not hear you preach again, just seeing your face, and knowing you are well and at peace, is the greatest happiness we can know.

I could see there were tears in her eyes, and I had to struggle against them myself, this old ox, this tiger, helpless as a child. I lay back on my futon, cushions propped up behind me, and took more rest.

*

My sleep was fitful, disturbed. I fell into a fever, turned this way and that. At one point in my delirium, I sat up and thought I saw Suio, standing at the end of my bed. I slept again, and when I woke he really was there, looking down at me, concerned.

It's you, I said.

He grunted.

So it would seem.

Good of you to visit, I said. Where have you been?

Here and there, he said. But I couldn't let you slip away without barking at me one more time. And I wanted another look at your ugly face.

I tried to laugh but it set me coughing. Suio helped me sit up, adjusted the cushions behind me.

So, he said.

Indeed.

He left a silence, then spoke, the words all-in-a-rush.

I have discussed matters with Torei. Things are going well at Ryutaku-ji and he will continue there. As for Shoin-ji, this old rubbish dump . . . Well, against my better judgement, I'll have a go at running the place and see how it works out.

Abbot Suio after all, I said.

Abbot Suio.

I bowed.

I am grateful.

Later I challenged him to a game of Go, for old times' sake, and he brought the counters and board. But I couldn't see clearly enough, or concentrate on the moves, and I barely had the strength to pick up the pieces.

This time I'll let you win, I said.

I had nothing left.

*

439

Next day a terrible storm swept through the district, battering Hara, bombarding Shoin-ji. Relentless rain poured down, the buildings shook and great bolts of lightning zigzagged to earth.

What do you think? I asked Suio. Are they opening the gates of hell for me?

Perhaps, he said.

There's a haiku by Matsuo Basho, I said.

I remembered old Bao reciting it to me.

> *How admirable*
> *Not to think life is fleeting*
> *When you see the lightning.*

Suio nodded, but when I was shaken by another spasm of coughing and spat up blood, he sent for the doctor.

My old friend Gentoku had himself passed to the other side, unable at the last to heal himself. His successor was a younger man, Furugori, all quick remedies and instant cures, with none of Gentoku's wisdom, his humanity.

He had treated me for a suppurating carbuncle on my backside. The curse of zazen, or too much sugar. It was agony, yet Furugori had showed no compassion.

Now he took his time in coming, waited till the worst of the storm was over. Didn't want to catch his death of cold. He had a fastidiousness, a fussiness in his manner, looked constantly disapproving. He took my pulse, holding my wrist.

Well? I said.

You eat too many sugared sweets, he said.

Guilty as charged, I said. I've eaten them all my life. And the remedy?

The same as last time.

Ah.

A purgative, he said. To flush it out of your system.

Get rid of all my sweetness.

He measured out a pinch of some powdered herb, told me to add it to a little water, swallow it down in a single gulp.

Then spend the night in agony, I said, crouched over the privy.

If that's what it takes.

Gates of hell, I said to Suio.

As the doctor prepared to leave, I asked if he had anything else to say about my health.

Nothing much, he said. There's nothing out of the ordinary.

I sat up as straight as I could, fixed him with my gaze.

You call yourself a doctor, I said, and you can't even tell when a man has just three days to live.

Suio and Torei glanced at each other. The doctor looked as if he had been punched. The young nun Erin dropped a bowl she had picked up from my bedside and it smashed to pieces on the floor.

Don't worry, I said. It was the bowl's time to die.

*

This very moment, what's to be sought?
Nirvana is here and now.
This very place is the Pure Land.
This very body is the Buddha-body.

*

The same young monk who had told me of Hakuyu's passing now asked if the master had really been 400 years old when I met him.

Words, words, words, I said.

All of it. All of it. Idle talk on the night boat.

441

A death-verse?

Torei had asked if I would write something. He was ready, brush in hand.

What more do I have to say? I asked him.

I recalled Shoju's reluctance to utter his final words. *I'll say it / Without saying it / Nothing more / Nothing more.*

There was one I had written that Bao had liked, about incense burning down, leaving just the fragrance. If only I could remember it.

But then Bao had quoted Mumon at me, said reciting a death-verse is adding frost to snow. Frost to snow.

Nevertheless, Torei was anxious.

All true poetry is death-verse, I said. Why not choose something I have already written?

He came back to me with a little tanka I had scribbled long ago, beneath a drawing of a swallow, flying.

> *Crossing the ocean*
> *of life and death,*
> *envying the flight*
> *of the swallow.*

That's as good as any, I said. But I'll make sure you hear my last word.

*

Last word? Last sound.

I had slept deep, woken from a dream. Looked around me and gave voice. Part mantra, part deep groan. The bellow of an ox. Like Ganto's last cry it would carry and resonate.

*

OM

*

Throw this old carcass on the funeral pyre and let it burn.

*

And then? Where am I now? What realm do I inhabit? This self, this no-self. He who was Nagasawa Iwajiro, he who was Ekaku, Wise Crane, he who was Hakuin, Hidden-in-Whiteness.

*

Where? In these words? In the mind of the one who wrote them and of you who read? You read them in a language I never knew, on the printed page or on some illuminated *kamishibai* screen you carry with you.

*

Expedient devices. Words on a screen. Name and form.

*

Idle talk. The night boat.

*

Is that so?

443

*

My childhood name was Iwajiro. I was eight years old when I first entered at the gates of hell.

ACKNOWLEDGEMENTS

There are many people I would like to thank for their contributions to the progress of *Night Boat*.

The late and greatly missed Gavin Wallace for encouragement and support, and particularly for facilitating a Creative Scotland grant for travel to Japan. Alex Reedijk at Scottish Opera for commissioning the libretto of my mini-opera *Zen Story* (with Miriama Young) and setting me off down the Hakuin road. Norman Waddell for his extreme kindness and generosity, welcoming me to Kyoto, sharing the fruits of the lifetime's research that went into his own definitive translations and compilations of Hakuin (running to five volumes). Yoshie Waddell for further extending that welcome and hospitality. Professor Yoshizawa Katsuhiro at Hanazono University, the foremost living Hakuin scholar, for allowing me deeper in to Hakuin's world and for graciously funding my trip to Tokyo to take part in his Hakuin Forum, linked to the fabulous exhibition he curated at Bunkamura Museum. Thomas Kirchner for looking after me on that trip. Cairns Craig for approving additional funding from CASS at the University of Aberdeen. Elizabeth Sheinkman, my wonderful agent, formerly at Curtis Brown, now with WME. All at Canongate, especially the indefatigable Jamie Byng, Francis Bickmore, as always an astute and unobtrusive editor, ably assisted by Jo Dingley, and Vicki Rutherford for patient copy-editing. My good friends in the Sri Chinmoy Centre – Sundar, Dhrubha, Jaitra and Pavitrata – for inspiring me to go to New York for the Hakuin exhibition at the Japan Centre, and Kusumita Pedersen for lending me a rare copy of Philip Yampolsky's book of Hakuin's writings. Brian McCabe for publishing part of the opening chapter in *Edinburgh Review*. Friends and colleagues who responded to individual chapters along the way – John Burns, Wayne Price and Alison Watt for positive feedback, Kevin MacNeil for his kind words, and Helen Lynch for continued support and invaluable close reading of several sections. Janani, always, for living with the work, for putting up with the process, for getting me to New York for that Hakuin exhibition, and for a final, painstaking proofing of the whole text. The biggest debt of gratitude is to Sri Chinmoy, my teacher of 40 years, a constant inspiration whose guidance has continued after his passing. To quote his final poem: *My physical death / Is not the end of my life. / I am an eternal journey.*